It was sheer heaven...no man should have a body this perfect.

She felt Nikos' hands on the zipper of her gown. Before she could react, she heard the sound of the zipper sliding downwards and cold air hit her skin. But that was just for a second before she felt Nikos' warm hands trace a path in her back. She didn't even have a moment to feel conscious about her body for his touch and his lips made her feel just how much he desired her.

He touched her as if he could not get enough of her. He touched her as if he worshipped every inch of her body.

"Let's finish this..." Nikos purred seductively.

That was when fear reared its ugly head and snapped Cassia back to the present. Her body still pulsed with desire but the fog of passion was lifted from her mind. She pushed at Nikos' chest and he let her go with a moan of complaint.

"We need to talk," Cassia said in between deep breaths.

"Now?!" he groaned.

"Yes. Now. This is important. This is about this marriage."

Nikos lifted his head and his gaze was as hard as ice. Cassia immediately regretted her words and wished that she could bring back time just so he could gaze at her with desire.

"You want to talk, right now?" he breathed. "Then talk." Then he claimed her lips again.

THE
BILLION-DOLLAR
MARRIAGE
CONTRACT

ALYSSA URBANO
(AerithSage)

This book is a work of fiction. Names, characters, places, and incidents are products of the author's imagination or are used fictitiously. Any resemblance to actual events or locales or persons, living or dead, is entirely coincidental.

For more information, contact the author at
a l y s s a m a r i e u r b a n o @ g m a i l . c o m .

Book design by Tania Arpa / Bronze Age Media, Inc.
h t t p : / / b r o n z e a g e . p h

To my mom and dad who always told me to get off the computer so my ass won't be as big.

To my brother who annoyed me ever since he was born.

To my grandmother who cooks the best food.

To my aunt who first introduced me to the world of books.

To all my Wattpad friends, followers and readers who first believed in my writing.

Prologue

"ARE you sure you want to do this, boy? Once you're in, there's no going back," an expensively dressed businessman asked the scrawny lad who was trying to look brave in front of him.

"Yes. I am sure. And I will do everything in my power to serve you well. There's no going back for me. I want this and I will see this through the end." The young man looked thin but his voice held so much resolve.

"Your name?" the man asked the boy.

"I have no name. I left everything behind before I set foot on this island."

"Good. Right now, you are our property. You have no past and we are your future."

"And it is a great honor."

"Very well, then. You did what was asked?" Instead of looking at him for the answer, the man looked at the guards standing behind the bastard.

"He did as he was told. He has managed to meet up with the buyers and the transactions all went smoothly. By the time the cops were alerted, he was already out of there," one of the senior syndicate members replied.

The young man reached for the bag containing the money from the transaction that served as his initiation. He handed it carefully and with pride to the man before him who then counted it with a huge grin on his face.

"You did great, boy! This is one of the biggest first takes I have ever counted! Welcome to the cartel."

The man grinned and pointed to one of his assistants who instantly walked towards the young man with a blazing coin held in a pair of tongs in front of him.

"This would hurt a bit. You can still back out now," the boss taunted.

"No. I want this. I will proudly wear the mark on my skin."

"Good. Hold out your arm." The young man did as he was told and then the red-hot coin was seared into his skin on the upper, innermost part of his arm. The pain brought him to his knees and tears to his eyes but he refused to cry out like the other initiates.

"From now on, you will be known as Sebastian Roman. Embrace your new identity. Embrace your new life. Now, go back to the city. We will call you when your services are needed. For now, enjoy the fruits of your initiation."

The boss then handed out the young man's share of the money. He used that money to secure him a ride back to the mainland and then towards the towering building of the Demakis Corporation. He committed to memory every inch of the structure and started envisioning his plans.

His vision was interrupted when he saw Stavros Demakis, CEO of the multi-billion corporation emerge from the building and quickly go inside his car. This was one of the men he hated most and the one he wanted to get his revenge on. Stavros' life was so different from his. The man was filthy rich and lived in excess while he had nothing. He didn't even have his family for his mother died because of the Demakis family.

The young man glanced at the burned mark on his skin. This was the start of it all. This was the instrument of his revenge on the people who hurt him most. He knew it would still be a long time, but he would get his hands on what was his due.

The young man felt rage searing his veins, and he tightly clenched his fists. He still couldn't do anything about it now...but he would...

One day soon...

September 15, 2003 (Later that Day)
Office of the CEO
Andrade Shipping International

"Stavros Demakis is here to request a meeting."

Costas Andrade of *Andrade Shipping International* turned his chair around and pressed a button on his intercom.

"Show him in," he replied to his personal assistant. The corner of his lips turned up in a sneer and his blood sang with triumph and delight.

He had waited for this meeting for a long time now. His arch nemesis would finally come to him grovelling.

Costas personally set out to ruin his competitor's shipping business. He just didn't expect Stavros would be able to hold out this long but it didn't matter. Everything he worked for was now in the palm of his hands.

Why did he do this?

Because forty years ago, Stavros Demakis stole Costas' intended bride. Yes, it was an arranged marriage but she was the most beautiful girl and Costas truly wanted her to be his. The girl, however, fell in love with Stavros and eloped with him, thereby crushing all of Costas' plans.

"Come in," Costas said when he heard a knock on the door.

His personal assistant opened it and nervously ushered Stavros Demakis inside. He felt a flash of annoyance when he saw Stavros. The man he hated most looked the same even after all these years, aside from his grey hair and the lines around his eyes. It seemed as though time had treated him more kindly than it had Costas.

"Please sit," Costas gestured to the couch in front of his desk.

Stavros folded his tall frame in the seat and glared at the man who ruined his company. He looked like a man who was only here because he had no other choice.

"Now, to what do I owe this pleasure?" Costas asked.

"You damn well know what this is about, Andrade! Every chance you got, you *ruined* me. Now, the bank and the board are pestering me because I am losing my company! I came here to tell you about it so that you could start gloating. That's what you wanted, isn't it? Now, tell me: are you happy now? In your own twisted version of justice, does this pay what I did years ago when I took your intended bride?" Stavros snarled.

Never. That debt can never be repaid, Costas thought to himself.

He clenched his fist under the table and fought for control. He sat back in his chair, feigning innocence while he watched the other man with amusement in his eyes.

"I don't know what you're talking about," he lied.

"*Bastarde,*" Stavros growled. Costas only raised an eyebrow. "All of this is because of Prudence. It all boils down to her. But you know what? I'd give it all up again for her. I regret nothing." Stavros dismissed Costas' beautifully decorated office with a wave of his hand.

Stavros' only sadness was that she died at such a young age.

Costas' eyes flashed with fury at Stavros' words but he quickly tamped it down for he did not want to give Stavros even a bit of satisfaction.

"I repeat, I do *not* know what you are talking about. However, I am aware of the financial situation of *Demakis Shipping*. I am willing to offer you a solution," he said with smug satisfaction. This was the moment he was waiting for.

Stavros looked as if he was going to have a heart attack after Costas' words sunk in.

"And what would this be?" he asked, his voice barely a whisper.

"A merger."

"A merger?!" he repeated incredulously.

"*Ne.* Combining the strengths of *Andrade International* and *Demakis Shipping*. I am willing to settle your debts and get the company back on its feet. But it's never going to be separated. The two companies will forever be merged as one."

"And what might this cost me, my soul?!" Stavros snarled incredulously.

"Contrary to popular belief, I am not a *devil* and this merger would not be signed with your blood. Nor will I have your soul. I have no use for it," Costas laughed, feigning amusement. But deep inside he was boiling with rage at how his enemy could still ridicule him on a time of need such as this.

"And what must I give up to gain your help and save my company?" Stavros asked.

"Your grandson."

"My grandson?! What does Nikos have to do with anything?!"

"He will wed my granddaughter, Cassia. Think of this as my safeguard. Their wedding would secure the merger and the ownership of the company would pass on to both of them. Your Nikos is legendary in business and my only heir, my granddaughter Cassia, knows nothing about its intricacies."

Stavros was drinking the coffee that Costas' PA gave him when Costas said the words. They caused him to choke on it so he set the cup down before the warm liquid sloshed all over him.

"*That girl?* Why do you need to secure a marriage for her? Are the rumors true that she's not right in the head?"

"*Silence!* I will not let my granddaughter be insulted like that! Cassia is a smart girl. She was just brought up by her mother in a different country and in a totally different culture. Let's just say that she's not yet used to this kind of life."

Stavros Demakis picked up his cup once more and sipped his coffee while he pondered on the merger. It sounded simple enough but he knew there was truly something behind the offer. Costas Andrade was not known for being a generous man. He tried hard to look for it but he couldn't quite find what Costas would gain from this merger.

"And what are the other details for this merger?" Stavros asked.

"I have some conditions. Andrade and *Demakis Shipping* will be merged as one. Nikos and Cassia's son will inherit everything. They would not be able to divorce each other unless there is an heir. If they do, the one at fault will lose all the money," Costas ticked the conditions off his fingers one by one.

"What do you mean by the one at fault?"

"Well for example, let's just say your grandson takes a mistress and it doesn't sit well with my granddaughter. If she chooses to divorce him because of adultery, then Nikos loses everything. Same goes if it's my granddaughter who is at fault. They would have to stay married for them to retain the company in their hands."

Stavros thought of Costas' words and he tried hard to find something wrong in those sentences. But no matter which angle he looked at it, it sounded like a valid offer especially when everything was placed in black and white. But he still had to be wary, for he knew Costas was a ruthless and devious man.

"Why are you doing this?" Stavros asked.

"Let's just say that I am feeling very charitable today. And I think your Nikos and my Cassia would definitely make a good match," Costas lied through his teeth. He knew that Nikos Demakis was a man not suited for married life. If the divorce occurred, the entire Demakis Corporation would fall into Costas' hands. Not only that, the added humiliation and the thought that the company fell because of Stavros' own grandson would surely kill the old man.

"Put all of your conditions in writing."

Costas grinned. "You will receive the papers within a week. And then I'll expect your reply within three days after you have received them. The negotiations will start the moment you sign those papers and then the merger itself will commence right after the wedding."

"Nothing is set in stone yet. Yet you sound so sure of yourself, Andrade," Stavros bit out.

"I *always* get what I want." Costas answered with a huge grin.

Chapter 1

Mesmerized

September 12, 2003 (Three Days Earlier)
The Emerald Hotel
Athens, Greece

JANN Arden's song, *'Insensitive,'* blasted through the entire grand ballroom of an exclusive five-star hotel which currently held a party that Cassia Andrade was forced to attend. She leaned over one of the marble pillars and sipped her drink while she contemplated all the things the other girls here had that she didn't.

First of all, they all looked like glittering princesses.

Well, that was bound to happen when one was born into so much wealth that they never had to work a day in their life. They were pampered right from the start and then raised to be the spoiled, snobby bitches they were right now.

Cassia snorted, exhaled and then tried harder to blend into the shadows.

To be honest, she tried as much as she could but she still stuck out like a sore thumb. She was like a duck in a room filled with gorgeous peacocks. She was not like these people. Yes, her grandfather was wealthy but she had not been born into the grandeur of wealth like these girls. She did not even know of her grandfather's existence until about a month ago.

Her parents died in a plane crash. Up until then, she had been happy. Her parents loved her very much. They may have had a difficult time scraping by financially but everything was alright since they had each other.

Then they died and orphaned Cassia at the age of twelve years old. Since then, she had been passed from foster home to foster home.

But her life changed one month ago, exactly after her nineteenth birthday, when her grandfather finally found her.

That was when she found out that her father was the only son of Costas Andrade, one of the richest men in the world. Her father was disowned because he married Cassia's mother, a common waitress. Her father gave up everything for her mother.

Now that her father was dead, she was Costas' only heir. After that bomb shell of a declaration, she was then swept into the glitz and glamour that was the life of the rich and famous.

"That was when I found out I would never fit in," Cassia muttered under her breath as she took another swig of the punch in her hand.

"Hey there, *fat-ass*," one of the women in the party snarled. Cassia ignored her. There was nothing else she could do but ignore these women who thought themselves to be the epitome of perfection.

"Hey hon, my dad owns a gym. Let me give you a free membership, okay?"

"Who did your hair? My poodle's hair looks so much better than that.

"When you shop for dresses, make sure it's the correct size. Not one or two sizes too small."

Again, she ignored all those taunts. But from all those words, it was the last ones that stung the most. Cassia tried everything to be refined, beautiful and smart like her grandfather wanted so that she could please him. But he was a hard man to please and instead of earning his love and his praise, she always earned his wrath.

The women sauntered by and Cassia knew she was not like them. They were like those models she saw on TV while she was short and plump. To top it all off, she had a face that no amount of make-up could fix. Her mother was so very beautiful and to her, her father looked like a Greek god. Yet somehow, fate and genetics laughed at that and produced Cassia.

Cassia snorted at her thoughts and scanned the beautiful ballroom.

Supermodels and sons of rich businessmen twirled around the dance floor in glittering silks and satins. They flirted openly with each other and looked as though they were having the time of their lives.

Cassia shook her head and refused to feel sorry for herself.

So what if no one looked at her with admiration?

So what if she was an outcast?

So what if no one asked her to dance?

She would just go through this ordeal to please her grandfather and then she would return home at the first available chance. She never belonged with this crowd. And she knew that she never would, for she was not beautiful and she was not accustomed to the lifestyle of wealth.

Suddenly, she was jolted out of her thoughts when somebody barreled into her.

"Whoops! S-sarreh din't see ya there," a drunken voice slurred.

Cassia spilled her drink on herself during the impact. She quickly reached over for a napkin and began to wipe her bodice. The drunken guy quickly retrieved the napkin from her.

"I'm so sorry. Let me do that for you," he offered with a sneer. He proceeded to wipe Cassia's bodice with a slowness that suggested lechery. Cassia gasped and stepped back from him but he tugged on her wrist and forced her to come into contact with his hard body.

"What's your problem, sweet thing? Shouldn't you be thankful that I am paying you some notice so that you won't have to blend in with the marble?" he whispered to her. She could smell the alcohol on his breath and it made her want to hurl.

"Please just let me go," she whispered as she tried to tug her wrist out of his grasp.

But even if the man was drunk, he was very strong.

"Let her go," another voice cut in. The pressure on Cassia's wrist eased and she opened her eyes.

Her gaze clashed with the most vivid green eyes she's ever seen. Immediately, her throat ran dry and her heart started to beat faster. She gazed at her savior and the first thought that popped into her mind was that he was the most handsome man she's ever seen.

He had jet black hair and a face which looked like it was sculpted by the gods themselves. Every inch of him was flawless but his most striking feature remained his beautiful green eyes. Right now, those eyes looked at her with concern.

He moved closer to her and Cassia realized just how tall he was. He towered over her by about a foot and she was already wearing four-inch heels.

"Are you alright?" he asked.

His voice slid through her like silk. It took her some time to reply but she was able to stammer, "Y-yes..."

"Good. Leave her alone, George," he said in a curt tone.

"Aaaw. Come on, Nikos. Don't be such a buzz kill. I just wanted to have some fun with her. She looked like she needed to be rescued from the wall."

Cassia flinched at his words and Nikos saw it. He shot her an apologetic look and her heart went out to him. Right now, she did not know if this was some case of hero-worship but she was definitely infatuated with this gentleman.

"I said leave her," Nikos repeated in a sterner tone.

"No. One good fuck may change her views on these kinds of things," George snarled.

Cassia flinched again and at the same time, she saw Nikos tense. George hand shot out and gripped Cassia's wrist. Before she could blink, she saw that Nikos launched his towering frame towards George and landed a solid punch to his right jaw.

George fell and clutched his bloody lip.

"What the hell, man!" he shouted.

George started cursing both of them but Cassia paid him no heed. She gazed at Nikos with a dumbstruck expression. That tender moment was ended when she noticed that everyone turned to look at them.

I wish the ground would open up and swallow me whole... Cassia thought to herself.

Everyone around them started whispering. Others sneered at her and sadly shook her heads. Cassia cringed at the thought of gossip reaching her grandfather and instantly dreaded the coming punishment.

"Again, I said leave her alone," Nikos said as he reached inside his suit and retrieved his handkerchief. He then tossed it to George who was still clutching his jaw.

Nikos turned towards Cassia. He lifted her hand and placed it inside the crook of his elbow. He leaned forward as if to whisper something to her and Cassia was able to get a whiff of the exquisite perfume he wore. Mixed with his masculine scent, it was a drug unlike any other.

"Come on, the least you can do is dance with me," Nikos told her with a small smile.

When she heard those words, her knees almost buckled. Sheer happiness raced through her and she wanted to jump up and down with joy. She managed to nod and Nikos guided her to the dance floor.

***

Nikos exhaled the breath he'd been holding. He really did not want to cause a scene tonight. Hell, almost every week he'd already been on numerous magazines and tabloids! It was all because of his playboy lifestyle.

Just right now, he punched one of his friends to rescue this girl he did not even know. For sure he'd be in another of those blasted tabloids.

Quick as a flash, the two of them became the center of attention and the only thing he could do to avoid reporters swarming around both of them right now would be to whisk her away to the dance floor.

Nikos waved his hand and it was as if someone hit the play button once more. The music resumed, people turned around to go about their business and conversation all around the party started once more. He then pulled Cassia close and placed his hand on her waist. She seemed stunned as he guided her onto the dance floor.

This was her first dance ever and she was so lucky to be in this hero's arms.

Effortlessly, Nikos Demakis led her on the steps of the waltz. He smiled at her when she stepped on his foot and adjusted his steps for her. With every sway, every smile and every step, Cassia fell deeper and deeper.

"I'm sorry about what happened," Nikos said after a long moment of awkward silence.

"Thank you for rescuing me..." Cassia breathed.

"It's nothing," Nikos replied in a clipped Greek accent that made Cassia's pulse skyrocket.

"I am Nikos Demakis."

"And I am Cassia Andrade..."

There was a long pause and Cassia noticed a different expression cross Nikos' face. It was something like surprise mixed with uncertainty. But it was gone in a flash and she thought that she must've just imagined it.

"Nice to meet you, Cassia," Nikos managed after a few seconds of silence. He never expected that the woman he saved was the Andrade heiress that everyone was talking about. He didn't envision that this was how they'd meet.

He tilted his head to the side and looked at her features. Yes, he agreed with what everyone was saying. She seemed plain, but if one looked at her harder and got past that first glance, it was plain to see that she had a fine facial bone structure. She also had skin so smooth and so pale that it looked as if it was glowing.

They called her fat but what Nikos saw was curves that made his mouth water. He blinked and tried to clear his head of these shameful thoughts. She was the granddaughter of the man that wanted to ruin his family! If he made her one of his conquests and broke her heart, the *Demakis Shipping Corporation* would surely plummet to the ground under her grandfather's wrath.

"The pleasure's mine..." she managed to reply.

They say time flies when you are enjoying yourself.

That happened to Cassia. All too quickly, the dance was over and she found herself craving to be closer to her savior. She wished he'd take her in his arms again and dance with her until the night was over.

But that was not to be. Cassia frowned a bit when Nikos let go of her hand. Then, he bowed and she realized that the song had already ended. She so desperately wished that it would go on for a little while longer for she really wanted to know him more.

It was as if there was something in him that called out to her.

She wanted him...*badly.*

"Thanks for the dance. I have to go," Nikos Demakis said as he picked up her hand and kissed it.

Then, he turned his back and walked towards his peers who started teasing him because he danced with her. He just shrugged as though it wasn't really a grave matter. He turned back towards her one last time.

When their eyes met across the crowded ballroom, he winked.

"I think I'm in love..." Cassia giggled.

Chapter 2
Sacrifice

"SEBASTIAN. Excellent as always. I expected no less from you."

Sebastian's chest puffed out with pride at his boss' words. In their world, you either lived by the rules or you died trying to fit in. It seemed as if the fates were smiling down at him. He just managed to secure police protection from a corrupt set of officials. Now, they were free to do their business in this city.

"The bosses will be pleased. For this, I will grant you a boon. Ask anything and if it is within my power, I will grant it to you."

Sebastian grinned. This was what he was waiting for.

"I need you to get me a job. I have a specific one in mind."

"A job? Why? You can live off your commissions!" his boss exclaimed.

"Let's just say that I have another ulterior motive...a personal vendetta."

His boss smiled menacingly. "Well why didn't you just say that? I love vendettas. Tell me about it and this job you want is yours."

September 22, 2003
The Amphitrite (Nikos' Yacht)
Somewhere in the Greek Coast

RIIIIIIIIIIIIIIIIING

Nikos turned and then groaned at the shrill ringing of his cell phone.

Who would dare interrupt him when he said that he didn't want to be disturbed and that all his calls and meeting be cancelled? He picked up a pillow and placed it over his head to drown out the noise.

"I think you better get that, *Cherie*," the woman beside him purred in a heavy French accent. He lifted the covers and stared at her exquisite features. She smiled at him and it was the smile of someone well-satisfied.

Her hair was tousled and her cheeks were still flushed from their recent bout of lovemaking. He smiled at her and she launched herself up his body and began kissing him eagerly. She was a renowned French supermodel and she was his latest mistress.

Nikos felt his body responding to her expert caress and he almost gave in. But they were interrupted once more by the incessant ringing of his phone.

He sighed and then placed one last kiss on her lips and stood up to retrieve his phone.

"Nikos Demakis. And this better be important," he growled.

His grandfather's laughter echoed in his ears.

"Nikos. I assure you that this is important," Stavros Demakis answered his only grandson.

"Nice hearing from you, *Pappou*... How are you?"

"Fine, my boy, but I am afraid I need to cut your vacation short. I need you here at the office as soon as possible. You know the current state of our company and I have some things I must discuss with you."

Nikos pinched the bridge of his nose and closed his eyes in a gesture of exasperation. He had planned his weekend with Marietta, for a really long time now. He had pursued her relentlessly but it was a long time before she succumbed to him. He wanted to cherish this moment of triumph when she was finally his.

But his time with her would have to be cut short for his grandfather requested his presence immediately.

"All right, *Pappou*...I will meet you in time for dinner," Nikos answered.

"Good. See you, son," Stavros replied and then cut the line.

Nikos ruffled his hair and then turned back to his pouting mistress. "I'm sorry but I have to go," he said as he reached for the drawer beside his bed and opened it. "For you." He opened a jewelry case that nestled a beautiful emerald necklace.

"*Oui! C'est beau! C'est parfait! Merci!*" she squealed as she showered him with kisses. Nikos laughed and quickly flipped her onto her back, rubbing his hardening shaft against her.

"I think we still have some time for you to thank me properly before I leave."

Several Hours Later
Demakis Corporation Headquarters
The Penthouse Suite

Stavros Demakis inspected his grandson from head to toe while he approached.

He noted the arrogant strides Nikos took and how he seemed to radiate power and authority with every step. He recognized that stance and it brought him several memories from his past when he was the same age as his grandson.

Stavros smiled in welcome while he shifted to hide the newspaper he was reading before Nikos arrived. It featured his grandson once more and the rumors that he was dating some French supermodel. Stavros knew Nikos' lifestyle even if his grandson didn't communicate with him often. It was not needed when he read about it in the papers almost every week.

Who could fault the boy for doing that anyway?

He was rich and he was young. Even though he was only twenty four years old, he already graduated from Harvard with a business degree. Right now, Nikos had his own money from buying and selling in the stock market. He also managed his own businesses while working for the Demakis Corporation.

Stavros then wondered how he was going to break the news to his grandson.

"*Pappou,*" Nikos greeted and he gave his grandfather a tight hug.

Stavros chuckled and patted Nikos' back.

"How have you been?"

"Excellent, my boy. And you?"

"Never better," Nikos replied with a smile.

Stavros walked towards his desk and indicated for Nikos to sit. Nikos folded his tall frame into the couch in front of the desk and awaited his grandfather's words.

"Nikos...you are aware of the situation of our company currently, right?"

Anger flashed quickly in Nikos' eyes and his entire body seemed to grow taut.

"Yes," he said through clenched teeth.

"It seems as if Costas Andrade has finally pushed us to our last limits," he breathed.

Stavros sighed, leaned back in his chair and pinched the bridge of his nose.

"Let's change the topic here first, Nikos. Have you met the Andrade girl? What do you think of her?"

"She's different from the women in her circle. She seems naive about this kind of world. Wait... *Pappou*, if you are thinking about asking me to date that Andrade girl to get her grandfather to be more amenable to us, you are probably wrong. I'd just end up breaking the poor girl's heart and Costas' wrath will be upon us further. Nothing will be left for us, not even the clothes on our backs," Nikos replied with humor.

Stavros sighed once more. His grandson spoke the truth. But the Andrade heiress was also their only way out of this tight mess.

"Nikos... Costas has offered us a way out "

Nikos leaned forward in his chair and regarded his grandfather with a curious gaze.

"What do you mean?"

"Nikos there's no easy way to say this..."

"Just say it straight to me, *Pappou*. You've never been one who beat around the bush," Nikos chuckled.

"Alright. Costas offers a merger of Demakis and Andrade Shipping. And we'd still be able to gain control of our company."

Nikos snorted. "That sounds like something the devil would offer in exchange for your soul."

"Ahh...but then it is not my soul he wants, Nikos...it is *yours*."

"Me? What the hell do I have to do with this? Why would he want me?" Nikos exclaimed.

There was a knock on the door and Stavros pressed a button on the side of his desk for it to open. His secretary came in with two cups of coffee. Stavros noticed the way that her eyes roamed all over Nikos and also the come-hither glances she threw his way.

Nikos just raised an eyebrow and turned the corner of his lips upwards in a smile. The secretary looked almost ready to faint.

Stavros coughed. "That would be all, Lydia. Thank you."

The secretary flushed a deep red and quickly exited the room.

Stavros sipped his coffee slowly in an attempt to postpone the inevitable for a little bit more. Another sigh escaped his lips and he leaned forward and looked at his only grandson and heir in the eye.

"Costas offers a merger that would save our company in return for you marrying the Andrade girl."

Nikos looked momentarily stunned. He took a deep breath and Stavros could see his hands shaking as he held his coffee cup.

"Say that again..." Nikos implored. His voice was barely a whisper.

"I apologize for this Nikos, but it is the only way. *Marriage*."

"This is his revenge on you, right? You stole his bride and now he wants to curtail my freedom? And what does he even gain from this?!" Nikos stood up and began pacing the length of the room.

"I don't know. But from what I've read in the contract, there must be no divorce. Or else, the one who filed for the divorce will lose all the money. Another one of the conditions is that you have to have a child and that child will inherit everything. Costas wants the fate of the companies tied to your marriage with his granddaughter."

"This is unbelievable!" Nikos spat.

"Right now, the entire Demakis fortune is in your hands, Nikos. What you do with that would determine our company's future."

Nikos ran a hand through his hair in frustration at his grandfather's words.

"I refuse! *Pappou*, I have my own businesses. They are flourishing! We will never become poor. I can still maintain this lifestyle that we have! I will get everything back for you one by one. This I vow! And I will make Costas Andrade pay!" Nikos vowed solemnly.

"I know you are a very smart man Nikos. And that you are very good with this business. But *Demakis Shipping* has been in our family for generations. I understand why you do not want to be saddled with this marriage. It just saddens me that there's nothing else I can do and that the whole business will become lost in my hands. I wanted you to inherit this. I wanted to see you sit at its helm and make it prosper even more...but I might not for this would be the end of our ancestors' hardships," Stavros whispered weakly.

He leaned back in his chair and Nikos noticed that his entire body seemed to sag. Gone was the ruthless business tycoon and in its place was just a frail old man. Nikos felt his chest tighten and he immediately regretted his words. But still, it was a huge sacrifice for him to make.

"*Pappou*...you cannot ask this of me," Nikos pleaded.

"I understand, Nikos. No one should impose something this big on you. And I will not hold this against you. Just go...I will talk to Costas tonight," he said in a defeated tone.

"*Pappou--*"

"Go, Nikos. I will deal with this," Stavros said and then pressed the button that opened the door once more.

Then, he rotated his chair and stared out of the window so that he would not be able to see his grandson leave, taking all hopes for the company with him. And Nikos Demakis turned his back and left his grandfather's office with a very heavy heart.

But before Nikos closed the door, he heard one last defeated sigh from his grandfather which tore at his heart.

A few hours later
Vrettos Bar
Athens, Greece

"Where are you?"

"At the oldest bar in Athens, getting myself drunk until all this crazy bullshit disappears," Nikos replied dryly. He perched atop one of the stools in the crowded bar while nursing a glass of brandy in his hands.

"A drink sounds nice. Mind if I come over?" his college friend Antonio Velez asked.

"Go ahead," Nikos replied and then gave his friend the address of the bar.

"Great. I am ten minutes away, my friend. Be right there."

Nikos ended the call and glanced one more time at the name of his friend.

Antonio Velez was one of the richest men in Spain. At a young age, he inherited and led his family's business. In all those years, their business of exporting the best seafood in the entire world flourished. While Nikos ventured into the hotelier business, Antonio ventured into the food industry. Right now, all of Nikos' hotels housed Antonio's restaurants making a more profitable trade for both of them.

"Hi there! You look as if you could use some company tonight." A blonde sidled into the recently abandoned stool beside him and slanted him a seductive look. She also leaned forward and bared her lovely breasts to his gaze.

Before Nikos could reply, she spoke again.

"You seem familiar...I think I have seen you somewhere," the blonde whispered.

Nikos inclined his head to the side and waited for her to recognize him.

"You're Nikos Demakis!" the blonde exclaimed and then clapped her hands together.

Her eyes lit up and Nikos could almost see the dollar signs flashing in them. All his life, women looked at him as though he was a walking bank account. They craved the things he could give them rather than the depth of a relationship, which was alright with him since he didn't want to form any attachments.

Yet why did this bother him now all of a sudden?

"So how about a drink at my place?" the blonde moved closer to him until her breasts were pressed to his arm.

"Hmm...some other time, maybe? I am meeting a friend here tonight."

The blonde pouted. "I could do things to you that no one has ever done before," she whispered.

Nikos almost snorted. He doubted that this blonde could do anything he hadn't experienced yet. At his age of twenty-four years, he had dated the most beautiful actresses, models who wrapped their long legs around him, ballerinas who were so flexible that they could take up the most outrageous positions, and many more.

"Sorry, sweetie. Not really in the mood right now," Nikos answered and took another swig of his drink. The blonde pouted yet again and left the stool to search for another rich man she could dig her claws into.

"Ever the ladies man," a deep voice drawled beside him.

Nikos chuckled and hugged his friend as he sat down on the stool that the blonde has just vacated.

"One brandy for my friend here, please," Nikos told the bartender.

When Antonio's drink arrived, he raised it in front of Nikos. "So what are we drinking to?"

"The end of Demakis International," Nikos replied with a groan.

Antonio raised an eyebrow and waited for his friend to continue speaking. When Nikos did not, Antonio sighed and then downed his brandy in one gulp.

"So the old man Andrade has finally succeeded, has he?"

"Apparently," Nikos replied.

"Hmm... I can sense that there is something more to this story," Antonio prodded.

"Costas Andrade told my grandfather that he is willing to offer a merger for Demakis and Andrade Shipping."

"No! Tell me I didn't just hear you mention a merger!" Antonio exclaimed.

"I just did."

"And what are the terms for this? Your grandfather's soul?" Antonio chuckled.

"Funny. I just said the same thing. No. No souls involved. Well, actually, there is one soul dragged into all of this - *mine*."

"How so?"

"In exchange for the merger, I have to marry Cassia Andrade."

Nikos expected his friend to utter a string of curses, or to spit his drink or smash it onto the marble countertop after his announcement.

What he did not expect was for Antonio to say "Ahh..." like it was a very trivial thing and something that made perfect sense.

Nikos frowned and poured himself another measure of brandy.

"I can sense that you expected a different reaction from me," Antonio said.

"Well, of course! I just told you that my grandfather wants me to marry the Andrade girl! I mean, have you seen her? Do you know her?"

Antonio raised another eyebrow. "As a matter of fact, I do. I know she is not accepted into the social circle because of her social awkwardness and her appearance. Which reminds me, where has Costas been hiding his granddaughter all these years? It's only now that I've heard of an Andrade heiress."

"Maybe she was raised in another country," Nikos snorted

"Maybe. What I can say is she is a sweet girl. She is like a breath of fresh air from all the women who wanted to have a look at your bank account before they would pay you any notice."

Nikos downed another drink when he realized that his friend was correct. There was truly something about Cassia Andrade that was different. She was not like the shallow girls who spent their life partying. There was meekness in her posture but there was intelligence in her gaze. Beneath all that, he could sense a strong spirit which was being overshadowed by her insecurities.

"*Hell.* I do not care," Nikos spat and gulped another drink. The bar started to spin and his head started to throb but he did not want to stop now. Besides, getting drunk tonight was the plan.

"What is truly so wrong about marrying her? She may not be as beautiful as the others but at least she's different."

"I don't want her. I want the ability to choose my bride for myself. If I had the choice, I won't be choosing for another ten or fifteen years! Most certainly not someone like her! I love my life too much! And I would not give it up for a wife that I did not even pick! I can't be forced to settle down right now!" Nikos exclaimed.

"I understand. But if this is the only way to save your family business...one that your ancestors worked so hard for! Is that not a small *sacrifice* to pay for your grandfather who raised you when your parents left?"

As usual, Antonio was right.

Nikos did not speak for a long while and proceeded to run his fingers through his hair.

"I do not know what to do," he finally admitted.

"Drink on it tonight and then think about it in the morning. I think that is best for everyone. Do not make hasty decisions, my friend, especially if there is a lot that depends on that *one* decision."

"And that is another fact I hate. I hate how the fate of Demakis International is on my shoulders. I hate how I am being forced into these circumstances."

Antonio placed his palm on Nikos' shoulder and squeezed. Then, he grabbed the bottle of brandy and poured them both another round.

"For now, let's drink to that." Nikos clinked his glass with his friend and they both downed their drinks in one gulp.

Suddenly, their drinking spree was interrupted when Nikos' cell phone rang. He quickly retrieved it from his pocket and glared at it as if it offended him so. However, his irritation was replaced by fear when he saw that it was his grandfather's personal assistant that was calling him.

"Nikos Demakis speaking."

"Mr. Demakis! Thank you so much for answering!" the personal assistant who had been with his grandfather for over twenty years now and had been like a mother to Nikos sounded very frantic. Dread filled Nikos' gut as he heard her.

"What happened?" he growled.

"Your grandfather suffered a heart attack! We are currently in the hospital right now. I found him passed out on the floor a while ago right after he talked to Costas Andrade and called the merger off. Do not worry too much. Everything's been taken care of and doctors told me that he is stable right now."

He used his shoulder to hold his phone to his ear while he retrieved his wallet and placed a wad of notes under his empty glass. Antonio sensed the urgency and grabbed the jacket he draped over the back of his chair.

"Has he woken up?" he asked.

"Not yet, Mr. Demakis. But the doctors say that he will be fine. They just advised us not to stress him out too much or he may have another heart attack," Maria told him.

Nikos clenched his jaw as he walked to his car.

"I will be there in about thirty minutes," he told Maria then ended the call. He explained the situation to Antonio as he walked back to his car.

He pulled out his keys but Antonio grabbed it from him. "You're drunk, Nikos. I'm not. I'll drive."

"This is all my fault," he groaned.

"What makes you say that?" his friend asked.

"He wouldn't be in this condition if I wasn't selfish enough to put my own needs before the company's. If my grandfather never recovered from this, I will never forgive myself..."

Nikos took a deep breath. "...Even if he recovers, I will *never* forgive Andrade."

While Antonio drove to the hospital, Nikos came to a solid conclusion...

For his grandfather, he could do this.

He could marry the Andrade girl and settle down so that they would have their company back. Then, he would work hard to rebuild Demakis International and repay Costas for every cent his family owed. It was time to stop being selfish and own up to his responsibilities.

If that responsibility was to throw away his lavish playboy lifestyle in return for a lifetime of hard work and a bride he did not want, then so be it.

Chapter 3

Borrowed Bliss

October 6, 2003
The Andrade Manor
Athens, Greece

"*G*ET dressed."

Costas Andrade's voice boomed across the hallway to the library. Cassia immediately jumped and then stood up when her grandfather entered the room. She folded her book and placed it neatly on top of the table. Then she waited for the yelling that always ensued when her grandfather sought her out.

Costas' secretary meekly followed behind him and then handed Cassia a beautiful gown made of blue silk.

"Another party, grandfather? Where am I supposed to go this time?" Cassia whispered softly.

"You are going to this party with Nikos Demakis. Now get dressed."

"N-Nikos Demakis?" Cassia parroted.

"Are you deaf, girl? I just said that. Now hurry!"

Cassia remained rooted to the spot while she clutched the beautiful dress to her chest. Did she just truly hear her grandfather say that she was going with Nikos Demakis?

It was a dream come true!

Cassia smiled and then moved out of the room with lighter steps. She felt like floating. She even pinched herself to check that this was truly real and not a dream. After thinking about him constantly for every day since she met him, this was like a gift from the gods. She just couldn't wait to see him again!

"Stop," her grandfather commanded.

Cassia stopped and turned around.

"You know the Demakis boy?"

"Y-yes..." she stuttered.

"Why are you still stuttering like a fool?! Have I not paid your tutors enough?! Isn't it enough that you still cannot grasp Greek. Now, you're also losing control of your English?!" Costas shouted and Cassia flinched.

"I'm sorry, grandfather," she muttered and tried hard to tamp down her fear.

"Do not call me that. Not until you have done something to make me proud to call you my granddaughter." Once more Cassia flinched in pain at the barbs in his words.

"How did you know Demakis?"

"We met at one p-party..."

"What do you think of him?"

"Err...he's nice..." Cassia's voice faltered as she said the words for she remembered what Nikos did for her at the ball. He was so gallant and he came charging like her knight in shining armor when she needed someone to rescue her.

Costas Andrade snorted and looked at his granddaughter.

She had love and adoration shining in her eyes. Clearly, she was besotted with the Demakis heir just like countless women around the world. Who wouldn't like the boy? At such a young age he was already a successful businessman with his own company and own line of businesses while at the same time helping out with controlling *Demakis Shipping*.

Costas realized that Cassia was so besotted and so naive that she'd make a great pawn in this elaborate game.

"Go and get ready," he instructed his granddaughter.

Cassia immediately bowed her head and ducked out of the room.

She entered her own room and was not surprised anymore when her team of hairdressers and make-up artists were there waiting for her. They had already set up their equipment and were impatiently tapping their feet on the carpet.

She knew they were the best and the most expensive team but she did not like their attitude. They always treated her as though she knew nothing. They went ahead with whatever they wanted to do even if she expressed her wishes that she did not want it.

She also knew that no matter how great their skills were, she'd never be as beautiful as the other girls.

Oh well...here I go, pitying myself once more.

Cassia shook her head and tried to empty it of those negative thoughts. What was important today was that she was going to meet Nikos Demakis. That would be enough to get her through the ordeal of being poked and prodded by the set of people who used every opportunity to point out all of her flaws.

"Please sit and we shall begin," the lead stylist told her.

Cassia sat and this was the first time she welcomed their ministrations for she truly wanted to look her best for her meeting with Nikos Demakis.

"Is this a special party, then?" Cassia asked after an hour.

She faced the tall mirror in her room and twirled around. For the first time in her life, she felt beautiful. She also felt her self-confidence rising, even if she hated that they dyed her brown hair and turned it into blonde. Maybe today she could shine like all those supermodels and actresses that Nikos dated.

Or maybe he was the kind of man who could look past the external.

"Who am I kidding? He's dating supermodels so how can I say he's the kind who looks past one's appearance?" Cassia muttered under her breath.

She snorted and then went back to inspecting herself in the beautiful, gilded mirror.

The team did a perfect job with her hair. It was coiled on top of her head with some loose curls framing her face and her nape. Pearls were also placed on her hair and they made her skin glow with every movement of her head.

She wore the blue dress that her grandfather's secretary gave her and it was very striking. It was simple yet very elegant. It only had one strap and it was fitted in the chest and waist area and then the skirt flowed down her hips and her legs. The light and almost sheer material moved gracefully with every step she took.

Cassia knew that this dress was a traditional Greek design altered to make it look more contemporary. It was brilliant! What made it even more beautiful was the brooch encrusted with diamonds and sapphires that was placed on the bodice of her gown.

Also, her make-up was flawless as always. Her eyes looked bigger and more luminous. Her cheekbones and her nose were made to stand out and her face was set to be more angular rather than plump.

Cassia then closed her eyes for a moment and wished with all her heart that the dress, the hair and the make-up would all be enough to make Nikos notice her.

October 6, 2003
The Grand Ballroom
Andrade Shipping International
Athens Greece

"I shall be bringing the papers for the initial proposal for the merger later during the engagement party," Costas Andrade told Nikos Demakis over the phone.

"Good. Then we can look them over and finalize everything before the wedding in a month."

"Yes," came the reply.

"All right. If there's nothing else, I'll be going. I still have to prepare for my own engagement party," Nikos said dryly.

His tone did not escape Costas who took it as a chance to spread further lies and start his vengeance both on his granddaughter and the grandson of the man who stole his betrothed.

"Nikos, I have something more to talk to you about." Costas tried to soften his tone so that it would sound as though he was a concerned grandfather. "Why do you think I offered your grandfather this merger when I was so close to ruining your entire family?" Costas asked in a concerned tone.

Nikos' hand tightened on the phone and he resisted the urge to hurl it across the room.

"Why?" he asked. His voice was barely a whisper as he tried to restrain his temper.

"My granddaughter likes you," Costas said in an affectionate tone.

"What?"

"Cassia...she told me so much about you. She told me how she met you at a ball and how you rescued her from a terrible experience. And since that day, she could not stop talking about you anymore. She wanted you and when my granddaughter wants something, I move heaven and earth to give it to her. Please do not break her heart."

Costas wanted to laugh at himself at how he sounded. Judging from the harsh breathing on the other line, Nikos was clearly buying it.

"So what are you saying here, Costas?" Nikos asked in a challenging tone. His temper already got the best of him after hearing Costas' words.

Now, it seemed as if a spoiled little girl had gotten her fancy on him and asked her dear grandfather to get him for her. Instead of looking at it from a point of view wherein Costas' main agenda was revenge, Nikos now saw that he was a bought husband for a spoiled heiress.

And that fact injured his pride even more.

"All I am saying here is that my granddaughter is smitten with you. And somehow, I err...I apologize for this but...somehow I made it look as though you wanted her too. She's a great girl. She'll never agree to an arranged marriage...so...make it look *real*. If my granddaughter sheds a single tear due to you, your family will pay, Demakis," Costas threatened.

"I hear you," Nikos replied through clenched teeth.

"Good."

"If there is nothing else, Costas, I really have to go and prepare for my own engagement party."

"There's nothing else. Just remember this conversation Demakis," Costas finished and then he pressed the button on his phone and ended the call.

As soon as the line went dead, Nikos flew into a rage.

He sat up from his chair and swept his arm across his desk sending all of the things there crashing into the floor. Papers and office supplies scattered everywhere. Glass went all over the carpet as his paperweight shattered.

His secretary entered the room and gasped at the mess she saw.

"Get out!" Nikos growled and the poor woman dashed away.

Right after she shut the door, Nikos collapsed in his chair and placed his head in his hands. He ran his fingers through his hair in both anger and frustration and resisted the compulsion to tug at the black strands.

"He will pay," Nikos vowed.

He then crossed his room and grabbed a bottle of brandy from the liquor cabinet. He took a hefty swig and wiped his mouth with the back of his hand. The liquor burned his throat just as Costas' words burned his pride.

One day, he promised that Costas too would burn like he did.

"Costas Andrade will pay for this. And so will his spoiled little heiress. I will rebuild Demakis International and repay Costas twice or thrice the price that this merger cost him. As for Cassia, her life will be a living hell married to me."

Another swig of alcohol and the fire reached his veins just as his anger had pierced his heart.

"I vow this: one day they will all pay."

Costas Andrade's Limousine
Somewhere in Athens
On the way to Andrade Shipping Corp Headquarters

Costas pushed a button and the privacy partition of the limousine slowly moved upward.

His granddaughter turned towards him and waited for him to start the conversation. Costas pushed another button and it revealed a hidden compartment with crystal glasses and a bottle of champagne. With deft fingers, he uncorked the bottle and poured two glasses.

He handed one to Cassia who took it with much surprise.

First, she did not expect that her grandfather was coming with her to this party. That had actually dampened her mood for she really wanted to have fun with Nikos and to get to know him better tonight.

Second, why were they having champagne? Was there something they should be celebrating?

"Aren't you the least bit curious as to where we are going?" Costas asked.

"I am, grandfather," she replied.

"Drink your champagne, girl. I am sure you'd want to be celebrating this with me." Costas said and then held up his glass in a salute.

Cassia also held up her glass. "What is the special occasion? What are we celebrating?" She asked to humor her grandfather. He wasn't normally in this kind of mood and she wanted to do everything she could to keep him this amiable.

"Why, your engagement of course," Costas announced and then laughed heartily and drank his champagne all in one gulp while Cassia stared at him with her mouth open.

"What?!" Cassia screeched. Then she quickly realized the mistake of her outburst and moved farther from her grandfather.

"Watch your tone with me, girl. And close your mouth or the flies will come in," Costas taunted.

Cassia took several deep breaths to calm herself.

When she first came to Greece to live with her grandfather, she often felt the back of Costas' hand for what he called her fiery temper. He always called her an insolent brat who inherited her mother's ways and hit her because of it. Now, she learned her lesson.

When she deemed that she was calm enough, Cassia spoke:

"What do you mean by saying that we're celebrating my engagement, grandfather?"

"Exactly that. You are not a stupid girl, are you? I just said that it's your engagement. It's as simple as that," Costas answered with a wry smile.

"And who might the groom be? And how come I do not know that I am about to be engaged?" Cassia snorted.

"Do not use that insolent tone with me, girl. Nikos Demakis asked for your hand in marriage. I think you have made a huge impression on him for he came to me and asked for you. In return, I decided to merge *Demakis Shipping* with our company. Sounds like a great deal, *ne*?" Costas said with amusement twinkling in his eyes.

Cassia knew that look. She knew it when her grandfather was mocking her. She also saw that look whenever he made a ruthless business deal or crushed his enemy. Right now, he had that look in his eyes along with another malicious gleam.

Yet at the same time, as Cassia went over the words in her mind, her heart started to beat a frantic rhythm. Only one phrase stood out: *Nikos asked for her hand in marriage.*

"N-Nikos...?"

"Yes. Nikos Demakis. I did not know that you had it in you to catch yourself a husband. And for that, I congratulate you. Nikos is a very intelligent man. He is cunning and extremely good in business. I think he will do well for our company."

Cassia remained silent for she still refused to believe any of this. She knew that Costas was cruel and this may all be some kind of a sick joke.

"I have to warn you, though. Nikos used to date actresses and supermodels. Of course, as his wife you will have a higher status. But men like that would tend to stray... If you can handle it, good. If you cannot, then just divorce him," Costas advised. He said it in a tone so casual that he sounded as if he was just discussing the weather.

Yet again, Cassia was forced to reel in her temper. She stared straight ahead and glared at the leather seats instead of glaring at her grandfather.

A few minutes of silence passed before Costas spoke once more.

"Now let's get a few things straight. And look at me when I am talking to you!" Costas shouted.

Cassia fought the urge to roll her eyes and inclined her head to the side to look at her only remaining family, who also happened to be the man she hated the most.

"Yes, grandfather." Costas allowed her to call him grandfather now for he was now in high spirits. He's finally getting what he wanted so he decided to be a bit more amiable to his *granddaughter*. He drank some more champagne and smiled as he prepared to deliver his lie.

"Good. I want this marriage to push through. Merging *Demakis Shipping* with Andrade Shipping would mean greater business for us —"

"Why? Isn't *Demakis Shipping* already about to close? I read in the newspapers that they are nearing bankruptcy and that there are a lot of controversies about their current business," Cassia interrupted.

"That is none of your concern! Your concern now would be your marriage to the Demakis boy. This merger is my concern and I am not asking for your opinion!" Costas snarled.

"But—"

"Silence!" Costas shouted and raised his hand to strike his granddaughter. However, at the last moment, he was able to control himself. He could not hit her now for it was her engagement party. If he marked her face somehow, people would talk. With that, he was forced to keep his temper in check.

"Now. As I was saying... Do everything you can to make people believe that this is real. There will be rumors that the marriage is just for the merger. But that is *not* true. Nikos met you and he asked me for your hand in marriage," Costas lied once more.

"Yes," Cassia replied in a very low tone. She still refused to believe her grandfather and she promised herself that she would get to the bottom of this mystery.

She finished the champagne in her glass in one gulp. Right on time they arrived at the driveway of *Andrade Shipping International Headquarters*. It was a tall skyscraper in the heart of the metropolis. Right now, the whole building had been transformed from a drab gray corporate headquarters and intoa glittering hall filled with decorations and festivities.

Hundreds of lanterns lit the driveway and a red carpet was rolled out in the center. Cassia watched her grandfather exit the limousine and then waited for him to open the door for her.

Once the door opened, she was forced to play the part of being Costas Andrade's dutiful granddaughter once more.

She placed her hand on her grandfather's arm and let him escort her. She also smiled to the media and forced a smile for him. She answered him politely when he made small talk, laughed at his jokes, and all other things.

Costas steered them into the heart of the crowded function hall which has been transformed into a grand ball room.

And that was when Cassia saw him.

He had his back turned towards her but her eyes immediately zeroed in on him. She noticed his tall frame and that he stood about a head taller than the crowd. She also noticed the rigid set of his shoulders and his defeated stance as he leaned against a marble pillar.

"Nikos!" Costas Andrade greeted.

Cassia noticed Nikos' body stiffen further before he turned around. And then he relaxed and smiled at them. And with that smile, Cassia was lost. Nikos strode towards them and Cassia thought that she must've just imagined the whole thing about his rigid and defeated stance.

He walked towards her and lifted her hand and kissed it. After that, the whole room erupted into whispers.

"Never mind them, *glikia mou*," Nikos said as he pulled her to his side.

For the first time since her grandfather announced that she was getting engaged to Nikos Demakis, she found herself believing that it was all real.

Nikos looked at her and smiled. Cassia looked up into his green eyes and sighed... He was just so handsome.

But she frowned a bit when she saw something different in his eyes.

His smile was warm, his voice was soft...yet his eyes were very cold.

Chapter 4
Engagement

TOMORROW *you get to meet the big boss, Sebastian. I've been bragging to him about you! So don't disappoint me, all right?"*

"I will never do that, sir."

"Excellent, son."

Sebastian's features hardened but he looked away so that the man in front of him would not see the sudden change. He was no man's son. He was nothing but a bastard. He and his mother were discarded by his father as if they were nothing but trash. And this caused the death of his mother.

His boss smiled obliviously as he counted the money before him.

"Sir...about that job. There's been a change of plans. I now want another one. I just realized that I hate working there and I now want something new."

"Pssh. I still do not know what your obsession is with these petty job requests when you already earn so much! But if it makes you happy, it is yours. I will pull strings for you and you may consider it done."

"Thank you, sir," he replied with excitement. He just started to lay down the puzzle pieces of his revenge. And one day, they would all come together.

One day soon...

October 6, 2003
The Great Hall
Andrade Shipping International Headquarters
Athens, Greece

Nikos took Cassia's hand and placed it on the crook of his elbow. Carefully, he led her towards the high table that was reserved for the two of them and their families. Once she was seated comfortably, he cast a sideways glance at her.

She twisted one side of her dress in her fingers as she kept on casting nervous glances towards the crowd. She scanned the people and her eyes landed on her grandfather. Nikos was very much surprised when her gaze did not consist of love and devotion.

Her gaze held hatred, sheer and utter hatred.

But before he could comment on it or ask why, someone clapped him on the shoulder. He turned around and met his friend Antonio's smiling face.

"Won't you introduce me to your beautiful fiancé?" Antonio drawled.

"Of course." Nikos grinned. He stood up and placed his arm on Antonio's shoulder.

"Antonio this is Cassia, my soon-to-be bride. And Cassia, this is Antonio...the greatest *pest* of my life."

Antonio chuckled. "Nice to meet you, Cassia. And contrary to what Nikos said, he is the pest in *my* life."

The moment that Antonio arrived, a great change took place in Nikos. He smiled a real smile for the first time tonight. After Nikos introduced Antonio to her, the two started to make jokes and Cassia also found herself smiling.

"Did you know there was a time that Nikos was not able to take an exam because he got so roaring drunk?" Antonio said in his thick Spanish accent then chuckled. Cassia giggled for his voice reminded her so much of Antonio Banderas.

"It was allhis fault! He was so heartbroken then that he needed some company to drink. And I went! The next thing I knew, it was midday already and the exams were done."

"Ahh...but my friend, I was able to make it and you were not," Antonio taunted.

"I will never forget that day, *compadre*. You don't know what I had to do just to be able to pass that semester," Nikos laughed.

Antonio glanced at Cassia and took in the warmth in her face. She stared at Nikos like he was some sort of hero. Also, he noticed the way she glanced nervously towards her grandfather as though she was waiting for some sort of tragedy to strike.

"Cassia...I apologize but I would have to borrow Nikos for a few minutes, alright? Business talks," Antonio asked.

"Sure. Go ahead," Cassia replied as she took her seat.

Antonio pulled Nikos to one corner of the room and both of them sat.

"I heard you trashed your office earlier," Antonio remarked casually.

"Yes. Costas got to me," Nikos replied in a hate-filled voice.

"What happened?"

"It seems that I was bought, my friend. Cassia liked me because I saved her from being humiliated one night. Then she decided she's got to have me. She then told her dear grandfather about it. And Costas, being the ever doting grandfather, he decided to offer the merger instead of thoroughly destroying Demakis International."

Antonio did not reply for a very long time. He kept staring at the decoration in the middle of the table and looked as if he was deep in thought. Nikos saw that his eyes also scanned the grand ballroom which was very elaborately decorated today.

The tables were covered with a pristine-white table cloth with gold at the center. In the middle of it were beautiful ice sculptures of Greek gods and goddesses. The center of the room now held a fountain that contained Atlas who held the world in his shoulders. The guests' dresses were also inspired by traditional Greek dress.

While Antonio was deep in thought, Nikos took the opportunity to scan his surroundings. Men and women who were dressed expensively mingled with each other. If this were an ordinary party and not his engagement party, he'd surely be on the prowl for a new conquest. Some of his old conquests like supermodels who did wicked things with him in bed were even here, along with many potential new ones. However, this was his engagement party and he should be enjoying this with his fiancé. But it felt like his funeral.

It hit him.

This lifestyle and everything in it was what he was giving up to save the family business.

He'd be giving up the women, the fast-paced living, the jet setting to whichever country and city he wanted, the late night parties, the countless mistresses, the gambling, the drinking and everything else.

Nikos shook his head to clear it of that line of thought and scanned the room once more. This time, his gaze flitted towards the waiters who kept on roaming the room bearing platters of *hors d'oeuvres*, shrimp cocktails, wine, and other drinks. His gaze also went towards the side of the room which was converted into a bar.

His hands itched to get a drink.

"You know...I still do not think that is the case. Have you looked at Cassia, my friend? She seems to be a nice girl and not like the spoiled heiresses we are used to."

"Well, some fruits look good on the outside but are rotten on the inside," Nikos scoffed.

Antonio shook his head sadly. "I still do not think that this is the case, Nikos. And I have a really bad feeling about this. What's your plan now?"

"I'll let her see what kind of husband she bought. And I'll make sure I drive her to another man so that I could file for divorce and all of Demakis International and Andrade Shipping will fall to my hands," Nikos said in a very determined tone.

Antonio sighed.

"Revenge is not a good thing."

Nikos raised an eyebrow and then threw back his head and laughed.

"Since when did you get so wise? Did you get a new job as my guardian angel or something?"

Antonio rolled his eyes also and laughed.

"I just can't shake this feeling that you're about to do something wrong."

"And now you have become an oracle or a soothsayer," Nikos teased.

"I see that your tongue is still as charming as ever! You best be coming back to your future bride," Antonio said before he stood up.

Nikos also stood up and started to follow his friend but Costas stood in his way.

"There you are. I've been looking everywhere for you."

"Ah, Mr. Andrade. You have the papers?"

"Yes. Here they are. You can review them and just contact my legal team for any changes. The final contract will be signed right after the wedding."

"All right then, I will get in touch. I will read through this and also have my grandfather and our legal team review it."

Costas then handed Nikos a thick envelope. Nikos raised his hand and motioned for his executive secretary to approach him. The man approached and retrieved the papers from him.

"If that is everything, I have to go back to my party," Nikos said flatly.

"That is everything," Costas replied with a smug grin.

Nikos excused himself and went back to find Cassia who was still sitting in the spot he left her in. She stared at the crowd warily and he noticed that she was twisting her skirts yet again.

"Cassia." Nikos called. Immediately, she raised her head and her brown eyes looked straight into his.

"I want to introduce you to my grandfather," Nikos told her.

She stood up and he took her arm and led her across the room and towards his grandfather

"Grandfather, this is Cassia, my future bride. Cassia, this is my grandfather, Stavros Demakis," Nikos introduced.

Stavros looked at Cassia from head-to-toe and then leaned forward and gave her a kiss on both cheeks.

"Nice to meet you, Cassia. And welcome to the family," Stavros said.

Cassia noticed the coldness in his tone and the way his eyes hardened like Nikos' did earlier.

She peered up at Stavros and tried to study his expression but his face remained blank. A second later, Stavros turned his back on her and continued talking to his fellow businessmen. With that, Cassia's spirits fell. She knew she was not welcome with Nikos' family.

"I guess that means your grandfather doesn't like me," she whispered in defeat.

"*Pappou* doesn't like a lot of people," Nikos replied dryly.

"What about your parents, then? Will they like me?" she asked.

"You don't have to worry about my parents. They are too busy traveling the world to pay me any notice. If they don't notice me then maybe they would not notice you too," Nikos muttered.

He realized later that he'd been rude and he quickly made amends.

"And it does not matter. It's not them who are getting married. It's us," he explained and even squeezed her hand to comfort her. She lifted her head once more and smiled at him.

And something tightened inside Nikos' chest at the sight of that smile.

"Thank you, Nikos..." she whispered dreamily.

With those words, Nikos was snapped back to reality for he realized that this girl truly had a bad case of infatuation with him.

"Well, time for the big announcement," he said as he took her hand and guided her towards the dance floor.

The moment they were in the middle, the music stopped and the entire crowd became silent.

"Good evening everyone. I know that some of you already know why we are gathered here tonight. And I also know that some are still baffled as to why. So let me announce this right now. The lovely Cassia Andrade has agreed to marry me and this is our engagement party! So tonight, help yourselves to the food, the wine and I bid you enjoy!" Nikos announced.

To make everything look real, he pulled Cassia affectionately towards his side and placed a kiss on her temple. He also felt her stiffen in surprise and then further melt against him.

He turned around and faced her then put his hand on her waist. With his other hand, he signalled the orchestra to play some music. Then he took her hand and they waited for the music to start so they could dance.

Nikos saw Cassia's eyes flare with panic.

"What's wrong?"

"I don't know how to dance."

"I seem to recall that we danced fine the first night we met," Nikos pointed out.

Cassia shook her head nervously and bit her lip.

"Don't worry. It's fine. Just follow my lead," he ordered.

Cassia nodded and with that, the couple took their first step which was followed by another and then another...

While they danced, Cassia finally realized that this was not a dream.

This was not a fairytale and that this was better than all the scenarios she came up with in her head.

This was real...

She was truly with Nikos Demakis.

She was now engaged, and in a month's time, she would be married to the same guy who took the lead role in all of her fantasies.

Chapter 5
Wedding

November 15, 2003 (More than one month later)
Antoniou Winery
The Island of Santorini, Greece

YOU look so beautiful, Cassia," Anna told her.

Cassia smiled at her and squeezed her hand. It was truly a good thing that her friend was here, for her nerves were eating her alive. Here she was in her room, in all her wedding finery, in the wait for the moment of her wedding to come.

"Come on, do a twirl for me, my friend. I want this to stay in my memory forever," Anna pleaded.

"Sure. By the way, thanks for being here. I don't know what I'll do without you," Cassia said, and with those words, her eyes started to fill with tears.

"No! Don't cry. You'll ruin your perfect make-up. And it's nothing! You paid for all of my expenses! Of course, I won't let the opportunity to travel pass me by. I'll never earn the fare here in my meager job back at home. And I'm really enjoying it here so far! So stop going all sentimental on me, all right?" Anna chastised.

Cassia laughed and wiped away her tears with a tissue before they could fall and ruin her make-up. Then she stood up and did a twirl for her best friend who had been with her since her parents died. They were once fostered together and stayed friends ever since.

Cassia wore a cream-colored wedding gown envisioned by one of the top international designers. She fell in love with it the moment she first set eyes upon it. The beading and the design in the bodice, where diamonds were embedded, was very intricate. The skirt of the gown fit her hips snugly and then flared out into a skirt with a very long train.

The train was a bit heavy but she still loved it. She twirled for her friend and they both laughed when she managed not to fall.

"You really look so beautiful. I never thought I'd see you like this," Anna said, and this time she was the one who wiped away tears that threatened to fall.

"Thank you, Anna." Cassia smiled as she hugged her tightly.

"Wait! We might wrinkle your gown!" Anna laughed.

"This is an expensive gown. I don't think it would get wrinkled that easily," Cassia teased.

"True," her friend agreed.

Cassia sat on the chaise once more and willed the time to pass away so that her wedding and her life with Nikos could start.

"So...tell me about this Nikos guy that you are marrying. What's he like? Every time I see him, he's polite and all. He's also really good-looking. But...I don't know Cass...he seems *cold* to me. There's something about him I can't quite fathom," Anna said thoughtfully.

Cassia tilted her head to the side and thought about her friend's observation of her fiancé. During the past month after her engagement, she went to all her social obligations with Nikos as her date. They also went together to the places and events for their wedding preparations.

Nikos was always on time. He was always perfectly polite, always immaculately dressed and always a perfect gentleman.

Just like Anna said, Nikos was a great man...he just seemed *cold*. And there was something else about him that was different.

Maybe it was the way his eyes looked as if they were filled with rage?

Maybe it was the way he looked at everyone in a cynical and calculating manner?

Maybe it was the way he held his body rigidly?

Cassia shook her head and let go of those thoughts. Nikos was a great man. He was very smart and he had made a fortune for himself already at such a very young age. Everyone had their faults so maybe his surly attitude was his.

"Nikos is really like that. But overall he's a great guy. Maybe he was just brought up in the kind of environment where everything's cold and has to be perfect." Cassia shuddered for that was how her grandfather wanted her to be, and sadly, she was far from perfect.

"Huh. Then why does it sound to me as though you are convincing yourself rather than saying it to me?"

Cassia glared at her.

"I don't know...I am not even sure about all of this...it's all so fast..."

"I agree that it's all so fast. What if your grandfather had something to do with all of this?"

"I don't know, Anna. Maybe he did. Maybe he didn't. I also put in the equation the fact that his company was almost ruined and that maybe this is all a business deal," Cassia sighed.

"If you know those things then why are you still marrying him?" Anna asked as she placed Cassia's veil in position.

Cassia didn't reply for she did not know how to tell her friend how much she wanted Nikos Demakis, so much that she was willing to overlook the fact that her brain was screaming to her that something was definitely wrong.

"Maybe I'm just selfish when it comes to him. I've got him, Anna. I don't want to let go. I believe we'd be great together. I can't wait to start my life with him."

"What if he's wrong for you?" Anna prodded.

"It's him for me. If this is wrong, I don't ever want to be right."

Anna sighed and when Cassia looked around, she saw that her friend had tears in her eyes.

"Now I know why you want to marry him, Cass. You've got it bad for him," she stated.

Cassia sighed. "I do."

"Then I wish you all the best on this marriage."

"Thank you, Anna. You're the best!" Cassia replied and hugged the other woman tightly.

Suddenly, there was a knock on the door.

Anna hurried to open it and Costas and his personal assistant rushed inside the room.

"Let's go," he barked. He wore a black tuxedo and his hair was slicked back. He also "brandished" an elegant wooden cane today.

She saw Anna roll her eyes before they turned and followed Costas out of the room. Cassia flipped her veil over her face and smoothed the skirts of her gown as they ascended the staircase and moved towards the open balcony with a beautiful view of the sea.

The view was truly breathtaking. The Greek coast was such a beautiful sight! The first moment that Cassia arrived and she was able to see the view, she was truly dazed. That was the second time she knew that it was possible to fall in love at first sight.

"This is it, princess. It's your time to shine," Anna whispered as she fixed the train of Cassia's gown on the floor.

She also handed Cassia her bouquet and the moment that her fingers touched it, her heart started to beat erratically.

Any moment now, the doors to the balcony would open. Then the music would sound and she would walk down that aisle. She'd say some words, exchange rings...

...And then she'd truly be married to Nikos Demakis.

Mrs. Cassia Demakis...

She stifled a giggle at the thought and concentrated on staring ahead of her while her grandfather bristled with impatience at her side. They were still maintaining the act that they were a happy family and Costas was going to give her away at her own wedding.

Cassia waited and waited but the doors still did not open. A few more minutes passed and a shiver of unease slid down her spine.

Suddenly, Cassia saw Antonio exit the room. He looked flushed and his face was pale. And by his frazzled appearance, Cassia immediately knew that something was wrong. Nikos' friend never lost control and he was always as immaculate as possible.

Yet right now, he looked as if he was on the verge of panic.

"What happened, Velez?" Costas hissed.

Antonio looked up and, for a moment, his gaze landed on Cassia. For a moment, he appeared stunned. Costas repeated the question but Antonio acted as if he did not hear it. Costas repeated the question for the third time and this time he was shouting. That seemed to snap Antonio out of whatever trance he was in.

He ran his fingers through his hair.

"There's a problem. But I am already taking care of it," Antonio answered. But when he said this, he was looking at Cassia and not at Costas who asked the question.

"What is it?!" Costas bellowed.

Antonio shrugged and then moved closer to Cassia. "I don't know what happened but someone might have spiked Nikos' drink before the wedding. He is now very intoxicated. Please give me some time to fix this," he answered.

Before Costas could reply or ask more questions, Antonio was gone.

"This is your entire fault!" Costas hissed at Cassia.

"How is this my fault?!" Cassia cried out in despair before she was able to stop herself. Her hands shook too much because of her wedding jitters. Furthermore, to find out that her groom was drunk was like a big blow to her ego.

"You insolent brat! Lower your tone! This is your fault! It's because of you that your groom has got himself drunk! He does not want to marry someone like you! A half-greek, half American bastard who grew up in the slums!"

Anna gasped and Costas glared at her and then inclined his head to the side.

"You want to know the truth? Nikos never wanted to marry you! I got him to do it so that they will not lose their company! I offered them the merger in exchange for marrying you! And I did it because I wanted revenge on his family. I want him to suffer. A man like him will definitely suffer with a bride like you! When he finally divorces you, as per the contract, I'll get all the money back! Then Stavros Demakis will surely die knowing that it was his precious grandson who lost him everything!"

"WHAT?!" Cassia shouted.

"Yes, dear girl. So you be good today. Nikos needs to marry you so he could gain back *Demakis International*. He needs you and his family needs you. Maybe he just wanted to drink some brandy to steel his nerves for the ordeal he has to go through today. Then got himself blindingly drunk!" Costas roared with laughter. "I would too if I had to marry someone like you."

Cassia reeled as if she'd been slapped. She looked at her grandfather and he shook his head at her and left. She could still hear his curses along with his laughter echoing across the narrow corridor.

She was so stunned that her bouquet slipped from her fingers at the same moment that tears fell from her eyes. Her entire body felt numb and she wished that the floor could open up and swallow her right at that moment.

"No...sweetie, don't. He did not mean that...you know that's not true. He's just a bitter old man," Anna whispered as she hugged her.

But even Anna knew that Costas' words already did their damage.

"Cassia...please...just allow some time...and then all of this would be well. It might have just been a prank by Nikos' friends or something. I think it was not his intention to get drunk at his own wedding."

"I think it's all true," she whispered.

"No! Don't say that! Come on, let's go somewhere you can sit," Anna said and tugged on Cassia's gloved hand and led her towards an empty function room.

"I knew it was too good to be true..."

"Stop this right now, Cassia! Get a hold of yourself! You know your grandfather hates you. He just said those things to ruin your day! You should not let him do that!" Anna screeched as she started pacing the room in frustration.

Cassia walked towards one of the couches and then sat. She stared at the floor and started to cry silently. A thousand thoughts flitted through her mind at the moment but the one taking the forefront was that all that her grandfather said was true.

Maybe Nikos was truly coerced with this marriage so he would be able to save his family's company. Maybe he just couldn't think of marrying her that he drank and drank until he got so wasted he couldn't even attend his own wedding.

Cassia sighed and tried to stop more tears from falling. There were hundreds of guests all waiting at the balcony. All of them were rich and famous. Most of them were Nikos' friends and the people who humiliated her before when she tried to fit in with this kind of lifestyle. By now they must've known what truly happened.

She was sure that by now their voices were hoarse from laughing at her.

"Cass! Stop it already! You'll ruin your make-up! And I am sure that this wedding is going to push through! Your grandfather is wrong, okay? Let's just trust that Antonio will be able to fix this. I'm just going to go and check out the status of things. Maybe he needs some help to get Nikos settled. Stay here, okay? I'll be back as soon as I can," Anna instructed.

Cassia heard the words of her friend but she was too numb to answer or to even nod. She just stared straight ahead and wished for her humiliation to end.

After what felt like an eternity later, the door opened and she looked up.

A young man with sandy-blonde hair and the bluest eyes she's ever seen entered the room. He was so tall and he looked incredibly handsome. He was wearing a waiter's uniform and held a tray in those two hands. When Cassia looked at him, he did a double take and almost dropped the tray of used glasses that he was carrying.

"I'm sorry. I didn't know this room was occupied," he told her.

"It's fine. Do you need me to leave?" Cassia sniffled.

"No ma'am...it's fine...you are welcome to stay here and I'll be the one leaving," he replied.

Cassia heard his footsteps and then assumed he was gone so she let her tears fall once more.

What surprised her was when a shadow loomed over her. She looked up and saw the waiter with his hand held out as he offered her a handkerchief.

"T-thanks..." Cassia stammered.

She accepted the item and then used it to wipe away her tears.

"You can also blow your nose if you want to," the waiter said in a teasing tone.

Cassia couldn't help it and a bubble of laughter spilled from her lips.

"There, that's the smile I've been waiting for. You know, brides should smile on their wedding day...not cry like their heart is broken."

"Not this bride," Cassia whispered under her breath.

Indeed, her heart truly was broken. The waiter seemed to have read her thoughts somehow and sighed.

"I heard what happened and I am sorry for it," he told her.

"Thank you," Cassia replied curtly.

"Would you mind if I sit here?" the waiter asked as he indicated the opposite edge of the sofa.

Cassia shook her head and she felt the other side of the sofa depress as he sat down.

"My name is Hector, by the way. Would you mind if I asked for your name?"

"My name is Cassia..."

"They say that the best thing to do when you're feeling nervous or in an unhappy situation is to talk about it. I hope I am not overstepping any boundaries ma'am but I would really like to help. I could lend my listening ear to you," Hector said with a warm smile.

Cassia wasn't able to reply for a long time for she was pondering what to tell him. She was very glad that he was here to take her mind off some things but she just didn't know what to say. It was definitely a long story and one that only seemed to happen in soap operas.

Hector mistook it for her unwillingness to talk and he stood up. Cassia quickly grabbed his hand and tugged it so that he would be forced to sit on the sofa once more.

"No! I am sorry. It's just that I am thinking of how I should say things to you..."

"It's alright, take your time," Hector replied and then he leaned back on the sofa and stared at the ceiling.

"Today, I thought I'd be marrying Nikos Demakis, a man almost every woman wants. And I thought I was special because he wanted me too. I thought he was able to see through my ugly face, my half-Greek, half-American background. I thought he was able to see that I am not as shallow as those dumb blondes and that I could have a very intelligent conversation with him," Cassia said and then more tears started to fall.

She used Hector's handkerchief to wipe all those away.

"Hmm...may I be blunt?"

"Y-yes," Cassia stammered.

"First, I do not think that you are ugly. You are very beautiful. I just don't think that blonde hair suits you and I do not think that is the original color of your hair. Second, what is wrong with being half-

Greek, half-American? I am half-Greek, half-American and I think there's nothing wrong with that. Third, I see the intelligence shining through your eyes. If you were given the opportunity to do whatever you want to do, what would it be?"

"I want to become a fashion designer," Cassia replied with all of her heart.

"Then why not go to college and make those dreams come true?"

"My grandfather won't allow it."

Cassia sighed. Hector was silent.

"What about you? Did you grow up here in Greece?" she asked.

"Yes. But this is actually my last day of work and my last day here in Greece. Later this day I'm going back to America and I'll be trying to make all of my dreams come true."

"What are those dreams?"

"I want to have my own business. I'd start with a few restaurants. I'm a really good cook, have I told you that? If there was time, I'd cook something for you and I'm sure you wouldn't cry again," he bragged.

Cassia laughed and something softened in Hector's eyes. He, too, smiled and the overall mood suddenly became light.

"I hope all your dreams come true. Invite me to the grand opening of your first restaurant. Okay? I want to taste that food you are bragging about."

"I most definitely will invite you. But I think that's still a long time in the future. Of course, capital is hard to come by. I need a big one for my business."

Again there was a huge amount of silence between the two of them.

"If a groom gets drunk on his wedding day, what does that mean? Be blunt please. I can handle it."

"Maybe his friends just played a prank on him..." Hector answered first to lighten the mood.

"Or?"

"...Or maybe he needed the confidence that the alcohol brings," Hector shrugged.

He flinched when he saw pain come back to Cassia's eyes.

"He really needed that to marry someone like me."

"No...don't put yourself down like that. Never ever see yourself through other people's eyes. If at first you do not respect and believe in yourself then other people won't either and they'll continue putting you down. You must show the world what you are capable of. Show them that you are better than those airheads," Hector lectured.

Cassia smiled amidst her tears.

"If there was only a way to escape this island..." Cassia mused.

"What if there is, would you take it?" Hector asked.

He sat up a little straighter and looked at Cassia directly in the eyes.

Cassia laughed, a hollow and bitter laugh.

"Me? Escape? That's hard. My grandfather has this whole place locked down with his security. And no one would dare drive me out of towards the dock. Even then, I'd have to wait for a boat to take me to the mainland and then wait for a plane. I don't have any ticket or any money with me..."

"I have a motorcycle. And I have a small boat I use to travel to the mainland. I can get you there. Speaking of the tickets...I have two. My girlfriend was supposed to return with me to America but we broke up. I can loan the extra ticket to you. Hmm...about money? I'm sure we can sell one bauble you have on you and there'll be plenty of money to start a life back home. If you sell all of your jewelry, I am sure you could even go to college," Hector explained with purpose.

In a flash, Cassia was already standing. Hope surged within her and for the first time, she started to believe that she could still make all her dreams come true.

"We can go home?" she said in a voice filled with longing.

"Yes," came Hector's determined reply.

"Let's go!" Cassia eagerly exclaimed.

Hector threw the door open for her and the two of them dashed down three levels of a narrow, winding staircase. Cassia's silk gown and her veil billowed in the wind as she ran.

And she never felt freer in all her years...

Cassia and Hector laughed as they both continued to run. Cassia slipped one time and Hector offered her his hand. Then hand in hand, they ran for their freedom...

Hector climbed in his motorcycle and it took a few tries before it was able to start.

While she was waiting for the motorcycle to start, doubts crept into her mind.

Was this truly the right thing to do?

If she fled, then Costas would win. The merger would not push through; Nikos would gain nothing and lose everything. But if she married Nikos today, and divorced him tomorrow stating that she was at fault and she had a lover...then she would get back at her grandfather. Nikos would get back the *Demakis Shipping Corporation* as their merger contract stated and her grandfather would be the one who lost everything.

After she had set everything right, then she could leave this life behind and go back to America where she could finally have the life she wanted.

"Let's go, princess," Hector said with a smile as he offered Cassia his hand to help her climb onto his motorcycle.

For a moment there, Cassia stood motionless as she debated what to do.

Freedom or revenge against her grandfather?

How could she choose when freedom was this close? When freedom just meant climbing on to Hector's motorcycle and throwing all caution to the wind?

But as always, her good heart won over and she sadly shook her head.

"I am sorry, Hector...I have to set everything right. I have to marry him today. If I do that and divorce him tomorrow, all the money will go to him and my grandfather would be left with nothing. You see, it's all because of Costas that all this happened to Nikos' family. I have to correct all my grandfather's mistakes. I have the power to do it and I will."

"Is that it then...is money truly everything?"

"For them...not for me. Wait for me in America. I'll try and find you. Hopefully I'll be on my way there tomorrow or within the week after I shock the world with my divorce."

"Such a kind heart, princess. Now I know why people step all over you. Just promise me one thing: never ever allow anyone to do that ever again. Hold your head high because you are better than all of them."

"I promise. But you have to promise me something in return..."

"Anything, princess," Hector replied.

Cassia smiled at the endearment.

Cassia reached over to her left wrist and unclasped her diamond and sapphire-studded gold watch. It was supposed to be her "something old and blue" for her wedding. But right now, it looked as if it was some silly superstition. Her wedding was a sham and she needed no good-luck charm in this part of her life. Besides, it would be better suited for Hector's purpose.

"Go and fulfill your dreams, and I still want to be present in that grand opening!" Cassia said with a tender smile as she reached forward and placed the watch in Hector's stunned fingers.

"No! I can't possibly accept this."

"You are the first person who's been kind to me in Greece. I have more where that came from and I know that you'll put the money to good use. Think of this as a loan from me. And when you're already making it big in the restaurant industry, you can always pay me back. And I won't take no for an answer."

"This is too much... I thank you for this gift. I vow that I will work harder and fulfill my dreams. And when the time comes that I am able to reach them, I'll buy you a treasure trove filled with these," he promised.

"I'll hold you to that promise."

"Last chance for freedom, princess...come with me," Hector said as he offered his hand once more.

It was tempting - oh, so tempting to just take his hand, forget everything and start a new life. But just like before, the other side of her won and Cassia shook her head

"I really have to do this."

"I understand. Well...see you in America!" Hector shouted over the roar of the motorcycle's engine.

With a last salute towards Cassia, he sped off into the driveway and then into the city.

Cassia watched him go with a heaviness in her heart.

When he was gone, she steeled herself and prepared to come back to her sham of a wedding. She would do this for Nikos' family. She would make her grandfather pay for all the times that he manipulated people's lives.

First Costas would pay...and then she'd be free.

Chapter 6
Nightmare

MAMA...I'm here," Sebastian whispered as he laid flowers above his mother's grave. *Today was her death anniversary and it was one of the days in the year that he hated the most. She would not be dead if not for Stavros Demakis. This was all his fault.*

"I will be away for a while. I've decided to move on, ma. I cannot stay this way. I want another kind of life. The one we deserve. If only you were here now, I would have bought you everything your heart desired..."

Tears stung his eyes but he dashed them back with his hand.

"But I will just settle for revenge on the people who did this to us. I will stop at nothing until we get what is our due. Because of that, I would have to leave. But I promise you, mama...I will never forget you. You're forever in my heart."

November 15, 2003 (A few hours earlier)
Antoniou Winery
The Island of Santorini, Greece

Nikos Demakis flung open the doors of his suite and stared out into the open ocean.

The breeze blew cold air towards his face and he closed his eyes in bliss. He arched his back and tilted his head towards the sun to feel the early morning warmth on his skin. Afterwards, he stretched and opened his eyes to watch the seagulls flying around and marveled at the freedom they had.

They could go anywhere they wanted to be and more importantly, they could pair with whichever seagull they wanted to be with.

Unlike him.

Nikos closed his eyes once more and sighed.

This was a beautiful morning. The signs were all pointing to this being a beautiful day. But not for him.

Why?

Because it was his wedding day.

Nikos snorted at the irony. Weddings were supposed to be fun things. It was when grooms looked forward to seeing their brides in that white dress as they walked down the aisle. It was the time that men were supposed to be nervous about starting a new life together with the woman they loved.

But that was not the case for him.

He did not want this wedding and he would have given anything just to escape his current situation. But giving away everything so that he wouldn't have to marry would really leave him with nothing. Not only would he lose all he had, he would also lose his grandfather's beloved company.

And there was no other way but to get this marriage over with.

Nikos heaved a great sigh at his inescapable reality.

He entered his room once more and glanced at the wrapped parcels placed in his table. All of those were gifts from his friends and he knew that they all contained the finest, most expensive wines and alcoholic beverages in the world. Suddenly he was transported to a few days back when his friends held his bachelor party for him.

"For your wedding, my friend."

One of his male friends laughed as he handed over a wrapped parcel.

"What is this?" he asked teasingly.

"The finest vodka in all of Russia. I give you this, my friend because I think you need some liquid courage to marry Cassia Andrade," his friend said and the entire group laughed, including him.

"I think I do. Thanks for this," he replied while he still chuckled.

The rest of the group whipped out their own presents which consisted of different bottles of the finest wines. He raised an eyebrow in inquiry which just made their group laugh harder.

"And this is to make it through every single day after the marriage. I suggest you use Dylan's absinthe for the wedding night," another one jested with a wink, and that comment brought on another round of laughter.

But the one that laughed the hardest was him. And it was at the expense of his own bride-to-be

Nikos walked over to the table and unwrapped said absinthe. He wanted to have maybe just one shot to calm his nerves today. His friends warned him that the absinthe was simply lethal but he was confident in his ability and his tolerance for alcohol since he had been drinking for years already. He even considered himself a connoisseur of the finest wines.

Nikos uncorked the bottle and read the label. He let it sit on the table for a few minutes to expose it to air as he tried to find a glass from the mini-bar in his suite. He sat on the stool in front of the marble countertop of the mini-bar and began to drink. The liquor was cool on his tongue and yet burned a path down his throat.

For the second time that day, Nikos found himself laughing at his current situation. Here he was, supposed to be wed a few hours from now and he was drinking just to be able to go through with it. He definitely did not want to be drunk but he just wanted the kind of buzz to make him not care about anything anymore.

With that, he poured himself another glass.

He even grabbed some lemon from the refrigerator to act as his chaser and wash away the bitter taste in his mouth. He downed another glass and then another before he found the will to stop himself.

Nikos knew his tolerance level and the amount he just consumed would definitely give him the buzz he wanted, yet was still far enough from being flat-out drunk. He stood up and then immediately felt that something was wrong.

His head was spinning and he had to brace his body on the side of the counter to avoid falling down. The room around him continued to spin and Nikos lost his balance. His hand immediately went to his head as he started feeling faint.

He frowned and then pulled himself up to a standing position. He reached for the bottle of absinthe which was still about two thirds full. He sniffed it and his body became taut with rage as he realized what happened.

Damn those bastards for spiking my drink!

That was his last thought before the world did another spin and he crashed to the floor, taking the bottle of liquor with him as he lost consciousness.

A few hours later...

"Shit, Nikos!"

"Wake up, goddammit!"

"Nikos!"

Nikos reluctantly opened his eyes and lifted his head. However, his brain felt as though it was laden with lead. He groaned and then closed his eyes and flung his arm across his face to block out the light.

However, his agony was doubled when the owner of the persistent voice started to shake him.

"Damn it, Nikos! It's your wedding! You should not be like this!" Antonio lectured as he ran his fingers through his hair in frustration.

He loosened his bowtie and released the buttons on his cuffs so he could move more freely and help his friend. While he did this, he also cursed fluently in Spanish.

He hauled Nikos to his feet and dragged him towards the bed, muttering curses as he tried to figure out what to do. He checked his watch and knew that the groom was definitely going to be late for his own wedding.

Antonio sighed in frustration and then walked outside of the room to call for Nikos' bodyguards. Three of them entered the room and he quickly started barking out orders.

"Strip him and then get him to the bathroom. Bathe the alcohol off him," he instructed. The bodyguards look baffled but they quickly hid their expressions when they saw the state that Nikos was currently in. They set to work and Antonio helped them carry Nikos to the bathroom. Then, he stepped out for he was also afraid to ruin his own tux for the wedding.

"You're going to pay for this one day, Nikos," Antonio growled low.

He exited the room to deliver the news to Nikos' bride and to her grandfather who was known for his ruthless temper. Antonio hated to be the bearer of bad news but there was no one else to do it.

Well, wish me luck.

Two Hours Later...

"Come on, drink a little more," Antonio urged as he handed the barely-awake Nikos some more coffee.

"Nooo. Lemme lone," Nikos slurred

"I can't do that! You are very late for your own wedding!" Antonio shouted in extreme frustration.

It only heightened another notch when Nikos started to laugh.

"Zat's the point! I don wanna go to that wedding!"

Antonio had the sudden urge to slap his best friend.

"You can't do that! We have been over this a thousand times over! Look at me Nikos," Antonio commanded and then tugged on the lapels of Nikos' jacket so that he would be forced to look at him.

Nikos' head lolled but he was able to look at his friend.

"Your grandfather's whole company depends on your marrying this girl. Remember your plans? You were going to do it and then you were going to do your best to raise your company from the shambles it's in. One day it can be independent from *Andrade International* and you can have your divorce and live the life you wanted. But for now, you have got to go through with this wedding!"

Nikos leaned back across the couch and closed his eyes.

His friend's words finally penetrated his haze-filled mind. He remembered the things he had to do and all the responsibilities that were in his shoulders.

"How? How am I to marry like this?" Nikos asked, his voice barely a whisper.

"That's what a best man is for," Antonio smirked as he clapped his friend on the shoulder.

Nikos accepted the cup of coffee and began to drink. He winced at the extra strong coffee his best man prepared for him.

"You know, Cassia is really beautiful today... You should see her."

"I know she's beautiful...but that'll be doubled coz I'm hammered," he teased and both of them laughed.

"Let's go do this, then?"

"Let's go," Antonio replied with a determined grin.

Two hours later, Nikos had enough coffee to be able to stand up straight. The room didn't spin anymore but instead, he felt terribly drowsy.

"Look now, Nikos. Here she comes, your bride," Antonio ordered.

Nikos lifted his head from his brief nap on his best man's shoulder and tried to look as attentive as he could as his bride walked down the aisle. However, he found himself nodding off to sleep every couple of seconds or so and just woke up when Antonio nudged him in the ribs.

Nikos opened his red eyes and tried to squint to see his bride. But his vision was blurred and all he could see was the white dress and the veil she wore. He couldn't even make out the details of the dress to complement her on it. She walked beside her grandfather who beamed like an idiot.

That was the last thing he saw before he dozed off once more.

"Nikos!" Antonio nudged his friend on the ribs. He sighed when he saw Nikos shake his head in order to remain awake. They were standing beside the aisle and Nikos leaned heavily on him in order to stand.

Without him, Nikos truly wouldn't be able to attend his own wedding.

Again, he sighed as he watched Cassia walking down the aisle. She had her head down and was staring at the floor instead of staring all teary-eyed at her groom like brides were supposed to. Antonio couldn't blame her. People were laughing at her because they had all heard about her drunken groom.

This was truly a huge jest if this was not his best friend's wedding. He would have laughed himself hoarse. But right now, the situation did not warrant any laughter and he sure as hell could not laugh after seeing the pain in Cassia's eyes.

Finally, she reached the aisle and her grandfather reached over to take her hand and give it to Nikos. But Nikos miscalculated and took Costas' hand instead of his bride's. He even had the nerve to laugh loudly.

Costas laughed too and then everyone followed suit. Antonio poked Nikos' ribs once more when he noticed that Cassia was staring at the floor as though wishing that it would just swallow her at that moment.

"We are gathered here today to witness the joining of Cassia Andrade and Nikos Demakis in holy matrimony. Marriage is a huge step in life for it brings two souls together as one. Two people enter a covenant with each other and they are bound forever. That binding starts with love. Their life together starts today."

Again, Antonio sighed and rubbed his temple when Nikos snorted at the word love. That act alone caused some of the guests to also snicker and point their fingers at Cassia's stony profile.

"Don't mind him, he's drunk," Antonio told Cassia in an attempt to lighten the mood.

She managed a weak smile for him and answered in a soft voice, "I can clearly see that."

And Antonio's heart broke for her.

"If there is someone who objects to this union, speak now or forever hold your peace."

Antonio saw Nikos raise his hand and it was a good thing he was able to stop it. He saw Nikos' intent before he carried it out so he was able to take hold of his friend's arm and pin it to his side.

"Mama why can't the man stand straight?" a child's voice rang clearly from the audience.

It was followed by a loud "Shhh!" from the mother and more laughter from Nikos' friends and ex-girlfriends who were also present in the wedding.

Antonio wiped his face with his hand and thought about fate playing a trick on all of them. *How could any day get worse than this?*

The best man tried to pull a straight face and tried harder to listen to the priest as he recited a bible passage from the book of Corinthians which spoke all about love. While he was listening, he kept an eye on the groom who still continued to doze.

The priest droned on and on about things about marriage that Nikos could not understand. All he knew was that Antonio nudged him whenever he had to stand. And when he was supposed to sit, he used it as a perfect opportunity for a little nap. He bowed his head so that it would look as if he was solemn and deep in thought about the things the priest was saying.

But the truth was that he could not understand anything.

He barely realized the essentials of the ceremony and he functioned as if he were a robot under Antonio's expert control. He even remembered smiling at his best man after Antonio caught him when he nearly pitched forward towards the floor.

"Do you, Nikos, take this woman to be your lawfully wedded wife, to love and to cherish, to have and to hold; and do you promise, forsaking all others, to cleave to her and her alone, for as long as you both shall live?"

Nikos did not hear the question and he did not understand the words. He assumed that it was just a part of the things that a priest must say so he remained silent. But he felt Antonio nudge him. He looked at his friend and Antonio mouthed the words *"I do"* repeatedly.

The priest coughed and repeated the question. Once more, this caused their beloved guests to laugh. Nikos finally understood it and he said "I do." But he said it in a voice which just showed everyone how drunk he was.

"Do you, Cassia, take this man to be your lawfully wedded husband, to love and to cherish, to have and to hold; and do you promise, forsaking all others, to cleave to him and to him alone, for as long as you both shall live?"

"I do," Cassia replied.

Antonio's heart broke for her once more when he heard that her voice was barely a whisper. He also heard all the heart and humiliation that Cassia kept bottled up inside of her.

"Please repeat after me," the priest instructed and Nikos obliged. But it took them several tries before he was able to finish his vows.

"Is there something wrong with the groom? He seems drunk. This wedding should be stopped," the priest whispered to Antonio.

"No!" he cried.

Then he coughed to right himself.

"He just had some nerves and we gave him some medication. He reacted badly to it and he became very drowsy. But he is fine. Please just bear with him. Thank you. We are almost at the end. It would be such a shame to have to reschedule," Antonio implored.

"Very well then," the priest agreed after a long silence which Antonio spent sweating bullets.

Nikos tried to say his vows once more.

"I, Nikos Demakis take you...err...Cassia... to be my lawfully wedded wife, to have and to hold from this day forward, for better or for worse, for richer or for poorer, in sickness and in health, to love and to cherish, till death do us part. By God's holy ordinance I pledge to you my faith..." Nikos managed to stammer after a few tries.

Antonio shook his head at Nikos who looked at him like a child awaiting praise for having said something so profound.

The priest turned towards Cassia this time and made her repeat the vows. And she did that in a voice that both the audience and even the priest himself barely heard.

"I, Cassia, take thee Nikos, to me by lawfully wedded husband, to have and to hold from this day forward, for better or for worse, for richer or for poorer, in sickness and in health, to love and to cherish, till death do us part. By God's holy ordinance... I pledge to you my faith."

Yet again, Antonio's heart broke when she heaved a great sigh filled with melancholy after she said her vows.

"The rings please?" the priest asked as he held out his hand to bless it.

A boy who served as the ring bearer approached the altar and offered Nikos the rings. Nikos bent low to receive it but almost fell towards the ground again so Antonio took it and then handed it to his friend.

Nikos fumbled with the rings before he was able to hold it steady.

He reached for Cassia's hand a few times before he was able to grasp it. Then, he noticed the engagement ring on her finger that he unceremoniously gave her at one of their dinners. He did not even bend his knee or any of those dramatics. He just presented her the ring in the middle of their dinner. She was so happy and enthusiastic about it that he felt like a giant fool immediately afterwards.

"This was my grandmother's ring," he told her as he touched the engagement ring.

Then, with his hands shaking, he went back to the task at hand and tried his best to place the wedding ring on her finger. But he was shaking too much and he kept on missing. With another sigh, Cassia held his hand and guided it to her finger. Finally, the intricately carved wedding ring fit perfectly on her finger.

"This ring I give as a token of my affection, sincerity, and fidelity. Will you wear it as a symbol of your own affection, sincerity, and fidelity toward me?" he managed to say.

He did not know the words and kept on glancing towards Antonio who patiently whispered in his ear what he should say.

"I will," Cassia whispered. Nikos frowned when he detected that she was crying.

Why would she cry at her own wedding? Or maybe they were tears of joy? But he looked closer and tried to peer at the sheer veil she wore. That was when he saw that she looked as if she was just told that this was her last day to live on earth.

He forgot that particular line of thought when Cassia reached for his hand to place the ring.

"This ring I give as a token of my affection, sincerity, and fidelity. Will you wear it as a symbol of your own affection, sincerity, and fidelity toward me?" Cassia repeated.

"I will," Nikos answered with a frown as he noticed that her voice shook as she cried.

Shouldn't she be ecstatic by now? She finally had the husband she wanted! She bought him and here he was, delivered straight at her feet. Shouldn't she be jumping with joy because she owns him now? Was she sad that he was drunk?

Well then that was just tough.

The contract only indicated that he had to marry her. It did not specify what state he should be in during that marriage. She would just have to deal with it.

"By the power vested in me, I now pronounce you man and wife," the priest announced and the audience clapped and cheered.

Nikos faced Antonio and gave him a huge grin.

"Thanks for keeping me up at my own wedding," he told his friend and Antonio rolled his eyes.

"You may now kiss the bride," the priest ordered.

Nikos smiled at Cassia.

A kiss...now that was something interesting.

This would be the first time he would be able to kiss his wife. How would it feel? Would her lips be as soft as it looks? Would she be passionate or would she be frigid?

Nikos thought of all these as he reached for her veil and lifted it. Slowly, he reached for her and cupped her chin with his fingers. He lifted her head and that was when he noticed her tear-stained face. He frowned when she averted her gaze but the audience was now cheering for him to kiss her. Well, he could not disappoint them.

So he bent low and placed his lips on hers.

Bliss.

He was more than right. They were soft, warm and inviting. He moved his lips over hers and she responded briefly with passion. But before he could kiss her further, he heard her sigh against his lips.

Then he stopped when he tasted her salty tears.

He frowned at her but before he could ask her if something was wrong, the crowd erupted into applause and the bridesmaids threw rose petals over their heads.

The ceremony was finally over but there was one last thing to be done.

They approached the priest and signed the copies of their marriage certificate. It took Nikos a few tries to grasp the pen but he was finally able to scrawl his signature at the document; a great feat for someone as drunk as him.

Then he pocketed the damned marriage certificate.

Costas Andrade approached him after that and clapped a hand on his shoulder.

"You have fulfilled your terms of the bargain. You have married my granddaughter. And now I fulfill my side," Costas said and then handed him a sealed envelope.

"The merger is complete. I have signed it. And I welcome you, my new grandson as the Chief Executive Officer and President of *Andrade-Demakis Shipping International*..."

And now it was a bit worth it for Nikos for he finally had what he wanted.

Chapter 7
Reality

November 15, 2003
Antoniou Winery
The Island of Santorini, Greece

THE signing of the marriage certificates was over.

Cassia was well and truly married to Nikos.

She breathed a huge sigh of relief mingled with embarrassment and horror over her current situation. She cast a furtive glance towards her groom who was now leaning on his best man as he started to fall asleep yet again.

Antonio led Nikos to the middle of the room where the photographer wanted to snap some photos of the bride and groom. Cassia couldn't help but be amazed as Nikos managed to stand by himself for a few minutes and even pose for the shots. Next came the shots with the family and with friends and with people she didn't even know. There were also shots with the people who laughed at her. Through it all, she plastered a smile to her face and kept on counting down the hours until this sham was over.

Antonio nudged Nikos and he opened his red eyes and blinked. It was time for them to move to the reception area. The people already formed lines to throw rice, rose petals and salt and sugar over their heads as a symbol of good fortune for their marriage.

Cassia smiled as they walked through it all. Nikos, on the other hand, did his best to try and walk straight as congratulations and felicitations were thrown at them from left and right from their guests. Cassia tried to keep a straight face as everyone congratulated her on her marriage and wished them the best but what she really was thinking was that this marriage would only last for a day.

Tomorrow, she would be free.

Tomorrow, she'd divorce Nikos.

She knew she'd shock the whole world but she cared only about shocking her grandfather and making him lose in his elaborate revenge scheme.

She just had to go through the humiliation of this day and then she's done. She could go back to America and live her dreams.

The sun started to set and immediately the place looked different. Dozens of lanterns were lit and the pool on the other side of the balcony was filled with floating candles. Servants entered the room and the balcony was transformed quickly and efficiently into a reception area.

The seats were removed and a dance floor was set up. Behind the dance floor, a high table was placed and Cassia and Nikos sat on the middle. The instant Nikos was seated Cassia noticed that he fell asleep yet again.

She let him sleep and just watched their guests silently. Beside the pool the bar was opened and their guests started flocking towards it for drinks. She wanted to go there and get a drink for herself to help her last through the night but then the photographer appeared and wanted to snap a few more photos.

This time, Cassia nudged Nikos and when he opened his eyes, she pointed at the photographer. He seemed to understand and moved his chair closer to hers. She watched him force a smile to his lips and wrap one arm around her.

A dozen flashes went off and Cassia blinked several times to regain her vision. When the photographer moved away, Nikos quickly let go of her and leaned across the table. He stared at Antonio who was now approaching and he had another steaming mug of coffee in his hands.

"Drink this," Antonio handed Nikos the coffee.

Nikos drank it and he seemed to become a bit more sober after a few minutes. Antonio pulled up a chair, sat beside him, and the two started to converse in hushed tones. Cassia turned to look at the other side of the room and tried to entertain herself.

People started making speeches about them and said their wishes for their marriage. Some were very serious but some were not at all. Those came from Nikos' friends. They made several jokes about settling down and married life that Cassia cringed with every word of it.

After hearing several derogatory speeches or "jokes" as they termed it from Nikos' friends, she just stopped listening altogether.

When a waiter passed by with some champagne, she took the opportunity to grab a glass. It was just right in time for it was Costas' turn to speak.

"To our guests, I bid you welcome. Today is a very special day for it marks a new beginning for all of us. Today, my only granddaughter and heir married one of the most brilliant minds in business. Welcome to the family, Nikos," Costas started.

Everyone launched into applause at his words and Cassia resisted the urge to roll her eyes.

She heard Nikos snort and she wanted to do the same.

"This day is also important for this is the day that *Demakis International* merges with *Andrade Shipping*. For this, I welcome yet another set of family in the form of thousands of employees across the globe. With Nikos and my granddaughter at the helm, I know that it will be a guaranteed success," he continued and everyone gave a louder round of applause.

"But above everything, what's important is family. And today, Cassia and Nikos start their life together. Nikos and Cassia, may the company flourish under both of you and I hope that you have a happy and fruitful marriage! Nikos, take care of my granddaughter, eh? If you don't, you'll have to answer to me. Also, I am expecting a house filled with heirs in the *very* near future." Costas winked and everyone chuckled.

Cassia, on the other hand, tried hard not to gag.

Costas raised his champagne flute and everyone followed.

"To Nikos and Cassia," he toasted and everyone raised their glasses in salute and drank.

The host took back the microphone and made some more comments that had everyone laughing. Cassia barely heard it because she was too busy counting the bubbles on her champagne to occupy herself

From the corner of her eye, she saw Nikos stand and offer his hand to her. She looked at him in puzzlement and he just shrugged.

"Time for the first dance as husband and wife," he said.

She noticed that he didn't slur as much now and knew that he was probably sobering up. It was great for she did not want him falling asleep on this dance.

She stood up and her heart started to beat wildly inside her chest. The moment Nikos touched her hand and placed it on his arm, her mind wandered back to their first dance. She recalled how much happiness she felt that night that one of the most handsome men in the room noticed her and was even gallant enough to save her from humiliation.

Oh how things have changed, she thought.

Last week she thought she was being married because Nikos took an interest in her. When she heard that, she was over the moon! Now, she knew that he was just being *forced* to wed her. Finding out about that felt like a nail had been wedged into her heart and all her hopes and dreams of a bright future were dashed to shards.

But then again everything was too good to be true and she should have seen that right from the start so that she could've avoided herself some heartache.

Cassia and Nikos reached the dance floor and the crowd started to clap.

The first few notes of the song were played by the orchestra and she closed her eyes in bliss. It was just so beautiful! It was one of the songs she loved so much. When she was a child, she told herself that when she married, she'd dance to this particular song: *The Way You Look Tonight* by Frank Sinatra.

She almost forgot that childhood vow but was glad that whoever arranged her wedding picked that beautiful tune. Well, she wasn't allowed to meddle with arrangements regarding her *own* wedding as per her evil grandfather.

Nikos took her hand and she placed hers on his broad shoulder. They began to sway to the music. Nikos looked down at her with an unreadable expression in his green eyes. Curiously, it looked something in between wanting to kiss her and wanting to strangle the hell out of her. Cassia suspected it was the latter. He was being forced into this marriage and he didn't want it. He *never* wanted her.

But she was going to correct that tomorrow.

After this wedding, she would talk to him and tell him about her plans. The only thing that she would ask for was help from him so that she could return to America, live there in peace and forget about the past months in her life as if they never happened.

And as per tradition, this dance was called the "Money Dance." Guests approached and started pinning money on Cassia's dress and Nikos' suit. This was an old tradition that signified luck and prosperity in the marriage. Halfway through the dance, they were nearly covered with it.

Someone must've poked Nikos with a pin because he yelped and then cursed. And Cassia just couldn't help it. She threw back her head and laughed. Nikos glared at her and then he, too, laughed. In that moment, Cassia found herself wishing that circumstances were different and that she was getting married to this great man for real.

While they danced, their guests started smashing their plates on the floor. It was another old tradition that signified wealth and abundance for the married couple. The tradition started in Ancient Greece and it was said to signify wealth because instead of being washed and reused, plates are thrown into the banquet or fireplace.

Cassia and Nikos both laughed as their guests truly enjoyed smashing their plates.

When Nikos looked at her, his eyes danced with laughter. She relaxed and smiled back at him. For a moment there, he seemed stunned. But the moment passed too quickly and the cold mask slipped back in place. Cassia's face also fell and she almost wanted someone to poke Nikos with a pin once more just so she could see the other side of him again.

"Nikos... I need to talk to you." Cassia finally found the nerve to say those words.

"Hmm? Can't it wait? We have the rest of our lives after all," Nikos brushed her off in a sarcastic tone.

Cassia heard the ice in his voice but she forced herself to understand. She placed herself in his shoes and if this was her, she'd be very bitter towards the marriage too. Maybe she'd also get herself drunk to go through with it.

Cassia sighed when Nikos let go of her hand.

The camera flashed and the photographer took several photos. She and Nikos posed for each one of them but her mind was running at a hundred miles per hour. Soon this night would end and she'd have to tell her husband about her plans. She just couldn't wait to tell him and she was sure that the right words would come to her later this night. Or so she hoped.

The night wore on and Cassia remained in her seat. One time, she went towards the bar and had some drinks with Anna. They giggled over everything and had the time of their lives at pointing out the flaws of Nikos' bitchy supermodel friends.

Nikos, on the other hand, partied as though he were a bachelor. He was with his friends and they hogged all the space in the bar. They kept on doing shots and daring each and everyone to do some stupid pranks. Cassia and Anna both rolled their eyes. But when she looked more closely, Nikos had this determined look on his face. Yes, he was joking with his friends and they were all drinking...*but not him.* What he had before him was a steaming mug that she concluded must have been coffee.

"Why is the bride all alone on a night like this?" Antonio drawled lazily and interrupted Cassia's musings.

Cassia laughed and then slanted a look towards him.

"Maybe because my groom is having the time of his life," she teased.

"Then maybe you should go get him?" Antonio suggested.

"No...look at him. He's having so much fun. It would be like grabbing a candy from a baby. Besides, we'll have lots of time for us afterwards," she said, referring to the month long honeymoon that her grandfather has planned for the two of them.

"You're right about that, Cassia...about this day—" Cassia raised her hand to interrupt him for she knew where this conversation was leading: Antonio was going to apologize for Nikos but it was not his fault so she wanted to hear none of it.

"Save it. There's no harm done. I should be thanking you. There wouldn't have been a wedding without you," Cassia said. And she meant it.

Antonio smiled with relief and decided to let go of the issue. Instead, they watched Nikos and the others in silence.

Hours passed and with each minute, Cassia grew even more bored. Usually, it was customary for the bride and the groom to disappear first because they just could not keep their hands off of each other another minute more. Usually, they'd be eager to start their honeymoon.

But not them.

There was no reason to rush because Nikos did not want his bride. They also did not have a flight booked tonight to go on their honeymoon. Tomorrow, they'd be using the Andrade private jet to fly to *Bora Bora* and spend a month there for their honeymoon; one that Cassia didn't plan on having.

If she succeeded with her plan, tomorrow she'd be using the Andrade jet for a different business: flying to America after her divorce.

So she just sat there and waited for her groom to collect her. All the while, she wished that he wouldn't be so drunk that he wouldn't be able to understand her plans.

Finally, after what felt like forever, Nikos was dropped before her by his drunken friends.

"Time for me to claim my bride," Nikos announced.

Cassia's jaw dropped and she gulped back her fear. Now she knew why he didn't drink like his friends: he was really looking forward to *this* part of their marriage.

She stood up and Nikos' rowdy friends started saying green jokes about his performance in the bedroom. Cassia cringed with every word. If this was really her wedding and it was not arranged and her groom loved her, she'd be looking forward to the events of this night. But that was not the case so she felt nothing.

No excitement, no anticipation; nothing.

Nikos took her hand and led her to his suite with long, quick strides. He kicked the door open and carried her in his arms across the threshold. When the door closed behind them, Nikos pinned her towards the door and his lips swooped down and claimed hers.

At first, she tasted alcohol on his tongue but a few more seconds of being surrounded by his exquisite taste and touch, and all thoughts fled. He lifted both his hands and placed it on the door on either side of her head, effectively trapping her inside as he deepened the kiss.

Her heart started to race.

"Now you're mine, Cassia..." Nikos murmured as he kissed a path down the side of her neck.

He pressed his body against hers and her belly clenched with desire. Before she knew it, Cassia found her hands wrapped around him. She clutched him tightly to her as if she couldn't get enough. She felt drunk with his kisses.

Like an addict, she craved more and more.

"Nikos..." her voice was half-plea and half-moan.

Nikos hands trailed lower and settled on her waist. His lips also traced a downward path and he licked and nipped on the skin of her neck. Her breath caught and her brain fogged with desire. She felt herself responding to his expert touch and she also wanted to feel his skin against hers. Her new husband must've read her mind for he shrugged his jacket off and pressed his body against hers once more. While he was kissing her, her hands were clumsily fumbling with the buttons on his shirt so that she could touch his bare skin.

"God, I want you...but I know I shouldn't," he whispered in between kisses.

Cassia moaned. She felt exactly the same way and it really did not make any sense.

Finally, Nikos was able to remove his shirt and her hands were touching the hard planes of his chest and abdomen.

It was sheer heaven...no man should have a body this perfect.

She felt Nikos' hands on the zipper of her gown. Before she could react, she heard the sound of the zipper sliding downwards and cold air hit her skin. But that was just for a second before she felt Nikos' warm hands trace a path in her back. She didn't even have a moment to feel conscious about her body for his touch and his lips made her feel just how much he desired her.

He touched her as if he could not get enough of her. He touched her as if he worshipped every inch of her body.

"Let's finish this..." Nikos purred seductively.

That was when fear reared its ugly head and snapped Cassia back to the present. Her body still pulsed with desire but the fog of passion was lifted from her mind. She pushed at Nikos' chest and he let her go with a moan of complaint.

"What?" he hissed.

"We need to talk," Cassia said in between deep breaths.

"Now?!" he groaned.

"Yes. Now. This is important. This is about this marriage."

Nikos lifted his head and his gaze was as hard as ice. Cassia immediately regretted her words and wished that she could bring back time just so he could gaze at her with desire.

"You want to talk, right now?" he breathed. "Then talk." Then he claimed her lips again.

This time, his hands got bolder and he tugged on the bodice of her gown. She wasn't wearing anything underneath it so her breasts were bared to his gaze. She sucked in a breath when she felt his hot breath against her nipples.

"Yes. This is important. About tomorrow—" Cassia began but Nikos held up a hand to silence her.

"I don't want to hear of your plans for our marriage. Can't we just take it one day at a time?" Nikos said through gritted teeth. He resumed his attentions and this time went for the other nipple.

"No. Please listen—"

"Just talk, I am listening," Nikos whispered against her skin.

Truth was, he wasn't interested in talking. He was more interested in the feel of her skin against his lips, her exquisite scent and the softness of her breasts under his hands.

"Nikos..." Cassia whimpered.

"Hmm?"

Then he moved his head lower and his tongue darted to lick one nipple. Cassia gasped and bucked underneath him. Her soft gasp just served to increase his desire further.

All protest from her disappeared when he took that nipple into his mouth and sucked. He switched to the other breast while his hand continued to tease the other. Cassia's legs turned to jelly and she would have fallen to the floor if it wasn't for Nikos' strength supporting her. When he felt her surrender, he bent and scooped her up and deposited her on the wide bed.

He gazed at every inch of her now that her gown wasn't hiding all that beauty underneath. What he saw tested his control further. Her skin looked so soft and creamy as though begging for his touch.

As he looked, Nikos also started to remove the rest of his clothing. He started with his shoes and his socks and then shrugged off the shirt that Cassia unbuttoned. He felt Cassia's eyes on him and when he raised his head to look, he saw that her desire mirrored his.

Her mouth parted on a gasp as he slowly bared his body to her scrutiny. Her hands clutched the sheets in anticipation as he continued stripping. When he didn't have a stitch of clothing on, her cheeks got even redder. He also saw a hint of fear in her eyes when she looked below his waist.

He joined her on the bed and gathered her in his arms before she could say anything. He melded his lips to her again and kissed all the protest and stiffness out of her body.

"I only get to be married once. We might not have got off to a great start but I guarantee I'll be giving you a wedding night to remember."

"Nikos...please...we really have to talk. Stop kissing me! I forget everything when you do that," she admitted on a groan as he covered her body with his.

"That's the whole point, *agapimeni*."

Nikos kissed a path from her lips, to her throat, then to her breasts. He continued down to her navel and parted her thighs.

"What—"

"Shh..."

"Oh, God..." Cassia moaned when he started his assault on her senses.

He held on to her thighs as she writhed and bucked under his caress. Her pleasure climbed higher and higher until her release slammed through her and she came apart, writhing and crying out his name.

She was breathing heavily as he rose over her and covered her body with his.

"Nikos..." this time she was clearly begging for his touch.

Cassia's body was on fire and she craved more pleasure from Nikos. Her initial fears were erased and she felt this was truly right. Surely, she could take this night and bury it deep in her memories as her one night with Nikos Demakis, the man who first made her heart beat.

Maybe this *one* night would be all they had and it would be alright...

Cassia gasped in pain as Nikos entered her but he held her tightly and murmured Greek words of comfort in her ear. He didn't move for a long time and just let her become accustomed to his size. Then, he kissed her again and ignited her passion once more.

When he started to move, Cassia held onto him like he was her lifeline. She was sinking in this tide of passion and desire and he was the only one who could save her. Her passion also engulfed him and burned him to the point of insanity.

Each movement drove them higher and higher. Each kiss ignited them more. Each touch made everything blaze. Soon, all was lost and only the two of them existed. Nikos plunged inside her over and over.

Cassia screamed his name and her nails raked down his back as she found that pinnacle once more.

"Cassia!" he also screamed her name as his release surged through him.

Afterwards, he was left shaken with the intense pleasure he received but also very much sated.

Nikos breathed heavily.

He knew his wife was a virgin yet from the numerous girls he'd bedded – supermodels, actresses and heiresses – he experienced pleasure with her the most. She was like a breath of fresh air with her open and unabashed response to his touch. She faked nothing and what she felt with him was genuine desire.

He found himself softening towards her and rethinking his views.

Well, what if the marriage wasn't so bad? What if they can make the most of this and maybe even grow to love one another someday?

Passion was a common ground and it could be a start for them.

"That was exquisite, *glikia mou*...now, we sleep and rest," he whispered.

He placed one last kiss on her lips and curled his body around hers and pulled the sheets over both of them. They spent the night peacefully in each other's arms.

Nikos woke up as sunlight streamed through their window. His stomach rumbled and he decided to get some breakfast. His wife was still asleep but he let her for he knew he tired her out the night before. They made love three more times before dawn.

Now, Nikos felt the aches and pains of that total of four times. On top of that was his headache from yesterday's hangover.

He took a quick shower then headed down to the hotel restaurant. He sat at a table by the balcony, ordered some coffee and grabbed the morning newspaper. As expected, the headline on the society page was his wedding with Cassia while the headline on the business page is the merger of *Andrade International* and *Demakis Shipping Incorporated* along with the announcement of him being CEO of the new mega corporation.

"Good morning, son."

Nikos looked up from his paper and saw that Costas Andrade sat on the chair opposite his.

He sighed and replied, "Good morning, Costas."

Costas smiled, "How went the wedding night?"

Nikos felt a spark of irritation at being questioned about something so private.

"As it usually does," he replied with a shrug.

"Looking at you, I am glad that my granddaughter pleased you." Nikos almost rolled his eyes but again, he just shrugged.

"I wanted to talk to you about the changes in the corporation. The merger is still fresh and I would need you in the Greece office to finalize more details. I'll also train and introduce you to the board so that you can take over easily."

Nikos nodded his agreement. "Anything else?" he asked.

"That's it. Enjoy your honeymoon but I think it will need to be cut short."

"No. I guess we'll be skipping the honeymoon first in order to get everything settled and just have it later this year. I need to be there during the company's transition. That cannot wait but my honeymoon can."

"I like that attitude. Business first," Costas said with a smirk. "Next order of business, I want to know where you'll be living with my granddaughter."

"My penthouse in Athens. It's closer to both companies."

"Well...she very much expressed her interest that she wanted to live still under my roof. Can't you give her that? She's still acclimating herself to Greece after living in America most of her life. It will break my heart also if she was parted with me. She very much agreed that both of you will live with me."

Nikos clenched his teeth. How dare she agree without telling him about it?

"I'll speak with her," he grated in a rough tone.

"She also expressed her disinterest with bearing your heir at this point. I do hope that you will respect that wish. She is young after all and she still has her life ahead of her. Maybe after three to five years?"

"If she wants all this, why can't she tell me herself?" Nikos spat as he found himself growing angrier with each word.

"She's still a bit shy and she doesn't know how you'll handle it. I'm really sorry about this, my boy...but there's one more thing: about your mistresses and your lifestyle. She respects your way and I already explained it to her. I spoke to her before I went down this morning and she wasn't really big on how your wedding night went. She told me she'd respect it if you still wanted to go with your mistresses. Just that you do it discreetly and keep her in the lifestyle she is used to."

Nikos finally understood. He stood up abruptly and his coffee spilled on the table. He clenched his fist. How could he believe they could have had a chance when she was one huge liar and schemer just like her grandfather!

"Now I think I know what you are getting at, Costas. Cassia wants to be married to me but she can't give up her extravagant lifestyle. She's not ready to work with the company yet that's why she still wants to stay with you rather than be a wife to me. She does not want to have my son and so she wants me to run along to my mistresses? Also, I have to keep giving her the lifestyle she craves which I think would cost me millions of dollars a year. Do I have it right?" Nikos snarled.

"Well, I really wanted to phrase it delicately...but you are correct. I am really sorry about this but this is how my granddaughter was brought up. I tried changing her but her ways are instilled in her. And I love her too much that I am afraid I also spoiled her."

Nikos threw his napkin on the table.

"Well if that's what she wants then that's what she'll get," he whispered in a deadly tone.

Without another word, he turned his back and left.

"Come in," Cassia said and the door opened.

A chambermaid came in bearing new linens.

"Housekeeping," she answered and looked at Cassia with something like pity.

Cassia dismissed it and grabbed some water from the fridge.

"Have you seen my husband?" she asked.

The woman's lips pursed and she turned to Cassia again with both pity and concern in her eyes.

"Mrs. Demakis, he is in suite three. But please don't say that this came from me," the woman said.

Before Cassia could ask more, the woman dashed out of the room.

Why did Nikos go to another suite? Was that one of his friends' suites? Cassia sighed and resisted the urge to pull at her hair. She didn't have time for these things now. She could not let the events from last night deter her from what she was supposed to do today.

She had to talk with Nikos and tell him about the divorce.

On the way to Suite 3, she encountered her grandfather.

"Good morning, Cassia," he said with one of his malicious smiles Cassia hated so much.

"Good morning," she replied tersely.

"Where are you off to little one?" he asked in a mocking tone.

"To find Nikos."

"I'm so sorry, Cassia...I didn't want you to find out this way...but Nikos is in suite three."

"And what about it?"

"It's not my place to tell you this...but you're my granddaughter. So you must know the way of things. Men are never going to be satisfied with just one woman. They will always stray. Remember that when you face him."

Cassia gritted her teeth and ignored her grandfather. She continued on her way towards Suite 3 and refused to think about her grandfather's words. He knew this was another one of his ploys to kick her harder when she was down. She knocked on the door but no one answered. She found the door unlocked so she quickly entered.

Cassia saw a woman sleeping on the bed and she was naked. Then, the door to the bathroom opened and out came Nikos with his hair still wet from his shower. He only wore a towel around his lean hips.

"Nikos—" Cassia gasped.

The woman on the bed stirred and Cassia came face to face with one of the most beautiful and famous French supermodels. Her name was Marietta and she was rumored to be Nikos' latest mistress before he had to marry her.

Cassia gasped in shock and took a step backwards.

"Oh it's you..." the woman purred.

Cassia's mouth fell open when she realized the implication of Nikos being here. How could he do this? How could he take her to bed on their wedding night and then go straight to his mistress' bed after?

Indeed, this was the last straw!

Her heart twisted inside her chest and she felt as if a knife has been plunged through. For a moment, she stopped breathing as sheer agony tore through her whole body. She knew this marriage was not real and she wished for only one night with Nikos before they went their separate ways.

Yet why did she feel like this?

"Please leave. I have to speak with my husband," Cassia calmly implored.

"Husband, huh? Well, that marriage contract and the ring is all you're going to get from him anyway. He's still mine," the woman said in heavily accented French.

Cassia felt the threat of tears in her eyes so she blinked them away quickly.

"*Mademoiselle,* I am not looking for a fight this morning. I just want to speak with Nikos. So if you could please leave us...that would be great," Cassia tried to stay calm as she said the words.

The woman inclined her head and slowly sat up on the bed. She shrugged then rose from the bed in all her naked glory. She even stretched before reaching for a robe beside the bed. Cassia saw red when she saw Nikos watching his mistress flaunt her body.

"What he saw in you, I never really know. Hmm...then again, maybe it's because of all the money to your name," Marietta told her with ice in her voice before she started to walk across the room.

"All right. Get out!" Cassia shouted. "Nikos, we need to talk."

"You don't have to tell me anything. Your grandfather already said all you wanted to say," Nikos replied in a bored tone.

"What? What did he say?!"

"That you don't want to live with me...you don't want to be my wife. You want to receive a big monthly allowance. Does that sum it up?"

"What? I never said that! Nikos, I came here to talk to you about something."

Nikos threw back his head and laughed.

"Do not lie to me Cassia. I am perfectly agreeable with your terms. I thank you for letting me keep my mistresses. So quit the wounded wife act at seeing me here with Marietta. You practically gave your consent for this."

"What?! I never said anything like that! In fact, I am wondering how you could jump from my bed to another's in such a short span of time!"

The man even had the gall to laugh.

He gave her a patronizing glare and spoke, "I have no wish to discuss my personal affairs with you. I don't even know why you are acting like this when you told your grandfather that I can keep my mistresses so long as I am discreet about it."

"Nikos...I never said anything like that. Can't you see that Costas is lying to you like he's been doing right from the start?"

"As they say, the fruit never falls far from the tree."

Cassia flinched as if she's been slapped.

"Nikos...please. Listen to me. I don't know what happened but Costas must've heard of my plans of divorcing you—"

"Divorce? Dear gods, where did you get that idea, wife?" Nikos asked in a mocking tone.

He finished dressing and turned to glare at her. He wrapped his arms around his chest and then casually leaned his hip on the side of the desk.

"Nikos—"

Nikos held up a hand. His green eyes burned with his fury.

"Stop it. There shall be no divorce. I think I know now what this is. You conspired with your grandfather for him to tell me to carry on with my mistresses, with my previous lifestyle. Then minutes after, when you found me in my mistress' bed, you now want a divorce. I see what's going on here," Nikos laughed and strode towards her.

He gripped her arms and forced her to look at him.

"You want the divorce and you want to blame me for it so that my family will lose everything and you and your grandfather will get your greedy hands on what we own!" he roared.

"It's not—"

"Silence! I will not listen to any more of your lies! I've tolerated enough, Cassia! You already have me! You have what you want! You bought me, correct? You just told your grandfather that you wanted me and he bought me for you! I've fulfilled the terms of the merger. I married you even though I did not want to! I even bedded you to completely seal the deal! Look at you. Who would go and marry someone like you? Good thing I was drunk or I would've run! Now just accept what fate has dealt your greedy little hands. We are married. This is what you wanted. This is what you're getting. There'll not be any fucking divorce and you'll have to deal with me for the rest of your miserable life!" Nikos snarled.

Cassia's eyes started to fill with tears at his hateful words.

At that moment, Hector's words came back to her.

"Such a kind heart, princess... Now I know why people step all over you. Just promise me one thing... Never ever allow anyone to do that ever again. Hold your head high because you are better than all of them..."

She promised him she'd never allow that again.

"You are wrong, Nikos. I'm as much a victim of this as you. My grandfather forced me to marry—"

Nikos threw back his head and laughed.

"Save it for someone who's dumb enough to believe your lies."

"If you would just listen to me!" Cassia shouted.

"Never ever shout at me," Nikos said through gritted teeth and tightened his grip on Cassia's hand causing her to whimper in pain. "If you think you can control my life just because you are my wife, then you are wrong. I will live my life the way I want. No one can tell me otherwise! Once is already enough."

He tugged on Cassia's hand and brought her towards the door.

"Stop it, Nikos! I don't deserve any of this!"

"You signed up for it when you asked your grandfather to buy me. Now, tell me princess: *was it worth it then?* Am I still the husband of your dreams? Or have you finally woken up to reality?"

This time Cassia's tears spilled over as she shook her head. She did not want to cry in front of him.

"You don't know anything about me Nikos. Stop presuming that you have me figured out! I told you that I was a victim of this too...if you would only listen, I can explain everything."

"I don't want your explanations! I just want you out of this room!" Nikos growled.

He reached for his bag and his luggage that was already packed.

"Here's the number of my personal assistant. Call him to ask for anything you need. Honeymoon's cancelled. I have too much work to do," Nikos kept on talking as he continued to rummage around his bag.

With each word, Cassia felt her hope and strength draining further.

"By the way, your grandfather told me you wanted to live with him. But if you change your mind, you are welcome to any estate of mine you want, except the one where I am currently staying. Don't like my houses? Go buy one for yourself. As for money, don't worry. Even before we got married, I already opened an account in your name." Nikos tossed her the calling card of his assistant.

Again, Cassia flinched but Nikos was beyond caring at this point.

"In case that's not enough. Here. Sky is the limit," he tossed her a black credit card.

Cassia ignored the card yet she paled even further at Nikos' gesture. Her vision blurred as more and more tears drifted down her pale cheeks.

How could he have gone from the tender lover last night into this hateful man before her today?

"Even if this marriage isn't real, I still can't believe that you are this kind of person. I thought you were a good man. It turns out I was wrong after all!"

Now it was Cassia's turn to laugh sarcastically.

Nikos scoffed.

"Yes. You are wrong. I am not the knight in shining armor that you bought with your money. I am just Nikos Demakis. I live my life the way I please. Don't go flaunting your influence over me and threatening me with a divorce. Whatever you are planning with your grandfather, it's not going to happen. I wed you because of money. Nothing more, nothing less. One day, I'll be able to repay every single euro and I'll throw all of it back into you and your grandfather's faces!" Nikos shouted.

Cassia flinched from his tone and yanked her hand so that she could free herself from him. However, Nikos grip was like steel.

"Let's set everything straight right now, *wife*. I will not let you dictate any part of my life, as I will not dictate yours. Live your life as you please and I will live mine as I please. Right now, what pleases me is to leave this place. I'm taking Marietta with me for she pleases me, not you."

Cassia opened her mouth to reply but before she could, the door opened and Nikos friends' including Antonio entered. They must've heard all the shouting and came here to investigate. Cassia heard Antonio groan as he saw the scene that was playing out before him.

"Whoah, Nikos! One day and you're already back with Marietta? Sweet," his rowdy friends cheered.

They added several lewd comments and did not even consider the fact that Nikos' wife was here at this very room and that she could hear every word. What added more salt to the wound was that Nikos laughed at the things his friends said.

"Have you no respect?!" Cassia shouted.

Immediately, everyone fell silent and some even stared at her as if this was the first time they were truly seeing her.

"Cassia...come...let us go and leave them be," Antonio offered as he took her arm.

She yanked her hand back.

"No! This is too much! I told you I was a victim of this marriage too but you did not want to believe me. You have insulted me at every turn when all I wanted was to help! I could have left and you wouldn't have had the merger but I did not for I felt as if I owed it to you. But I owe you nothing! *Nothing!* And I sure as hell don't deserve all the humiliation that you're giving me! Getting drunk at your own wedding and then flaunting your mistress in front of me? You may all be rich and educated but you know nothing!" Cassia shouted as she reached the end of her patience.

"Take those words back. I will never let you speak ill of my friends and of Marietta," Nikos snarled close to her ear.

"No! Never! I do not deserve all of this! *You* do not deserve *me*."

Nikos threw his head back and laughed. His friends did the same.

"I think you are living in an illusion. *You* do not deserve someone like *me*," Nikos growled while his friends laughed and nodded in approval.

"To think that I suffered through everything just for this. To think I considered defying my grandfather just to give you back all you lost. But no, you do not deserve even a single penny."

"So what are you saying? Are you threatening to go to the lawyers and tell them it's my fault and you want a divorce so that all the money goes to you according to our contract? You can't do that. You won't be able to prove anything. I'll fight you every step of the way," Nikos threatened.

"No...but I can do something worse. You know, I considered divorcing you today and telling them I had a lover so that all the money would go back to you. You would win and my grandfather would lose his revenge scheme. I want no part of the money and to think I was willing to give all of it up. *Now*...I don't think so," Cassia said in the bravest and iciest tone she could muster.

She smiled when she saw that this time it was Nikos who was stunned speechless.

"I don't believe you. You are as cunning and as conniving as your grandfather. Like him, every word that comes from those pretty lips is a lie," he shouted.

"Nikos, stop it!" Antonio ordered. He surged forward and placed a restraining hand on Nikos' arm.

"Stay out if this," Nikos growled.

He yanked Cassia back and stared at her. This time, Cassia tugged her hand away and rubbed some blood back to her wrist.

"Go on, Nikos. Go live your life the way you please and I'll live mine. For all that I've been through, I'll make sure I make your life a living hell," Cassia said sweetly.

"Get out!" Nikos shouted and he pushed Cassia towards the door.

She stumbled and fell on the corridor and Antonio ran after her. He helped her to her feet but she denied any further assistance. Then, she did what she promised Hector: she drew herself to full height and held her head up for she truly believed that she was better than all of them.

"You made a big mistake, Nikos. One day you'll realize that."

Then, she walked away without another backward glance.

Cassia went back to their suite and grabbed her belongings that were already neatly packed for her supposed honeymoon. As she waited for a taxi, she saw Nikos boarding his private yacht with his mistress. His arm was wrapped around her while she was giggling at something he said. He stepped onto his yacht and never even looked back.

Then again, maybe she was not supposed to forget *all* of it.

She'd remember this day. She'd remember Nikos and the pain he dealt her. She'd remember how much she thought she loved him and how he smashed her heart to pieces. One day, she'd have her revenge.

One day she'd make him pay...

Chapter 8
Change

"SEBASTIAN? Is that you? I haven't heard from you in a long time!"

"Sorry boss. I've been busy. And since I moved, I was under a different boss. This one is way more demanding."

The boy's old boss laughed.

"I know. The place is demanding and so the bosses must be demanding too. It's harder to survive there than here. The law there is much more difficult. Too many people to bribe."

"Tell me about it," Sebastian laughed. "But besides that, it's great here. How about you? How have you been all these years?"

"Excellent, boy. Excellent as always!"

"Glad to hear that."

"Why does your voice sound different. You seem happy. Hmm...is there a lady involved?" his boss queried.

"Maybe..."

November 8, 2013 (Ten Years Later)
Cassia's Penthouse Apartment
157 West 57th Street, New York City

"Good morning everyone! And we are back to our show, "Lifestyles of the Rich and Famous!" This is your host Melanie."

"...And Arthur Cornwell bidding you a great day ahead!"

Cassia brushed her teeth while pulling on her high-heeled shoes at the same time. She was running late for a presentation after oversleeping. The TV sounded in the background and she groaned loudly.

She forgot to flip the channel towards the news and was now stuck listening to a talk show that scrutinized lives of people she did not care about.

"And who is our celebrity for today, Melanie?" the co-host of the television show asked.

"He's hot. He's handsome. He's dashing. He's a debonair. He's sex appeal on legs. Aaaand...he's also one of the richest people in the world with a brain totally wired for business and making tons of money! Today, we'll check out the life of the definitely rich and definitely famous, Nikoooos Demakis!"

Cassia muttered a muffled curse around her toothbrush. But somehow, she found herself gravitating towards the television to see what the show would say about her husband. The first part of the show described Nikos' early life. He was described to be a very intelligent boy who always had excellent grades but was the most unruly child.

It was also discussed how Nikos' parents married young and then weren't quite ready to settle down in one place and build a family. Because of that, they left Nikos in Greece with his grandfather while they continued travelling the globe.

Cassia dismissed the information with a shrug. She already knew some things about Nikos' past and why the hell would she want to know anything more?

She finished brushing her teeth and then started on fixing her makeup. She glanced at her watch and realized she still had time if she could forego her early morning caffeine fix.

It was a hard decision to make but she quickly decided that there was much more she needed to do rather than buy her usual coffee.

She sat on her sofa and then opened her laptop so she could check her presentation whether her designs were already good. She checked each slide for a flaw and smiled when she found none. The TV droned on and on in the background but she was too preoccupied to notice it.

"Nikos Demakis is also known for the many supermodels, actresses, heiresses and other women that he dated!" the male host exclaimed.

"Who would blame him? He's hot and he's rich. I'd date him myself if he'd have me!" the woman replied with a giggle.

Cassia rolled her eyes at that. Women kept on throwing themselves at Nikos Demakis. They did not know the evil that lay beneath the face of a Greek god; that beneath the facade of an angel was the soul of a devil. They did not know the pain that he was capable of inflicting on someone.

Cassia shook her head to clear it of past bitterness. She stood up and decided she couldn't go without her morning coffee after all. It was just that this time, she'd have to go and fix it herself instead of buying. With a sigh, she stood up and headed straight towards her kitchen to get the coffee maker working.

While she was waiting, she leaned her hip across the counter and listened to the show.

"Ahh...but that's where the controversy lies. You see, Nikos Demakis is a married man. For nearly ten years now, he has been married to Cassia Andrade, the only heir of the Andrade fortune. The fact is that dozens of magazines, tabloids and paparazzi catch him in the arms of different women while he is currently married! And this is no rumor, mind you. For during the different balls and social functions he attends, it's not his wife hanging on his arm but someone else!" the host called Melanie replied with a wry grimace.

"Ahh... The man likes to play the field, so to speak."

"Yes. And rumors say he only sees his wife once a year. It's on their wedding anniversary. No wonder there's still no Demakis heir running around."

The two hosts laughed and then a series of pictures of Nikos and the different bimbos he dated were flashed across the screen. Again, Cassia rolled her eyes and snorted. He hadn't changed one bit.

But before, when there would have been a twinge in her chest at seeing those pictures, now there was none. She was really perfectly happy where she was. There was nothing that could take that happiness from her right now.

"Whoa. I could not believe the luck of this guy! He dated Marietta, the French Supermodel? There. Are. No. Words," the male host said this in a tone filled with unconcealed envy.

"And all you can do is drool, huh, Arthur?"

"Just wait, Melanie. I'll make myself a billionaire and then I'd play the field like that too," Arthur laughed.

More images flashed and the hosts kept on discussing all the women that Nikos dated. Again, Cassia ignored it and focused on her laptop.

Throughout the course of ten years, she'd read about Nikos and his conquests in all the magazines.

At first, it filled her with a burning need for vengeance along with the need to rip the magazine to shreds. But now, she was totally indifferent. One could even say that she's become immune. She couldn't care less which slut Nikos dated and what he did with his miserable life.

Cassia drank her coffee and suddenly, her day seemed brighter. With a smile on her face, she focused on her work and started editing her designs. Her hands flew across her tablet and the stylus came alive in her expert fingers.

However, her attention was snagged by the television when she saw a picture of her and Nikos from their wedding.

"Pathetic," Cassia whispered to herself the moment she scrutinized the picture and saw that Nikos was clearly drunk while she was trying to appear as inconspicuous as possible.

Well, no more.

That Cassia was a thing of the past. She was dead now. And a totally new Cassia was in her place. She would never allow anyone to treat her the way she was treated all those years ago. She would never let anyone mock her.

She was successful now. During the past ten years, she had made a life for herself.

Her thoughts drifted back to ten years ago and towards the exact moment that she left Greece. She left with her heart broken, a great sense of injustice and a need for revenge.

Leaving Nikos caused an uproar and she was sure she would've been beaten to death by her grandfather had she stayed. Thankfully, she was able to book a flight to America with Antonio's help and she was out of the country before the media got hold of their situation.

For a whole month, her grandfather called her. He shouted and cursed at her over the phone for her rash decision. She told him everything but he simply did not understand. He kept on repeating to her that it was her duty to stay by Nikos' side. Finally, she had the courage and told him to fuck off for she was going to live her life the way she pleased.

Afterwards, Costas cut off all ties with her.

Technically, what that meant was that he cut off her credit cards, closed down her bank accounts and disowned her in front of the public media.

Well, good riddance!

Being poor was not new to Cassia. She came from that life and she just returned to it after pretending to be one of society's finest and failing miserably. She did not need her grandfather's money. She lived alone before and she could do it again. She worked two jobs just to be able to support herself through college.

Throughout the years, Nikos still maintained several credit cards for her along with a bank account where he deposited her yearly allowance. For her, the sum could feed an entire country. She could have taken advantage of his money and wasted it all to get back at him.

But she *didn't*.

She wanted no part of it.

She touched it only once when she needed money for college but she paid the double the amount she took when she started earning.

And after a grueling four years in College, she finally had her degree in Fashion Design!

She survived it all because of her determination to prove herself. Another factor to her success was that Hector was by her side. She found him a few months after she returned to America when she read in the newspaper about him opening his very first restaurant.

She ate there a few days after the opening and she didn't know which of them was more surprised when they saw each other there. He sat down with her that day and told her everything about how she helped him reach his dreams.

Then it was he who helped her reach hers.

He was her light in the darkness; her confidence boost during the times she stopped believing in herself. Now, he was a huge part of her life. She wouldn't have been able to make it this far if it weren't for him. Yes, Hector was not all that perfect. He had his bad moments: he was always so busy. She always felt as if she came second in his life. But she understood him for he also wanted to chase his dreams and make his spot in the world like her.

Because of Hector and her hard work, she was now *Cassia Adrasteia*, renowned designer.

Yes, she used a pseudonym when she was designing for she never wanted to be associated with her grandfather or with Nikos. She wanted to make a name for herself and that was what she did.

Now, she was the owner of one of the most successful fashion shops in the world, *Cassiopeia*.

She was very proud to call it hers for it came from her own sweat and blood. It was born from her hard work and her determination to prove to others that she was capable of making her own path.

"Two years ago, there was an event which was said to have changed Nikos' life forever. He and his friend Antonio Velez disappeared for over a month with no trace whatsoever. And our sources say that the two of them were kidnapped!" Arthur explained.

"How horrible!" the co-host replied.

"Yes. However this was not proven for the PR team of Demakis-Andrade International have negated this issue over and over again and refused to give out any statements. But trusted sources say that the two truly have been kidnapped and held for ransom."

"So that means they paid, right?"

"Hmm...sources say that they escaped with the help of someone from inside. And then they just miraculously returned one day, thin and worse for wear. But the statement that they gave the media was that they took off on an adventure and went mountain climbing. Yeah, right," the host said sarcastically.

Cassia scoffed.

She heard those rumors all those years ago and she received a call from the PR team of their company. When she heard about it, she felt a hint of fear and worry but when she asked what happened to Nikos, she was told that they couldn't tell her any information for it was classified and Nikos did not allow it.

Yet again, she realized just how much Nikos valued her and thought of her. She let the issue go and just agreed to do what the PR team demanded so that they could all shut up and leave her alone. They just asked her not to say anything and that her husband was fine. She gave all the necessary statements to placate the media as dictated by their PR department.

But she did not believe Nikos had been kidnapped. Maybe he just enjoyed too much time with one of his mistresses.

Or, if it was true that he was kidnapped, then karma took a really long time to catch up with him.

Cassia glanced at her watch once more and then turned her laptop off. She leaned against her couch and cradled the coffee mug in the palm of her hands.

"And how is Nikos now?" the female host asked.

"Well... I'd say he's back in top shape. Business-wise, Demakis-Andrade International is booming! They are now the top shipping company in the world and that is with Nikos Demakis and his wife Cassia at the top of the company."

"That is great! Yes, almost two years ago, Costas Andrade who is Cassia's grandfather had a heart attack. Since then, he has been confined to his bed. And it seems as though whatever scandal happened ten years ago, after Cassia and Nikos' marriage, was put to rest because Costas claimed Cassia as his heir once more. He even left her in charge of the Andrade side of the company which has its headquarters in New York."

This time, Cassia sighed.

Yes, it was true. More than two years ago, Costas had a heart attack and a stroke. Doctors said that half of his body was now paralyzed. When Cassia first heard of the news, all she thought about was that karma also took a long time before it hit the cold-hearted Costas Andrade.

But the goodness of her heart won and she returned to Greece to visit her grandfather. He was her only living relative after all.

Nothing much was said between them when she visited. All Costas told her was that she would now be responsible for half of the company and that he expected her to run it together with Nikos.

Cassia refused but the old man took a different route this time. Instead of shouting at her about her responsibilities, Costas told her that this should have been her father's legacy. He should have been the one handling the business and it was what he was groomed for all his life. He told her that he was happy during the brief time he ran the company but that was before he met Cassia's mother. After he met her, he then dropped everything else and ran away with her.

That little story made Cassia feel guilty and nostalgic.

So, she agreed to run half of the company. It was not for Costas but for her father. She would make all her father's dreams and visions for the company come true. But there was one condition: she'd be doing it in America and not in Greece.

Surprisingly, her grandfather agreed.

During the last two years, she had tried managing both half her company and her own business, *Cassiopeia*. Everyone told her she would fail. But she did not. Once more she proved everyone wrong by rising to the top.

"Hmm...what about Nikos' own business? The Nostos Chain of Hotels, Restaurants and Shopping Malls?"

"Ahh...this is where it differs. For years, Nikos' business was at the top. But now, there is a new contender. This is the one endangering Nikos' business with its stiff competition! This is none other than the Petrides Corporation."

"Please enlighten me about this Petrides Corporation," Arthur told his co-host.

"This is owned by a man named Hector Petrides who came straight from the gutter and worked his way to riches. Just recently, he was on the cover of Time Magazine for his exemplary business skills which quickly turned him into a multi-millionaire. His dream started with a small restaurant in which he was both the owner and the head-chef. From there, it all went uphill."

"Sounds too good to be true!"

"I agree! It kind of sounds like a fairy godmother just waved her wand and all his wishes came true. But you know, some people seem to have all the luck in the world. Some of them really deserved it, and I'd say Mr. Petrides deserved it. Maybe one day, he'll be the one featured here, right?"

Cassia smiled after hearing those words.

After watching the entire talk show, she could say that this is her favorite part. She couldn't care less about Nikos Demakis but Hector Petrides was her whole world. Together, they discussed their dreams and together, they made them come true.

Now, they were reaping the fruits of their labor.

Finally, they are where they envisioned themselves to be that time that they talked ten years ago.

The talk show spouted more facts about Nikos and his business but Cassia wasn't listening. They also discussed Nikos' latest rumored mistress but yet again, Cassia didn't care. She only glimpsed at the face of the girl and she knew that it was one of her models.

"Then again, Nikos can do whatever he likes," Cassia muttered to herself.

She stood up and dumped the empty coffee mug in the sink. She picked up her laptop, her files and her car keys. She took one last glance towards the television and switched it off.

She then exited her penthouse apartment and drove herself to work. Today was a big day for she would be organizing the biggest fashion show in her career. Also, this would be one of her biggest charity works, for her designs would be auctioned and half the proceeds would go to the orphanage that she was sponsoring.

Cassia was snapped out of her thoughts when she heard her phone ring. She quickly dug her phone out of her purse and connected the Bluetooth headset to her ear.

"Hello?"

"Hi, princess," a familiar voice drawled.

Just like that, a smile came to Cassia's lips.

"Hello, yourself," she replied.

His rich laughter slid over her like silk and her smile widened. This man was the reason why she no longer cared about Nikos and about revenge. This was the man that changed her life and helped her become a better person. This would be the man she would marry one day after she freed herself from Nikos Demakis.

"Where are you?"

"On my way to work."

"Good luck with that fashion show. I know you'll amaze them as always."

"Thanks. And Hector, good luck with securing that deal with the bank for the new site of your restaurant," Cassia said cheerfully.

"Thanks, darling. When that restaurant is finished, you and I will be the ones cutting the ribbon again," Hector replied.

Cassia laughed and she heard Hector sigh.

"So... are you doing anything tonight?" Hector asked.

"Hmmm...let me check my schedule. One moment," Cassia said and acted as though she was looking for something when she was just smiling like a teenage girl with her first crush.

"Alright. I'm sorry I am not available. Upon checking my schedule, I have a date with a Mr. Hector Petrides at ten pm in that five-star international cuisine restaurant that he owns," she teased.

"Ah...you're breaking my heart, princess. How can you date someone else like that? I won't survive this. I'll die with a broken heart," he answered melodramatically.

Cassia just couldn't stop herself and she burst out laughing. Her conversation with Hector continued and it was filled with laughter and sweet words.

Before she knew it, she already arrived at her office.

"I have to go," Cassia told him with a sigh.

"All right. Can't wait for tonight. See you later, princess," Hector told her and then cut the line.

As Cassia exited her black Porsche, she had a smile on her face and a ton of extra energy to get her through this day. This was a critical point in her career and she would do everything she could to turn it into a complete and utter success.

Her smiled widened even further when she remembered that she was going to have dinner with Hector later. Finally, she was going to tell him that she'd made her decision, that she already had an answer to his question.

And she just couldn't wait for tonight...

Chapter 9
Broken

THEY say people find peace in their sleep; that it is the time of day when everything else is quiet and both your mind and body rests.

But not for Nikos Demakis.

In sleep, he was haunted by his nightmares which all started after he was kidnapped more than two years ago. Sweat dotted in his entire body and the bed covers were fisted in his hand. He thrashed on the bed as he was deep in his nightmare.

The sound of gunfire and explosions echoed across the large highway, followed by panicked cries and moans of pain. Nikos was shoved downwards by his body guards but not before he felt a searing pain in his side.

"Antonio!" he shouted.

He saw his friend across the highway and sagged with relief when he was unharmed. He placed his hand on his side and he felt the sticky warmth of his blood. His side felt as though it was burning but he clenched his teeth to keep himself from shouting.

After a few minutes, he lost consciousness from severe blood loss and pain.

When he woke up, he was sitting beside Antonio and he was tied to a chair. His skin felt cold and he felt very weak. His throat was dry and his head throbbed. Someone yanked on his hair and he was forced to raise his head. Then, a newspaper was placed on his chest and there was a flash as his picture was taken.

He heard many voices and there was only one thing he heard clearly: they were asking for ransom money. Whoever they would be sending this video to would have a week to prepare what they asked for or he and Antonio would both be dead.

He drifted in and out of consciousness and his head rolled. He heard Antonio trying to wake him up but he was too weak.

So *this* was how it felt to die.

No dramatics.

No memories of your life flashing before your eyes.

No grim reaper with a scythe waiting to escort you into the afterlife.

There was just pain and then the slow descent to unconsciousness. At that point, the women, the cars, the money didn't even matter. Nothing did.

But there was one thing Nikos saw, though. It was something most unexpected for him. He saw his wife, Cassia, a wife he just saw a couple of times over the years. He could count on his fingers and toes the number of words he said to her over the years after their marriage.

He saw her standing in front of him in all her wedding finery. She was exquisite and she took his breath away. He saw her more clearly now than he did on their wedding. The disappointment in her eyes also tugged at something inside his chest.

That image would haunt him forever.

Next, he saw her underneath him. Her eyes were closed as he thrust over and over into her wet warmth. Then, her eyes flew open and she cried out his name as she splintered in his arms.

It was another image of her he'd gladly take to his grave.

The next time that he gained consciousness he smelled burning metal. Antonio was asleep on the floor beside him. He seemed unharmed and Nikos sighed with relief. He tried to look around his surroundings to gauge how much time has passed but he saw that they were inside a room with no windows and his wrist watch had been smashed. There was no way to tell the time.

Nikos tried to move and loosen the ropes binding his wrists but he just ended up chafing them raw. He heard the masked men laugh and then hold up the burned metal that was still glowing red.

They began to walk towards him.

He realized their intent and he started to panic. They wanted to cauterize his wound to prevent it from bleeding further and since there was no way for them to take him to a hospital, they were going to do it the primitive way.

"NO!!!" Nikos shouted through the gag in his mouth but it just came out as a muffled cry.

He found the strength to struggle but the men in black masks just laughed at him and shook their heads.

With every step they took, the fear inside him heightened until the point that he wished that his death would just come and claim him right now. But no. No matter how he wished, the Grim Reaper never came for him.

Someone yanked on his hair and then he felt his shirt being torn from his body. It was followed by sheer agony and the smell of his flesh burning. It was the kind of pain that was too much that one almost passed out from it; the one where all the nerve endings in your body felt as though they were being electrified. Nikos cried out and struggled but it was to no avail.

"Noooooooooooooooooooooooooo!!!"

Nikos Demakis jerked awake.

He sat on the massive bed and noticed that the sheets were twisted around his legs. His throat also felt raw; he must've been shouting in his sleep again. He flung the covers away from him and crossed the room to drink some water. Once his thirst was satisfied, he held the cool pitcher against his cheek.

Another nightmare.

Just like the other nights before this.

When was it going to end? When would he be able to have one whole night that wasn't plagued with visions of his haunted past?

There was a knock from the door and Antonio entered.

"I apologize if I disturbed your sleep," Nikos said quickly.

His friend shook his head and sat down on the chair near Nikos' bed.

Nikos walked towards the window and moved the drapes to the side so he could gaze outside and see the beauty of the waves crashing against the shore.

"So, I guess the latest doctor also didn't work out?" Antonio inquired.

Nikos shook his head.

Since the time he was kidnapped, he had been seeing several psychiatrists to help him with his nightmares. They all diagnosed him with Post Traumatic Stress Disorder. But he didn't need their medical terms. He needed a cure for his nightmares. He wanted uninterrupted sleep.

So far, none helped.

His latest physician was one of the most expensive psychiatrists in the world yet he wasn't able to do anything. No amount of medicine or counseling could help him sleep well at night.

"I hope I didn't wake up Elise and Anton," Nikos told his friend.

"No. They are still sleeping soundly," Antonio replied with a huge grin at the mention of his wife and son.

If there was one positive thing that happened when they were kidnapped, it was that Antonio met Elise.

Before, he was almost married but it proved to be one hell of a failure. Antonio believed that his ex-fiancee, Mara, was different even if Nikos and all their other friends told him otherwise. They were right for she turned out to be nothing but a gold-digger who wanted to sink her claws in Antonio's money.

Now, Antonio had Elise and she was truly different. She was the daughter of the man who organized their kidnapping. Even though she grew up in a world filled with greed and violence, she retained her pure heart. Elise pitied Nikos very much when she saw the condition he was in and the regular beatings he received. Because of that, she helped Antonio nurse him during their one-month captivity.

That was when the two fell in love.

When they escaped, Antonio took Elise with him and from that time on, he never let her go. They got married a few months later and after a year, they had little Anton who was his father's pride and joy. Nikos was here in Spain now for Anton's first birthday.

Right on cue, Anton started to cry and Antonio left the room to grab his son. A moment later, he returned and sat on the chair he previously vacated as rocked his baby back to sleep.

"He's adorable," Nikos commented.

"He is," his friend agreed.

"You know, you're his godfather and you haven't held him even once since he was born."

Nikos laughed nervously. "He looked too fragile then. He still does now. I am afraid to drop him or squeeze too much."

"You won't. Come on, just give it a try."

Before Nikos could reply or complain, he felt the weight of the baby in his arms and there was nothing he could do but to hold him securely so that he wouldn't fall.

"Is this correct?" he asked nervously and Antonio laughed.

"A bit awkward but you're fine."

Nikos looked down and Anton's eyes opened and gazed at him. The baby smiled and something twisted in his chest.

"It's the best feeling in the world when I hold him in my arms. It's like I am holding a miracle."

"Yes," Nikos gasped.

He didn't know it but he was also smiling to the baby and swaying so he could be lulled to sleep.

"Even more if that is your own son you are holding," Antonio pointed out.

Nikos' heart gave another squeeze as the thought hit him hard. What would it feel like if he held his son in his arms for the first time? What would it feel like seeing him the moment he was born? What would it feel like when his daughter held his hand? What would she look like? Would she have brown hair and brown eyes as well?

Nikos' thoughts drifted towards Cassia...

Wait...why was he even thinking about her? They were never going to have a family together. Their marriage was not that sort! It was nothing but a business arrangement.

Nikos sighed as he looked at Anton's perfect features.

Truth be told, he was jealous of Antonio. The man had something he wanted most: *a family*.

Nikos laughed to ease the tension.

"I can't have that."

"Why not? You have a perfectly lovely wife. Have you seen Cassia lately? She's changed so much! I could hardly recognize her."

"I haven't seen her for four years. Before, we always saw each other for our anniversary. Just for appearances' sake. She stopped coming when Costas had his heart attack. She did not even come when we were kid—"

"She was not informed," Antonio cut him off.

Nikos scoffed.

"She just doesn't care. She vowed to make my life a living hell, remember?"

"Nikos...she's busy."

"With what? Shopping? Wasting my money? Then it's no wonder she's beautiful now. Maybe she spent it all on plastic surgery. I see the accounts that are being sent to me. How come she needs eight new fucking houses? And just where does she spend millions of dollars?" he snarled.

"It's for chari—"

"Save it! I don't want to hear where she spends the money. It's hers to do with as she pleases," he replied.

The baby stirred in his arms and reacted to the hostile environment. It looked up at him with fear and something twisted in his chest yet again.

Before he knew it, he was crooning to comfort the child.

"Here...let me get him. I think it's time for him to go back to Elise. Then you and I will talk."

"There's nothing for us to talk about. Not Cassia."

"Hold that thought," Antonio told him.

He carefully retrieved his son and walked out of the room. Nikos sat and resumed staring at the window.

For the first time in a long time, he let his thoughts drift back to his arranged wife.

How was she doing now?

A long time ago - he couldn't remember when - he heard something about her name being linked to fashion. He couldn't remember the details also but he remembered distinctly that it was about fashion. So was she a style icon now? Is that where she spent all *their* money?

What was she doing with her life? How did she spend her time when she was not wasting money? Did she have a lover now?

He felt a surge of possessiveness go through him and he clenched his fists. He remembered their wedding night and the passionate way she responded to him. He remembered touching every inch of her and achieving her surrender. *She was still his*. No man should have touched her.

So she can't have a lover, but you can?

He shook his head at his traitorous conscience. But it was right. He had no right for he didn't honor his marriage vows either. He'd spent years dating several women and discarding them just like he did before he was married.

Yet there was one thing he couldn't admit out loud.

It was that Cassia still haunted his thoughts whenever he was with them.

In bed, he remembered her. He remembered how she smelled, how soft her skin felt and the sound of her cries as he drove her higher and higher to her pleasure.

That night, ten years ago, he believed that they had a chance. But come morning, he was presented with more lies and deceit. So he cast her out and hurt her.

But his actions were justified, right?

Cassia was the reason why he has not found the girl he truly wanted to settle down with. Now, time was ticking for him. He was thirty-four years old and he still didn't have a family.

Another pang of loneliness hit him in the chest and it was a heavy blow. He bowed his head and felt the cold touch of the glass on his forehead.

But then again, he did not deserve a family. How could he when he couldn't even sleep at night? How could he sleep beside his wife without waking her up with his nightmares? How could he let his son sleep when he would be screaming through the night?

How could he find the right woman for him when he, himself, was a broken man?

Antonio arrived and sat.

"We have to talk."

"You already said that earlier."

"I always say that yet you never listen."

Nikos sighed and then ran his hand through his hair in frustration. He sat on the chair opposite Antonio's and placed his forearms on the table.

"What?" he hissed.

"I don't like the way you're living your life. It's like you're just being forced to exist."

"I am. And how can you say that I'm not living my life? I have! *Andrade-Demakis International* is now the most successful company under my hands! I have worked hard for that and everyone can see the results. My hotel and restaurant business is also flourishing and I am spending my time trying to make it more successful! Now tell me again how I am not living."

"That's work. And you work very hard, Nikos. I know your work drives you. But I remember a certain man from the past. He had great visions and he always had enthusiasm and hope shining in his eyes as we planned for our future while we were still in the university. I don't see that man now, Nikos. All I see is a robot programmed to work hard every day of his life with no emotion or enjoyment."

"I am not a robot. I'm just a broken man. Nothing can fix me now and I will forever be haunted by what I suffered."

"Then you're an idiot. You have everything to live for, you just don't see it. First of all, you have a marriage you should start now. You have a wife you think the worse of. But the truth is Cassia is one of the most kind-hearted people I know."

Nikos scoffed. Now why did the conversation shift towards his *wife* once more?

"Kind-hearted spoiled brat?"

"That's not true. You know if only you would look closer, you'd realize that all you believe about her is a lie. A lie you built so that you could distance yourself from her. You crave connection yet you shun everyone away, Nikos. And I am sick of it."

"What do you want me to do?!" he snarled in agitation.

"For starters, you could go to Cassia. Apologize for the way you behaved. Ask her to for another chance for you and your marriage. This time, don't mess it up. If you want a family of your own, do it now before it's too late. Get to know her. Spend some time with her. And maybe you'll find out she's the one you've been looking for all along," Antonio challenged

Nikos was silent for a moment and then he threw his head back and laughed.

"I doubt that. If there's someone out there for me, I haven't met her yet."

Antonio shook his head sadly.

"Well then, if you do not like that approach...let me remind you of this. You have to have an heir. Cassia is supposed to be the mother or else both corporations slip through your fingers. And if you do, your son or your daughter will inherit everything. Let me tell you also that it has been ten years. Cassia is not getting any younger. She's already twenty-nine and you are thirty-four. I really think it's time for both of you to settle down."

Nikos continued laughing.

"I don't even see myself being with her. How can we start a family when we're so hostile to each other? She hates my guts, Antonio. She would sooner stab me with a knife than go to bed with me."

"Well, I can't blame her. Did you ever give her a reason to like you? All you've been showing her is that asshole side of yours," Antonio replied and Nikos glared at him.

"What do you want me to do?"

"I've been telling you that over and over but you don't listen. My friend, what I want you to do is to start living your life again, and if you want what I have, better make up with your wife before it's too late. As the saying goes: *You never know what you have until it is gone.*"

"Wise words as ever, Antonio. When I am talking to you it's like I am talking to an old soul in the wrong generation. But no amount of wise words will make me change my mind about her. Not now, not ever."

"An old soul in the wrong generation?" Antonio barked and then he laughed. "It's just that I've been through so much in the past that it made me wiser."

Nikos just sat back and nodded. He knew perfectly well what Antonio had been through. There was a time in Antonio's life when he was in worse shape than him. But his friend had struggled through it and emerged a much better man.

Antonio stood up and then sighed. Slowly, he started to walk towards the door.

"Well, at least I tried," he whispered under his breath.

"Stop matchmaking for the two of us Antonio. We're like oil and water; we will *never* mix."

"Is that really me you're convincing, Nikos? Or is that yourself? What is it about Cassia that every time I mention her, you look as if you want to run far away yet your eyes light up with life at the same time?"

Nikos gritted his teeth and placed his head in his hands. Why did he get the feeling that something really terrible was about to happen? Why did he get this sudden premonition that something big was waiting for him in the future? And why did Antonio's words feel like they were nothing but absolute truth?

"I'll never be with her, Antonio. She's not the one for me. Never have been, never will be."

Chapter 10
Reunion

W*HAT do you mean 'he screwed up'?!?"* Sebastian shouted.

"Something went wrong with one of the shipments. One of the cops smelled it and I think the entire mission was discovered and all the drugs were confiscated. Several of our people were arrested."

"What do you mean by 'something'? I want concrete answers! Our jobs and our lives are at stake when we commit errors! Do you know what this will cost us?!"

Sebastian stood up from his desk and towered over the man who stood in fear in front of him.

"I want answers and I want them now! Find me the person who made this mistake and we will make him pay!" he hissed.

"Right away, sir." The terrified man backed away from Sebastian and made his way towards the door.

"Return here without the answers I am looking for and you are a dead man."

November 8,2013
Nostos Restaurant
The Bellagio, Las Vegas

The deep sultry voice of the singer at the lounge accompanied by the beautiful chords of the piano and the violin made Cassia Andrade close her eyes and hum to one of her favorite songs: *When I Fall in Love* by Celine Dion.

"Would you like another glass of champagne, mademoiselle?" the waiter inquired.

Just like that, the serenity of the moment was shattered.

"I'm fine," Cassia replied with a smile. She lost count of how many glasses of champagne she'd already had while waiting for Hector, who was already two hours late.

Cassia glanced at her watch and then sighed. She'd known Hector for almost ten years now. He was really a great guy. However there was one thing about him that she couldn't categorize as good or bad: his workaholic attitude.

She understood him for she herself came from poverty. Cassia knew that Hector just wanted to make his mark in the world and to never be poor and an outcast again, but sometimes, he was just pushing it too much. Like today, he was late again because something came up at work.

This was one of the things she disliked about Hector. He was always late, always busy. When he was with her, he'd frequently get a call and then he'd drop everything and go. Oftentimes, he promised that they'd just reschedule but that usually never happened.

Cassia loved Hector.

She really did.

But this was one of his least endearing qualities. Sometimes she didn't know where she stood in his life. If they ever created a family, would Hector lessen his work hours so he could be with them?

Or were they going to continue to live a life like this and she'd just be adding children that would also beg for scraps of attention from their father?

Again Cassia closed her eyes and tried to let go of her negative feelings. She just focused on trying to listen to the song.

Instantly, she was taken back through time by her memories. In her mind's eye, she saw her parents. Her mother and her father were both smiling at each other as they both danced around the kitchen while her father hummed this beautiful melody...

When her father saw that she was looking, he scooped her up into his arms and also danced with her.

"Do you know that this was the song that was playing when I first saw your mother?" her father whispered to her.

"It's beautiful, daddy," she giggled.

"Not as beautiful as you, princess."

When Cassia opened her eyes again, she was back to reality – a reality wherein she wanted what her parents had but was almost sure that she was not going to find it.

Hector really tested her patience sometimes. However perfect he may seem to others, she always felt there was something lacking, something she was looking for that she couldn't find in him.

"Daydreaming without me, princess?"

Cassia opened her eyes and saw Hector standing in front of her. He looked very handsome in a suit and with the ambient lights of the restaurant, he looked even more breathtaking.

"Hi, handsome," she greeted.

Hector leaned down and placed a kiss on her lips.

"Cass...sorry I'm—"

Cassia stopped him from apologizing by placing her finger on his lips.

"No worries. I understand. It's work," she told him.

He nodded and exhaled very loudly. He leaned back in his chair and began rubbing his neck in a tired way.

"Got problems?" she asked.

"Yes. Competition is a hard game," Hector replied.

Hector's primary competition in his business was none other than her estranged husband, Nikos Demakis. Though Hector was cunning in business, Nikos was ruthless. He was called the Einstein of the Corporate World for a reason.

"I'm not worried. I know you got this." Cassia smiled sweetly.

Hector returned her smile and then took her hand. He kissed the back of her hand.

"You realize you're the cause of my success, right? You're the first person who believed in me, and because of that belief I'm where I am today."

"I do understand that because that's how I feel about you too."

Hector's entire face softened. His tiredness even seemed to fade away from his body at those words. He leaned forward again and there was this twinkle in his eyes.

"Cass...I know I've asked this a million times already. I know that your answer is always the same. But today, I am still hoping that it would be different. Cassia...would you want to be with me, in every sense of the way?"

Cassia's breath caught in her throat again, just like every time Hector asked that question. All those times before she always told him no. She had several reasons and each of them was different every time: she was busy with college, she was just launching her career in the fashion industry, she wanted Hector to concentrate with his business first, she just launched her shop *Cassiopeia*, she wasn't ready yet.

But another reason aside from those already mentioned was the fact that she just couldn't let Nikos have his freedom and all of the money before. She promised to make his life a living hell but the only thing she has done so far was to be absent in his life, which didn't really make a big difference.

When she fled Greece, she promised to herself that she'd have her revenge for all those times she was humiliated. But as time passed, she found herself less and less inclined towards that revenge. Her time and concentration went to her studies and then further on to her business.

Like all wounds, hers was healed by *time*.

Now, she realized that she had placed her life on hold for a long time just to spite Nikos. But it had no effect for the man had skin as tough as iron. For all she knew, he might've forgotten her already like the other women who came and went from his life.

Now, she was twenty-nine years old...

She had a successful career and she could already say that she reached her dreams. Now, she wanted a change in her life. She wanted to settle down with the man she loved and take a chance at happiness with him. She wanted to have a family. She wanted to have a child whom she would love as much as her parents loved her.

She was finally ready to let go of her need for vengeance, her hatred for Nikos Demakis and her life as the Andrade heiress.

She was ready to move on and take another giant leap of faith.

"I'm ready, Hector...and I want to be with you."

Those were the words that Cassia wanted to tell Hector. But the man had waited too long for her already. She wanted to make it special for him also.

But she was nervous and she wasn't good at these kinds of things and the only thing she was able to blurt out was: "Yes."

The smile on Hector's face disappeared and for a full minute, he sat there speechless with his jaw hanging open. Then, he shook his head and stared at her.

"S-say that again...Cass...I don't think I heard you right."

"I said yes, Hector," she repeated.

Hector stood up so fast that the water before him spilled on the table and the glass rolled towards one side. In a reflex movement, Cassia also stood up to avoid getting wet. Before she could blink, she was enveloped in Hector's arms and his lips were on hers.

She laughed while her eyes started to fill with tears of joy at Hector's reaction.

"I'm going to make you happy, Cass. And for starters, I'll try not to spend too much time at the office. I promise," Hector whispered.

Cassia laughed and kissed Hector on the lips. "I'll hold you to that promise, okay? Please don't be late for the fashion show!"

"I'll *never* miss it for the world."

Hector turned around and faced the other people on the lounge.

"This wonderful woman has just agreed to marry me!" he shouted just as the beautiful song ended.

He smiled widely and gave her a kiss on the lips. The room erupted into applause and shouted their congratulations and best wishes for the newly-engaged couple.

Cassia stared lovingly into Hector's beautiful eyes and wished that she would find whatever it was that she thought was missing from their relationship. Or that she could forget whatever it was so that nothing would impede their happiness anymore.

November 13, 2013
Nikos' Penthouse
Las Vegas, Nevada

"Nikos Demakis speaking," he answered curtly.

"Daaaarling..." a seductive voice replied.

His mouth twitched as he recognized the voice of his French mistress, Marietta, on the other line.

"Hello. I haven't heard from you in a while," he replied with a lack of interest.

"I became busy. There was this movie I had to do. And I knew you were busy as well. How are you?"

"I'm good. Yourself?"

"Never better. Especially now that I am talking to you. I know this is totally random, but are you in Vegas by any chance?" Marietta purred.

"As a matter of fact, I am."

"Perfect!" his mistress screeched.

He was in Las Vegas because of a business venture. His casino was losing profit because of his competition's newest gimmicks. He had to retake the market so he was here personally to oversee the running of the casino. Aside from that, his personal assistant reminded him that in two days time, it was his tenth wedding anniversary with his *wife*.

He flinched as he remembered the word, like he did every time that her name was mentioned. He also sighed. He would have to get used to it now.

He also made a mental note to ask his personal assistant to call her secretary and schedule for lunch or dinner on their anniversary day. That will be the time he would tell her of his plans.

Those plans were settling down with her, trying to coexist in peace, getting to know each other, being in each other's lives more often, and finally trying to build a family. He did not know how she would react to that but surely she would like the idea? It was she who wanted to marry him in the first place.

Yes, she was mad at him for what he did to her on their wedding. But surely, ten years was a long enough time to forgive and forget, right? Especially when he himself was willing to throw away their past, along with all the lies, and start anew?

"Nikos! Are you there?" Marietta's heavily accented voice snapped him out of his musings.

"Yes."

"I said will you meet me at MGM Grand later tonight? I am hosting this charity fashion show auction...then maybe we could grab some drinks afterwards?"

Nikos checked his watch and tried to remember if he had any meetings scheduled tonight. When none came to mind, he decided that he also needed some company. Maybe Marietta was exactly what he needed to get his mind off things.

"What time?" he asked her.

"The show starts at eight. Around ten, the auction will be done and it's just the after-party."

"I'll be there at eight. I don't have anything to do so I think I'd rather watch."

"Perfect, darling! I'll get you front stage tickets. I have to go. Call me when you're there and I'll meet you to give you tickets. Oh, and if you want to stay for the after party, bring a mask. It's a masquerade ball. Till later, baby!"

And the line went dead.

Nikos placed his phone down, took off his diamond cuff links, his suit and then unbuttoned his shirt and removed his pants and shoes. He entered the bathroom and let the hot water slide down his skin as he placed his hands on the cold tiles of the wall.

He'd gone without socializing for quite some time now. This charity auction may be just what he needed to meet his friends once more and gain some new contacts for his business.

One hour later...
The MGM Grand Hotel
Las Vegas, Nevada

Nikos Demakis sat in the front row of the catwalk as various skinny models in lingerie paraded before him.

He smiled with satisfaction as he realized he had dated some of them. Some looked at him with flirtatious expressions while some looked at him with anger. Those were the ones who wanted more and were bitter when he ended the relationship because he couldn't give them the *'more'* they were searching for.

Aside from eyeing the models, he also took in the details of the designs. Actually, he was a connoisseur of beautiful things and this set of designs really caught his eye. He often bought his mistresses expensive clothing to placate them and to not have things so complicated when he broke things off. Those were nothing compared to this.

Now, he made a mental note to ask his personal assistant to buy the clothing he sent out as gifts in this shop instead.

The parade went on and on and he grabbed his pen and noted the designs he wanted to buy later. Earlier, it was explained that the proceeds would go to the numerous orphanages that the owner of the shop sponsored.

Then, he focused back on the show. Overall, it was very organized and he found himself enjoying his night, something he hadn't really done for a long time. He made another mental note to meet the designer and congratulate him or her on a very successful event.

He loved everything about it.

He loved how the ambiance and the music complemented the theme of the show. He loved the designs, the models chosen and the way they were asked to parade the clothing. He also loved the fact that this show was for a good cause.

But all good things come to an end.

Time flew so fast that Nikos was surprised when they announced that the show was already over. For the last part, all the models came out wearing evening gowns with their masks on. All their evening gowns were designed by the owner of the fashion line and he concluded that this was what all of them would be wearing for the after party.

Finally, the designer exited the stage and everyone stood up and clapped. He also clapped and he was even more amazed when he saw that it was a woman. His heart skipped inside his chest and for some reason, he felt as if he knew her.

He studied her and looked at her from head to toe. She had gorgeous brown hair that fell down her back in a mass of beautiful curls. Her skin looked so soft and it was a bit toned as if she spent some time under the sun. But what he noticed most about her was that she had curves that could make any man's mouth water. He couldn't see her eyes through the mask but he could see her lips which made him want to kiss them all night long.

All those were just physical characteristics.

He also counted in the fact that she had a brilliant mind for her designs were absolutely exquisite. Her gaze fell towards him for a moment, and he saw her stop. The instant their eyes connected, he felt a jolt of electricity go through his entire body. Again, he couldn't help but feel that tingle of recognition.

Her lips parted and he knew she must've felt the same way too...or maybe it was just his imagination for she quickly looked away.

Her reaction to him made him all the more certain; he just had to meet her.

***

"Hi! Are you enjoying your night?" Cassia asked her guests. All of them nodded and began to chat with her enthusiastically about her designs. They also told her that they were sure that they were going to bid for a lot of her designs tonight.

Cassia smiled and marveled at her success. Overall, this night was perfect! It was everything she envisioned it to be. The show and her designs were a success! She was sure she would gather a lot of profit for her numerous charities later tonight.

There were just two things that dampened her spirits: the first one was that Nikos Demakis was here.

When her eyes connected with his, she felt as if she was back in Greece. For a moment there, she was taken back to the time when she was still a naive girl who blindly followed her grandfather's wishes. She was also reminded of the fact that she was so infatuated with Nikos Demakis at one point in time

Then he looked at her with desire in his eyes. During that moment, memories of their wedding night arose. He had looked at her that way as he kissed her and mastered her body. But that desire was worth nothing. The next morning, he came straight to his mistress' bed and chose her over his own wife. Then came all the humiliation.

She steeled her resolve and looked away. She wore a mask and he'd never recognize her anyway. She would just have to avoid him for the rest of the night. He wouldn't recognize her for they hadn't seen each other for a couple of years. Several things had changed. One of them was that she wasn't blonde anymore. Her hair color was back to its natural brown. Also, she wasn't fat. It all melted away in college when she had to work and study at the same time.

As for the second reason she was not a hundred percent happy: *Hector wasn't here*.

He promised her he wouldn't miss this fashion show for the world. But he did. He said something came up in his work again and that caused him to miss his flight to Las Vegas. And then he was also running late due to traffic.

Cassia shook her head and sighed. Well, it seemed as if she had her answer: she would always come second in his life. His business would always take first place and the most room in his heart.

"All right, then. Please enjoy the rest of the night," she told her guests and then moved away to entertain other guests.

She was stopped on her way when a man walked towards her. Her breath caught in her throat when she realized it was none other than Nikos Demakis.

"Hi." Nikos drawled.

"Hello," Cassia replied.

Her heart started beating a furious rhythm inside her chest but she willed herself to be calm. She would not show Nikos any fear. If possible, she'd never reveal her identity. But he would know about this sooner or later. Well then, she'd just remove her mask when the perfect opportunity came.

"I just wanted to commend you on your designs. They are excellent. Far more superior to any other I've ever seen. They are very unique and creative."

"Thank you," Cassia replied and then she tilted her head up. "I think you are a man who doesn't give complements easily. So your words must be true," she added in a flat tone.

"That is true," Nikos laughed.

He grabbed two flutes of champagne from a passing waiter and passed one to her. She took it and thanked him with a nod.

"So...what brings you here to my show, Mr. Demakis? You didn't strike me as the man with a taste for fashion."

"How'd you know my name?

"Everyone knows Mr. Nikos Demakis

The corner of his lips turned up in an arrogant smile. "Well, I was just in town. And this was a great event. I thought I'd go. This is for charity too which just makes it all the more interesting."

".Hmm...what you said is true. I hope you bid for some pieces later tonight for charity."

"I'd bid for it because it's an excellent design. It, being for charity, is just a huge bonus," Nikos replied.

Cassia smiled and marveled at how sweet Nikos' tongue was when it wasn't lashing out cruel words for her. He was just like this because he didn't even recognize her plus the fact that he was *flirting* with her.

"I am a direct man, Ms. Cassiopeia...so I'll just say this straight away. Would you like to have dinner with me some time?"

Cassia laughed. Nikos truly did not recognize her. *And now, what?* He was planning to make her one of his conquests? One more to add to his list of successful women he dated? Another notch in his bedpost?

Well, been there, done that.

"Unfortunately, no."

"So quick to say no? Can't you think about it?" Without another word, Nikos grabbed her hand and inspected it.

"No rings," Nikos pointed out.

Cassia laughed once more and snatched her hand back. She extended it in front of her face and made a point to look as curious as she could be as she studied it.

"Hmm...you're right. But there *used* to be. No matter, we'll get divorced soon," she pointed out.

Nikos couldn't help but feel satisfaction as she said that she was getting divorced soon. He badly wanted her.

"See...so you are getting divorced, then? Come to dinner with me. I think your husband won't mind that now, will he?"

Cassia knew that it was the perfect opportunity to reveal herself. No other moment could be as perfect as this one.

She removed her mask and waited for comprehension to dawn on Nikos face. *But it didn't.* Instead, his eyes grew heavy-lidded with desire and mild curiosity.

"You tell me if you would mind, Nikos. You *are* my *husband*, after all," Cassia said.

She watched as his jaw dropped and recognition and shock crossed his beautiful green eyes. The two expressions warred and she saw a muscle throb in his jaw.

Before he could say another word, she laughed and then turned around and walked away from him.

Chapter 11
Auction

WAS it true or was it all a figment of his imagination?

Nikos watched Cassia walk away with all his muscles locked in place. His jaw would have dropped had he not controlled himself.

When she laughed it was like a punch to his gut. The first thought that popped into his mind was that it was not really her. But upon looking more closely, indeed it was her. Now he knew why he thought he recognized her the first time he saw her on stage.

She had the same beautiful brown eyes and the same facial features. But now, all the fat in her body melted into perfect curves; the kind that made a man want to hold on forever.

Another thing that changed was that she was no longer blonde. Instead, she was now a brunette. And it looked even better! Nikos' stomach clenched and so did the hand holding the champagne glass. He shook his head and turned around to lean against one of the marble pillars.

He could not believe that he had just been flirting with his own wife!

He definitely needed a stronger drink.

He walked towards the bar and sat on one of the stools.

"Give me your best scotch," he told the bartender who quickly went to work on his drink. While he was waiting, his eyes roamed the room.

Now that his shock has faded, his logic was back.

For the first time tonight, he realized that the famous designer that owned the fashion line *Cassiopeia* was none other than his *wife*. He took one more look around the room and noted the success of the event. If she organized this herself, then he had to admit that she was good. If not, then she had a good set of staff to do this for her.

The bartender slid his drink towards him and he took a long swig.

She was his wife yet why did he not know about this? Is this where all the money that he gave her every year as her allowance went? Were the houses she bought with his money the locations where she built her shops?

With this train of thought, he took another hefty swig of his drink. It burned a path down his throat but he welcomed it for he now knew that this was reality and he was definitely not dreaming.

Antonio had raised some valid points and he tried to tell him about Cassia's life now but he did not let his friend talk. Why? *It was because he did not care.* He did not want anything to do with her because to him, she would forever be the woman who stole his freedom and built a web of lies around their marriage.

Over the years he reasoned that, because of her, he could not find the woman for him. She took his choice away and now he was stuck with her. Especially since his family prided itself on never having any divorce. Once they married, it was for life and divorce was certainly out of the equation.

But then again, Antonio argued that Cassia was not in his life for ten years and that they only saw each other once in a while. Cassia basically had no influence on his life and he was free to do whatever he pleased and date whoever he wanted; which was what he did.

But over the course of ten years, he never even had a serious relationship. He never found a woman he could give his heart to; never found one he wanted to marry. Because of that, he carried on with his life and still searched. Then there came a point that he simply gave up. Maybe he was not suited for a family life and maybe he was just incapable of feeling an emotion as deep as love.

Nikos ordered himself another drink before he went back to his thoughts.

He stared at the ice cubes in his scotch as he pondered the recent events of the night.

In two days, it would be his and Cassia's *tenth* wedding anniversary. Ten years of marriage and they were no closer to each other than the day they were wed. He loathed her and she loathed him. He decided that he would take Antonio's advice and to try and make Cassia agree that it was time they both settled down.

Why the change of heart when just a few days ago he was convinced that he would never want her?

Well, it was due to the fact that he thought he would never find the woman for him anyway. Time was running out. He refused to wait some more for someone that may never come. Plus, he had a duty to his family. He had to have an heir with Cassia or everything he and his ancestors worked hard for would all go to waste.

Demakis International had been with his family for generations and he refused to let it end with him. No matter what, it must stay in his family and the only way to do that was to pass it on to a child that was from both Cassia and him as stipulated by their contract.

And since he gave up the notion of falling in love, he might as well do his duty. He may not love his wife but he sure as hell would love his son or daughter. Maybe when he was holding his own child in his arms, he'd stop being so *gods-damned* jealous of Antonio and his perfect family life. For a long time, he felt as though there was this huge void in his life and maybe, just *maybe*, it was what he needed to fill it.

He needed an end to this kind of playboy life and he was finally ready to settle down. He was willing to sacrifice it all again just so he could have that. He was even willing to make peace with his *wife*. Maybe they could even have a civilized relationship once they got past all the hate.

With that thought in mind, he flew to Vegas from Greece two days early with the intent of scheduling a dinner with Cassia on their wedding anniversary which was on November 15th, two days from now. During that dinner, he planned on discussing his plans with her. He believed that she would agree quickly. If not, he'd apologize for his behavior ten years ago and ask for a chance.

But why would she not agree? She was the one who wanted him in the first place. Maybe the idea of them living together and her having his child would even make her faint with joy.

"One Gin and Tonic please."

A man slid into the stool beside Nikos thereby pulling him out of his thoughts. He looked to his left and then his whole body clenched and he frowned.

"Petrides," he hissed.

Nikos looked at Hector Petrides from head to foot and noted the expensively tailored Italian suit, the gold Rolex watch studded with diamonds and his shiny leather shoes. Every inch of him screamed wealth and Nikos could not believe that the man started out as a waiter somewhere in Greece, according to reports.

The man's brown head whipped towards him and surprise registered in his eyes.

"Demakis," the man replied in an equally nasty tone. "What a pleasant surprise! Didn't think you liked these kinds of things."

Nikos shrugged at his best competition in the hotel and restaurant industry.

"I know the host," he replied. "And you? Didn't think this was your kind of thing either."

"Well, I know the designer," Hector replied as he grabbed his drink from the bar.

He slid off his stool and winked at Nikos. Then, he walked away without another word.

His brows furrowed in confusion as he watched Hector disappear in the crowd. He couldn't help but be suspicious about Hector's last statement.

"Good evening everybody!" Marietta greeted.

Immediately, the people started to go to their tables to be seated since the auction was about to start. Nikos slid off his stool and went towards his table near the front of the stage.

He smiled and nodded politely to the people seated at the same table. He also listened to their polite conversation and answered some of their questions. Then, the auction went on and Nikos bought most of the things at an outrageously high price just so he could please Cassia.

Marietta beamed at him all the while for she thought it was for *her*.

Nikos noticed it and made a mental note to sever all ties with her before he would go and talk to Cassia. Since he had known Marietta for a long time now, he couldn't help thinking that the French supermodel-turned-actress believed that she was going to be a permanent fixture in his life someday.

But that was never going to happen.

He had to get things straight.

Nikos lifted his head and watched as several jewelry pieces were paraded for the auction. This time, he let the men who came here with their wives win the bidding. He thought that it will be more appreciated by the wives of his colleagues as a sweet gesture rather than let those beautiful gems just sit in his vault.

Nikos eyes darted towards the side of the stage and he saw Cassia smiling with tears in her eyes. Earlier that night, the charities where the proceeds of this auction would go to were introduced. An amount was set as a target. But because of the generosity of the men here, his own high bids and Cassia's excellent designs, the target amount was met and even tripled.

The sight of the smile on her face moved something inside him but he quickly shook the feeling away.

"Thank you everyone for your generosity! Our target of five hundred thousand dollars has now been achieved! What's more is that we now have one million and five hundred eighty thousand dollars! Now, can't we close this at one million six hundred thousand dollars?" Marietta's voice rang clear across the room. "How about a kiss from our beloved designer, Miss Cassiopeia for that twenty thousand dollars?" she suggested.

The guests chuckled and so did the designer herself. She threw her head back, exposing the long column of her neck, and then laughed.

The sound was like a soothing balm to his fractured spirit.

He was about to raise his hand and bid for that kiss when a voice beat him to it.

"I'll take that kiss!"

Nikos' turned towards the sound of the voice and he saw Hector Petrides with his hand raised in the air.

Rage blazed inside of him along with a surge of possessiveness. His earlier suspicion was pretty much confirmed: Hector and Cassia had some kind of relationship. His vision turned red and his hands clenched at his side. All his self-control went towards stopping himself from standing up and hitting the bastard in the face.

That was *his wife* Petrides is bidding *a kiss* for!

Nikos raised his hand. "One hundred thousand dollars."

Marietta laughed and so did the entire crowd. They thought it was a joke and that he was simply being very charitable. It was true. But behind that reason, he did not want anyone else kissing Cassia. They may not have the perfect marriage but she was still his wife.

Besides, he hated Hector Petrides and didn't want him to win.

Hector turned towards him and one corner of his lips turned upwards in a smile.

"One hundred and fifty thousand dollars."

Hector just sealed his fate even further. There'd be no mercy for him now. Nikos would make sure his business went down.

"Three hundred," Nikos retorted

"Wow. This is some sizzling competition. But I understand for Miss Cassiopeia is truly stunning in her gown. I thank her for also designing the gown that I am wearing. And to Mr. Demakis and Mr. Petrides, thank you so much for your kindness. That's one hell of an expensive kiss, huh?" Marietta quipped.

She also winked at Nikos and he just ignored her.

People laughed some more but Nikos did not care. He'd even give a hundred million dollars just so that Hector could not kiss Cassia.

"Four hundred," Hector said quickly.

Nikos decided to bid double.

"Eight hundred thousand dollars."

Nikos noticed that Petrides looked uncomfortable now. He sat back in his chair and just smiled around at the people and even for the media who leapt into action and took several pictures.

He knew the headline for tomorrow's gossip columns would be that he was interested in the famous designer of Cassiopeia. But what they did not know was that she was already his wife. A fact he also did not know when this night started.

"Mr. Demakis, a moment please?" one of the reporters approached him.

"Sure," he replied with a smile. He darted one glance towards Cassia and Hector but Hector hadn't bid yet. Maybe the bastard was still checking how much money he still had in his bank account.

"Rumors say that you are going to be racing at the *Monte Carlo Grand Prix* again this year after so many years of being out of the racing circuit. Is this true?"

Nikos smiled and the reporters waited with bated breaths.

"What can I say? Racing is my hobby and it shall forever be in my blood," he replied with a smile.

At that answer, the reporters went wild and started throwing more questions left and right. Because of the noise they made, he did not hear Hector's last bid. Because of his preoccupation, he forgot that he was bidding for a kiss from his own wife.

"One million dollars."

Cassia and Marietta both turned to look at him. The French model looked at Nikos with curiosity while Cassia looked at him with expectation in her eyes. When he did not bid further, disappointment flashed across those beautiful features.

Cassia shook her head and scolded herself for feeling this way.

Earlier tonight, she was so happy at the stunned expression on Nikos' face. She was so happy with the scene she made. Her entire night was perfect and she couldn't wish for anything more. The fact that Hector still made it just added to the joy that she was feeling.

But when Nikos bid for her kiss, she nearly fainted. It was as if something inside her was unlocked and she was back to the same girl that was infatuated with him years ago. It unlocked some sort of longing inside her and truthfully, she was overjoyed.

When she turned to look at him, their eyes met and she saw possession written across his features. It was the same expression her wore when he looked at her on their wedding night.

Finally, he was noticing her again.

Cassia reveled in it even though she knew it was wrong.

With each bid against Hector, she was secretly thrilled. When Nikos was interviewed by the reporters and he wasn't able to bid anymore, she was disappointed.

Cassia laughed and gave herself a mental shake.

How could she still feel something for that man after all he did? How dare she hope for something? Cassia closed her eyes. She told herself she was incredibly stupid and naive to feel this way. Hadn't he hurt her enough? Why was she still holding out for even crumbs of affection from him? Had she not vowed to have her revenge? Had it not been ten years and she had finally moved on?

Had she not found love with Hector and agreed to be with him?

She was done with Nikos Demakis.

He had caused her enough heartache to last her a lifetime. She would do well to remember that so that seeing him would not resurrect any old feelings. Those feelings deserved to be locked in a steel vault then buried in the deepest part of the Pacific Ocean where it would never ever see the light of day again.

Feeling more composed, she looked at Hector and plastered a smile to her face. She even winked at him and the audience laughed.

"A kiss from the designer of Cassiopeia who looks really lovely tonight, by the way...for one million dollars! Going once...going twice...sold! To Mr. Hector Petrides!" Marietta announced.

Cassia laughed when Hector launched himself towards the stage to claim that kiss.

"You're late," she whispered.

"I'm sorry, princess...I'm trying hard. I really am. But today's been a very unlucky day," Hector groveled.

"Kiss me and it'll all be better. After all, this particular kiss cost you a million dollars," she teased.

"Ahh...such arrogance, milady," Hector said with a small bow as he took her hand and pulled her closer towards him.

Hector then turned towards Marietta and announced loudly, "Oh and I'll add that twenty thousand dollars too so that it'll be closed at two million six hundred thousand dollars," he even winked and the audience went wild.

Nikos turned his attention back to the auction when the guests started to clap and cheer. At the same time, he saw Hector Petrides race towards the stage and jump up towards Cassia.

Fuck it. He was too late.

Because he was too preoccupied with the reporters who crowded his table he forgot all about the bidding. Now he lost against his business' best competition and one of the men in the world that he hated the most.

He saw Cassia smile at Hector and the two exchanged whispers.

Something tightened inside Nikos' chest when he realized that the two had truly known each other for a long time now. They had an intimate look when they gazed at each other.

Were they lovers?

Before he could ponder the thought further, Hector's fingers cupped Cassia's chin and tilted her head upwards. He decided to look away for he was feeling so much rage and possessiveness that he could barely control himself.

But he just couldn't do it.

He watched as Hector's head dipped and his lips claimed Cassia's. The moment their lips touched, he saw Cassia sigh and then close her eyes. It was like their wedding kiss all those years ago. He was drunk at their wedding but he clearly remembered that first kiss and that precious sigh. He also remembered all the passionate and timid kisses she gave him on their wedding night.

Now, it was not him she was sighing for but Hector Petrides.

Nikos looked away just as he felt something inside him clench and then *shatter*.

Was it his heart? Maybe? Maybe not.

Perhaps it was just all his *pride*.

Chapter 12
Strangers

"S-SIR...we can't find them anywhere..." the man's weak voice echoed across the small room in which he had been held for two days now.

"You know I do not tolerate incompetence in my team," Sebastian said through clenched teeth.

He raised his fist once more and aimed another punch at the man's already bloody and swollen face.

"Please...g-give m-me another ch-chance..." he stammered.

"There'll be no second chances. Not even for me when it comes to something this big. We're all dead men," he whispered.

He retrieved his gun and smiled as he aimed it directly between the terrified man's eyes. He opened his mouth to beg for his life but Sebastian didn't give him that chance.

He laughed as he fired.

November 15, 2013
The King's Suite, Royalty (Nikos' Hotel)
New York

"Did Cassia confirm that she will come for dinner?" Nikos asked his personal assistant.

"Yes, sir. Mrs. Demakis confirmed that she will be attending dinner at 8pm, *Le Bernardin* restaurant. The whole restaurant is already reserved for both of you," his efficient assistant told him.

"Good. And James? Have you ordered the flowers?"

"Yes sir. I have also called *Cartier* and asked for a selection of their most beautiful necklaces. I found a diamond and ruby necklace. Would that suffice?"

"Yes. I trust your choice. It's always excellent," Nikos complimented.

His assistant had been with him for over ten years now. He was more efficient than ever and for that, Nikos compensated him well. James pulled out his cell phone to confirm the purchase. Nikos' would just drop by the store before dinner to pick it up. He glanced at his watch and it was only 4 pm. He still had to get a lot of work done before he could go to dinner with his *wife*.

"Have you finished the papers regarding the *Higeshima deal*?" he asked.

"Yes, sir. They are waiting at your desk."

"Good. We have to get that finalized before I leave for Monaco next week."

"Yes, sir."

Nikos picked up the stack of papers on his desk and began to read. After the first few paragraphs, he became absorbed. It was as if the outer world ceased to exist and it was only him and his papers.

Work was the only thing that occupied his mind and tried to keep the nightmares at bay. So when he couldn't sleep at night, he just poured more and more of himself into his work.

It felt like the blink of an eye but hours had passed and it was already time to leave.

He grabbed the keys to his Lamborghini Aventador and made a mental note to pick up the flowers and the jewelry. Today was his tenth wedding anniversary with Cassia.

He snorted at the thought for he really did not feel married.

But all of that was now going to change...

November 15, 2013 (Earlier that day)
Cassia's Penthouse Apartment
157 West 57th Street, New York City

Cassia placed her phone between her ear and her shoulder as she tried to organize a huge stack of papers neatly in an envelope. At the same time, she struggled into her high-heeled shoes.

"You've got the divorce papers?" the person on the other line asked.

"Yes, Hector. Got them."

"And you know what to say already?"

"Ugh. Of course I do!" she shouted and Hector chuckled.

"All right then, good luck tonight princess. Break a leg. Bring home the bacon...all that jazz."

This time, it was Cassia who laughed. "All right, then."

"When this is done, we'll go for that *Bora Bora* vacation I promised you. One week. And I won't be bringing my cell phone or my laptop. I swear!"

"Mmm-hmm," Cassia murmured in a disbelieving tone. "But I'll give you the benefit of the doubt. If you bring any of that, I'll throw it to the bottom of the ocean," she warned

Hector's deep chuckle echoed over the phone.

"Agreed, princess. I'm still in California. See you in two days for our celebratory dinner."

"Yeah. Bye," Cassia said with a smile.

She placed her phone in her bag and checked her desk for anything else she would need tonight. Then, she checked her reflection in the mirror. She placed light makeup only and wore a simple black dress with her high-heeled pumps. For her jewelry, there was a simple pearl necklace around her neck and the diamond-studded watch that Hector gave her around her wrist.

It was his first gift to her and he gave it after he made his first million-dollars. When he presented it to her, he told her it was his replacement for the watch that she gave him during her wedding day with Nikos. The value of her new watch was triple the value of the one she gave him.

To date, it was her most favorite jewelry piece *ever.*

Every year, for their anniversary, Nikos sent her some jewelry. Or maybe his assistant did. She didn't see him as the type who would bother by going to a jewelry store and selecting a piece himself.

His assistant was who she always spoke with whenever it was about attending company business, declining social invitations or returning the gifts. Cassia really made it a point to speak to James, Nikos' assistant, and not to Nikos himself.

And always, she sent the gifts back just like she did with the wedding and engagement ring he gave her all those years ago. She mailed those back to him the moment she set foot in America.

Now, it was their tenth wedding anniversary. A great feat for most couples. But not for them. For they *never* were truly married. It was all a great sham. A big fat lie.

But all of that was now going to change...

November 15, 2013, 8:00pm
Le Bernardin Restaurant
New York City

A limousine picked Cassia up and drove her straight to one of the finest restaurants in New York City. She cringed at the lavishness of the limousine but it was arranged by Nikos' assistant and she just went along with it. While the limousine made its way through the heavy traffic, she mused about the lifestyle Nikos was used to.

He was born a billionaire and pampered like a prince. To him, this type of extravagance was just normal. But to her, to someone who was born in a lower middle class family and who just now reaped the rewards of her hard work, this was a bit *extravagant*. And this extravagance reminded her of her grandfather's ways.

As they got nearer to the restaurant, Cassia's heart started to race. She opened her bag and sighed with relief when she saw the envelope that contained the divorce papers.

This was it.

The time had come. She was truly going to be free of Nikos Demakis. She was finally letting go of him, this sham of a marriage, her ties to her evil grandfather, and the money and status that came with her name.

She was finally saying goodbye to *Cassia Andrade-Demakis* and continuing her life as *Cassia Adrasteia*.

All she needed was to get through this night.

But why did this feel like it was the hardest thing she was about to do in her entire life?

She jerked back to reality when the driver opened the door and held it for her.

"Okay, show time," Cassia whispered to herself.

She then schooled her features into the expressionless mask she always wore when dealing with people she didn't particularly like. She was not the scared little girl anymore who meekly stood by in a corner while she was insulted by everyone. She had backbone now and she would not let herself be treated in any manner less than what she deserved.

Cassia entered the restaurant and saw that it was empty. The lights were dim and there were several candles that filled the room with a soft glow. It was elegant yet not too much. On the far side of the restaurant, a stage was set-up and a female singer softly crooned a beautiful love song.

Usually, on a night like this, the restaurant would be crowded. But now, it was reserved for just two people. It would have been a romantic gesture had it not been from someone like Nikos Demakis.

She felt a wave of regret cross her entire body. Nikos was not the sort of person who would organize this. Or maybe not for her but for his numerous other lovers.

For him, she was the evil one; the antagonist to his life story. The reason he was married at an early age.

And to her, he would always be her infatuation gone horribly wrong.

Nikos waited patiently at the restaurant. He arrived early with the flowers and the jewelry. As usual, his assistant did an excellent job. Well, he had lots of practice because he was always the one who chose Nikos' gifts for his mistresses.

He sat at the only table that was lit and asked for a bottle of wine. He sipped the finest *Le Bernardin* as he pondered on how his life would change from this night forward. He also thought of how to tell Cassia that he now wanted to give their relationship a try.

Should he say it to her directly? Should he sugar-coat his words?

The door opened and Nikos' head whipped towards the entrance of the restaurant.

Cassia walked in as the exact epitome of class and elegance. His breath caught and he felt his mouth run dry at the sight. She wore a simple black dress and matched it with a pearl necklace that just made her neck seem longer and added an ethereal glow to her face.

Oh how she had changed from the Cassia he knew before.

He watched as she glanced at her surroundings, as if she could not believe what she was seeing. Just like that, he was taken back ten years ago when he took her to different places after their engagement was announced.

She looked at things as though it was her first time seeing it. She enjoyed the little things the most, as though she'd never encountered them before!

All the while, he thought it was an act.

How could an heiress not have been to one of the finest art galleries in Greece? How could someone like her not know how to act in a five-star restaurant?

He immediately pinned it down as something like a ploy to look innocent. And he hated her for it.

But now...he was slowly rethinking his judgment. She had not seen him yet but she took note of her surroundings as though the sights were the most fascinating things in the world. He also noticed the look of regret in her eyes before it was replaced by something like anger.

Her searching gaze finally found him and her features hardened. Gone was the awe in her eyes and now coldness took its place. She took quick steps towards him and before she was able to reach the table, he stood and held out the chair for her.

"Nikos," she greeted.

"Happy anniversary," he told her and handed her the huge bouquet of flowers.

"How thoughtful," she said with a hint of sarcasm, fully aware that it was James who chose it.

But Nikos was unaware of her sarcasm. She glanced at the huge bouquet of roses and sniffed the elegant blooms. She couldn't help it and a smile touched her lips at its beauty.

A waiter approached to take the bouquet and she gave it to him.

Nikos waved his hand and another waiter approached them and handed them menus.

"Have you been here before?" Nikos asked in order to start a conversation.

"No. Not yet. But I have heard of this place," Cassia replied distractedly as she perused the menu.

"Then, let me order for you. The lady will have the Crab Salad. And I will have the *Kindai Maguro*," Nikos told the waiter.

"Excellent choice sir. And for dessert? Or shall I ask again later?"

"Later will be fine."

"Err…wait. Cancel the crab salad and I'll just have the *Kobe Beef*, please," she said with a smile.

"Excellent choice also, madam," the waiter grinned.

"Their crab salad is the best," Nikos pointed out with a frown after the waiter disappeared

He was used to ordering for his female companions and they always loved what he chose for them. Today, he chose the crab salad for Cassia because it was one of their best dishes. Also, he took in the fact that women usually were very conscious of their weight and tended to eat less.

"I can order for myself, thank you very much. Plus, I can't eat that because I'm allergic to crabs," Cassia said in a flat tone.

Once again, Nikos was struck with the realization that he knew nothing about the woman he was married to for ten years now.

"I apologize. I'll keep that in mind."

For a long while, there was silence between the two of them. They had nothing in common and they did not know each other at all. This was how their past dinners were.

The waiter came to their table and poured some white wine. Cassia took hers and sipped it slowly as she stared around the beautiful interior of the restaurant

"So how's your business?" Nikos asked.

"It's going great. I'm opening a new shop in California soon."

"You should put some in my malls too. I'll check for open slots and I could give you a call," he offered.

"That's nice of you. But I think I have more than I can handle right now."

"Alright, just tell me if you need anything."

"Alright," Cassia replied.

But what she said inside her head was *'I'll ask Nikos Demakis for help when hell freezes over.'*

Over the years, she learned to be self-sufficient.

Whatever happened, she was never going to ask Nikos or her grandfather for any help.

She'd rather *suffer* than beg.

Once more, silence reigned between them.

Cassia took a deep breath and then exhaled. She tossed back the entire content of her wine to boost her courage.

"Nikos—"

"Cassia. I have something—" they both said at the same time.

"Uhh...you go ahead," Cassia told him.

"Thank you. I was just thinking. It's our tenth year anniversary and we barely know anything about each other. To each other, we are practically strangers," Nikos began.

Cassia resisted the urge to roll her eyes.

"I know we didn't start out at the correct footing. But past is past and I think it's the perfect time to move on."

At his words, Cassia grinned.

Could it be that he was now thinking about the divorce too? Then it would be perfect! He would just need to sign the papers today and she would be filing it tomorrow. Within a short span of time they would both be free!

"I know exactly what you mean," she agreed.

"And in order for us to start our lives together...I suggest, we start getting to know each other, build a good relationship between the two of us and start living together as a wedded couple. I have decided to cut down on my traveling and spend more time in Greece. I will be giving you the choice of which house I own that we would turn into our permanent home."

Cassia's jaw almost hit the floor at his words.

This guy truly had some nerve! How dare he think that he could just say some words and they'd act like a true wedded couple?

At the same time, a sense of impending doom along with a giant burst of anger filled her.

"Say that again..." she said in a whisper thinking she just heard him incorrectly.

"Well...I'd say it's past time we set aside our differences. We are married after all and we should start acting like a married couple. Maybe even start a family someday. We're not getting any younger and I think that this is the perfect time in our lives for this. Personally, I am ready to settle down," Nikos said in a tone that stated he meant business.

Acting like a married couple? Starting a family? Settle down?

Was she going crazy or did she actually hear him right?

A bubble of hysterical laughter welled up inside her. She then leaned across the table and released everything. Her stomach cramped and she had difficult time breathing as she was consumed by her fits of laughter.

"What's so funny?" Nikos asked.

She saw that he was scowling and that his hand was holding his wine glass very tightly that his knuckles already turned white.

"*You*. You make me laugh, Nikos. You think you can just invite me to dinner after everything that's happened, after all the pain and the humiliation. And after ten years! You think you have the right to waltz into my life and announce that you are ready to settle down. And it follows that I must drop everything and run to you with tears of joy in my eyes? Is that how you envisioned this to be? It's absurd!" she ranted and then laughed once more.

"Which part of this do you not like, Cassia? This is what you wanted right from the start isn't it?" Nikos wore a frown as he asked her this.

He leaned forward and placed his arms on the table. He regarded his wife with a confused expression.

"Hell no, you arrogant bastard!" Cassia shouted loud enough that it shocked the waiters hovering around the place.

Nikos stood up and glared at her.

"Calm down," he ordered.

"No! This is preposterous!" she threw her napkin down and stood.

"What?!" Nikos hissed.

"You—You—" she stammered as she tried to find the words in the middle of her rage. "Ten years and you've not changed one bit!" She threw her hands up in exasperation. It was better than her doing what she really wanted to do at the moment: to beat the arrogance out of Nikos Demakis.

"What? Isn't this what you want? Isn't this what you asked your grandfather for ten years ago?" Nikos repeated in a condescending tone.

Cassia shook her head and laughed hysterically.

"And like what happened all those years ago, you're still wrong Nikos. I *never* wanted to marry you in the first place. It was my grandfather who arranged it. I blindly went along with his wishes because I thought you wanted me. On the day of our marriage, I found out that he forced you. What I planned was to marry you and then get our marriage dissolved the next day so that you would have your company back and my evil grandfather would have nothing, like I told you all those years ago. But I think you know what happened next."

"You lied to me and caused a scene!" Nikos exclaimed.

"No, Nikos. *You* did. You started that by going to your *own* wedding drunk. But I let all that pass because I would be having my revenge on my grandfather the very next day. I took the humiliation thinking that when morning came, I would be free of it all. And that was why I came to you and your mistress' room. That was what I wanted to talk to you about. Looking back on it now, it was a pretty stupid thing to do."

Cassia laughed once more. But this time, it was a bitter kind of laugh.

Nikos' entire body became taut with tension.

How dare she lie again? Did she think he was a fool to believe the words coming out of her mouth?

Yes. That was what all of her words were. *Lies*. Nothing but lies. After ten years, she still decided to stick with that story. Was he wrong about thinking she changed at all?

"You will cease that nonsense this instant!" Nikos commanded.

"No. *You* cease that nonsense. Ten years is quite enough, thank you very much. Now let me tell you why I actually agreed to this dinner."

She reached for her bag and pulled out the envelope. Angrily, she ripped it off and slammed the stack of papers down the table.

"I am done with this. Nikos, I want a *divorce*."

Cassia took a deep breath and then continued, "I don't care about the company. You can have it for all I care! I won't ask for any money from you and you can keep everything we own together. Just sign the damned papers and let's get this farce over with."

This time, it was Nikos jaw that almost dropped to the floor.

After he got over his initial shock, a muscle ticked in his jaw because of the anger he was feeling. Several emotions churned through him at the moment but only one word repeated inside his head like an endless loop: *divorce.*

Seeing that Nikos was momentarily incapacitated, Cassia continued:

"And I agree with what you said earlier. We are in the best time of our lives to settle down. And I, *myself,* am ready to settle down. Just not with *you.*"

Chapter 13
Divorce

NIKOS was seething.

Nobody managed to rile his temper like this in a really long time. Usually people cowered before him. He was Nikos Demakis; a billionaire and the owner of the largest shipping company in the world. He was not used to being told he couldn't have what he wanted.

He took one glance at the divorce papers in front of him and deemed it as a huge pile of rubbish. Then, he reached for his wine and poured himself another glass.

"There will be no divorce," he said with finality.

"What did you say?"

"I said there will be no divorce," he repeated.

Right on time, the waiters who tried to appear oblivious to what was happening, came and brought their food. Nikos opened his napkin and placed it in his lap. Then, he picked up his knife and fork as if nothing extraordinary was happening.

But Cassia was livid.

"Nikos. I said I want a divorce! You just cannot say no!" she shouted.

"I can and I will. When you wanted the marriage, I said no but I couldn't. Now I am saying no because as I told you, there's been no divorce in my family since the beginning. We believe that marriage is forever. So as with what I did ten years ago, you will just have to deal with it."

"Why you—you..." Cassia stuttered.

She could not believe the nerve of Nikos Demakis!

How dare he say those things to her after she just told him the entire truth! Ten years forward he still didn't believe a word she said!

What irritated her more was the fact that he just sat there eating his dinner as though this was the most normal thing in the world.

"Nikos. I don't think you understand the situation."

"I do. And my word is final. No divorce," he replied with a slash of his hand in the air.

"I will not stop just because you said so. I will file this in the courts and do everything I can. I will not stop until I am free of you!"

"Go ahead and publicize our private affairs, *agape mou*. The media will not let you go and you will not be able to work in the anonymity of the shop you built in another name," Nikos explained.

"I don't care."

"Ah. So this is more important than the business you worked hard on? Tell me, Cassia. Why the sudden change of heart? Have you met someone?" Nikos inquired.

He placed his knife and fork down and looked at her as he waited for her answer. His appetite was gone anyway. He raised an eyebrow as he waited for her reply. He dreaded the answer but at the same time, he truly wanted to know if the reason she wanted this divorce was to go marry someone else.

His chest tightened.

"None of your business! And I want this because I want change in my life. I want to start living a life of my own and this is one of the ties to the past that I still have. I want to get rid of it. Through this divorce, you will have the company secured in your name. You will even have my grandfather's company. Is that not what you wanted when you married me? You will have all that when we're divorced! Plus the fact that you'll now be free to marry someone else! So please just sign the damned papers!" Cassia shouted.

"I will not. And I already told you why. Go ahead and file those papers. Turn our lives into a media frenzy. But know that I will be contesting the divorce every inch of the way. It will take you years before you get rid of me."

"Years will be better than being shackled to you for life. I cannot believe that you have the audacity to tell me that you are now willing to give this marriage a chance. As if I didn't have a choice about it at all! What do you think I have been doing for the past ten years, Nikos? Pining for you? Waiting for you to turn around from your mistresses and your wealthy lifestyle and take notice of me?" Cassia snorted.

Nikos opened his mouth to reply but Cassia beat him to it.

"No, Nikos. I tried to better myself. Contrary to what you believed, I was not born an heiress. My grandfather disowned my father for marrying my mother who was a waitress. I grew up in a small family. But then they died and I was fostered from different homes. I lived on scraps to get by. When I was eighteen, my grandfather finally acknowledged me and I knew of the wealth we had. I thought my life was going to change forever but it just turned for the worse. And during the past ten years, I spent it all trying to reach my dream. Now, I am where I wanted myself to be. I think it's high time that I enjoy my life too."

It felt as if an ice dagger was plunged directly through his heart.

"Stop lying, Cassia. Your grandfather told me that he could not bring you up himself because he was too saddened by the passing of his son. That's why he sent you to America where you studied in the finest boarding schools. Stop your sob story for it will not make me sign those papers."

For what seemed to be the hundredth time this night, Cassia laughed.

"You'd believe my grandfather but not me? You know nothing about me, Nikos Demakis. Talking to you is like talking to a brick wall. Believe what you want about me. No matter how hard I try to explain, you just don't believe me. Then to *hell* with you. I will still file the divorce and there's nothing you can do to stop me."

Cassia stood up, picked up her purse and the papers. She completely ignored the large bouquet of flowers he gave her and also the expensive jewelry. Without another glance towards Nikos, she turned around and walked out of the restaurant.

And when she was safely ensconced inside the limousine, that was when she let all her pent-up tears fall.

With shaking fingers, she took her phone out of her purse and dialed Hector's number. She just needed him right now. She needed to hear his voice and hear his reassurance that all would be well and they would work through this.

But he wasn't picking up and she was going straight to his voicemail.

"Hector, it's me... It's been a rough night. Call me please."

November 17, 2013 (Two Days Later)
The King's Suite, Royalty (Nikos' Hotel)
New York

Nikos pored over several papers on his desk and it effectively blocked out the rest of the world again. He did not know how much time he worked but he did it so that he would forget the events that happened during the last two days.

He heard a knock on the door and he lifted his head. His assistant entered.

"Sir, Alex Smith says he is here to see you."

The corners of Nikos' mouth turned up in a smile.

Alex was his long-time friend and was the best mercenary, detective, body guard, and spy anyone could ever need. He was ex-CIA and became a rogue agent. They'd been friends since college but Nikos wasn't even sure that Smith really was his last name.

"Show him in," Nikos instructed.

He stood up from his desk and stretched his cramped limbs. He placed his hands in his pockets and waited for his friend to enter the room. This visit truly was a pleasant surprise and he just couldn't wait to catch up but at the same time, he was also a bit apprehensive about what Alex's visit meant.

The man was very tall and he had hair the color of sand. Today, Alex wore a suit but it could not disguise the power in his bulky frame. Beneath that suit were muscles born from perfecting several martial arts and countless hours spent in the gym in order to continue being fit. And he needed to be fit. Especially in his line of work.

"Alex," Nikos greeted.

"Nikos!" the other man clasped the hand he offered and they embraced like old brothers.

"You didn't have to come to my suite. I could have treated you to lunch on one of the restaurants downstairs," Nikos laughed.

"Just have them bring it up here. I think we are overdue on a long chat. We can talk about your work almost anywhere. But you know *my* work. Your guests will have a heart attack if they overhear what I've been up to," Alex replied.

"True," Nikos laughed again and then he pulled out his phone and barked several orders for James.

"So while we're waiting for our food, how have you been?"

"Great. You know how much I love my work. And as of today, there are plenty of people wanting to hire my services. But I am working on a case. That is why I am here in America."

"That's what I thought. You weren't the sort of type that took vacations."

"Yes. And I agreed to this meeting with you because I believe you know the person I am currently investigating. He is involved with smuggling drugs along with other contraband items into the country. I believe he owes the drug syndicate a huge amount of money and the way they're asking him to pay is by including their items in his shipment for his business. He also owns some high-end hotels and some dealings take place there."

"Everybody would suspect the cheap hotels for this kind of things. But never the high-end ones. Sounds like this person is in deep trouble."

"He is," Alex agreed.

"And who is this person?"

Alex reached behind him and withdrew an envelope. He then, pulled out some photos and spread it over the desk.

"His name's *Hector Petrides*. I believe he's your biggest competition in the hotel and restaurant world."

Nikos cursed under his breath. He looked at the photos that were spread on his desk. He couldn't help but feel smug as he realized his best competition in business and with his wife was basically *screwed*.

"No wonder he's made it to the top quickly! It was because he had some illegal help. And no wonder he's got so much money!"

Alex laughed. "And you play fair and square, my friend?"

"Most of the time," Nikos replied with a laugh.

"So what do you know about him?"

"Just the usual. He's one of those rags to riches type."

"I have intel that he's now in hiding from the drug syndicate. I think there was a problem with one of the shipments. It was delayed and he lost them a lot of money. Right now, anyone who knows him or who is close to him is in deep trouble." Alex explained.

Then he peered up at Nikos as though awaiting some kind of reaction from him.

Nikos noticed his intense stare and immediately his heart started to race. He had a feeling that his friend's next words won't do him any good at all.

"You have no idea, do you?" Alex scrutinized Nikos' expression. His friend truly appeared to be clueless.

"About?" Nikos asked.

"About why I really am here...I discovered something. I thought you should know."

"Go straight to the point, Alex," Nikos barked.

Alex reached towards one of the photos and withdrew one that looked as though it was taken at some kind of lounge. The man in the photo clearly was Hector Petrides and he was dining with a woman who had her back turned.

Alex gave him the next photo and this one was of Hector's dinner companion. His heart stopped completely when he realized that it was none other than his wife.

"Show me everything," Nikos commanded in a hoarse voice.

"Are you sure? You know that I am a thorough man," his friend replied hesitantly.

"Yes. I know you came here because of this. Now, show me."

Alex reached behind him and pulled out another folder. This one contained all the research he had done on both Hector and Cassia. He gave it to Nikos and noticed that his friend's hand shook with anger as he flipped through the photos.

Alex was there during their wedding years ago.

He admitted that he was a different man then. He had laughed along with the others at the thought of Nikos getting married and had laughed equally harder at the catastrophic events. It was public knowledge that Nikos and his wife did not live together and that Nikos carried on having his affairs.

But something must have changed for him to react this way...

Nikos' jaw almost dropped the moment he saw Cassia's smiling face in one of the pictures. Then, his heart started to race and fury flooded his veins. His emotions were evident in how his fingers shook as he leafed through the photos. His breathing became harsher and his entire body became rigid in posture.

Nikos flipped through several pictures. One was dated about four to five years ago when Cassia finished college. She was in a toga and smiling beside Hector who looked so proud of her. She waved around her diploma and her eyes shouted her happiness to the world.

The second photo was Cassia cutting the ribbon of her first fashion shop. Yet again, it was Hector who was beside her. Next it was Hector cutting the ribbon to his first restaurant and Cassia was standing right beside him and holding his hand. There were several photos of them throughout the years. Every new shop Cassia opened, Hector was there for her.

Nikos finally understood.

He was right. It was Hector Petridcs she was having an affair with. No wonder they kissed like lovers during the auction. This was also the reason she was asking him for a *divorce*. She said she wanted to move on with her life but the truth was she wanted to settle down with Nikos' greatest competition.

He snorted when he thought that Hector was still his competition even when it came to his own *wife*. He hated the fact that he was there through the years with her and he was not. He should have been the one with her during her life's greatest achievements and not Hector.

But you never cared, Nikos.

He brushed her off ten years ago and was even happy when she left Greece to go and live her life somewhere else. He didn't even inquire as to what happened to her. He just continued on sending her the money she wanted. He was happy that he still got to continue the playboy lifestyle he loved so much.

Without another thought about her, he had carried on with his life.

So this train of thoughts about being there during the greatest accomplishments in her life was a big fat nonsense. Maybe he was just feeling a bit possessive of her because technically she was still *his* wife. Nikos shook his head to clear his thoughts and then flipped through some more photos.

"She's in danger from this drug syndicate, Nikos. Good things she's known as Cassia Adrasteia, the famous designer. That will make it a little harder to find her. But when they learn of her, they will get her so that they could lure Hector in. I don't know anything about your marriage but I assumed you wanted to know this information."

"I do. Thank you, Alex."

"What are friends for?" Alex laughed.

"What do you plan on doing about Hector Petrides?"

"Believe it or not, I'm hired by the government for this particular mission. It's about the drugs. I have to find their location, how the shipment goes and all those details. For this, I need Hector Petrides. Once I have everything, all his deeds would be exposed and he'd be imprisoned."

"I see."

"Do you think your wife knows about all of this?"

"I don't know."

"But do you intend to tell her?"

"Of course. She's convinced herself that she wants a divorce from me. Now I know that it is so she could go with Hector. Can I keep these other pictures for evidence?" Nikos asked.

He picked up the folder that contained pictures of Hector and the drug syndicate. He also took the picture that showed Hector with his back towards probably millions of dollars worth of drugs.

"Sure. What do you intend to do now?" Alex asked.

"There'll be no divorce. I'll keep her safe."

"If you need any help with your security detail, let me know. I know the perfect men for the job," Alex offered.

"Once again, thank you for this Alex. One more thing though, I have to ask...have you heard anything about the ones who kidnapped me?"

Alex bowed his head.

"I'm sorry, my friend. Not as of yet. I have tried and tried to find information about them but they cover their tracks well. I have followed everything that Antonio's wife told me but I always hit a dead-end."

"I understand. It's all right, Alex. I know that you are doing your best."

There was a knock on the door and the waiters came in and brought their food. The conversation was much lighter this time. They talked about each other's work and compared the differences. They also reminisced about their past and how they always got into trouble as teenagers.

As their lunch progressed, Nikos started thinking of the ways that he could use this information over Cassia. Now, he could force her to go with him and insist that it was for her safety.

And if she didn't know anything about Hector Petrides' activities yet, then surely she was in for a huge shock.

Chapter 14
Rescued

THERE'S *been a change of events. The higher-ups would spare all of us if we pay the amount of what was lost."*

A chorus of murmurs went around Sebastian's men at this spark of hope. The drug cartel never gave second chances but it seemed as though fate was throwing them a bone.

"But how can we pay millions of dollars?! The latest drug shipment was a big one and it was worth too much!" one of his men cried.

"The men in charge of the shipment disappeared off the face of the earth," one of Sebastian's men reported. They'd searched for weeks but to no avail.

"We are still the head of this territory and the blame will fall on our shoulders for this slip-up," another interjected.

"Unless we find a way, we're all dead men."

Suddenly, Sebastian had an excellent idea. His men looked at him as though they thought he finally lost all his screws when he smiled and then laughed.

This was a perfect opportunity. He could get money and have his revenge at the same time. The timing couldn't be any more perfect. Besides, he'd waited too long already...

"I have a plan. Exhaust whatever resources would be needed. I expect you to succeed or we are all dead men."

"What do you want us to do, boss?"

"Get me Nikos Demakis."

November 18, 2013 (The Next Day)
Cassiopeia
Fifth Avenue, New York City

"What do you mean you won't be able to make it?" Cassia breathed into the phone.

"I'm sorry, princess. There are so many things I have to do right now. I won't be able to make it to our dinner later and I also won't be able to go back the rest of the week. I'm not sure when I'll go home but something's come up. I'll call you and keep you informed, I promise," Hector explained. His voice sounded strained and he spoke too fast.

"Hector...you promised that you would try. You said that you would try and be here more often."

"I am trying, princess. But I can't escape this. I have to tell you something and you must listen to me carefully..."

Cassia stopped trying to take inventory of the shelves in her store and focused more on her phone conversation. Hector's hurried rate of speech and his serious tone gave her the impression that this was really important.

"You know you can tell me anything, Hector."

"There are some things I have done that I know you won't be able to forgive, Cassia. But know this, no matter what happens...I love you. I truly do. You are the only thing in my life worth fighting for," he said.

"Now you're scaring me," she replied. There was a wobble in her voice and Hector sighed when he heard it.

"I've done things..."

"What things?"

"I can't tell you about them, Cassia. Knowing more would just place you in greater danger. I'm trying to protect you as best as I can. I am hiding now. I involved myself in something big and now that I don't want to continue anymore, they won't allow me to leave. They are forcing me to their will. These are the only things I can tell you."

As dread filled her, Cassia replied, "What did you do Hector? What is this error you are talking about? Is this about money? You know you only have to ask."

"No... Cass," Hector sighed with frustration. "This is bigger than you or me. Just know that I am doing everything I can to fix this. Soon, I'll go home and we can spend all the time we want together. For now, please understand," he pleaded.

"As if I have any choice."

"Cass, there's one more thing I have to tell you. You have to leave your apartment. Take a vacation for a week or two? Go to some beach and stay there."

"What? I just can't take off like that! My work depends on me and I have a lot of commitments for the next few weeks!"

"This is for your own safety. Please, Cassia, just follow me this once without question. Do this for me. Those who are after me might know of my connection to you and they may hurt you to get to me. Please just pack up and leave. Make as many phone calls as you want and take your laptop so that your work won't suffer! All I ask is that you leave the city and spend some time in a faraway place."

"Hector--"

"Cassia, please," Hector begged.

Something in his tone said he was desperate. For now, Cassia decided to believe him.

"Fine. But you will have to meet me wherever I choose to go. We'll hide together," she bargained.

There was a long pause on the other line wherein she only heard Hector's rough breathing then he said, "I'll try, Cassia. I'll try and finish everything right away so that I can be with you as soon as I can. Please understand..."

"Hector, whatever it is that you've done, you know I'll always be here, right? You can tell me and I won't judge you."

"I know. But I'm not ready to tell you now. Give me some more time," he sighed. "I don't deserve you, princess. You will forever be my greatest treasure."

Cassia's eyes misted with tears and she found it difficult to swallow through the sobs that welled in her throat.

"I love you, Hector."

"Not as much as I love you, princess."

Silence descended over them. She would hold Hector to his promise that he would fix everything and that they'd soon be together.

"Cassia, I have to go. I'll call you as soon as I can. But I'll be using another number so that they will not be able to track me," Hector told her.

"I understand. Bye, Hector. Keep yourself safe and return to me as soon as you can," she urged.

"I will. And I will be counting down the hours until we are together again."

Cassia stared at her phone for a couple more minutes as she replayed her conversation with Hector over and over again. She tried searching for clues as to what predicament he was in but everything was so vague.

She sighed and went to the computer to straighten things out. It was a good thing that it was still early and there were no customers yet. She could still do whatever work she could and at the same time make plans for her impromptu vacation.

She sat and began answering her numerous emails. Afterwards, she sketched some changes to her designs and made a note to start searching for the perfect fabric to create them with. Then, she took out her planner and pondered which meetings she would have to cancel or postpone for another time. When she was sure that her schedule was cleared, she searched for vacation packages to the places that she wanted to go to.

After careful consideration, she decided to settle on going to Hawaii.

Then she made a list of everything she would need on that vacation.

Nikos stretched his legs out in front of him.

Then he stretched his hands in the air, arched his back, popped his neck and yawned widely. He had been awake all night as he finalized some papers about the *Higeshima Deal* he was working on. Higeshima Corporation is a shipping company in Japan. Due to bad management, the once prestigious company became bankrupt. But Nikos saw its potential so he wanted to buy the company and take over. If all goes well, the *Higeshima Corporation* will now be under the *Andrade-Demakis Corporation* and this will expand the company's reach in Asia. Soon, they will also conquer the Asian market and this was Nikos' goal for the next five years.

But before that happens, there was still so much work to be done.

Nikos stretched his arms again and leaned back. Now, the sun was nearly in the middle of the sky and he's just finished.

He was at the penthouse suite of his hotel but instead of relaxing, he finished a mountain of work. He decided he'd take some brunch, drink his sleeping pills and go straight to bed while wishing for a dreamless sleep.

Suddenly, his phone rang. It was not a registered number so he hesitated in picking it up.

"Nikos Demakis, speaking," he drawled in a bored tone as he stifled yet another yawn.

"Nikos! It's me Alex. Thank God you answered!"

"Alex? Why? What's wrong?"

He heard the note of distress in his usually calm and unshakeable friend.

"Just got intel that says they already know of her. Hector called her earlier this morning and they traced the call. The person I've assigned to guard her just reported there are several suspicious men outside her shop. I'm on my way," Alex explained hurriedly.

Nikos heard the screeching of tires in the background and he knew that this was a dire situation indeed. His heart started beating faster as adrenaline flooded his system. He tucked the phone between his shoulder and ear and ran towards the table where he hastily retrieved his keys and wallet.

He ran towards the elevator as he continued speaking to Alex.

"Where is she?"

"*Cassiopeia.* Fifth Avenue," Alex replied and the line went dead.

Nikos pocketed his phone and cursed the elevator for going so slowly. His mind emptied of any other thoughts except for the desperation to get to Cassia. He didn't even have time to think why he was acting and feeling this way about his wife who was practically a stranger.

The moment the doors opened, he bolted across the lobby and towards his car. He painted the road black as he burned tires in his haste.

However, one look at the traffic and he knew he wasn't going to make it as fast as he wanted to. He banged his palms on the steering wheel and cursed the city to hell for its heavy traffic. At the same time, he sent a prayer for Cassia's safety to whoever might be listening.

Then, he pulled out his phone and decided to warn her.

Cassia's phone rang again for what must have been the twentieth time already. She glanced at the screen and saw that it was Nikos. For the last fifteen minutes, she pressed the Ignore button repeatedly. She even considered switching it off for the frantic ringing was driving her crazy.

"What?!" she hissed.

"Thank the gods you finally picked up! Listen to me. Go to the back of your store and stay there. You're not safe. Do not open the doors for anyone!" Nikos barked.

"What? That's absurd! I cannot close my shop! It just opened and there are customers already! If this is a prank or a drunken call, then let me tell you, Nikos, it isn't funny."

Cassia hung up but before she could place her phone down, it rang again.

"Leave me alone!" she shouted.

"Cassia. Please. Listen to me. You are in danger. Just go to the back of your shop and wait for me there. I'll explain everything later."

She laughed and moved away from her register. She went closer to the glass that contained the mannequins dressed with her most beautiful designs.

"Are aliens coming to get me, Nikos?" she asked sarcastically as she looked at the skies. "I'm staring outside and the heavens look clear to me. No sign of flying saucers or something," she teased.

Cassia didn't disregard Nikos' warning fully, however. She also scanned her surroundings while taking cover by the pillar near the glass. Nothing was out of the ordinary. She shook her head and berated herself for taking Nikos' word seriously at all.

"Cassia, this isn't a joke!" Nikos shouted. He considered throwing his phone because of his frustration but what good would that do?

He heard Cassia laugh and his anger and desperation just spiked up another notch.

"There are men out there who are out to get you. Get away from the glass, lock your shop and hide!!!" Nikos roared.

Cassia's laughter was cut short and Nikos heard her gasp. It was followed by the sound of glass breaking and falling. There was a muffled thud like a body hitting the wooden floor.

"Cassia!" Nikos shouted.

There was no sarcastic reply this time, only a groan of pain.

His entire body tightened with fear. He stepped harder on the accelerator. He weaved through traffic and thanked the gods that his hobby was racing. He could certainly put it to good use now.

By the time he made the turn towards Fifth Avenue, his heart was beating so fast that he half expected to have a heart attack.

He jumped out of his car and ran towards Cassia's shop. However, he was stopped short when he heard the sound of gunfire and the window of the taxi beside him shattered. He ducked then hid behind one of the nearby cars and used his arms and legs to crawl nearer.

He lifted his head for a second to survey his surroundings and saw the front of Cassia's shop. Broken glass and bullet shells were everywhere. The mannequins lay on the ground and some had several large bullet holes.

His wife was on the floor and his heart squeezed inside his chest. He saw red and all thoughts fled except the need to get to her. Without thinking, he leapt over the car and ran to her.

"Get down, you fool!" He was yanked hard mid-jump and forced down to the ground by Alex.

Nikos struggled but Alex held him down effortlessly with one hand while his other hand held his gun. His eyes darted around and when the sounds of gunfire stopped, he lifted himself from the cover of the taxi and fired several shots.

"You won't be able to save her if your brain is blasted to bits on the pavement!" Alex hissed.

"I have to help her!" Nikos shouted.

"Nikos! Stop this insanity and use your God-given brain to assess the situation!" Alex hissed and then smacked him in the head.

Those words, along with the stinging pain near his temple calmed Nikos enough for rationality to creep back into his brain.

"Where are they?" he asked.

"Some are already inside the shop but they don't dare approach Cassia because she is out in the open. If they go nearer, my team and I will be able to take them out. So they're staying near the back and shooting at everyone who tries to approach."

"Cassia is left there vulnerable. What if your team shoots her?" Nikos said through gritted teeth.

"They won't shoot her; they're damned good. The men won't shoot her either because they need her. If the going gets tough, the most they can do is take her hostage until they can negotiate with us for a way out. When they emerge, my snipers will take care of them," Alex told him and pointed to a spot above the buildings.

Nikos saw a glint of metal and he felt slightly reassured.

"Do the police already know of this?"

"Yes. They know my name too and who's backing me up on this case. They won't interfere unless I ask them to. They know my team and they know we can handle it," Alex answered.

Nikos breathed a sigh of relief. He placed his full trust and confidence in Alex and his men. They were the best in the field.

"What do we do?" Nikos asked his friend.

Alex completely understood what he was feeling.

He had been in situations like this hundreds of times before. Every time that he was on a mission, he felt the thin line between rationality and anxiety. Sometimes he crossed that line and went into full blown panic. But that was what got a soldier killed.

With time, he learned to control his emotions. Rationality played before emotions. He always used logic no matter what the situation.

"Sit here and wait," he answered.

Alex reached into his back pocket and retrieved a pistol for Nikos. He handed it over to his friend.

"For your protection. Still know how to use that thing?"

"Of course, I do," he snarled.

Once more, Nikos lifted his head and looked at Cassia. She looked so helpless on the floor that his heart squeezed with every breath. Her eyes were closed and his gaze zeroed in on the blood surrounding her.

Alex gripped him by the collar of his shirt and looked straight into his eyes.

"Calm the *fuck* down!"

***

"I can't," Nikos' voice broke as replied.

A thousand emotions assailed him at seeing her like that. He did not understand why he was feeling this way. He hated how he couldn't think. He hated how he couldn't function logically or rationally and could only panic.

Alex must've noticed his slip and looked at him from head-to-toe.

"I didn't realize you felt this strongly about your estranged wife," he teased in an attempt to lighten the situation.

"Just get her out of there," he pleaded.

Suddenly, a black massive Hummer skidded to a halt on the street before them.

Out came more men dressed in black. They were reinforcements of those attempting to kidnap his wife.

"Shit," Alex muttered at the same time that Nikos cursed under his breath in his own native tongue.

The mercenary lifted his hand and touched his earpiece. He barked several orders to his team. Nikos didn't understand a word of it for he was looking at his wife.

He saw her chest rise and fall and it calmed him a little bit. But fear still twisted his gut when he saw that her beautiful features were twisted in a mask of pain.

"Stay down," Alex commanded.

One of his men threw an Uzi submachine gun to him. Alex quickly grasped it and the roar of gunfire echoed as he squeezed the trigger, discharging a storm of bullets. Three men dropped dead while the others ran for cover.

Nikos looked to his left when he saw a flash of black and saw more enemies come from the other side. He then relied on his reflexes as he lifted the pistol from the ground and fired several shots. He missed several times as he did not have a steady hand like Alex.

While the sound nearly made him deaf and the recoil hurt his hand, all he could think about was how these men intended to hurt his *wife* and how he would never allow them to. He had to protect her. So he focused and fired again.

He was so focused on his left that he left his back unprotected. The moment he turned around, he was suddenly rooted to the spot when a gun was pointed to his face. He took a deep breath and sent his elbow into the man's ribs. It made him drop the gun and Nikos kicked it out of reach. He aimed another punch towards the man's nose and the force made him stagger backwards. Nikos then dived towards the discarded weapon and fired a hole into the man's skull.

He almost gagged at the sight but he kept himself in check by staring at the other direction and taking in several breaths of air.

Suddenly, he was flashed back to another scenario. It was two years ago and the scene was *exactly* like this. Only that it was him who was bloody and it was his bodyguards firing against the enemies to keep him and Antonio safe.

But they were outnumbered.

Immediately, he felt fear and panic sliding down his spine.

No. *Not now.*

Nikos shook his head and tightened his grip on the pistol.

He could not be weak. Not at a time like this. Cassia and Alex needed him.

He shook his head and focused harder. Alex threw him a magazine clip and said, "Cover me." Nikos nodded and reloaded his pistol. The two of them crouched low and moved slowly to the front of Cassia's shop. Suddenly, the men ran outside the shop. When he saw that they didn't have Cassia, he aimed the gun at the bastards and squeezed the trigger. He did this until he ran out of bullets and none of them was left standing.

The sound of gunfire stopped and the only sound that could be heard was the sound of the police sirens in the distance. He lifted his head and saw several bodies on the floor. There were more of them piled outside Cassia's shop.

"All cleared," one of Alex's men told him. He and Alex stood up and ran inside the shop.

He was almost afraid of touching her in fear of causing her more pain. Her eyes opened and sheer terror was written all over her face.

"Shh...it's me, Cassia. You're safe now," he crooned as he gently brushed the hair away from her face. He wanted to lift her into his arms but he was too scared to move her because of her injury.

"Nikos..." she sighed.

He ran his hands down her arm, not caring one bit that he was already covered in her blood. He checked her for injuries and saw a bullet hole near her shoulder. His grip on her tightened as his fury overtook him once more. He let her go when she winced and he cursed himself for being a fool.

Nikos withdrew his handkerchief from his pocket and used it to press Cassia's wound and stem the bleeding.

She winced again at the pain and he felt like his heart was being clawed out.

"I'm so sorry, *glikia mou*..."

Her eyes slowly drifted shut. Nikos was so shocked that his heart stopped beating for a second. But when he saw that she simply lost consciousness, it was as if air was let back into his lungs and he could breathe and function again.

"Medics are on their way. But judging the wound, I don't think the bullet hit any major arteries. She'll be fine," Alex told him.

"But why isn't she awake? Why is there so much blood?"

"It's a wound, Nikos. There's bound to be blood." Alex rolled his eyes. "As for her being deeply asleep, I think she might have also been hit with a sedative so they could snatch her away more easily. This is better; she won't feel the pain," Alex continued.

Nikos only nodded because his throat suddenly felt too tight to form any words.

The medics arrived and they carefully lifted Cassia onto a stretcher. They rolled her towards the waiting ambulance and when one of the wheels hit a rock, the stretcher was jolted so badly.

"Careful!" Nikos roared.

Everyone flinched, including Alex. The medics nodded apologetically to him and this time, they wheeled Cassia faster but more gently. Nikos climbed onto the ambulance and he glared at everyone inside as though threatening them to just try and tell him that he couldn't be there.

Alex also climbed in and the ambulance made its way to the hospital.

Nikos held Cassia's hand while the ambulance hurtled through the streets of New York. All the while, he was thinking that her safety was now his main concern. They would go somewhere safe. He'd hire hundreds of men if need be just so he could protect her.

He cursed under his breath, shocked at the intensity of his own thoughts. Alex was right. Since when did he care so much? Since when did he feel this way about the woman who destroyed his life?

Nikos comforted himself by thinking that she was still his wife. No matter what, they were bound before God and before man. Naturally, he had to care at least a bit. Naturally, he had to feel at least some emotions for her.

Also, if she died, what would happen to their contract? Would he forfeit all rights to the company he worked so hard for? Death was not part of their contract and he did not know how this would affect his life.

Yes, surely that was the reason why he felt this way.

He just had to protect her. It was one of his responsibilities as her husband. Now he'd never let her out of his sight.

She would come with him. He did not care if she did it willingly or if he would have to chain her to his side.

Chapter 15
Taken

November 18, 2013
Presbyterian University Hospital of Columbia and Cornell
New York City

"*Do* it gently!" Nikos shouted.

Everyone in the emergency room of the hospital already lost count of how many times Nikos Demakis delivered this outburst. By now, they shouldn't have flinched at his tone for they should have been used to it. But it was just so loud and came unexpectedly that all the doctors and his attendants still winced.

Cassia sighed and rubbed her temples.

"Please have him sedated. Or sedate *me* instead. Anything. *Please,*" Cassia begged.

Her head pulsed with a headache from pain and then also from Nikos' bellows. Also, his mere presence brought her pain. But she did not discount the fact that she would not have been here if only she heeded his and Hector's warning earlier.

What the hell was going on?

First Hector told her to take a vacation and then Nikos told her that she was in danger. Cassia shook her head and rolled her eyes. She was too tired and distraught with pain to think clearly right now. She would just have to think about it some other time.

The young doctor smiled at Cassia and Nikos felt his temper flare up more.

He was about to shout but the doctor stepped back from his wife and said, "You're all done."

"That's it? She won't have to be confined?"

"No, Mr. Demakis. It's just a flesh wound. The bullet went through her shoulder and did not hit any major blood vessels or any bones. She just needed to get a few stitches and to rest that arm. I'll be giving her some medications for the pain. But aside from that, she can go home," the doctor announced.

"Can she travel?"

"Provided that it is not a rough journey and that she takes her medications on time and gets plenty of rest, I see no reason as to why she cannot travel."

"Thank you, doctor."

"Wait, Nikos. Travel?"

"*Ne*," he confirmed. "We will be going to my island in Greece where you will be safe."

Her eyes widened with rage. "Are you serious? Hell no!"

"We will talk about it later."

The doctor hurriedly moved away from Nikos and back to his own desk.

"Scared the crap out of that young doctor with all your glaring and shouting," Alex announced from behind him.

Nikos only glared at him.

"By the way, the additional security I hired for you just arrived."

"Thank you, Alex. Again, I find myself indebted to you."

"It's nothing. Though I really want a Lamborghini for Christmas," Alex teased with a wide grin. "I trust you have everything handled here? I have to go and search for those men and for any evidence they might have left behind."

"Yes. I have kept you from your assignment long enough. Thank you for all your help today. Call me when you need anything."

"And you call me when you find out anything from her," Alex whispered and with a soft smile he walked out of the emergency room.

"Alex!" Cassia called out. He stopped on his tracks and turned around to look at her.

"Thank you for what you did today. Thank you for saving me."

He threw her a mock salute and then turned around once and walked out of the hospital.

After a few more seconds, Nikos went to Cassia who was still sitting in bed. He nodded to the bodyguards outside the room and they moved in closer.

"I'd just settle the bills and we'd get going," Nikos told his wife.

"I'm sorry, I don't have my purse. I'd just pay you back when I get home."

His entire body stiffened at her words.

She was *his* wife! Of course he'd pay for her hospital bills! He was damned rich he wouldn't go poor from paying damned hospital bills. There was no way he'd let her pay him back.

"No. I'll pay for it," he said through clenched teeth.

"Fine, Nikos. Whatever you want," Cassia lazily drawled with a roll of her eyes.

Quite frankly, she'd had enough of this day.

First there was Hector's very short and uninformative call. He just told her that he was hiding from something and that she must hide too. But she decided to follow him so she made reservations for her vacation.

Aside from that, she also got shot and was caught in the middle of a gunfight. Then she was brought to the hospital and had to endure Nikos.

At this point, she'd do and say whatever he wanted just so she could go home and rest in her apartment.

Nikos came back a few minutes later, his mouth set in a grim line.

"Can you walk?" he asked her.

"I got shot in the arm, Nikos, not in the legs. I can manage," she replied. "But thank you for everything you have done for me today. And your friend, too."

A muscle throbbed in Nikos' jaw and his hands clenched tightly into fists. By the gods, this woman drove him to insanity!

He counted to ten and forced his breathing to become even so that he could calm down. Cassia had just been through a rough ordeal and she should not be stressed further.

"Let's go then," he said as he offered her his hand.

He sighed with relief when she took it. Her touch was like a brand. It sent heat down his arm and electricity down his spine. Unbidden memories of their wedding night rose to his mind. He felt himself responding to her closeness and he cursed himself a fool for the hundredth time.

He must not think about these things right now.

The bodyguards Alex hired for him quickly flanked both of them. When they left the hospital they were immediately on alert. Even when they were inside Nikos' SUV, they didn't relax their guard.

The moment Cassia's back touched the plush leather interior it looked as though tiredness overwhelmed her entire body. She squirmed until she found a comfortable position and closed her eyes.

Nikos looked at her and he stifled the urge to gather her in his arms and hold her close. Then he reeled with shock at his own thoughts.

Now where did that come from?

He stopped himself from reaching across the space between them and placing her head on his shoulder or brushing that stray lock of hair away from her cheek.

He knew she wasn't ready for that yet.

Neither was he.

They'd just end up having another fight and he'd rather they both reserved their energy for later. He knew she would not like it when he told her that he really intended to bring her to his private island in Greece. There was also the inevitable talk about what happened earlier and what Hector Petrides had to do with all of this.

After a few more seconds, Cassia's breathing evened. Nikos told his driver to drive slowly. He reached under him and pulled out a small pillow and a thick blanket. He placed the pillow under her head and wrapped the blanket around her.

Then, he contented himself by sitting back and looking at her while she rested.

A few minutes later he looked down and noticed the dried blood in his shirt.

He crinkled his nose in disgust and decided that a bath would be the very first thing on his list to do once they arrive at the on his plane. For now, he just grabbed a hand towel from the back of his car and placed emptied the remaining contents of his bottled drinking water on it. He rubbed it on his skin until all traces of the blood vanished. He then grabbed a new shirt and changed.

After an hour of being driven through New York City traffic, Cassia opened her eyes and looked wearily at her surroundings. She seemed to be confused but when she looked at the man beside her, the haze in her eyes quickly cleared.

"Nikos? My apartment is at 157 West 57th Street. Where are we going?"

"Somewhere safe," he replied tersely.

"Where exactly is that?"

"I told you. My home. My island in Greece."

"I thought that was some sick joke! You can't seriously consider bringing me to Greece!"

This time her voice was more of a growl. Nikos could definitely hear the threat behind the question.

"We will go to Greece," he said firmly.

"No way!"

Her voice was loud enough that the driver flinched and swerved to the right. Nikos quickly grabbed Cassia so that her injured shoulder wouldn't hit the door of the car. He cursed in his native tongue as he held her tightly but she pushed him away and he was forced to let go.

Nikos decided to vent his anger on the driver instead. He barked loud and low and told him to be more careful next time.

"There's no way in hell that I am going to Greece with you, Nikos Demakis. No *fucking* way."

She said his name with such disdain that he winced.

"Yes, you are. I will keep you safe there, Cassia *Demakis*." He emphasized her last name and this time it was she who flinched.

He had hoped that she would sleep throughout the ride to the airport but it seemed as if the fight would have to happen early.

Nikos rubbed his temples and faced his spitfire of a wife.

"Cassia, we will go to Greece so that you will be better protected. I live in a private island so it's much better. It's safe and it's built like a fortress."

"I don't care! I can protect myself, Nikos! I also have money! I can hire a team of bodyguards!"

"Their loyalty can be bought. When it comes to security, I trust only my own people and Alex's. My home is in a small island that can only be reached by boat or by plane. It's a convenient location."

"Again, there's no way I am going to Grecce with you, Nikos. You hear me? No way!"

"Remember our anniversary dinner at the restaurant? Well, just think of this as the start of us spending time together," he suggested.

The man truly had some nerve.

"I already told you no! Have you forgotten that I'll be divorcing you?! Have you heard nothing of what I've told you?" Cassia seethed.

"Hearing and understanding are two different things. Yes, I heard you but I chose ignore what you said. I told you that divorce is out of the question. There will be no divorce, ever. Now, the only option left is whether you want to make the rest of our lives hell or if you will try and work with me to attain some sort of peace between us."

Cassia glared at him and then threw her head back and gave a sarcastic laugh."That's never going to happen. In your eyes, I am a lying, money-grabbing, spoiled bitch."

"I will reconsider all your past lies and behavior if you, too, would decide to bury the past so we could both move forward," Nikos declared calmly.

"No."

"Very well then, choose the hard way. We are still going to Greece. End of story."

"I can't just go to Greece! My life and my work are here! I have several social commitments!"

"We can always fly back for those if needed. My private jet is at your disposal. By the way, from your shop, I saw that you were already planning for a vacation. My assistant saw the list and the things you've packed. I asked him to bring all of it and to go back to your apartment and get the others so that you'd have everything you need when we land on Greece. I have several free rooms in my house and you can convert one of them into your office or studio."

"Everyone will look for me!" Cassia shouted.

Nikos just raised an eyebrow.

"Then I'll tell them you're with me; that we are in our home in Greece. It's natural for a husband and wife to get together."

"But...but—" Cassia spluttered.

"Ran out of excuses, *agape mou*?"

Her jaw fell open at the arrogance displayed by the man in front of her. She wanted to say a clever retort but the shock and fury going through her body seemed to also numb her brain. Instead, she looked out of the window and took several deep breaths to calm herself while thinking of another excuse.

"I can't go to Greece because I have a vacation planned with someone."

Nikos lifted a brow in query and then leaned forward and placed his chin in his hand.

"By all means, tell me. Is it with Hector Petrides?"

"None of your business."

"It is my business because you are my wife and you are under my protection. You carry my name and everything you do has an effect on me and the company."

"I didn't give a *shit* what you did all those years, Nikos. I didn't bat an eye when you dated all the supermodels in the world. I did not lecture you with *'because you are my husband, every bimbo you dated reflects on me and the company.'* So don't give me that reason. It's bullshit."

"I didn't know you kept tabs on me all those years, *agape mou*. Contrary to popular belief, I did not date all the supermodels in the world. That would have been impossible." Nikos grinned.

Cassia snorted, "Don't think too highly of yourself."

Nikos chuckled. She infuriated him unlike any other person and it was a refreshing change.

"We are still going to Greece. My word is final. There are things going on here that you don't know anything about. Things connected to your attempted kidnapping and to your Hector Petrides," the last few words came out as a low growl.

Cassia snapped at attention when she heard Hector's name.

"What is it about Hector? What happened?" she asked in a shrill voice.

Nikos' lips pursed into a tight line.

"This conversation will be reserved for later until you are well enough for it," he answered.

"Don't treat me as an invalid! I can handle anything!"

"I doubt it. Trust me on this one, Cassia. We'll talk about this. There's a proper time and place for everything. For now, rest and don't do anything ridiculous. I'll have you guarded all the time so there's no use escaping," Nikos told her as he crossed his arms over his chest.

Cassia grabbed his arm and squeezed.

"Please, Nikos. I have a right to know. I can handle it," she swore.

He sighed and ran his fingers through his hair.

For a few minutes, he gazed out the window contemplating as to whether he should tell her or not. She had a right to know but he felt like he didn't have the proper words to tell her. Then maybe evidence could speak for him at this point.

"Hand me my briefcase in the back, will you?" he asked the bodyguards who sat behind them. They handed it to him and he retrieved an envelope from it and handed it to her.

Fear raced down her spine when she saw several pictures of Hector.

"What is this?"

"Alex believes that Hector Petrides has been involved in several illegal activities. Years ago, his business was failing and in order to save it, he struck a deal with the devil. The devil was in the form of one of the drug lords from the one and only Greek drug cartel."

Cassia's hand shook as she flipped through the photographs.

"He's been the instrument of this drug cartel to ship their drugs to the United States in return for their protection for him and for more and more money for his business."

"No..."

"Alex is working on this case. He's been tracking that drug cartel as one of his assignments. He stumbled across Hector's involvement and further unearthed his involvement with you. Alex came and told me you were at risk."

"No! This isn't true! Hector is not involved with drugs!" she cried.

She tried to deny it repeatedly but deep down she knew there was some truth in what Nikos was saying.

About five or six years ago, Hector's business *had* been failing. He talked to her about closing everything and he was so beat up about it. She even offered him a loan but he didn't want to accept. One day, he told her he had the money to reopen his business and it flourished ever since.

But...

Also starting that day, Hector had less time for her. He was always away on what he said were business trips. When he returned, he was more stressed than before. When they went out on dates, he often received a call and then he would just simply disappear.

What baffled Cassia was that Hector was now at the top of his game. He should be able to always take a break and enjoy the money he got from his hard work! He had a highly competent staff to which he could delegate the running of his business for a few days so that he could go on a vacation.

But he always said no.

He always told her that there were things he should handle by himself and could never delegate. She did not understand it back then but she just assumed he was one of those people who were perfectionists and wanted to do everything themselves.

I could never be more wrong.

Tears filled Cassia's eyes as her shaking fingers took hold of one of the photographs where drugs placed in boxes were being hauled at the docks then placed inside vans painted with the logo of his hotel. There was also a clear photo of him supervising everything.

It was truly damning evidence.

"This isn't possible..." she whispered.

Her vision was already clouded by tears but she hastily wiped them away so she could gaze more at the photographs and the written report in front of her.

"Cassia..." Nikos' voice shook. He frowned when he saw the tears in her eyes and reached out towards her but she slapped his hand away.

"What is this?" Cassia gasped.

She lifted a photograph and then showed it to him. It showed the body of a boy, someone who could not be more than twenty, and there was a bullet hole in his forehead.

Nikos pursed his lips and grabbed the photograph from her.

"We believe it's one of the waiters from Hector's staff who found out what the shipment contained. He was killed because of the knowledge he bore."

Cassia's stomach rolled and nausea overwhelmed her. She covered her mouth and tried to breathe deeply to avoid being sick. At the same time, a heavy feeling of dread settled over her shoulders and her tears turned into huge sobs.

She picked up one photograph of Hector where his face was clear. She gripped it tightly and raised her other hand to trace along the edges of his handsome features.

Uncaring about who was listening, she cried her heart out.

"Cassia...shh..." Nikos gathered her in his arms.

He kissed her temple as he tried to comfort her.

"Now, I hope you understand why I have to protect you. Hector fucked up somehow and now the entire cartel is after him. They would use you to get to him."

Cassia sobbed harder when she realized the truth in his words. This was why Hector sounded so frantic when he last spoke to her. This was why he wanted her to take a vacation and told her she wasn't safe.

"I won't grant you the divorce either. I can't have you go to someone like him. The life you believe you'll be having with him is all an illusion. He can't give you something normal. The drug cartel would always come first. There's no escaping them."

Cassia gasped in outrage and pushed Nikos back.

"How dare you speak like that?! You know nothing, Nikos! Hector is a good man! I know that his desperation for his business caused him to do this! But his intentions were pure! He did this because his business was all he had! Desperation drives even the best men to sin and to do what they don't want to! *You* should know, right?"

Nikos sucked in a breath after hearing her question.

"You were forced to marry someone you believe is equivalent to a spoiled heiress and a monster when *Demakis International* was about to be snatched away from your family!"

Nikos opened his mouth to argue but Cassia kept on speaking.

"What makes you any different? Please stop making accusations and stop pointing fingers! You are just like him!" Cassia snapped.

Her words chilled him to his very core. He could not accept that she was comparing him to Hector.

But he also couldn't help the tightening in his chest as he realized what she told him was true.

Later that Day
La Guardia Airport
New York City

"Before we board the plane, I need to go to the bathroom."

"There's one on the plane. You can just go there," Nikos replied dryly as he looked up from the newspaper he was reading. They were seated in the VIP lounge of the airport while they waited for his private jet to be ready.

"No. I have to go now."

In truth, she needed to escape his presence so that she could call Hector and ask him about what she just learned.

Nikos sighed, "Very well then."

He nodded to two of Cassia's guards and asked them to escort her to the nearest comfort room. The guards thoroughly checked the stalls before they let Cassia inside. After she was done with her business, she began looking for pay phones.

But there were none.

She poked her head outside of the door and called one of her guards.

"Can I borrow your phone?" she whispered.

"Ma'am, I do not think that is wise," the guard told her firmly.

"I have just been attacked and my store has been ruined. I need to call my assistant to have leave instructions about the shop and about what happened earlier. In a few minutes, I'll be flying to Greece and I'll be leaving the poor guy alone to handle everything that happened."

"I advise that you discuss this with your husband."

"Haven't you noticed that he's a busy man? Besides, I have a few instructions for my assistant regarding private matters that he need not bother himself about. I promise I will just be quick."

Reluctantly, the guard handed her his phone.

"Please be quick, ma'am. I think the jet is almost ready."

Cassia nodded to her guard and then closed the door and went to the farthest part of the bathroom where she was sure they wouldn't overhear any conversation.

She quickly dialed Hector's number. He told her last time that he'd change his number but she prayed that it was still the one he used.

His phone rang but he didn't pick up. She decided that she would just leave him a message and waited for his voicemail.

"Hector... It's me Cassia. Something happened and I—"

"Cassia?! I told you not to call. It isn't safe!" he cried frantically.

"Hector...listen. Something happened. My store was attacked. There were men who came there with the intent of kidnapping me—"

"What?! Are you okay? What happened? Where are you?"

"Calm down, Hector. I'm fine. Just a little bit shaken. I was shot in the arm but it's only a flesh wound and I already had it tended by doctors. I was just in my shop while packing my things to go on that vacation as you ordered. Before I knew it, the glass shattered and there were men barging inside my store."

Hector cursed under his breath.

"Cassia...I don't know what to say. This is all my fault."

"Hector...I know this is not the time to talk about this...but Nikos told me several things. And I just have to know."

"What did he say?" Hector's tone was icy.

She never heard him use that before.

"He said that you are part of the Greek drug cartel."

There was silence from his end for a long time. Finally, he sighed.

"It's true Cassia. But I don't want to be with them anymore. I wanted to end it all so I could be free. I did it for you! For us! I talked to them about it and they agreed on one condition. There was a last shipment. It was bigger than anything else. I think it was worth close to a billion dollars," he confessed.

"What happened?" she asked hesitantly.

Each word from him broke hear heart. But she needed to know the entire truth.

"I failed that shipment. Something happened. I don't know what. Maybe someone heard about it and stole everything. Maybe someone fucked up from my team. It's lost and no matter what I do, I can't retrieve it...I failed them Cassia..." his voice broke on a sob.

"Hector... it's going to be all right. I promise you."

"It's not! That mistake is going to cost me my life! This is why I am hiding! This is why I want *you* to hide! We'll never be safe. What happened to you is my fault."

"Stop it, Hector. It's not," she reprimanded.

In fact, it was her fault. If she did not press him so much about wanting more of his time, then he wouldn't have begged to be released from the drug cartel.

Hector took a few seconds to calm himself down.

"Where are you now?"

"That's what I was calling you about. Nikos swept in on the scene and decided he'd whisk me away to Greece for my safety. I told him no but the man is immovable on this."

"What'?!" Hector's tone suddenly changed, "Where in Greece would he be taking you to?" This time his voice sounded menacing.

"He just mentioned something about a private island. That's all I know."

"Cassia. I'm afraid about this. I don't want you with him. I know we can't be together because of all the danger...call me selfish, but I still want you with me. I can't let you be with him. "

"Don't worry, Hector. It will be all right. You have nothing to worry about with me and Nikos."

"Promise me you won't return to him. Promise me this," Hector begged.

"I promise."

"You know I love you, right?"

"I know."

Thirty Minutes Later
Nikos' private jet.
La Guardia Airport, New York City

Nikos held her hand as they climbed up the steep ladder. They entered his private jet and Cassia's jaw dropped. Drool would've fallen from her mouth had she not closed it quickly.

Everything here was truly *lavish* and *extravagant!*

It was like those that she saw in movies, only this one was bigger and better. There were only a few seats and they looked like a more expensive version of a *La-Z-Boy*. On the far side of the wall, there stood a large, flat screen TV. It was a large plane but the interior looked like the living room of a grand mansion.

Cassia went straight to the chairs but Nikos tugged her hand.

"Let me tour you to the bedroom first. We'll stay there after we take off so you can rest."

Before she could react to his words, he opened a door and gently guided her inside. Her eyes widened when she saw the large bed there. On the left side was another door.

"If you need to use the bathroom, go first. I want a shower before we take off," Nikos told her.

She nodded and entered the bathroom. At first, Cassia fumbled around because it was really hard to pull down her pants because one of her hands was placed in a sling. But after much wiggling and awkward tugging, she was able to relieve herself.

Once she exited, she saw that Nikos had a fresh change of clothes in his hands. He instructed her to go outside and strap herself in one of the seats for they would be taking off soon. She did as he asked and found herself dozing off as she waited for them to leave. A few minutes later, Nikos also strapped himself in beside her after having a few words with the pilot.

Strapped in her seat, Cassia drifted off to sleep as the plane left New York City.

When she woke up, she was on the massive bed in the room and Nikos was also sleeping *beside* her.

She jolted and then quickly sat up. Pain flared in her shoulder. She gasped and flopped back down on the bed in pain.

Nikos felt the bed dip and heard her groan of pain. He stretched his arms and pulled her closer.

She struggled and he opened his bloodshot eyes which stared at her in confusion. When the fog in his brain lifted, he quickly rolled off the bed and shook his head. *Damn it,* did he just snuggle with his wife?

To cover up his actions, he reached for her medicine on top of the drawer. He also opened the small refrigerator and handed Cassia a bottle of water.

"Here. It's time you take your pain pills," he said as he handed her the bottle and her medications.

Cassia took it and greedily drank down water.

"How am I here? And why are you here?" she hissed.

"I carried you here because you were out like a light the minute your back hit the cushion. I am here because I need to rest too. This is the only room here on this plane and it's been one hell of a day. I am tired."

Wow. She didn't even wake up when he carried her?

"It's a pretty large *plane*," Cassia commented.

She hoped Nikos took the hint and left her alone.

"It's a pretty large *bed*. Besides, I cannot fit on one of the couches. Don't worry; injured women are not my type," Nikos grinned and then rolled over on the other side of the bed.

She glared at his back and stopped herself from throwing one of the pillows at him.

After a few minutes, Nikos' breathing evened and Cassia knew he was asleep. She relaxed and within a few minutes, also fell deeply asleep.

Nikos opened his eyes when he heard the intercom beside the bed ringing.

He took a deep breath and the tantalizing smell of vanilla made desire bubble in the pit of his stomach. His mind traveled back to the past when he last smelled that on Cassia's skin during their wedding night. He was hit with an intense need for her as vivid images of that night flashed through his brain.

He lifted his head and sought out that delightful aroma.

Cassia's hair was fanned out in the pillow and most of it was near his nose. Apart from that, as he came to alertness, he realized that his hand was resting on something soft—*Cassia's hip*. His entire body was spooned around her and her legs were tangled in his. Nikos was hit with a larger bolt of lust and he felt himself hardening against her.

The moment was shattered by the shrill and incessant ringing of the intercom. He sat up with a curse and grabbed the receiver.

"Yes?" he answered.

"We will be landing in fifteen minutes, Mr. Demakis," the pilot informed him.

He rubbed the sleep from his eyes and glanced at his watch. Then, he stilled with shock.

Damn, it's been ten hours already?

He *never* slept that long. Usually it was only three or four hours, maximum. But now, he'd slept for more than double his usual time and there wasn't even a hint of the nightmares that usually plagued him. He couldn't remember the last time he slept like this.

Was it because of the events that happened this day?

His gut clenched and another voice spoke inside his head.

Maybe it's because of her...

"Alright, we'll strap ourselves in," he replied and then set the receiver down.

He took a few more minutes to get his bearings and willed himself to be calm. He felt really rested and for the first time in a long time, he felt a great sense of well-being.

He sighed and reached across the bed.

"Cassia...wake-up, *agape mou*. We're in Greece."

It took a few more gentle shakes before Cassia roused.

"What time is it?" she asked.

"I think the sun's just about to rise."

"Where's your home? Is it the one in Athens with your grandfather?" Cassia asked as they strapped themselves in. It seems as though sleep also took out her crankiness.

"No. I do not live with my grandfather anymore. I have my own home."

Nikos clasped her seatbelt for her for she could not use her right hand.

"Where? Santorini? How are we going to go there?" she asked

"No. A private island. Skorpios. We'll land at Athens first. Take a car towards the docks. And we'll go there by riding my yacht."

Cassia's jaw fell again at that revelation.

"Skorpios? Seriously? Wow. I applaud you at the way you showed off *all* your shiny toys today, Nikos. I loved the way you topped it off with an island worth millions of dollars," she half-mocked and half-groaned.

Skorpios was one of the most exclusive islands in Greece. It used to belong to an old Greek Tycoon before Nikos managed to get his hands on it. People said it was so beautiful that it was likened to *Paradise on Earth*. The fact that it was a private island meant that there were no overexcited tourists, no busy establishments, nothing to interrupt a perfect vacation.

"Yes. *Our* home's beautiful. By the way, it's not millions of *dollars*. It's millions of *euros*," Nikos bragged.

Cassia snorted.

She knew she would *love* the island.

She knew it was very beautiful.

But what she hated about it was that Nikos called it *their* home.

She had no intention of sharing any home with him even if he was the King of England and they were to live in the Buckingham Palace itself.

Chapter 16
Captured

WHAT did you do?!" Sebastian roared.

"We couldn't get hold of Nikos Demakis. He was simply too slippery. But we knew we needed a source of money so we tried to capture his wife instead."

A muscle in Sebastian's jaw ticked with anger at his men's incompetence. Also, another emotion assailed him but he tried to push it away.

"What happened?" he asked in a deadly whisper.

"We failed because the mercenary, that bastard Smith showed up. It seems as if he was watching her and he knows of us already."

This time, his hands itched to draw his weapon. Alex Smith had been too much of a nuisance to him already.

"Many of our men died and they escaped. Now we've lost them."

The man flinched after he delivered his report. He waited for his boss' burst of anger but he seemed deep in thought.

Sebastian's phone rang and he moved away from his men when he saw who was calling. It took him several minutes before he returned to them with a smile on his face.

"They're in Greece. If my guess is correct, they'd be heading to Demakis' private island. Get them there."

"Right away, boss!"

"And Kristoff? Do not fail me this time."

November 19, 2013
The Amphitrite (Nikos' Yacht)
Somewhere in the Greek Coast

"It's going to be a thirty minute ride to the island. Make yourself comfortable," Nikos told Cassia and gestured towards the deck where there were several plush chairs. "The sun will rise in a couple of minutes. It's a beautiful sight to watch up deck," he added.

Cassia quickly climbed and settled herself on one of the sofas. She chose one near the railing of the boat and closed her eyes as she savored the cool air against her cheeks. She looked excitedly to the horizon. It had been a long time since she enjoyed life's simple pleasures like looking at the beauty of the sun as it rose.

While waiting, she found herself dozing off but she instantly awoke when she was picked up from the sofa and cradled into a hard male body.

"Wha--?"

"Shh. There are people following us. We have to go below deck where it's safer," Nikos whispered.

Cassia craned her neck to catch a view of what was happening before they went to hide. She noticed three smaller vessels behind theirs. She also saw their bodyguards with their weapons drawn. Two of them were behind Nikos, quickly ushering him below deck.

Fear took hold of her once more and she tightened her grip on Nikos. The moment he closed the door to their bunker below deck, the unmistakable sound of gunshots were heard.

"What's happening?" she hissed.

"Get down!" Nikos shoved her on the floor.

He covered her body with his and Cassia lifted her hand to cover her ears. The sound of heavy gunfire was followed by the shouts of her guards and their assailants. Cassia's fear increased with every minute that passed. Nikos continued to hold her against his body to protect her but when she looked up she saw that he was pale and that his body was clenched tightly.

The two guards who were with them in the room crawled towards the door. When the sounds of mayhem stopped, they quickly dragged one of the tables towards the door as a buffer. Then, they reached for the radio behind them and tried to communicate with the others.

No one answered.

Their guards tried to radio the tower near the docks. Cassia sighed with relief when she heard another voice. Her guards quickly relayed their situation and asked for backup. Nikos also added that they should call Alex Smith for he was his head of security and gave them the number. Now, all they could do was wait.

"Nikos—"

"Shh. It isn't over," he whispered in her ear.

Cassia shivered at the thought. She saw the fear in Nikos' eyes and it made her panic. He was a calm and composed man and if there was something that caused him to be like this, then their situation was really grave.

Suddenly, the door was kicked open.

Cassia screamed but her loud cry was drowned out by the sound of more shots fired. There were muffled thuds as bodies fell onto the wooden floor. Then there came the metallic stench of blood. Quick as a flash, she was jerked upright and shoved behind Nikos.

"Greetings, Mr. and Mrs. Demakis," one of the masked men approached them.

"Stay back!" Nikos shouted.

"Don't worry. We're not here to hurt you. We only need you to come with us willingly."

"What do you want? The boat? Take it! It's yours!"

"I already told you what we want. We want you to come with us willingly and no one gets hurt."

The man approached them and Nikos aimed a kick at his groin. He landed a solid hit to the man's privates and he doubled over in pain and growled something in Greek that Cassia didn't understand.

All the remaining armed men quickly rushed towards Nikos and separated both of them.

"Cassia!" he shouted as he kicked and punched his way towards her.

But he was trapped and he was only one man against many.

"Nikos...please...stop it. You'll just hurt yourself further," Cassia pleaded.

Two men also grabbed her and tied her hands behind her back. This caused her arm to throb painfully and she felt as if her wound was reopened. She was not able to stop the gasp of pain that escaped her lips.

"No! Don't touch her!" he shouted.

There was a crazed look in his eyes and it made Cassia very afraid of him. She remembered the rumor about his kidnapping. Now, she was thinking it wasn't a rumor at all. Nikos wouldn't be this afraid if he had not experienced it firsthand.

"Stop struggling, Mr. Demakis, or we'll carve her skin," one of the men shouted.

He appeared to be their leader. He grabbed Cassia, retrieved a serrated knife from his pocket and held it against her neck.

Tears spilled from her eyes and Nikos' throat clenched with fear. When he was kidnapped, he was also held like that. He could still recall the fear he felt then and how he felt when he thought he was truly going to die. Now, his wife was facing that.

"Let her go!" he snarled.

"Behave and we will," the leader replied.

Even though it was hard, Nikos let the fight leave him and he just slumped forward in his captors' grasps.

"Good."

He was hauled to his feet and then dragged from the lower bunk. Cassia was also dragged behind him and he winced with her every gasp of pain. They were led up the deck and transferred from his yacht to one of the boats.

They were forced to sit on the edge and their hands were tied to the railings on each side of the boat.

When the men left them, Nikos moved closer to Cassia.

"Are you all right?"

She nodded.

"I swear I am going to get us out of here. I won't let them do to you what they did to me before," he vowed.

Her eyes widened. "I had no idea that the rumors were true Nikos. The company's PR department covered it all up. They didn't even tell me what happened. I'm so sorry."

Nikos' gut clenched. Antonio was right. It was not that she didn't care what happened to him; she simply did not know.

"Don't be. It's all in the past now. But I won't let it happen again. We will escape as soon as we can," Nikos replied.

The men approached them again and placed blindfolds over their eyes. They've been travelling maybe over an hour or close to an hour. Maybe they were already near and the men didn't want them to see the location. Their bound wrists were removed from the railings and then they were tied together. Nikos' right hand was handcuffed to Cassia's left.

They were led from the boat toward some sort of vehicle. More minutes passed before the vehicle went to a stop and they were dragged by their kidnappers once more.

Their blindfolds were finally removed and both Cassia and Nikos blinked at the brightness of the lights.

"Welcome to your new place. It isn't as good as the luxury you're used to. But then again, you don't have any choice," the man laughed and his men followed.

It was a small, windowless cell. There was a pallet and some blankets in one corner and then a toilet and sink in the other one. Aside from those items, there was nothing else. The walls were also bare and it was made of cement and not bricks.

"What do you want with us?" Nikos growled.

"Man, I just work here. Save your questions for the boss. But what I can tell you Demakis is that you seem to have pissed off the wrong people."

What?

Where did that come from? Nikos racked his brain for a list of his enemies.

He knew he had many because of the competition in the business world. But he didn't know of one who would go to great lengths such as kidnapping him.

He simply had no clue.

"Money? How much do you want from us?" Cassia asked.

"Ma'am, again, I just work here. Better ask the boss. I think he'll be arriving pretty soon," the leader sneered.

Who could these people be? Was this truly just all about the money?

If it was, it would be easy. Once he gave them whatever they wanted, they'd be set free. But if the leader was right and there was something about revenge in this, then they were doomed. They wouldn't be leaving this island at all until the person's idea of vengeance had been satisfied.

"You two best behave until the boss arrives. If I catch anything funny, you're in for some serious trouble," the man told them before he turned around and left.

The door shut after him and they were plunged into total darkness.

Cassia panicked instantly and Nikos felt her jolt. He quickly wrapped his arms around her.

"It's okay. I'm still here," he whispered softly.

She relaxed a bit and he felt her lean against him.

"What are we going to do now?"

"We are going to find a way out of here. I do not know if this was the same island that Antonio and I escaped from but I have a feeling it is."

"Can't we just give them whatever it is they need?" Cassia asked hesitantly.

"If there was one thing I learned before, it was that these people never really negotiate. If they're in it for the money, it would be easier. But you heard what the man said. If I pissed off someone then this may be something about revenge. Maybe one of us pissed someone off enough that they had us kidnapped."

Cassia was silent for a long time as she tried to recall if she made any enemies.

"I don't think someone hates me enough to do this. Well, maybe my grandfather then," she scoffed.

"Why would Costas want to do that?"

"I don't know. He hates me. If ever I pissed someone off, I think it's him."

Nikos gritted his teeth as he let her lie roll through him. How dare she lie to him about her grandfather again? It was a well-known fact that Costas doted on her. She was his only granddaughter and heir! He gave her everything! He even caught him for her when she set her eyes on him. How dare she say this now?

"Cassia, stand up," Nikos ordered. "I need to check our cell for anything we can use and if we could really escape."

They were still handcuffed together and in order for Nikos to walk around their tiny cell, he would have to drag her with him. Cassia stood up but she winced in pain from her wounded shoulder. Nikos approached the bars and tested their strength as he pulled. They didn't budge.

He sighed and slammed his palm forward.

"Now what?"

"We watch the guards. We find one that would be easy to bribe."

"Bribe?"

"*Ne.* In these men's world, money is everything. If we find one that would clamp its jaws on the bait then maybe we could escape."

"I hope we find one," she sighed heavily.

"I will keep watch. You take some sleep first."

She nodded and they both settled back to one corner of their cell. Nikos grabbed the blanket from their pallet and wrapped it around his wife as best he could. When her breathing evened and she was deeply asleep, he bent his head just so he could inhale her sweet vanilla fragrance – a small reprieve from all the chaos.

***

"Call whoever has access to your money and tell them to wire one hundred million dollars to your account now!" the harsh words were followed by a punch that made Nikos' lips bleed.

He was sitting on a simple wooden chair with his hands tied behind his back. He was so weak from the beating he received that he was barely awake. His kidnappers then doused him with cold water which instantly made him alert.

"No," he growled.

The leader of his kidnappers raised his hand and his goons began to punch Nikos in the chest and in the stomach. He tried to curl into a ball to avoid the pain but his bindings restricted him. One punch to his chest knocked all the breath out of his lungs. He also felt that the stitches in his wound were torn and that it was bleeding freely again. He spat out blood but still he refused to do what they wished.

"Last chance, Demakis. Do it!"

"No!"

"Have it your way then."

The leader then reached into his pocket and withdrew a jagged knife. He approached Nikos with an evil glint in his eyes and waved the knife in front of his face.

"Let's see if you'll still look that pretty when we carve the hell out of your body," his captor said and then all the men inside the room chuckled.

***

Cassia jerked awake when she heard Nikos shout and felt the chains binding them together yank her arm. She felt his body twisting in their cold, dark cell and she instantly reached for him. Sweat covered his forehead and also his entire body. She squinted against the dark and saw that his eyes were closed.

"Nikos!" she shouted as she shook him awake.

He was still screaming and she was afraid that any time now, their kidnappers would come to investigate.

"Nikos. Please. It's all a bad dream," she explained when he finally opened his eyes.

The feral look was back in his gaze and his eyes looked terrified. Cassia forced him to look at her and she gazed deep into his eyes.

"Nikos. It's me, Cassia. You're fine. It was just a nightmare."

The tension in his body eased a little bit and he started to look around his surroundings. He focused back on Cassia.

"No...it's not a nightmare. We're here and in the same situation so it's all real..."

Cassia winced at the pain in his voice. Good thing it was dark or he would've seen the pity in her eyes. Nikos was a proud man and she was sure he would not appreciate those emotions for him.

"It may be real. But you said we're going to escape here. I believe you, Nikos," she said to calm him.

The lights were switched on and brightness flooded the room. After a few seconds of adjusting, Cassia was able to see every inch of their cell once more. The door to their cell opened and two trays of food were pushed inside.

Cassia was so thirsty that she began to reach for the water. Nikos stopped her by grabbing her hand.

"That may be drugged or poisoned."

Reluctantly, she huddled back to her corner.

"Suit yourself." The young man who brought their dinner shrugged.

"Hey, Eddie, get your ass back here!" one of the other men outside shouted.

The boy who brought their dinner rolled his eyes and cursed.

"Coming!"

Eddie continued to curse and mutter insults about the other men as he pushed the second tray inside Cassia and Nikos' cell.

"Those good for nothing assholes just sit on their asses all day doing nothing and they get paid thrice of what I get. *Fucking damned unjust world*," the boy kept on muttering.

He placed another glass of water inside their cell.

"It isn't poisoned lady, you can drink that. They don't pay me enough to poison your food," the boy informed her before he turned around and left.

The lights were switched off and they were plunged into darkness once more.

"I think he may just be our way out of here," Cassia whispered after the boy left them.

"Maybe..."

Nikos thought hard for a few seconds.

"...if we play our cards right."

Chapter 17
Closer

"*T*ELL me about yourself," Nikos told Cassia after they were silent for what felt like hours.

A day may have passed, and they were still stuck here. She was bored out of her mind, but she also did not want to talk to Nikos. They needed to stick together to survive but she still couldn't get over what happened between them in the past. She could be civil to him but that was still a far cry from being friends.

"Why should I?" she replied.

"We don't have anything better to do, and I know you are bored."

She sighed and finally relented. For the next hour, she told him all about her shop and her passion for design. He was a great listener. He never interrupted her but gave his opinions and inputs when needed. He also commended her for being able to go far.

Over time, she found herself relaxing and telling him more. At first it was just general facts but after a while, she told him the problems of her shop. She was surprised when he gave her excellent solutions based on his business expertise.

"Where do you live? Is your permanent residence your apartment in New York?"

"Yes. It is the most accessible one. I fell in love with that apartment the first time I saw it."

"What I am thinking is that your apartment, even though it's one of the most expensive apartments in New York, is still nothing compared to the other eight estates that you bought. Yet you chose not to live in one of those."

She rolled her eyes and huffed in irritation.

"Nikos, those estates were donated to charity. Seven of them are now orphanages and one of them is a safe haven for stray cats and dogs. I bought all of them with the money I got from my shares to the company."

She could have slapped him and he wouldn't have been more shocked than how he was feeling right now.

"You bought those with your own money? Then what about the yearly allowance I gave you?"

"Still sitting in the bank account you opened for me. I never touched them. Well, I did once when I needed money to start my shop and pay off my college tuition, but I repaid it in double plus the interest when I started earning."

"Why?" he asked incredulously.

"I never wanted your money. Contrary to what you believed all these years, I am not a gold-digger."

He sighed and ran his fingers through his hair. His wife was an irritating woman, but he was also finding out that she was a complex one. He was right with his assessment of her the first time they met: she was different than the women of the elite circle, including all the gold-diggers and social climbers that he dated.

At first he wasn't that jaded when it came to women but after dating several with the same attitude and inclination, he just grew tired. Another factor that influenced him was what happened to his Antonio and his ex-fiancee, Mara.

Nikos took her hand and linked his fingers with hers. Then, he frowned.

"I remember at the party I asked you about rings. Where are yours?"

Cassia raised an eyebrow. "Where's yours?"

"It's in my safe in Greece."

"Then that's also where mine is. Along with all the baubles you asked your assistant to send me for my birthdays and our anniversaries for the past ten years." She shrugged.

"What? Why?"

He was close to losing his mind at this point. He wanted to reach up and pull at his hair in his frustration.

"I mailed them back to your assistant the day after our wedding when I flew back to America. I mail whatever your assistant sends me back the very same day I receive it."

"Why?"

She glared at him and retorted, "The same reason you aren't wearing yours, Nikos. Our wedding is a sham. It's nothing. I want nothing from you."

"Don't say that."

"It's true," she snapped.

"During the period after our engagement when we were supposed to get to know each other, I found out that we had nothing in common. I told myself our marriage was doomed from the start. But during our wedding night when you showed me your passion and told me about your life, my view changed. I actually believed it could work out. But you and your grandfather ruined that with all your lies."

Cassia laughed hysterically.

"I thought you were the sun and the moon. I was so infatuated that I was blinded. I couldn't wait for the day that we were going to be married! I only realized I was wrong right after Antonio told us you were drunk on our wedding day. My grandfather told me that he just forced you to marry me so you wouldn't lose your company. Unlike you, I believed in us right from the start. That changed when you showed me what kind of man you were the next day."

Nikos sighed. They were back to that story, again. What's more, she was blaming him!

His first reaction to everything she said was to scoff and call out her lies but he remembered that he promised to bury their past and move forward. Maybe he could give her the benefit of the doubt for now and see where her story was going?

It was hard but it wasn't impossible.

He looked at her hazel eyes to see if there was any trace of a lie.

There was none.

"What would Costas gain from lying to you?"

"I don't know. He hated me ever since. Maybe because my father ran away with my mother? They say that I look like my mother and maybe he sees her in me. For that, maybe he wanted to punish me." Her tone was indifferent but he could see the pain and anger in her eyes.

"Your grandfather told me that you wanted me, and since he loved you, he offered a merger in return for marriage instead of ruining my company."

She snorted. "He doesn't love anyone but himself. He planned everything from the start. Maybe he told you that he bought you for me so you will hate me even at the start of our marriage. Which you did, by the way. I think he made sure we will *never* be happy." She leaned her head against the stone wall. "Maybe he was hoping that you'd treat me badly because of his lies. Then it would follow that I'd grow unhappy and file for a divorce."

Nikos exhaled slowly. If everything she said was true then Costas Andrade truly was the devil incarnate.

"Or maybe I was right about what I thought the day after our wedding. Maybe Costas told me that you didn't care if I went to my mistress because he hoped that one day you'll catch me and file for divorce. If that happened, then I would be at fault in the courts and as per our contract, I would lose the company."

"I guess you're right about that too," she sighed.

"Cassia...I am turning my back on everything negative I've known regarding you. I am willing to give this marriage a chance. I am willing to put my full trust in you and believe everything you tell me. Please do not lie to me.

"I never lied to you, Nikos. *Ever.* You chose to believe my grandfather but not me. Tell me why everything is my fault?" His mouth opened to reply but she continued, "I fancied myself in love with you, remember? You were my whole world..." She looked straight into his eyes.

"...why would I lie to the man I thought I *loved*?"

The lights were switched on and the boy who brought their meals came in.

He opened the door slightly and pushed the tray of their food inside. Cassia gasped when she saw that his left eye was purple and swollen shut. His cheek was also bruised and his lip was cut.

"What happened to you?" she asked.

"None of your business, lady."

Nikos accepted the tray and sat near the bars of the cell. "You can tell us anything. If you need to vent your anger or talk about it, you can tell me. I have nothing better to do with my time," Nikos whispered.

The boy sighed and Cassia was surprised when he sat down.

"I failed them. They ordered me to go to a bar with them and deliver cocaine to a buyer. I did everything they told me except checking the money. It turns out it was fake." He sighed and banged his head against the bars.

"I really needed that money," the boy added.

"How much was the cocaine?"

"About twenty thousand euros."

Cassia's gasped at the amount and her eyes widened when Nikos took off his gold, diamond-studded Rolex watch and handed it to the boy.

"Sell that and you'll be able to repay them. There will still be extra for whatever you need the money for."

The boy's jaw dropped and his eyes widened as Nikos' closed his hand over the watch. "No! I can't take this!"

"You can and you will. Use it for what you need." Then, Nikos stood up and returned to the corner of the cell. Cassia watched as the boy sat there stunned. He never took his eyes off the watch even as tears filled his eyes. After a few minutes, he hastily wiped away his tears and got up and left without another word.

The next morning, Nikos woke up screaming again.

Cassia shook him frantically and he saw the relief in her eyes once he finally became alert. He then realized that something was different. The lights were on and he was able to see everything in the cell.

He felt as though something bad was going to happen.

That was when he saw them.

The men were in front of their cell and they were looking at him with evil gleams in their eyes. Without thinking, he shoved Cassia behind him again just as the men opened the door to their cell.

"Trying to cause a disturbance, were you? Trying to scream for help? No one can hear you in this island," the leader leered.

"No! He was having a nightmare! That's all it was!" Cassia answered.

The men laughed and looked at Nikos like he was too weak and beneath their notice.

"Usually, in situations like this, it's the lady that screams and the guy acts all brave," one of the other men said.

The other howled with laughter and Cassia realized that they were drunk. Her fear for their safety increased. She knew drunk men tended to do impulsive and stupid things. She was proved correct when the men entered their cell and hauled Nikos to his feet. She was yanked along with him for they were chained together.

One of them retrieved the keys to their handcuffs and removed it. She rubbed at her sore wrist as she glared at them.

"Where are you taking him?!"

"We're just going to teach him how to be quiet. Maybe pound some sense into him. Maybe even discipline him for disturbing us," their leader answered.

Nikos struggled and tried to kick those who were holding him but one of them punched him hard in the stomach. He uttered a groan of pain and then fell limp.

"No! Please don't hurt him!" Cassia recalled Nikos' nightmares and her heart ached for him.

But there was nothing she could do. The men closed the door and switched off the lights.

"I hate rich men. Don't you, Kristoff? I hate how they just had to be born and the world was already laid at their feet," one of the men told their leader.

Cassia memorized every inch of his face and his name.

"Nikos! No! Please let him go!"

"Shut up, lady or we'll take you too. I know the boss instructed us not to touch you but what he doesn't know won't hurt him right?" Kristoff, told her. Then he added to the men, "I want my turn with her first,"

"Sure. Then we can pass her around. That would be one hell of a night."

She heard their captors' lewd jokes along with their footsteps getting louder.

"No!" she shouted and ran to the corner of her cell.

"Don't touch her!" Nikos shouted.

He rammed his shoulder into the man on his left, whose head hit the wall. When he had space to move Nikos extended his leg and aimed a powerful kick to the one on his right. He hit the man's stomach who then doubled over with pain.

"Son of a bitch!" Kristoff shouted.

He pulled his gun out and aimed it at Nikos' head. "One more move and you're dead."

"Nikos!" she called out after him but the only response she got was the men's laughter.

Nikos stilled. When he was held at gunpoint before, his life flashed before his eyes. Now, all he felt was sheer determination to live. He couldn't leave Cassia defenseless at the mercy of these men.

Cassia moved towards the bars of her cell when she heard the sudden silence. She trembled in fear when she saw Nikos kneeling on the ground with a gun pointed directly at his head.

"No! Please! Don't hurt him!" she shouted.

Cassia kept on shouting in the hope that she would be able to distract them from hurting Nikos. Or that maybe she could plead enough. They ignored her and picked Nikos up. They dragged him away from her, and with every step they took, her fear for him increased.

She couldn't see anything anymore and the only thing she heard were their footsteps. It was followed by grunts and the sound of rattling chains.

After a few more minutes, the torture ensued. Nikos grunts of pain along with their captor's maniacal laughter rang across the empty corridors. She recalled his nightmares and bile rose in her throat. There was just something different now, though. He didn't scream for mercy. He didn't beg. He shouted out in pain and cursed but he never gave in.

Tears fell from Cassia's eyes as she was forced to listen. She huddled in the corner of their cell and covered her ears with her hands for she couldn't take it anymore. After a few hours, she fell asleep still crying.

Cassia woke up when she heard the doors to their cell being opened. She stood, just in time to catch Nikos as they threw him inside. He groaned in pain as she dragged him to their pallet. Their handcuffs were placed back and the leader aimed another kick at Nikos before he left. It hit him on the back of his leg and his knees crumbled.

She knelt beside him and looked at him before the lights were switched off.

Nikos' left eye was swollen shut, his face marred with bruises and there was a cut across his left brow that still bled. He was also taking shallow breaths which meant that there could also be an injury to his ribs. Cassia lifted the shirt he wore and ran her fingers down his chest gently.

Nothing seemed to be broken but there were several large bruises and small cuts. She cringed when she saw one bruise that was in the shape of a foot. When they got out of here, she would make sure that those who were responsible for this would suffer for what they did.

She continued her examination until she ran across a large scar in his side. The skin there looked whiter and shiny. It was raised and smooth and Cassia knew this was a scar caused by a burn. She had several small cigarette burns from one of her foster families who punished her by turning her into an ash tray when she did something wrong.

She had nightmares as a child because of that. But looking at Nikos' scar, it was bigger therefore it was more painful that what she experienced.

Could this be the one that caused all his nightmares?

This was not the time to think about those things. She stood up and reached as far as the handcuffs would allow without disturbing Nikos. He was unconscious, and that was a welcome relief from his pain.

She gathered water using one of their drinking cups and tore a strip from their thin blanket. She washed it clean to the best of her abilities using only one hand. She used that to clean Nikos' wounds. He groaned and flinched but did not wake up and Cassia thanked all her lucky stars for that. She did her best to clean him and wipe away all blood and dirt.

When she was finished, she sighed and sat back against the wall beside her husband.

She wished that their escape would come soon. She couldn't take it if anything more happened to Nikos.

And one of these days, she could be next.

During the last two days, both of them spoke to the boy who brought their food. Nikos spoke to him more and threw out subtle hints about several injustices. He also made the boy feel as if he truly understood him. He agreed with whatever the boy shared with them about his life here and Nikos made him feel as if he mattered.

She waited for the next time their meals would be brought. Since their cell was dark and windowless, that was the only thing she could use to tell the time. The next meal that would be brought to them would be their breakfast and Cassia would make sure that their plans to escape would already be fulfilled.

She almost dozed back to sleep when the door opened and their food was pushed inside. She stood up to move towards the boy but was surprised when he knelt beside her.

"It was unfair what they did to him. You must get out of here, lady. I heard them say they are planning to do something to you tonight."

Cassia's jaw dropped open in shock. Then her muscles locked with fear. The boy shook her.

"You must take him and leave! There's no more time to waste! They're not here. The ferry which brings supplies to the island is here, and there are only a minimum number of guards. I can help you escape! But we must hurry!" the boy whispered.

The heavens truly had been watching over her.

"Where are we escaping to? How do we get off this island?" she asked

"I can lead you outside this facility. Once you're outside, follow the trail to the woods. You'll come across a cabin. That belonged to the boss' daughter before. They do not know of that. You can hide there. I believe there's a satellite phone you can use."

"I can never thank you enough...wait! How do I know this is not a trap? Why are you helping us?"

"I thought this was all for money. We are poor and we really need the money. I need it for my mother to buy her food and medicine. Turns out that wasn't the case. They kidnapped you for some kind of revenge. They never wanted money. I overheard them talking about ways they could torture and use both of you. That wasn't what I signed up for.

Besides, you two seem to be good people."

Cassia opened her mouth to thank the boy but he lifted his hand to stop her.

"We could sit here discussing this or we could go. *Now.* They will be back anytime soon."

Cassia shook Nikos awake. He opened his eyes and the first thing she saw in them was terror and panic.

"Shh...it's me. We're getting out of here."

Nikos nodded and tried hard not to make any noise as he stood up.

His body hurt all over and it cost all of his effort not to cry out in pain. As stealthily as they could, they followed the boy through a maze of corridors. Relief flooded Cassia when there were not many guards around.

The main trouble came in the form of the guards from the entrance doors. There were two of them and they were wide awake, alert and heavily armed. The boy motioned for them to go inside a small cabinet to the side.

"What are we supposed to do now?"

The boy thought hard and looked at Nikos from head to toe.

"He can't fight at that state so it's going to be you and me, lady. We can sneak behind them and hit them with something..." he trailed off and looked around the cabinet for something they could use.

The boy grabbed two wooden mops and handed one to Cassia.

"Use this and hit them on the back of the head. Swing hard for we only have one strike with this. Do *not* hesitate," the boy told her.

Cassia nodded but her mouth ran dry with fear. What would happen if they got caught? They would only beat Nikos further and then they would carry out their threat of raping her.

She shuddered at the thought and gripped the mop tighter. She could do this. This was the last hurdle and then they'd be free.

"On my signal, we walk towards the wall. Don't make any noise. Wait again for my signal. Then, we strike. After that, you take him and run as fast as you could before they can alert the others."

The boy moved towards the door but Cassia stopped him.

"I don't think you belong with this kind of life," she told him as she removed her diamond earrings, her necklace and her watch. She handed all those to the boy who again seemed stunned.

Her action made a memory flash through her mind. She recalled doing the same thing for Hector and her heart ached when she realized she missed him so much.

"Take this and start a new life somewhere. Go to America. Or find us in Athens. I'll give you more if you need it. Go to the *Andrade-Demakis Corporation* and look for Cassia Demakis. I'll give you whatever you need."

The boy looked shell-shocked for a moment and then tears misted his eyes. Cassia wiped them away and smiled at him in encouragement.

"Thank you for this," she whispered as she held his hand.

"I hope you make it home. Let's go, lady," the boy replied.

He motioned for her to follow him. The boy looked left and right and then silently walked towards the wall. Cassia squeezed Nikos' hand and he nodded to her before she followed the boy. She tried to mimic his movements as best as she could to avoid creating any noise.

They sneaked up to the two guards who, luckily, were busy having a conversation about a hooker they both shared last night. The boy positioned himself behind one of the guards and Cassia did the same. She gripped the wooden mop as tightly as she could and prepared herself to swing.

She prayed that they would succeed as she waited for the boy's signal.

He nodded to her, and without wasting any more time, the two of them reared back and then swung the mops with as much force as they could. It hit the back of the guard's skull with a sickening thud. The impact jarred her wrists and she watched as the guard went down with a grunt, their blood staining the floor.

"Go!" the boy hissed.

Nikos stood up and limped towards them as fast as he could. Cassia met him halfway and supported him by placing his arm on her shoulders.

"Will you be okay?" she asked the boy as they passed him by.

"Yes! I'll hit my head on the wall and pretend to be knocked out near your cell. They will believe that you overpowered me and escaped.

Once they are busy searching for you, I'll escape."

"At least tell me your name before we go."

"Jason," the boy whispered.

Cassia and Nikos followed the barely visible trail deep in the woods. There was another, well-worn path that they were sure would've led to the beach but that would be where most of their captors were. The beach would also be the first logical place they would look. The wisest course would be to trust the boy's word and look for the cabin.

Nikos still groaned in pain and limped as they trekked through the dense forest, but no complaint escaped his lips. They stopped as often as they could for rest. Nikos was still bruised and battered all over, and he could only take a mile or two before he collapsed.

After a few more minutes, his steps slowed and his eyes drooped.

"Just a bit more, Nikos. I think we're nearly there,"

"Leave me here. It'll be faster that way," he panted.

Cassia resisted the impulse to punch him.

"Stop that! What if they catch you again? You'll be in a much worse state than you are in now!" she lectured. She tugged on his good arm until he stood up again. Truth be told, her shoulders ached from carrying much of his weight already but she, too, never complained. "Come on. Once we're there, you can rest all you want."

"I don't have the energy to walk anymore."

"I'll talk to keep you awake."

"Good idea. Tell me why you hate me so much."

Cassia laughed at the absurdity of his demand.

"Boy, where do I start?" she mused as she walked forward and kept Nikos' arm around her.

She stared at her hand and started ticking off things.

"One, you came to your own wedding drunk. Two, you believed all my grandfather's lies but not me. Three, you spent our wedding night in my bed, making love to me but when the next day came, you were back in your mistress' bed."

"Go on," he said tersely.

"Four, you humiliated me in front of your friends and family. Five, you're an arrogant and selfish jerk."

She looked at him and asked, "Should I continue?"

"Yes."

"I think the arrogant and selfish jerk part pretty much covers everything. How about I give you some advice for the future? You gave me business advice after all. I think I should return the favor."

"Alright then," he replied.

"Just a piece of advice after we're divorced and you're courting another woman: pick a gift yourself. Don't let someone else do it for you. The flowers, the jewelry you sent, it's all him. It's irritating and insulting how picking a gift for someone in your life is too much of a chore for you."

"Noted. Anything else?" he asked through clenched teeth.

"I've got *a lot* more."

He was silent for a long time as they continued to walk through the dense forest. Maybe he was thinking about all the things she said?

"I'm sorry, Cassia," he whispered.

She was stunned when she heard those words. Her steps faltered before she was able to right herself. Did she hear him right? Did the almighty Nikos Demakis just apologize?

Yes. Ravens also just turned white and pigs flew.

"I'm sorry...I know how much you hate me and it must be hard to help me all this way. Thank you for not leaving me," Nikos told her.

"I can never leave someone behind no matter how much I hate him. Besides, once we get out of here, we'll go our separate ways again and we'll never have to bother each other. Especially if you grant me that divorce."

"No divorce."

"Oh well, a woman can dream," she laughed as they started to make their way towards the cabin once more.

The sun had nearly set when they found the cabin. When they approached, Nikos stilled.

"This place looks familiar," he told her as he released her. He limped ahead of her towards the door and tried to push it open. It was locked. He lifted the flower pots beside the door and lifted the key. He held it up and smiled at Cassia.

"I was right. Antonio and I were held in the same place before. This was Elise's cabin. And she still kept the key in the same place."

"Elise?"

"Antonio's wife. She was the daughter of one of the higher bosses of the drug cartel. But she helped us. When I was wounded, she tended to my injuries without anyone's knowledge."

Nikos slid the key inside the lock and cautiously turned the handle. When they were sure no one was inside, they went in and Nikos barred the door. He flopped down on the bed and dust flew everywhere.

"Everything is as I remember it. I really think no one was here during the past two years."

"Okay then. Where can we find a lamp or something? We need to have some light before the sun sets. Hmm...there's a fireplace here. Maybe something to start a fire?"

"*Ochi.*" He shook his head. "The smoke will be visible from afar. I think there's a lamp by the table and a set of matches."

He pointed at another small, dusty table that seemed to be some sort of writing desk.

Cassia lit the candle and placed it inside the lamp. She raised it high so she could see the inside of the cabin.

"How about water?"

"Elise and Antonio got water from a well behind this cabin."

"Alrighty then. Now for some food," Cassia muttered to herself as she opened the cabinets near the stove.

What she found inside were several canned goods. She lifted the light so she could read the expiration date. The fates must have been on their side right now for it had around three months more before it expired.

"Hungry for some pork and beans?" Cassia joked as she faced Nikos who just raised an eyebrow at her. "Well, beggars can't be choosers, Mr. Demakis," she chastised.

Cassia opened another cabinet and there were medical supplies inside.

"Well, we are very lucky indeed. I'll go get us some water and we can cleanse those wounds. But I'm afraid we'll eat our dinner cold because we can't build a fire." She shrugged.

Before Nikos could offer to help, Cassia was already out the door carrying a small wooden bucket with her. She went to the well and tied the bucket to the rope. She laid it down carefully and gathered a small amount of water. She sniffed carefully to check if it was safe. She deemed it safe enough so she gathered more. Humming to herself, she went back to the cabin and poured it on the larger bucket by the fireplace.

It took six more trips before she filled it.

Nikos watched her as she worked. She rolled her sleeves up and took the bucket back and forth. He marveled at her strength and felt frustrated that he couldn't do anything to help her. He was so useless just like two years ago when he couldn't have survived without Antonio and Elise.

Now, history repeated itself, and it was Cassia, his own wife, who he depended on for his survival.

Something clenched inside his chest at the thought of how weak he was. But as he looked at her, another totally different feeling assailed him. She was dirty and her shirt was torn and filled with blood. She had dark circles under her eyes and her skin was pale.

Yet no one seemed more beautiful.

"Please tell me there's something I can do to help you," Nikos told her after her sixth trip. His pride also couldn't take any more beating.

"No. The water is filled now and I think this should last us through the night," she replied.

She looked for a wash cloth and cleaned it by the sink. Then, she took the smaller bucket and knelt beside him by the pallet.

"Let's get your wounds cleaned." She dabbed at his wounds with the cloth then placed some antiseptic over it.

He flinched every time but almost shot off the bed when she grabbed his hand. She examined his wrist and Nikos watched her closely. Her eyes were still the most beautiful and vibrant he's ever seen. Right now, they were filled with concern and curiosity. Her lips were still a temptation. It invited him to lean forward and capture it with his own.

She gently twisted his hand and pain shot up his arm. He couldn't help the groan of pain that escaped his lips.

"This looks broken, Nikos. We would have to set this before the bone heals all wrong. You would have to bear with the pain for a while."

"Wait. How about you? Have you cleaned your wound?" He pointed to her arm.

"Yes. I have already cleaned and re-bandaged it while I was gathering water from the well."

Nikos looked at her incredulously. "Are you sure you know how to do this?"

She nodded.

"Wait! At least tell me how you know so that I can be sure."

"I told you that when I was younger, I was passed from one foster home to another. Not all of them were nice. Some were physically abusive. I learned to do what needed to be done." She left it at that and Nikos felt his rage climbing. His jaw clenched and he made a mental note to find those who hurt her and make them pay.

"Trust me on this, Nikos. I have a splint here and we can tie it up afterwards."

She looked at him with so much concern in her eyes that he just gave in.

"Please don't scream," Cassia said as held his hand. "On the count of three. One, two—"

She didn't finish the count and tugged on his hand to reset the bone. He bit on his knuckles to prevent himself from crying out and then cursed continuously after.

"I thought you said on the count of three!" he hissed.

"Well, if I counted until three, you'd be all tense because you're bracing yourself for the pain. It would be harder that way. On a positive note, the worst pain is over," she told him as she carefully splinted his wrist and then taped it.

"If you can stand for a moment, I'd like to dust that bed before you suffocate in it."

He obeyed. She dragged the mattress outside and pounded on it. Then, she took the blankets and shook them too. Nikos tried to help her fix the bed but she just swatted his hand away.

"Rest now. Dinner's coming right up."

Again, Nikos watched as his heiress wife hummed as she tidied the kitchen. When she deemed everything was clean, she set the table and opened the can of pork and beans.

Nikos marveled at how domestic everything seemed.

Cassia looked like she belonged in the kitchen and she wasn't even squeamish about all the dirt. This was no behavior of an heiress, of someone used to living in luxury. Besides, she even tended to his wounds and placed a splint on his wrist. How had she known how to do all this?

He started to rethink his views about her being a spoiled heiress.

As they said, actions spoke louder than words.

Cassia went to the bed and sat on the edge. She handed him his plate along with a spoon.

"Yum," she said sarcastically as she took her first bite.

Nikos laughed and started eating too.

"Look on the bright side. You opened that yourself. At least you can be sure that it isn't poisoned," he told her.

"Well, I think some of my optimism is rubbing off on you. It's nicer than you frowning and sulking all the time."

"I do not frown nor do I sulk," he contradicted.

"You're doing it now," Cassia pointed out and then she laughed once more.

Nikos couldn't help but laugh too. Her laughter was so infectious and her acceptance of their situation humbled him.

"You're more handsome when you smile," Cassia blurted out before she could stop herself. She blushed and just finished the rest of her food to avoid saying more stupid things.

"Handsome, huh? Well, let me just say that you've also grown more beautiful over the years. Forgive me for not recognizing my own wife at the fashion show."

Cassia blinked. At his words, the easy companionship she had with him faded. Instantly, she was reminded about their anniversary dinner wherein he callously declared that he now wanted them to live together and start a family to fulfill the terms of their contract.

It was like her happiness bubble was popped and doused with cold water. Abruptly, she got up and deposited her plate in the sink. She started scrubbing it like everything about it offended her.

"Did I say something wrong?"

"What? No. I was just thinking about something else. I found the phone by the way. But it's solar powered and there are panels on the roof. Right now, there's no charge and I think something's wrong with the panels. So I guess we wait for tomorrow before we can make that call."

"All right, then. But it's weird that there's solar panels and even a phone in a cabin like this," she laughed.

"Elise was always prepared. This was her cabin and that phone was what she used to help me and Antonio. I also noticed the facility we were in. There's no electricity on this island. It's all solar powered and maybe Elise got hold of a panel or two."

"She seems like a great woman," Cassia said with a smile.

"She is," he agreed.

Nikos looked at his wife with curiosity. What was going on in her mind right now that all the laughter suddenly died from her face? Was it him? Did he do something wrong?

He tried to recall his last words to her and found nothing. Still, she didn't talk to him and the silence stretched on and on. There came a point that he couldn't take it anymore. He racked his brain for topics for a good conversation.

"How did you get so handy with things? How do you know all this?" he gestured at the now clean room.

She sighed heavily. They have been through for what felt like a hundred times already. He never believed her once.

"I wasn't really born into riches, Nikos. I already told you this. I was with my parents in America when they were alive. When they died and no one claimed me, not even Costas, I was sent to the foster system. I lived in different homes where I learned how to do housework so I could earn my keep."

This was one of the lies she told him before. But was it really a lie?

"And about my wrist?"

"Mine's been broken twice."

"What happened?

She sighed. "I was pushed down the stairs twice," she replied in a dead tone.

Then, she turned towards him.

"Why are you asking me all this, Nikos? I know you won't believe me. I told you this before and you called me a liar. What's changed?"

Nikos was at a loss for words.

When he was through thinking of all the things happening in his life recently, he found Cassia to be asleep on the moldy couch. He was too weak to carry her to the bed so he just covered her with a blanket.

He took a few more minutes just looking at her. Her features were relaxed and she was even more beautiful when she wasn't glaring at him. He suddenly found himself smiling and before he knew it, he bent and placed a kiss on her forehead.

Nikos shook his head at his sudden burst of tenderness and returned to the bed. He was reluctant to close his eyes for he didn't want to scream from his nightmares and alert their kidnappers to their location. So he just lay there and listened to her even breathing as she slept, watching for any signs of their captors.

Dawn came and the silence was interrupted with the chattering of Cassia's teeth. Nikos immediately stood up and brought his blanket to her and covered her with it. It was cold but they couldn't build a fire for it would easily be seen by their enemies.

He tucked the blanket edges securely around Cassia but she still shook with the cold. Nikos muttered a string of curses when he felt that her skin was like ice.

He sat beside her on the sofa and gathered her in his arms. Her eyes immediately opened and panic set in.

"Shh...it's me." he whispered as he rocked her.

"N-n-nikos...can- we l-light that f-fire now?" she stammered.

"I'm so sorry. We can't. They'd find us."

"It's s-s-o c-cold-d."

"I know. Trust me on this?"

She frowned but nodded. He lifted the covers and heard her gasp of outrage as he slid in beside her.

Nikos pulled her to his chest and placed her cold hands on his neck. He gasped from feeling her icy fingers on his skin. He rubbed her arms and her back with his uninjured hand and then wrapped the blankets more securely around them.

Her entire body stiffened against him in protest but after a few minutes, she relaxed and sighed.

"That's nice," she whispered.

"Radiant warmer at your service," he teased.

"Thanks."

"Anytime, Cassia."

After that, both of them fell asleep; warm and comfortable. Nikos didn't plan on sleeping but with the feel of his wife in his arms and her exquisite vanilla scent he loved so much, the moment he closed his eyes, he was a goner.

Daylight streamed through the windows making Cassia groan.

She didn't want to get up yet as every part of her ached. Her shoulder felt as though it had been hit by a sledgehammer. Her legs felt like dead weight from walking around all day and her other arm ached from hauling water from the well.

But she really had to get her day started if she wanted to survive on this island and not get caught by their kidnappers.

With another groan, she opened her eyes and got up from bed.

"Good. You're already awake. Breakfast is ready," Nikos told her.

He gestured to the table which was already set with two plates filled with pork and beans. Cassia winced and Nikos laughed.

"Beggars can't be choosers, remember?"

She laughed when he threw her own words back at her.

She was also glad that he could already stand, even though he was still limping. The swelling in his eye had already lessened and his bruises were turning a darker shade of purple. Overall, he looked better today.

Suddenly, the events in the early parts of daybreak came crashing back to her and she averted her gaze. She just spent the night cuddling with none other than her ex-husband! Well, maybe that could be excused because she was really, really cold and they could not start a fire for fear of their kidnappers finding them.

Besides, there was no other way to keep warm so it's fine. Right?

No, traitor.

Her conscience chose that moment to intrude on her thoughts and she groaned.

You liked it even when you weren't cold anymore. You liked feeling his arms around you. You liked his smell and the fell of his hard chest against your palms. You liked feeling his soft breaths against your cheek. His closeness reminded you of that one night you spent together.

She cringed at her thoughts. This was *wrong*. Being near him evoked a lot of memories and emotions in her. Those were things that she buried a long, long time ago. She wasn't the naive girl who fell in love with him anymore.

But everything now chipped at the ice that she surrounded her heart with. Her armor was weakening and he hadn't even so much as kissed her! He just held her and she was nearly insane with desire for him!

Cassia mentally shook herself.

Stop it.

Her life was much better now and she couldn't throw everything away just because of *lust*.

"Is something wrong?" Nikos asked her.

She glanced up from her plate of pork and beans and shook her head.

"Nothing's wrong but you haven't eaten anything. I've been watching you push your food around your plate."

"Umm...guess I'm not that hungry."

"You'll need your strength, Cassia. Eat up."

He was right. Danger still held them by their throats and she would need every ounce of strength she possessed. She also needed to eat to keep her brain shipshape.

Cassia sighed and started to eat without really tasting the food. Her thoughts were still on the complex man sitting before her.

"Do you think we should leave?" Cassia asked after a long period of silence.

"I think we're safe here for now. First, they would comb the shore area. They think that's where we'll go and they'll tighten the security on ferries and boats with access to this island. I think that will take them a day. While you were asleep, I tried to circle the area. If by any chance, the kidnappers can find this cabin, they would be coming from that direction." Nikos pointed towards the trail they came from. "The other side only contains a denser portion of the woods. So I doubt they'd be coming there. If we hear them coming, we can go out the back door of this cabin and lose them in the forest."

"Sounds like a great plan. What about the phone? Is it already charging?"

"I'm afraid the solar panels have been damaged. Only one is working and the wires have also been damaged. I can repair those wires but it may take some time. The soonest we can make that call may be by tomorrow."

"Great," she muttered.

Nikos ignored her. He cleared the table and began to lay out several tools and wires. He placed the solar panel on one side and inspected every inch of it.

"I'm going to refill our water supply and then maybe go around for a walk."

Nikos looked up and she was pierced by his green eyes.

"Be careful," he warned.

"Always."

Cassia returned a little past noon. She was breathless from the long hike she took. She wanted to get a lay of the land. Unfortunately, she was not able to do that but she found something else.

"Good news or bad news?" she asked Nikos.

His brows were furrowed as he concentrated on repairing the solar panels. Also, there were several dirt streaks on his cheeks but he couldn't look any more handsome if he tried.

Cassia cringed at her thoughts. *Don't go there, Cassia.*

"Bad news."

"Okay then. We only have two cans of pork and beans left. I guess that's for lunch. Then no more."

Nikos raised an eyebrow.

"Good news?"

"I found a stream nearby and we can bathe there and also get fish. Assuming one of us knows how to fish."

Nikos' green eyes glittered with amusement. "Well, we'll have to learn if we want to eat tonight, right?"

"But how're we going to cook it?"

"Ever eaten sushi?" Nikos asked with a huge smile.

"Yes. I *hate* sushi," Cassia answered. She wrinkled her nose.

Nikos' smile turned into a bark of laughter.

"Maybe we can cook the fish when it's already dark so that the smoke won't be that visible. We'd have to do it quickly, though."

"Can we risk it?" she asked.

"This is a dense forest. I doubt they'd see a little bit of smoke at night. Hmm. Better yet, let's cook it from afar where there's a thick canopy of trees. Let's cook near this stream you found."

"Great idea," she replied and they grinned at each other.

Cassia sighed.

Why was it so easy to be with him like this when ten years ago he was always stiff and formal beside her? She'd never seen this side of him and it made it all the more difficult to guard her heart against him.

But she had to.

This was all a trick. He was just nice to her because they were thrown together in this disaster. They needed each other to survive and he'd gain nothing by alienating her. But when they were rescued and when they went back to their lives, they'd be like they were before – *strangers.*

She repeated those thoughts to herself over and over as she tried to refreeze her heart and rebuild her armor.

For she *couldn't* repeat her mistakes from ten years ago.

A few hours later, Nikos was waist-deep in the water trying to catch fish with his bucket while she was perched on top of a rock, laughing at him.

"Stop! You're scaring the fish away!"

"Stop laughing at me! Do you know how hard this is?" Nikos hissed.

Cassia already caught two large fish while Nikos still had nothing. He was wet from head to toe and failing miserably.

"Damn it!" he cursed as he slipped and fell in the water.

He rose from it, cursing and sputtering. Cassia continued laughing as he turned to her.

"You think this is funny?" he asked through clenched teeth.

"It really is," and she *howled* with laughter once more.

Cassia clutched her stomach and laughed as Nikos tried over and over again. After an hour and he still had nothing, he finally conceded.

"You didn't catch anything. But look on the bright side: you are clean now since you've had a bath," she teased.

Her laughter was cut short when she was suddenly doused with cold water. When she opened her eyes, Nikos held his bucket over her head with a smirk on his arrogant face.

"Why you—you—" she never got to finish the sentence as she decided to pounce.

She fell from the rock and into the water taking Nikos with her. When they resurfaced, they began splashing each other like two rowdy children.

Cassia gave it all she had and didn't relent. Nikos did the same and soon enough, both of them were tired and dripping wet. And they were both laughing.

"Okay. Stop. I call truce," Cassia surrendered. Her arm throbbed from her exertions and she knew Nikos' aches and pains were punishing him as well.

"Truce," he agreed as he breathlessly waded towards her rock and sat beside her. He looked around and listened carefully for the kidnappers might have been alerted by the noise of their childishness.

"If catching fish was a competition, I won today," Cassia gloated.

Nikos scoffed. Then he leaned back and lay down across the rock.

"I haven't had that much fun for as long as I can remember," he sighed.

Cassia's heart immediately went out to him. She remembered his nightmares, the night he was tortured and the scars she saw when she cleaned his wounds.

She also lay down on the rock and looked at the sky.

"What happened two years ago, Nikos?"

He stilled and the mask he always wore slid back into place.

He never spoke to anyone about his kidnapping, except for the doctors he consulted to help him. Even they had difficulty in having him open up about what he experienced. But right now, only one question from her and he ached to spill everything. Something in her called out to the pain he carried inside him. He turned to his side and looked into her hazel eyes.

He saw concern there. No judgment. No pity. No curiosity. Only *concern*.

He started recounting his tale.

"Antonio and I were on our way to a business conference. Suddenly, there was an explosion and the car I was in swerved to the side. Then, they fired on us. I felt a pain in my side and realized I was shot."

Her eyes widened. Now she knew where the scar on his side came from. But why did it look like the skin was burnt?

"From there on, I drifted in and out of consciousness. Maybe it was from blood loss. I would have died if they didn't do anything about it."

Nikos gritted his teeth as he flashed back to the scene. He recalled how they dug out the bullet and then seared his skin to close the wound. Shame washed over him as he heard his own voice crying and begging for them to end his torture.

He looked at Cassia to gauge her reaction. She reached for his hand and squeezed.

"They will pay, Nikos. We will make them pay for all they did to you two years ago. And for what they did now," she vowed.

Her eyes were bright with unshed tears. They were not of pity or judgment. She cried for him because she shared his pain. His heart ached at those words.

"How did you manage to get off the island?"

"First I'll tell you about Elise."

She nodded.

"She was the daughter of one of the leaders of those who kidnapped us. But she was not like them. At first, Antonio and I thought she was sent in to torture us. She came to our cell carrying her knives and a whip."

He breathed in deep and summoned the courage to continue.

"She asked for a bucket of water and threw it over me. She laughed and so did all the guards. She asked them to leave and then told us she was not the enemy. She'd help us but we had to scream as loud as we could."

Nikos gave a bark of laughter. He remembered the look of confusion on Antonio's face when she told them she'd help but they had to shout as though they were being beaten within an inch of their lives.

"She laid down those knives and retrieved medical supplies from under her dress. The water she threw over me was so she could clean my wounds and avoid an infection. She really did help me while Antonio and I screamed. We didn't trust her at first but she came back night after night."

"I guess that's when Antonio fell in love with her?" Cassia said with a small smile.

"Yes. I was still too weak then but when I wake up during the night, I saw her sitting outside our cell and the two of them were talking. Before the sun rose, she was gone."

"She helped you leave the island?"

"Yes and no. She wasn't allowed to leave the island either so she couldn't smuggle us out, if that's what you're asking. But she found a way to help. We were about to be transferred to another place where they would keep us. Elise overheard them and she told us. Antonio asked her to contact Alex and she did. When we were transferred to the place, Alex and his team were there waiting."

"What about Elise?"

"Antonio grabbed her and carried her to the helicopter himself. He refused to let her go. He didn't want her to go back to what she did in the island. He told her she deserved a better life and that he would give it to her." Nikos smiled. "They were married a few months later."

When he finished with his story he saw Cassia dash away her tears with her hands. Then, she smiled at him and he felt as if a huge burden was lifted off his chest.

The doctors were right after all. Speaking about what happened in the past truly did help. Maybe the problem was that he never really opened up about everything. He chose the bits and pieces that he shared. And when he spoke, he always believed that people would look down on him with pity. He hated that.

Now, he felt *free*.

Before he could think further, he dipped his head lower and his lips met hers. She gasped as he deepened the kiss and he used that opportunity to dart his tongue inside and taste her.

It was *exquisite.*

It was exactly how he remembered it ten years ago. Maybe even *better*.

Cassia's first thought when Nikos kissed her was that she should punch him in the face but there was another part of her that wanted this. He kissed her just how she remembered in her dreams of their wedding night and it set her blood on fire.

She sighed against his lips and threw her uninjured arm around his neck to pull him closer. She returned his kisses with a passion of her own as she ran her fingers through his hair. Nikos groaned and she truly became lost.

Nothing else existed but him and her and the pleasure they felt in each other's arms.

Just like their wedding night ten years ago.

Cassia felt as if she was doused with another bucket of cold water when she remembered that night. She gave herself to him fully, asking for nothing in return. She just wanted to make memories with him that she could take with her when she left.

That night was perfect.

But the next morning, Nikos showed her his true colors. She then realized it was true what they said that the devil wore the face of an angel.

She pulled back and scrambled away from him.

"Cassia...?"

"We have to go. We still have to find somewhere we can cook the fish without being seen before the sun sets."

She took the bucket and placed the fish inside. Without waiting for Nikos, she sprinted towards the opposite side of the stream.

Nikos pushed himself off the rock.

He also ran a hand through his hair in frustration. What was the matter with Cassia? One moment she was very sweet and tender and the next she was back to being a spitfire. He had her in his arms and was kissing the hell out of her one minute and the next she pushed him away and disappeared.

He shook his head and set off to follow her.

"Women. The day that men understand them is the day of the apocalypse," he muttered to himself.

He also gave himself a mental shake but no matter what he did, he could not forget the events that recently transpired. Now, he was even more convinced that he wanted his wife back. Her passion for him was still the same like it was ten years ago.

Maybe, no matter how small, she still felt *something* for him. She could deny it all she wanted but it was clearly there.

For the first time in a long time, he felt a spark of hope. Maybe Antonio was right and that he was not really living his life anymore. Now, he felt truly alive for he had a purpose. He'd win back his wife whatever it took.

He was ready to forget his biases in order for both of them to move on. Also, something happened in the past which wasn't their fault and he would discover that.

This time, nothing else would come between the two of them.

Nikos sat quietly in the dark as he and Cassia ate their fish.

Earlier, they cooked the fish over the fire then took it back to the cabin to eat. Since that event by the stream, Cassia still hasn't talked to him. When he tried to ask her a question, she simply replied with a yes or a no.

Even when he teased her, she ignored him. He found himself missing the easy camaraderie they shared these last few days.

"Cassia, if this is about what happened earlier...I'm sorry."

She only grunted in reply and went back to eating her dinner.

"Cassi—"

"I don't want to talk about it Nikos, okay? I'd also appreciate it if it won't happen again."

"Why?"

"You know why! Everything between us is over! I've moved on with my life and you've moved on with yours. We are getting a divorce! It's best that we don't complicate things further."

"Cassia, you know how I feel about the divorce. I won't allow it."

"Well that's just tough then."

"We have to talk about this," he implored.

"I don't have anything more to say, Nikos."

"I want another chance, Cassia. I know you wanted me ten years ago. I want that back."

Cassia scoffed.

"Damned arrogant, aren't you? Whatever I had for you ten years ago, you already killed it. Nothing's left, Nikos. You don't even deserve anything from me."

"We already spoke about what happened in the past, Cassia. We could discuss it more and you'd know what happened was all a misunderstanding."

"I explained that ten years ago but you did not believe me. And talking about things doesn't set them right, Nikos. It's over between us."

"You say that yet I know you still want me. Your lips say one thing but your body says another."

Cassia laughed.

"Don't mistake *lust* for something else."

"Lust? Lust is two people scratching an itch, Cassia. But when I kiss you, you melt. You sigh against my lips just like you did ten years ago."

"Don't turn nothing into something, Nikos. It's over between us. I have Hector now. I am happy with him. I've agreed to marry him that's why I need a divorce from you. *Now.*"

Nikos' patience ran out after hearing Hector's name.

His blood pounded in his ears and his heart thundered in his chest. How dare she mention another man's name? His blood heated and his entire body roared with possessiveness. He's show her who she really belonged to.

She just had to forget about Petrides for he was *never* letting her go.

"Marriage is for life, Cassia. *No divorce.* I won't let you go to Hector Petrides. You're mine."

He tugged her to his chest and then claimed her lips once more. But this was unlike any other kiss before. This one was a brand of possession, a stamp of ownership. It was fierce and demanding. He kissed her as though he was never letting go.

Nikos placed his hand on her nape and held her steady as he deepened the kiss. His other arm wrapped around her and brought her into contact with his hard body.

Cassia's senses reeled at the onslaught. She knew she should be fighting this. She knew she should push him away. But even to save her life, she could not do it.

This felt so perfect that she just couldn't let it end.

Deep in her subconscious, this was what she's been dreaming of for ten years now.

As Nikos kissed her, she also realized what she thought was missing in her relationship with Hector.

Passion. Desire.

When Hector kissed her, it was nice but it didn't set her body on fire for him the way Nikos' kisses did. He made her melt with even just one glance the way Hector never did.

He backed her up against the wooden table and lifted her against it without breaking their kiss. He separated her legs and stepped between them. She moaned again when she felt the evidence of his desire against her.

Nikos unbuttoned the blouse she wore and slid it gently off her injured shoulder. Somehow, she also found herself lifting her hands to unbutton his shirt. She sighed with bliss and ran her palms down the hard ridges of his muscles.

Nikos flinched when she touched his scar.

He didn't like anyone to see or touch it for it reminded him of the horrors he experienced. This was why, after he was kidnapped, he never let another woman get close. For over two years, his bed was empty. For more than two long years, he hadn't felt another's touch.

This was also why he was ravening for her.

Nikos took his time admiring the creamy swell of her skin that he uncovered. Before she had any chance to be self-conscious, he stepped closer again and covered it with his hands. She moaned against his lips and her grip on his arm tightened.

He removed her bra and placed his hand on the middle of her back. She arched her back against him to make herself more accessible for his mouth. With the first suck, pleasure shot down her spine and pooled low in her belly. He moved to the other nipple and she moaned his name.

"You're mine, Cassia," he whispered against her ear after he gave one tentative lick.

She shivered in his arms but this time, it wasn't from the cold.

Her head spun and she opened her lips to contradict his statement but what came out was only a breathless gasp for he slipped his hand inside the waistband of her jeans. Finally, he touched her where she craved him the most. She was so wet for him that he almost came right then and there.

He prayed to all the gods listening for control. He wanted to make this night last and he wanted to savor her. This wasn't a dream. She was really here in the flesh and he wanted to make it special.

"Tell me you're mine," Nikos whispered as he kissed a path down her neck. "Tell me."

Her only reply was a sharp intake of breath.

He unzipped her pants and drew them down her legs. Her underwear soon followed. He knelt by the table and parted her legs. Then, he used his fingers and his mouth to drive her wild and make her soar.

He knew she was nearly there and he lifted his head.

"Don't stop. Nikos..." she pleaded.

"Tell me you're mine," he repeated.

She was silent for a long time. She merely closed her eyes and lay down on the table.

Telling him that she was his was like admitting what her greatest fear was: that she *never* really moved on. That somehow she still wanted him and that she still had feelings for him no matter how deeply buried they were inside of her. That she was just in denial all this time.

Telling him would be admitting what she's known but feared and kept a secret for ten years of her life...

"I'm yours," she whispered in defeat.

He stood up, removed all his clothing. She felt him pressing against her.

"Tell me this is what you want."

Nikos forced down his desire and wrestled with control. He had to make sure she wanted this too. He'd waited for this for ten years and he didn't want her to have any regrets. It would be hard to pull away but he would do that for her if that was what she wanted.

"I want you..."

Without wasting another moment, he pushed inside her. This time, it was he who moaned her name. She heard him whisper endearments in Greek and she held on to him tightly.

"...like I've *always* wanted you."

He started to move. His breathing deepened as pleasure assailed him. He cupped her jaw and forced her to look at him. He wanted to see her face as he made love to her. He saw her desire mirrored in his eyes and he knew she wanted him as badly as he wanted her.

She bucked her hips and heard his quick intake of breath. Once more, she opened her lips to his and the sensation of their tongues twining almost sent him to his knees. He pulled back to look at her and the way her features were twisted with pleasure would forever be in his memory.

She drew him back to her by wrapping her arms around him and moving her hips against his. He couldn't take more of this wicked temptation and he succumbed to it. He moved against her faster and harder, and she returned his passion equally and clutched him.

He bent his head and flicked his tongue against her nipple. Then he sucked and it was just too much. Cassia shattered in his arms as she moaned his name.

Her climax triggered his.

"Cassia!" he writhed against her as ecstasy consumed him.

Afterwards, he carried her carefully to the bed. He was much stronger now and he also made sure that he was careful of her shoulder and his broken wrist.

He didn't give her time to think, for he didn't want her to have any regrets. The moment that she was settled on the bed, he pulled her against his chest and laid her head on his arm. He placed one last sweet, lingering kiss against her swollen lips and pulled the covers over them.

"Sleep..." he whispered.

Chapter 18
Escape

"WHAT do you mean they escaped?!" Sebastian roared.

He was on a plane to Greece. He'd anticipated finally getting his revenge but now he was being told that the man he hated the most was gone.

"They knocked two guards out and ran. We did not find them right away because most of the men were busy down on the docks for the latest shipment and recruits."

"They couldn't have escaped on their own. There's a traitor within us. Find him and make him pay."

"Noted, boss."

"Find Demakis and his wife. Now!"

November 23, 2013
A stream near Elise's cabin
An unknown island in Greece

"God, I am the stupidest human being alive!" Cassia shouted.

She woke up today naked in Nikos' arms. And she wasn't even cold!

The moment she opened her eyes, the events of last night came crashing down. She carefully extracted herself from his arms, left a note as to where she was going and then ran all the way there. She screamed and cried, kicked some rocks and cursed herself.

How could she sleep with Nikos Demakis?

Cassia laughed bitterly. Sleep wasn't really the technical word.

Cassia smacked herself on the forehead. How could she let that happen? How could she sleep with the person who hurt her most? Hadn't once been enough? Hadn't she been hurt enough to last her a lifetime?

She cursed and stomped on the muddy ground. Then she cringed when she remembered telling Nikos that she was his.

"I'm yours, Nikos..."

"I want you like I've always wanted you."

"I'm stupid! I've gone officially insane!" she laughed hysterically and kicked another rock down the stream.

She pulled at her hair and considered hitting her head on one of the trees if only that would make her forget.

But another part of her brain kept on telling her that last night was perfect.

She'd dreamt about making love with Nikos Demakis. In her dreams, they'd made love hundreds of times in a hundred different ways. But that was all they were: *dreams, her innermost fantasies*.

But last night, it was all real.

And it was *perfect*.

She couldn't have dreamed a better scenario.

Still it was wrong though.

She just betrayed Hector after agreeing to marry him!

But technically, she didn't betray Hector, for Nikos was really her husband. In fact, she was betraying Nikos with Hector.

Cassia gave another sarcastic laugh. Now, even her conscience was reasoning out with her and it was taking Nikos' side!

No. This insanity must end. There simply was no future for both of them. Everything that happened last night was a *mistake*; nothing more.

Cassia was snapped out of her thoughts when she heard men's voices and footsteps. Her heart raced and she immediately hid herself behind one of the large rocks. She waited for them to pass, and as quietly as she could, she ran back to the cabin.

Nikos woke up with a smile on his face.

Last night was *perfect*.

It was better than his dreams, better than any other night he spent with a woman before. He opened his eyes and frowned when Cassia was nowhere to be seen. It would've been better if he woke up with her in his arms and maybe he could've made love to her again this morning.

Her place in the bed was still warm. He saw a note beside the bed. She wrote that she just went to the stream.

He sent a silent prayer willing her to be safe.

Now, back to business.

He looked outside and noticed that the sun was already high in the sky. It was noon! He overslept again. Why was it that when he was with Cassia, he didn't have those nightmares? Why could he sleep like a baby when she was near?

He sighed and went to the table. He was distracted when he recalled what happened last night at that particular table. But then he forced himself to concentrate.

The solar panels had been fixed yesterday and he hoped that the satellite phone would be charging by now. He checked the wires and saw that they were fine. Joy surged through him when he saw that it was already charging!

"Come on, open please," he muttered as he punched in some buttons. When the screen lit up, he wanted to jump up and down with joy.

He immediately dialed Alex's number.

"Alex, it's me—"

"Nikos?!" Alex exclaimed.

"Yes. It's me—"

"Where the hell are you?!"

"I don't really know the name of the island. I was mostly unconscious when we were here. Ask Antonio. Elise will know. I'm on the same island where we were first kidnapped."

"I'll assemble my team and we'll be there as soon as possible. Are you and Cassia alright?"

"Yes, we are. Just minor injuries."

"Good! I will also send medics. Your yacht was found in the middle of the ocean after the bodyguards I sent with you were able to radio for help to the mainland. Antonio and I have been going crazy ever since. I flew here as soon as I heard."

Nikos heard Alex cursing.

"I've locked on to the signal of this phone. We're coming for you as soon as we can. Stay off the beach or the docks, that's the first place they'll look. Stay hidden and we'll come find you."

"Alright."

Suddenly there were two beeps. The line was cut for the phone went dead. Nikos stared at it and tried to turn it on again but the battery was drained. Well, their fate was all in Alex's hands now.

"Nikos!" the door flew open and Cassia ran to him.

"What happened? Are you all right?"

"Yes. But we have to go! I saw men by the stream and they are coming this way. We have to leave!"

He was immediately spurred into action. He grabbed their blankets along with the medical supplies. Then he grabbed her hand and they exited the cabin through the back door. They ran as silently as they could deeper into the woods.

"Where are we going?" Cassia asked him after they walked for several hours.

"We just have to find a place to hide. The solar panels were fixed and the phone was charged. While you were out, I got through to Alex. He's coming for us."

"That's great! When do you think will they arrive?"

"Maybe in a couple of hours."

"So we just have to sit and wait?"

"Yes. Preferably in a safe location," Nikos answered with a grin and her heart jumped.

They continued their search for a safe place. The sun nearly set when they found a small cave near the mountainNikos spread one of the blankets on the damp ground. They sat together and wrapped the other blanket around both of them.

He noticed that instead of curling against him, Cassia leaned against the wall. He gritted his teeth, for he was sure what was running through her mind: regrets over what happened last night.

"Talk to me, Cassia."

"We've been over this before. When you kissed me by the stream I already told you that we couldn't be together. But I know that it takes two to tango so it's a huge fault of mine too."

Nikos cupped her jaw and forced her to look at him.

"You just admitted that you're mine, Cassia. I won't let you go. Whatever we had in the past, we'll sort it out and start anew."

"You think it's that easy? And how can you say that we are going to sort through all of our issues when you won't believe a word I say?"

"I'm willing to listen now. We've been married for ten years, Cassia. But we've barely begun this marriage. Give us another shot."

"You were the one who ruined it!"

"I am not arguing with you about whose fault it is, alright? It's not important. What's important is that both of us move on."

"You know, if this is all about the contract and about us having an heir...it's *not* needed. Grant me the divorce and I'll say I am to blame. I'll say I took a lover so that everything will go to you. You'll also gain control of the Andrade side of the company. You don't need to sacrifice yourself again."

"It's not that. I want *you*. I want a family. I believe we can become happy together. I want to be with you, and I want you to be the mother of my children."

Cassia's heart melted at his words.

But she'd been on the receiving end of his sweet words before only for him to take it all back and replace it with bad memories the morning after.

"I can't. I have Hector now."

"If you really loved him, Cassia...you wouldn't have responded to me the way you did last night. We can keep arguing about this and it will never end. I won't let you go."

Cassia sighed and turned away from him.

"Say whatever you want, Nikos. When we get off this island, we'll return to our normal lives and you will know what all this is - it's just a *mistake.*"

"Never," he sighed before he pulled her in his arms and turned her to face him.

"I'm sure you will return to your mistresses and your crazy lifestyle the moment we are free of this island. How's Marietta by the way? The woman you slept with after you came straight from our wedding bed."

"I did not sleep with her that morning," he responded in a flat tone.

Cassia whirled, "What?!"

"I didn't. Believe it or not, during our marriage, however recent that may be, I was completely faithful to you."

Cassia laughed.

"So you were just casually coming out of the shower in her suite and she was naked on the bed?"

"No. I went there to shower before my flight. I went there after I spoke with your grandfather. He told me several things. Basically, he told me that you didn't want to be my wife and that you only wanted money and your freedom. He said you didn't even want to live with me. I didn't return to our suite because I was so angry at you so I decided to bathe in one of my friends' suites. I saw her coming out of hers and she told me she was headed to breakfast. She granted me access to her room and I went there and bathed. I didn't know that she came back on the bed naked. I found out the same time as you."

"You lie," Cassia spat.

"I have never lied to you, Cassia. You can ask Alex about it. He was the first one I asked to lend me the shower in his suite. He saw Marietta offer hers," he answered in a sincere tone.

Cassia stilled as she processed what she just heard. Was Nikos telling her the truth? He really did not sleep with Marietta that morning?

"Why didn't you correct me when I thought wrong? Why didn't you throw her instead of asking her to stay? You chose her over me, Nikos!"

"I was wrong about that...I apologize...but I was so angry with you and your grandfather that day. I thought that you both lied to me and played me for a fool again. You dented my pride and I wanted to retaliate."

"What exactly did my grandfather tell you that day?"

Nikos ran his fingers through his hair.

He tried to recall the conversation in his mind and then told her everything. He had this suspicion that it was all Costas' fault. That old man manipulated everything. Maybe he also did it to his granddaughter's marriage.

"He lied!" she shouted.

"I realize that after everything you told me."

She frowned and clenched her fists.

"When I woke up, the first thing I did was to look for you. A maid told me you were in another suite so I went there to get you. I encountered my grandfather and he told me about you and your mistress. He told me I had to understand for men have needs and tend to stray..." Her voice wobbled, betraying the emotion she tried to kept bottled. "He really set out to ruin us before our marriage even began."

She was silent for a long time and he could almost see the gears in her mind turning.

"I think he wanted you to be the cause of our marriage falling apart. I think he wanted me to find you with Marietta and file for divorce. That leaves you nothing and he gains everything through me. I was his puppet then and he was the one who pulled my strings. Besides, if the merger fell apart because of you, your grandfather would have been devastated."

Nikos' jaw clenched.

She was right.

He felt a pang in his chest as it was now truly clear that what happened before was all a misunderstanding. It was all caused by a bitter old man who wanted to play God and wreak havoc with their lives.

He was ready to give their marriage a chance ten years ago. If Costas hadn't ruined everything, their lives would be totally different now. Maybe they'd be happy. Maybe his Greek island would have been filled with laughter from their children; perhaps a boy who inherited his business acumen and a girl who had Cassia's passion for art and her beauty.

The anger fled from her eyes and instead they misted with tears. Maybe because, like him, she also felt regret for the time that was wasted?

"Nikos..."

She reached for him.

He was about to kiss her but the moment was ruined when they heard heavy, running footsteps.

Both of them immediately stood up and hid behind the larger rocks. Nikos shoved her behind him and they stayed silent as they waited for the men to pass. But the sound of their footsteps lingered.

Cassia cursed under her breath when she saw that they left one of the blankets. It was out in the open and the men would immediately see it. She was about to reach forward and grab it but a beam of light was shone across the cave and directly onto the blanket.

Then the footsteps stopped.

"They're in here!" one of the men shouted.

They heard Kristoff's laugh and saw him pick up the blanket.

"Mr. and Mrs. Demakis...you may come out now. Let's do this the easy way so nobody gets hurt," he called out in a menacing tone.

His laughter echoed across the dark cave again. Fear struck Cassia and she squeezed Nikos' hand. She saw the promise in his eyes. His look promised that he wouldn't let anything happen to her.

Cassia feared so much for him. If they get caught, she knew he would suffer the beating he received two nights ago, maybe more. They'd be merciless this time. Maybe they'd even carry out their threat of raping her.

If they got caught, there'd be no chance of an escape this time.

The men entered the cave and their heavy footsteps nearly drove her insane with fright. Nikos pushed her against a wall and covered her body with his. When one of the men reached them, Nikos kicked him and sent him scrambling backwards. He tugged on her hand and they sprinted towards the entrance of the cave.

But it was no use for there was more men waiting outside. Hands grabbed at her and she tried to fight them off as best as she could. Cassia kicked and clawed her way out but there was just too many of them. Her heart beat faster with fear and at the same time, she was filled with a sense of hopelessness. She was terrified about being captured again for she knew what awaited them.

She saw Nikos fighting but he, too, was overpowered.

Once more, their hands were bound. She heard Nikos' cry of pain as his broken wrist was tied behind his back.

Kristoff emerged from the mouth of the cave with a huge grin. He headed straight for Nikos and kicked his ribs. Nikos fell down sideways and the men laughed.

"Not so tough now, huh?" the leader taunted.

Another man punched him in the face. Cassia recognized it as one of the guards they knocked out. Nikos said nothing and just spat out blood on their feet.

"No! Stop it, please!" she shouted.

The leader cupped her jaw painfully and forced her to look at him.

"Tonight you are ours," he declared in a lewd tone.

He forced her to her feet and they began the long walk back to their facility.

The sun was about to set when the woods thinned and they were able to see familiar path to the beach again.

"I'm sorry, Cassia," Nikos whispered to her before they were forced back to enter the cold, dark place that served as their prison.

"It's not your fault," she told him.

Suddenly, the man beside Cassia fell. She screamed when she saw their eyes stare sightlessly ahead. She screamed again the moment she saw that there were bullet holes in their heads. But she didn't hear any sound of gunfire so what was used could have been silenced weapons.

Two more of their kidnappers fell. Those were the ones holding Nikos. When the rest of their kidnappers saw their fallen comrades, they immediately went into alert. The men around her crouched and Kristoff started to shout orders in Greek. Nikos crawled towards her and forced her head down.

"Trust Alex to come in the nick of time," he told her and there was hope in his voice.

More shots were fired and the men were all shouting. Cassia barely understood a word they said.

"When I say run, we run to the other side of the bushes. We're not safe here. Got it?"

She nodded.

Nikos counted to three and then they stood up and ran. She took his arm and placed it around her shoulders again so that she could help him. Their kidnappers saw their escape and chased after them but the men were all immediately cut down in a hail of bullets. Cassia looked up as they ran and saw that there were several snipers perched above the thick branches of the trees.

When they reached the bushes, two men emerged from it and ushered them closer. They wore black turtleneck shirts with Kevlar vests over them. Then, they wore black cargo pants to which various weapons were strapped.

One of them pulled his mask off and Alex's relieved face came into view.

Cassia and Nikos both sighed with relief.

Alex barked a couple of orders into his earpiece and then they were moving. Several men were left behind to cover their back. The others surrounded Nikos and Cassia and killed anyone who tried to follow them.

After another long walk, they were now in Alex's boat. He sat beside them as the medic tended to them. When their wounds were treated the boat sped off to the mainland.

"Anyone hurt?" Alex asked

Both of the former captives shook their heads.

"Stay here. You're safe here. Let me just see to my men and we'll see if we can find any evidence or if there are any of your kidnappers left alive. I sure as hell hope there's at least one of those assholes left for questioning."

"Their leader is the tall, black-haired man. His hair is up to his shoulders and he has a scar on his left cheek," Nikos told Alex

"I'll do my best," Alex replied with a malicious grin.

Some of Alex's men followed him back to the forest while more stood guard in the boat. The medic quickly tended to their wounds. Afterwards, they made themselves comfortable as they waited for Alex and his men.

Cassia woke up and the boat was already moving. She did not know how much time has passed. She looked around and saw Nikos was sleeping peacefully beside her. Alex sat beside Nikos and he was leafing through a stack of papers.

"What happened?" she asked groggily.

"We went back and gathered as much as we could. We have their computers and all their files. But their leader got away," Alex hissed. He looked so disappointed that Cassia wanted to soothe him.

She placed her hand on his shoulder and looked into his eyes. "Thank you for saving us, Alex. I know you did your best. Don't worry, I'm sure you'll be able to catch Kristoff soon."

Alex's eyes softened and he covered her hand with his.

"Thank you, Cassia. Nikos is sleeping and you should too. Get some rest. I know how difficult the past few days were for you. I'll wake you up when we're in the docks."

Cassia nodded and obeyed Alex's orders.

About two hours later, they reached Athens. The moment they arrived at the docks, there was already a large crowd waiting for them. Most of them were people from the media. Immediately after they went down, there was a barrage of flashes from their cameras. Also, microphones were thrust at them from every direction.

There were so many questions thrown from left and right that Cassia couldn't even properly hear one. Her mind reeled from the sudden noise.

"Is it true you've been kidnapped?"

"Please tell us what happened, Mr. Demakis!"

"Is it true that the Greek drug cartel is involved here?"

"How much did you pay as ransom?"

Alex barked an order and his men began to circle them and herd the reporters back.

Nikos turned towards them and said, "No comment for now. You'll receive a detailed statement from our public relations team."

After that, they were led to a waiting limousine.

The instant the doors opened, someone that Cassia recognized from the past exited and threw herself against Nikos.

"*Cherie*! I was so worried! It's all over the news and I flew here as fast as I could to see for myself that you're safe!"

She hugged Nikos tightly and rained kisses on his face. Through it all, Nikos just stood there.

Suddenly, it was as if Cassia was plunged in ice-cold water.

Maybe he slept with her. Maybe he didn't.

But what was clear now was that they had enough of a relationship for her to fly all the way here and act this way. Nikos didn't even push her away which just cemented all her beliefs.

How could he do this to her again?

Cassia felt her heart breaking once more.

Everything that happened between them was a mistake. They were all lies. It was just part of the elaborate game that Nikos was playing with her.

He lied when he told her he wanted her. He lied when he said he wanted another chance for their marriage.

Nikos saw her walking towards the other limousine and he was snapped out of his trance. He pushed the clinging Marietta away and grabbed her arm.

"Cassia...it's not what you think..."

"Yes. You're right, Nikos. I thought you were sincere with everything you said. Turns out I was wrong."

She climbed aboard the vehicle and slammed the door. She was surprised when Alex climbed in beside her.

"Cassia...it's not—"

"Not a word, Alex. Please. Let's just go."

Thankfully, Alex did not push the issue further. He just patted her hand and let her be.

She faced the window and let her tears fall...

Three days later and she was on the plane back to America. Again, she left without saying goodbye.

She laughed for her situation was really nostalgic. Ten years ago, she fled Greece in the same situation. Before, her heart was broken and so was her pride. Because of that, she vowed revenge against Nikos.

Now, her heart was broken but there was no more of her pride to break. It was her own damned fault that she was in this situation. She never learned.

As the old adage went:

Fool me once, shame on you. Fool me twice, shame on me.

Chapter 19
Chase

November 26, 2013 (The Next Day)
Athens General Hospital
Athens, Greece

*I*T took one more day after Cassia left before Nikos Demakis awakened.

His body was battered and bruised, and he needed the time to recuperate. He had a broken wrist, two broken ribs, and several cuts and bruises. When he woke up, the first thing he asked for was his wife.

But she was nowhere to be found. Instead it was his personal assistant, James and Alex who sat beside his bed. He never got to talk to her after she saw him with Marietta, and they rode in separate vehicles to the hospital. When they arrived, they were treated immediately and separately. He was heavily sedated for he had more injuries than her.

"How're you feeling?" Alex asked.

"Like I've been run over by a truck. Where's Cassia?"

James and Alex looked at each other.

"Err...she's gone back to America."

"What?!" he roared.

He struggled to sit up and his friends helped him.

"When did she leave?"

"Yesterday. I think she misunderstood Marietta's presence here,

Nikos. I saw the look on her face. That was how she looked like ten years ago when you threw her out."

Nikos flinched. Marietta truly brought him nothing but heartache-- along with a pounding headache.

"For years after our affair ended, she wanted to get back with me. I told her it was over. But she kept coming back. Maybe I should have asked for a temporary restraining order," he sighed.

"I think I can have her assassinated. Say the word," Alex teased.

Nikos rolled his eyes. He wanted to go to Cassia right now and explain. He wanted to see her smile again and know that it was him who caused it. This time around, he wouldn't let a misunderstanding separate the two of them.

"No need, Alex."

"I'd do it for free for Cassia. I hated how she looked when she boarded that plane. I knew what she felt was killing her and it damned near killed me too," Alex groaned.

"Prepare the private jet, James, and prepare all necessary documents. We're going to America."

His assistant flinched and paled.

"Sir...I'm sorry but that's not possible at this time. First of all, you're not yet cleared for discharge. Second, the board of directors is already waiting for you and your report. I have already given a statement to our PR Department for damage control but the board members themselves want to see you. Then, there's the *Higeshima Deal* which will commence in about a week."

"Cancel everything, I need to go to America," he said without preamble.

"Sir. I strongly advise against this. You would also have to release your statement to the press. Give me two weeks sir and after that I will clear your schedule."

"Two *fucking* weeks?! Is there no other way?"

"I'm afraid not."

He sighed and flopped back down on the bed.

"Call a flower shop in America. I'd like to send Cassia flowers."

"Excellent, sir. I'll choose one and have them sent to her right away."

He shook his head. "*Ochi*, James. Call them and I'll choose one, myself."

Nikos didn't know who was more shocked with his declaration: Alex or his assistant. Alex raised an eyebrow at him while his assistant hid his surprise better and proceeded to do as he was told.

A moment later, Nikos was lost in a wide selection of flowers. At first, he spoke with the shop manager who then tried to explain to him in great detail how the bouquets looked. But Nikos couldn't choose based on words. He wanted the best for Cassia so he asked for a video call so he could see everything. He even asked the shop manager what the different colors and blooms meant.

He was on the phone for more than thirty minutes before he was able to make a selection.

December 23, 2013
Cassiopeia
Fifth Avenue, New York City

"Delivery for Mrs. Cassia Demakis?"

Her staff all rolled their eyes at the same time. They looked at each other to check who would be accepting the deliveries. The task fell to Anna, Cassia's best friend and general manager for Cassiopeia.

"When is he going to stop? It's got to the point that it's irritating and pathetic."

"I've told him to stop but he says he won't until I forgive him," Cassia replied with a sigh.

For the past month, Nikos had been sending her flowers thrice a day. The first week, it was accompanied by letters. He kept on explaining that there was nothing going on with him and Marietta.

He explained to her that they'd broken up a long time ago and were only acquaintances but she refused to let him go and had been pestering him ever since. He explained that he knew he was mistaken for not setting her right and telling her they didn't really have any future together.

Cassia ignored all of it and threw the letters in the trash. She didn't care if Nikos was with Marietta or not. She was done with him. She'd been a fool twice and she wouldn't open herself up for a third time.

Cassia pulled her phone out of her pocket and glanced at the screen.

Still no word from Hector.

She returned to New York as he came out of hiding just to make sure she was safe. He picked her up at the airport then drove her to her apartment. She ached to tell him about the ordeal she suffered but he was too busy talking on the phone to notice her.

She just sat there in his car as she waited for him to finish.

Then, he dropped her off at her apartment and told her he couldn't stay. He ordered her to stay put and that he would contact her.

But it had been nearly a month and still there was *nothing* from him.

She was snapped out of her thoughts when Anna handed her another wooden case for her to stack on the shelves.

"I'm just curious, you know. He wants to apologize but he's never been here and it's been a month. If it was me, I'd have come here in the flesh."

"He's busy. There are a lot of things that have been going on with the company. There's this deal that's been falling apart and then he had to handle the media after our kidnapping."

"Why are you even defending him?" Anna glared at her.

Cassia shrugged, "I'm not. I'm just stating facts."

The doorbell rang again.

"I'll get it," Anna said as she ran towards the door.

Cassia finished placing the boxes back on the shelves and dusted her hands. She was so tired and she just wanted to return home and buy herself take-out dinner.

"Err...Cassia, speaking of the *devil*."

"What?" Cassia grabbed her purse and followed her friend to the front of the shop. There, she saw Anna glaring at Nikos.

Her breath caught in her throat as she saw him in the flesh. He was still as handsome as ever. He wore a finely-tailored gray suit and was holding another bouquet of flowers in front of him. This was the biggest and most elaborate one yet.

"What are you doing here?" Cassia spat.

"I came to see you. I would've come sooner but there were a lot of things I had to do."

He handed her the bouquet of roses and Anna took it from her.

"Okay. You saw her. Now you can go."

Anna shooed Nikos away and the two glared at each other.

"I was hoping we could talk."

"There's nothing for us to talk about, Nikos."

"There's a lot for us to talk about. Hear me out, Cassia. Please?"

"No."

Cassia grabbed Anna's purse from the table near the register and handed it to her. She tugged her friend outside the door and both of them locked-up the shop as quickly as they could.

"Let's go."

She grabbed Anna's hand and went to the other side of the street where her car was parked.

Suddenly, she was lifted off her feet and carried over Nikos' shoulder.

"Put me down you brute!" she shrieked.

"Hey!" Anna shouted.

The people in the vicinity all turned to look at them with curiosity. Some looked at Nikos warily.

Nikos smiled that charming smile of his at everyone who turned to look. "Just settling a domestic dispute with my wife. She's being stubborn," he told them. The others turned away and continued what they were doing.

"Miss, is this man really your husband?" one man shouted. Nikos heard the man's companion order him to call the cops.

"No need! He's my husband. *Unfortunately.*"

Some laughed. The man and his companion turned and walked away. When no one else paid attention, Cassia pinched Nikos' arm.

"Put me down now! You're causing a scene!"

"*Ochi.* I'm kidnapping you so we can talk and you can't do anything about it," Nikos told her as he brought her to his car.

He nodded to his bodyguards and they opened the door. Their faces remained completely blank to what Nikos was doing. One of them even held Anna back.

"We're going to talk, you and I. And you can't run away this time. I refuse to have another misunderstanding keep us apart."

He gently placed her inside the car and climbed in after her.

She tried to get out but the doors were immediately locked and only the driver could unlock them.

"Let me out of here!" she screeched.

"My hotel. Drive," Nikos told the driver who quickly sped off.

December 23, 2013
Nostos Hotel
New York City

Nikos dumped Cassia on the bed and sat beside her.

He pinned her arms by her sides so she couldn't escape and looked straight into her hazel eyes.

"What's the matter with you?" he hissed.

"Me? It's you who kidnapped me here!"

"*Ochi.* No. I mean what happened to you? I thought that we were okay back on the island and then you suddenly disappear on me! You didn't reply to any of my letters or emails and did not answer any of my calls."

"Well, I thought that since you already have Marietta with you, you have everything you need."

Nikos stiffened and then he sighed. He finally realized what was going on here. Alex was right.

"That day back at the docks...it was nothing. Alex told me she wanted to come see for herself that I was fine. She thinks we're still together but we've broken up a long time ago. She keeps on thinking there's still something else between us. There's nothing, Cassia."

"Lies! From the looks of that, she's still your mistress—"

"After I was kidnapped, I didn't sleep with anyone for two years!" he cut her off.

Nikos took several deep breaths to calm himself. He stood up and faced away from her.

"I told you I am a broken man, Cassia. I've never even slept peacefully after I was kidnapped. I can't because every time I close my eyes, I am drowned by nightmares. I haven't been with anyone else because I can't trust them to look at my scars...I can't trust them enough to fall asleep and let them hear what torments me. If you want, I can contact all the doctors I've seen and ask for my medical records."

"N-no..." She remembered waking him up from his nightmares well enough.

"I just want you to know I have wanted to come here since the day you left me at the hospital. They asked me to stay for three more days before they cleared me for discharge. Then there was the media frenzy because of our kidnapping. Then I had to fix the *Higeshima* deal."

"I am aware what happened with that and I am happy that it pulled through."

"*Ne*. But it took me almost a month before I could come here. So I sent you flowers and letters in my stead."

Cassia scoffed, "Your assistant did, you mean?"

"No. I remembered what you told me when we were in that island. This time, it was me who chose all of that."

Her jaw dropped.

"Y-you did?"

Nikos nodded.

"I am serious about wanting another shot at our marriage, Cassia."

For the first time tonight, she was speechless.

"I am never letting you go. You are going back to Greece with me."

Her ire came back in a snap just like that. "*What?!*"

Nikos just raised an eyebrow for he was sure she perfectly heard him.

"We are not going back to Greece! It was a disaster last time! And I could not leave my shop just like that!"

"It's final, Cassia. We are going to Greece. I hired more security this time. We are going to Athens by plane and then we are going to take a helicopter to go to my island. I am not taking any chances with our safety now."

"We've had this argument before, Nikos. I have a life here. I can't just take off on a whim."

"You can. And does that life still include Hector Petrides?" he snarled.

Cassia lifted her chin.

"I heard he was hiding from the drug cartel. Alex told me he lost an entire shipment worth about a billion dollars. There's no going back from that Cassia. Either he finds the shipment or he's a dead man. He'll never be with you. Have you spoken to him in the last few days?"

That struck something deep inside of her. Hector hadn't talked to her for more than a month already. During that time, over and over, she had thought about their relationship. They were great friends but they never really had much when it came to a romantic relationship.

Hector was never there.

When he was, he was busy and preoccupied. He was never open to her and she lately found out about the dark secrets he harbored - secrets which nearly cost her life.

How were they going to have the family she wished for when he was never going to be free of a drug cartel?

They never released their people. Once you were in, you were in for life.

She glanced down at the ring she wore. She slid it off her finger and placed it in her bag. She was waiting for Hector to talk to her so they could end their relationship. Once she spoke with him face to face, she would be returning his ring.

They were really better off as friends; they would never work as lovers. She had to talk to him and end it all before it got even more complicated. It wasn't something easy and it hurt, for he'd been there for her for the longest time.

But it had to be done.

"He's not in my life anymore," she whispered.

"Good. It will never work between the two of you," Nikos said as he knelt in front of her and took her hand.

"And you think it will work out between us, Nikos?"

"I know it would. I'll do *everything*," he vowed.

"This is all going so fast. Can't you give me some time to think about it instead of forcing me to Greece?"

"I can't. I've waited for a month already," he groaned.

She sighed.

"Then at least give me tonight, I have a night out with my friends. I'll take as many bodyguards as you want. Just let me go."

"Tell me where you'll go and I'll drop you there and pick you up myself. And you must always be within the line of sight of your bodyguards."

She nodded but sighed and rolled her eyes, "Fair enough."

"So what time are you supposed to be there?"

"Around two hours from now."

"Great."

He grinned and took her hand.

"Where are we going?"

"Dinner, of course."

Nikos didn't let go of her hand as they made their way from the penthouse suite to one of the most elegant restaurants in his hotel. It was always full and you had to have reservations a long time prior to eating there. Unless of course, like Nikos you owned the hotel.

Like a perfect gentleman, he helped her to her seat. The waiter introduced himself and they were handed their menus.

"I've heard of this restaurant for a long time now but it's the first time I've actually been here."

"This is a great place. It is owned by Antonio, by the way. His restaurants are in all of my hotels. Antonio is an excellent chef and a businessman. We started this when we were fresh out of college."

"Wow. I never knew Antonio was a chef."

They placed their orders and resumed talking. Nikos told Cassia all about Antonio, his wife and their newest addition to the family. He told her how adorable baby Anton was and how he drove his parents crazy.

Cassia laughed and she realized she was really enjoying herself tonight. Nikos kept on entertaining her with his brilliant stories about his travels, the business and almost everything else under the sun.

She was never bored and she found herself wanting to visit the places he's been. He told his stories so vividly that it was as if she was experiencing it firsthand.

She also marveled at how fun it was to eat dinner and talk. Usually, when she was with Hector, she was silent as he had to talk to somebody on the phone. If he was not on the phone, he was busy checking his emails. They never really talked.

Cassia glanced at her watch and saw that it was almost time to go to her friends.

It was true what they said: time really flew when you were enjoying yourself.

December 23, 2013
Club Harmony
New York City

"I'll pick you up at exactly 2AM. Would that be all right?"

She nodded.

"Have fun then. And please always stay where your bodyguards can see you."

Cassia nodded and watched as Nikos sped off in his black Lamborghini.

She hurried inside the club and was met with the loud music and crazy lights. She went through the throng of people who were grinding at each other on the dance floor. Several men stopped her and asked her to dance, but she just smiled and shook her head.

She and her friends had a VIP booth on the second floor of the bar. Cassia evaded more men asking her to dance and quickly climbed the stairs. She entered the VIP room reserved for them and breathed a sigh of relief when the music wasn't so loud anymore and she could hear her own thoughts.

Going to clubs and dancing wasn't really her *thing*.

"Earth to Cassia," her friend said as she waved her hand in front of Cassia's face.

"Hmm?" she murmured distractedly.

"You're zoning out. Repeatedly," Arlene, another one of her friends and most loyal customers pointed out.

"Oh, sorry. It's just that I really have a lot of things on my mind right now."

She thought of Nikos and how much she enjoyed their dinner. She kept on telling herself they had nothing in common but it turned out, they did. Tonight, they never ran out of anything to say and she found herself immensely enjoying his tales.

"Humph. Maybe in your head, you're still in bed with your handsome hunk of a husband," Arlene giggled.

Cassia told her friends before what happened when they were kidnapped.

She frowned and then snorted, "I'm not."

Arlene raised her eyebrows and then leaned closer and stared into her eyes.

"Did he finally send enough flowers to make your house and your shop collapse? What is up with you guys now? Did you forgive him?" another long-time friend named Isobel asked.

Cassia sighed and took another sip of her cocktail.

"Aha! I knew it!"

"So, spill."

Cassia rolled her eyes heavenward.

"I don't have anything to spill."

"Clearly, you do," Jenna disagreed.

"Cassia, come on! Are we not your friends? Tell us what's bothering you! Maybe we'd be able to help. We're also married, you know," Arlene persisted.

"Yeah, we could give you great advice," Isobel quipped.

"You're not married, Isobel! How can you give her advice?" Jenna laughed.

"I'm not. But I know that men are devious little creatures. Also, I know how much pain they can bring and I've dealt with it. So if that's what is happening to our friend here, I think I can give pretty good advice in that area."

They were all silent after that for they knew Isobel's past.

Cassia sighed. "Thanks, Izzy," she said affectionately.

"Don't keep us in further suspense!"

"All right, all right..." Cassia murmured under her breath. "It's just that...I don't know what to do with Hector anymore and Nikos just complicates everything!"

Isobel scoffed. She really hated Hector right from the start.

"What did Hector do now?" Arlene asked in an irritated tone.

"Besides never being there, you mean?" Isobel interjected.

Cassia rubbed her temples. "I don't know what to do anymore. I thought he was the perfect guy—"

"Excuse me, Cassia. Pardon the interruption but...he's not."

"I agree with Isobel. You were just too blind to see all his faults."

"We've told you this over and over again. You keep on telling yourself he's great but he's not. First of all, he's never there for you. When you guys talk, it's always about him."

"Plus the fact that there's just something evil about that man," Isobel shuddered.

"True. When you look at his eyes, it's like he's hiding something deep, dark and sinister."

For another ten minutes, her friends continued to rant about how they hated Hector and outlined his faults. For the first time, Cassia listened to them and compared what they were saying to the things she experienced when she was with him.

All of it was the truth.

She had her eyes closed during their relationship and now they were finally opened. It seemed she was wrong about everything and she kept her eyes and ears shut during the entire relationship. He stayed by her side throughout the years but he was preoccupied with his own business. He wasn't there or he was late during her accomplishments but she was in every one of his.

Then, there was the issue of his temper.

"I swear he's bipolar or maybe he has multiple personalities," Isobel pointed out.

"How come?"

"When we're with him, he's like sweet and all. Then he gets this call and he flies into a rage! So scary! Then, it's like he switches off everything, and he's back to being sweet. It makes me feel like he's just acting."

Jenna was right. That always happened. There was even one time that Hector slapped her. He quickly apologized and told her that it was an accident. She believed him but since then, she did everything not to rile his temper.

Cassia sighed. She truly had to end things with Hector. There was simply no future for them and it looked like she was just convincing herself he was perfect all along.

"You all know how my marriage started, right?"

Cassia decided it was finally time to talk about Nikos. She needed some advice on what to do about him. He was the only aspect of her life wherein she couldn't think rationally.

"Yes, we do. Which brings us to another important topic. Have you forgiven him? Has the relationship between the two of you gone from enemies to lovers?"

"It's not like that...I don't really know what's going on right now," Cassia groaned.

"So spill the story," Isobel said with a wave of her hand.

"On our tenth wedding anniversary, we had dinner and he told me that he wanted us to start being a true husband and wife. He wanted us to start living together and for me to provide him with an heir. I threw it back to his face and laughed. Then we got kidnapped."

She breathed in deep before continuing

"...I've spent time with him on the island and found out several things from our past. All of it was a lie and a misunderstanding caused by my grandfather. He orchestrated all this and we were both victims."

"Victims? What about what he did to you after your wedding night? He slept with another woman, remember?"

"No. He didn't. Marietta climbed into the bed just as he was showering. It was his grandfather's suite. He didn't know she was there."

Her friends looked at each other as if they did not know what to say. Some looked as though they weren't sure if they would believe what she just said.

"When we were together it resurrected feelings I'd buried deep. I felt things I shouldn't. When I look at him now, I see the guy I fell in love with ten years ago. Sometimes it's also as if he's giving me a promise of what's to come if only I gave in and decided to stay with him for good. It freaks me out because I like it! I like how being with him feels!

It's bad because when I'm with him, I forget the past ten years and instead hope that I'd have ten, twenty, maybe even a hundred years with him if I could..."

Cassia's words trailed off and she found that all pairs of eyes were on her. Her friends knew exactly what she was feeling, especially the married ones. They knew that when love hit, it hit hard. Love made you forget past mistakes and gave you hope for the future.

"So what's the problem dear? What's holding you back?"

"A lot of things! I still have Hector to consider—"

The moment she said Hector's name, everyone else groaned.

"We're done discussing him. He's old news," Arlene declared.

"You deserve someone better and I think if you open your heart. Nikos is that someone," Jenna told her.

"Amen to that," Isobel replied.

She raised her glass in a toast.

The others also raised their shot glasses and drank. When the alcohol was done burning a path down their throats, they turned back to Cassia.

"What do I do?" she moaned. She covered her face with her hands and wished that the ground would just swallow her right now and end her torment.

Her friends waved their hands towards a passing waiter and ordered another round of shots for all of them. When the new batch was placed on their table, Isobel leaned forward and looked her straight in the eyes.

"Life is a gamble. There are no sureties. If you want something, you have to take a leap of faith," Isobel lectured.

"Wow, wise words, Izzy!" Arlene interjected and all of them laughed.

Isobel just rolled her eyes. "As I was saying, what I suggest is for you to give him a chance. Say, give him two weeks and lay down your rules. If by the end of two weeks, you find out that you're really incompatible, leave and never look back. At least you tried. But if he makes you fall in love with him again and everything's great...then it's happily ever after for you guys."

Isobel had a point.

But if she opened her heart and gave Nikos another chance, she'd be vulnerable to another wave of pain! Then what if it all didn't work out?

What would happen to her then?

"But...I can't...it's hard. I don't want to be hurt again."

"You know...the guy is trying and you're putting up this wall because you're afraid to get hurt. It's not fair to him, Cassia," Arlene told her.

"There's never a constant thing in life and love and you can never predict what will happen. All you can do is give it a chance and hope that everything works out in the end. We told you to give Nikos a chance and that chance entails you removing all negative thoughts regarding your relationship. Remove your biases, my dear, and the happiness will follow," Isobel advised.

Her friends all had a point.

After everything that happened, it was really hard to trust Nikos. She felt as though everything was too good to be true and that if she so much as blinked, all of it would change again. But Nikos was really trying while she was too afraid to give him a chance.

Could she take that blind leap of faith and hope that he was there to catch her?

"So what's it going to be?" Isobel asked.

"You're right girls. What else do I have to lose other than my heart which I already gave him ten years ago, anyway? So I'm thinking that I'm taking that leap of faith. You're right; it's time to settle down."

The girls shouted their glee at that statement, and they congratulated their friend by downing another round of shots.

"Okay then, we have something else to celebrate tonight! Drink up, me hearties yo ho!" Isobel imitated Captain Jack Sparrow from the Pirates of the Caribbean.

At this point, Cassia's stomach hurt from laughing so much and her heart truly felt light. It was as if a huge burden had been taken off her shoulders.

"And then we go dancing!" Jenna shouted.

Her statement was met with another round of giggling and shouting. This time, Cassia giggled and shouted along with them.

She just couldn't wait to take that leap of faith with Nikos.

Chapter 20
Falling

"I cannot believe that it's been a month and we still do not have them! How many times must you fools fail before we finally get Demakis so we can stop hiding?" Sebastian growled.

"Boss, his security is tighter. Even his wife's. If we try, we are going to lose more men and only risk exposing ourselves."

"I have trusted you for too long now and all you did was fail. I'll just do things myself!" He turned and grabbed his phone.

"Get everyone ready, we're flying to Greece. It's time I took things in my own hands."

December 23, 2013
Nikos' Car
Near Fifth Avenue

"Had fun, *agapimeni*?"

Nikos took her hand and lifted it to his lips as he waited for the light to change.

"Lots and lots," Cassia tried to keep her voice from breaking.

She shuddered as Nikos kissed her wrist.

"Good. I've asked your assistant to pack your things. They are waiting for you at the airport. I asked regarding your schedule and so far you do not have anything. But if you need to work or something comes up, the jet is at your disposal."

Nikos ran his hand through his hair and placed it back on the shift as the light changed. "I want to take you somewhere you've never been. But the 100th anniversary for *Demakis Shipping Corporation* is in a few days and we have to be there."

"Okay," she replied with a shrug.

Nikos looked dumbfounded. "What? No argument?"

She rolled her eyes. "None. Would you like me to give you one?"

"No! It's just new. That's all. I quite like it," he grinned.

"One month, Nikos. I am giving you one month. I am putting my full trust in you and willing to give whatever we have a try. If by the end of one month we still don't work out, you have to let me go."

Nikos' smile widened.

"One month? You're mine by that time, *glikia mou*. I accept your challenge."

He turned those green eyes and their full ferocity bore into her. She saw his joy reflected in them and her heart skipped a beat.

"You better not hurt me, Nikos. This is the last chance."

"I won't."

He sealed his promise with a kiss.

December 25, 2013
Nikos' Home
Island of Skorpios, Greece

"Wake up, Cassia...it's Christmas!"

Cassia groaned and rolled over. She was not really feeling well this morning. Her stomach churned and she was nauseated. It was definitely something she ate last night at the Christmas Party they attended. Or maybe she caught some kind of stomach bug?

"Come on, *glikia mou*. You'll miss all the presents I have for you."

She felt the bed dip and Nikos was sprawled beside her. Then, she felt his lips trail a path across her neck while his finger drew lazy patterns on her hip. Her cheeks flamed when she recalled what they did last night.

She groaned and tried to cover her face with a pillow. The pillow had

Nikos' scent and it was enough to set her blood on fire. He nibbled on her earlobe and she shivered with desire.

"All right, I'm up," she sighed. She moved slowly to keep the nausea at bay.

"Great!" Nikos sped off across the room and brought back several items which he dumped on the bed.

"First things first."

He handed her an envelope. When she opened it, it was filled with different cheques addressed to the charities she sponsored. The amount on the cheque made her eyes wide and knocked the breath out of her lungs.

"Nikos...this is...I have no words! Thank you!" she stammered.

Before she could stop herself, she threw her arms around him and hugged him tightly. The world tilted to the side and bile rose in her throat but she didn't care.

He laughed at her enthusiasm. "There's more."

He gave her a small box. She tore the wrapping paper and opened it. Inside was a key.

"That's the key to your new car. It's a Hummer and it's in the garage downstairs. I got sales-talked into buying it because of how safe it is. It's practically built like a tank and your safety matters to me a *lot*."

She had the urge to roll her eyes. Nikos was so paranoid about these things that it was sometimes funny. What was she going to do with a car the size of a truck? How was she going to drive and park something that big?

Oh well, it was the thought that counted.

"Do you like it? If not, I could have that replaced."

"No! I love it."

The uneasiness faded from his face and it was replaced with that heart-stopping smile. Cassia moved past him on the bed so she could reach for the gift she bought for him. She only had one day to shop here in Greece and she spent it trying to find something for him. It was hard for she didn't know much about what he liked and if there was something he needed.

She grabbed it but he handed her another box before she could give him his. She looked into his eyes as she tugged the ribbon and she saw hope and sincerity in them. There was also a hint of fear and vulnerability. She snapped the lid open and was greeted by the sight of her wedding and engagement rings.

"The engagement ring belonged to my grandmother. She gave it to my grandfather for him to give their son's bride when the day came. But my mother didn't like it so my father bought her a new one. *Pappou* gave it to me and I gave it to you."

"It's beautiful..."

"I know we're still in that trial period but nothing would make me happier than if you wore them again. I want people to see those when we go to the *Demakis Shipping International* anniversary party."

He held up his hand and gave a nervous laugh. There was a glint of gold; he was wearing his own wedding ring.

Her heart melted. He was really trying and doing his best to make this work. She held out her hand to him.

"Put it on me, then."

He pulled her closer and enveloped her hand in his.

"The first time I did this, I was too drunk to know what I was doing. I just wanted to find a place where I could lie down and sleep. Now, I do know what I am doing. With this ring comes a promise. I promise to give you all of me: my fidelity, my trust, my love..."

He placed both rings on her finger and bent his head to kiss her knuckles. Her breath caught at his words and she felt a blush heat her cheeks. All her life, she'd never heard words more romantic. She'd read them in books and heard them in movies but she never had them being spoken to her...

Until now.

"Am I winning your heart yet?" he whispered.

It had become a habit of his to ask her those words. It had been three days now and every time he told her something sweet, a gesture or a gift, he jokingly asked her that.

In truth, he was getting there but she didn't want to answer his question right away. He had a lot to make up for and she refused to concede at once. She also refused to acknowledge that she was falling fast for her own husband.

January 8, 2013
The Andrade-Demakis Shipping Corporation

Athens, Greece

"Have I told you that you look exquisite tonight?"

"Nope. I believe you haven't," Cassia replied.

Nikos smiled and patted her arm which was wrapped around his as they waited to be announced into the grand ballroom.

"Well, dear wife, you look absolutely ravishing. All of them pale in comparison," Nikos told her sweetly as he gestured towards the women scattered around the foyer.

Cassia snorted as he pointed towards tall, svelte models that she thought she really didn't compare to.

"I should only have eyes for you, remember?" Nikos teased and Cassia slapped his arm and rolled her eyes. She was feeling a bit queasy again but she attributed it to nerves.

This was a grand party for the 100-year celebration of the Demakis side of the corporation. It was a lavish event and there were several notable people in the crowd. Cassia fanned herself to chase away the nausea.

She also felt a bit tired and this she blamed on jet lag. After Christmas, they flew to Barcelona to be with Antonio, his wife and their son. She enjoyed meeting them, and holding little Anton in her arms made her long for a baby of her own.

During the past few days, Nikos toured her around Barcelona. He relayed her stories that Antonio told him about his home. She enjoyed herself too much. When Nikos set his mind to being a charmer, he really pulled out the big guns and she couldn't help but be swept away.

"Mr. Nikos Demakis and his wife Mrs. Cassia Andrade-Demakis, CEO and major shareholders of the *Andrade-Demakis Shipping Corporation*!"

The two of them were announced and they descended the wide staircase towards the grand ballroom. All eyes were on them for this was the first time they were seen together after they being kidnapped. Both of them painted smiles on their faces and waved at the crowd.

Cassia was decked out in a beautiful flowing lavender gown. It was wide at the sleeves and tight on the waist. The cleavage was so low that she thought Nikos' eyes were going to pop the first time he saw her in it.

Truth be told, she really chose this dress to vex him. She designed it herself and she knew he would feel all possessive over it and ask her to change. But he took one look at her and his eyes clouded with desire. She still remembered the look of pure need that he gave her and shivers of desire slid down her spine.

"You like it? Aren't you going to ask me to change? What will people think?" she teased.

"They will think that you are the most beautiful woman there and I am the luckiest man. They will see you and they will envy what I have because they can only look. But I can touch and all of it is mine," he rasped in that deep baritone of his.

She shook her head to clear it of those thoughts and focused on walking towards their table. She and Nikos were in the middle of the raised table and on either side of them were the board members and the company's major stockholders with their wives.

Nikos stood up and started his speech:

"Thank you, everyone, for coming. First of all, a pleasant evening to all of you. Welcome to the celebration of the one hundredth year of *Demakis Shipping Corporation*! Of course, this is now merged with Andrade International. Yet another great feat for us," Nikos began. "We have encountered many threats: competition, the changing economy, global modernization, challenges of the weather and so much more. But we are still here one hundred years later. We not only have ships but also planes, cars, trucks, and hundreds of thousands of employees across the globe. What started as one small ship is now an empire. We are stronger than ever! For this we are very thankful. So everyone, please raise your glasses to the continued strength of our company and may good fortune continue to smile upon us."

The room erupted into a round of applause and everyone raised their glasses and toasted the continued success of the company.

"Let the party begin! Please do enjoy yourselves!" Nikos said with a smile before he sat down.

The music resumed and the waiters started serving the food.

Nikos was busy with the board members who kept on engaging him in conversation. He kept on glancing apologetically to Cassia. Even if he was busy talking, he took her hand from under the table and never let go.

"I'm so sorry," he mouthed.

"It's okay," she whispered with a smile.

"You should go with your friends for now. I am very bad company because they all want to speak to me."

"I'll go and do that. I think I'll get myself drunk too so that I can finally have payback for what you did on our wedding."

Nikos groaned and shook his head.

"I'm kidding," she laughed. "Find me when you're done. You owe me a dance."

She winked and then stood up and crossed the room towards the bar.

Cassia spent the time glancing around the room and looking for her friends who were also attending. She found Isobel perched atop one of the bar stools and drinking shots like there was no tomorrow.

"Whoa, Izzy. Slow down."

"I don't want to slow down. He's here, Cassia."

"Who? The one I told you about. The man who made me hate the rest of his species." That got Cassia's attention and her eyes quickly scanned the room.

"Who?"

Isobel sighed, "It doesn't matter."

"Tell me, please! I am dying of curiosity about him!" Cassia tugged on Isobel's hand.

Isobel rolled her eyes and cursed under her breath when she saw the Senator who her father forced her to date walking towards her.

She mustered a fake smile and glanced at Cassia apologetically when the Senator asked her to dance.

Cassia instantly pitied her friend. There couldn't be any girl who hated the male species more than her friend Isobel. She hated men and sworn herself off dating but her father, the President of the United States, was forcing her to.

"She's here," Alex told his friends.

Both Antonio and Nikos straightened and they quickly scanned the room. Their eyes locked on one specific woman. Cassia and Isobel were totally oblivious about the conversation between the three men and how three pairs of eyes were on them.

"It seems like Cassia knows your old flame," Antonio told Alex as they watched Cassia and Isobel on the bar. He nodded quietly and continued to sip his drink.

"She's grown more beautiful with the years. I still remember the two of you back in college," Nikos commented. He was glad at being granted a reprieve from all the people who wanted to speak to him. Now he could kick back and enjoy the party with his friends.

Alex sighed and took another glass of champagne from a passing waiter.

"Too bad for me then that she thinks I've been the villain all along."

"Then maybe it's time you tell her the truth of what happened. It's clear to me that you still want her even after all these years. You've not maintained a serious relationship since the two of you broke up."

"Whoa there. Maybe it's because of the fact that I've been in the military and then the mercenary business that's why there's no time for me to *chase* a relationship?" Alex snorted.

"Keep telling yourself that, buddy. It's clear that you're still smitten with her just like you were in college," Nikos teased and Antonio nodded his agreement.

"Why don't you just tell her the truth? Maybe she'd give you another chance."

"It isn't that easy. Besides, she hates my guts. But I promise you...I'll get her back. I've just seen an offer for a job as her head of security. I think I'll take it." Alex's grin was filled with so much mischief.

"I do not think I like that smile," Nikos groaned.

"Of course. It's clear that he's plotting something," Antonio agreed.

Alex just continued grinning.

"Please don't do anything stupid," Nikos pleaded.

Alex turned around and winked then he disappeared amongst the crowd. Antonio and Elise also made their way towards the dance floor and started dancing.

Nikos was left alone so he went in search of his wife. He found her with her friends, and excused them so they could also spend some time dancing.

"Enjoying your night?" Nikos asked her.

"Hmm...let's see. During the brief time I was away from you, I've already been cornered by about three of your exes. It's the usual thing, nothing serious," Cassia told Nikos as they swayed to the slow melody.

"How did you handle yourself, *agapimeni*?"

"I handled myself well, I suppose. The days when they can put me down are so over."

Nikos threw back his head and laughed.

"You're priceless."

"I am, so you better be sure that you understand my worth before I slip through your fingers."

"Ahh...that already happened once, *glikia mou*. I won't let it happen again," Nikos vowed as he pulled her closer to his chest.

He knew the truth now and he would never let her go. A man was only given one shot at happiness when it came to a woman. He believed she was that shot for him.

Cassia laughed and the sound slid through him like silk.

"You better not be thinking about any of them. Because if you are, I'll cut your balls out and feed them to you."

Nikos raised an eyebrow. "My wife is pure evil," he laughed.

"Nikos," a familiar voice rasped.

Nikos turned around and saw his grandfather, Stavros Demakis.

"*Pappou*!" he greeted as he embraced his grandfather, "I didn't know you would be here."

"I really did not want to go, son. It's just that I heard you were going here with your wife. I just had to see you for you haven't visited me for a long time," his grandfather said in a sad tone.

"I'm so sorry, *Pappou*. I've been very busy and a lot of things have happened."

"We have to catch up about a lot of things. Shall we?" Stavros pointed to the bar.

Cassia noticed that Stavros Demakis was pointedly ignoring her.

"Go Nikos." She smiled at them both.

Nikos reluctantly left her and went to the bar with his grandfather.

"So, how are you, son?"

"I'm fine. Excellent. And you?"

"Never better. Nikos, I'll get straight to the point. I am here for a reason. I heard that you are spending time with your wife. Are you back together?"

"Yes. We are giving this marriage a try," he replied dryly.

Why was his grandfather interested in his marriage all of a sudden?

"Nikos...it's been ten years. You have worked very hard and the company is flourishing. Costas Andrade is now weak. He won't be able to manage anything. That's why he depends on you. You can now repay him every cent we owe. Here's your chance to gain your life back."

Nikos' entire body stiffened after hearing his grandfather's words.

"Pay Costas Andrade and divorce his granddaughter! I know how hard this was on you ten years ago. I am sorry that marriage to her was the only way. But you've suffered enough, Nikos. Now, you can reap the rewards of your hard work. You can divorce her and marry someone of your choosing."

"Pappou—"

"Listen, Nikos. That girl isn't for you. I know she's like her grandfather. Now, you don't have to stay with her. You don't have to let your life be dictated by that piece of paper that's your marriage contract. You can now be free."

Nikos sighed and gulped down his drink. *"Pappou,* I know you want what's best for me. Cassia is the best thing in my life. She wasn't who I first thought her to be. All Costas Andrade told me when I married her were lies. He made me believe the worst of her, made me think that she was greedy and wanted to divorce me so they'd get everything. Now that I've spent time with her, I've fallen in love."

"Nikos—"

*"Pappou...*love is exactly as you told me it was. I remembered all your stories about *yiayia."*

When Nikos was young, Stavros told him a lot about his *grandmother*, whom he loved so much. He taught Nikos a lot of things about love too.

"I can't let her go now. She's different. This is real, *Pappou.* I'm not dictated by that contract we signed anymore."

"Do not make hasty decisions, son!"

"This is not a hasty decision. Believe me, I've thought about this a lot. This is our chance to be together and set everything right like we should have ten years ago."

Stavros Demakis was silent for a long time.

"I cannot believe I am hearing these words from you, Nikos. Since what happened two years ago, you've changed a lot."

"Well, kidnapping takes a lot out of you," Nikos teased in an attempt to make the mood lighter. "Besides, she makes the nightmares go away, *Pappou*. When I'm with her, I dream of a future together. A *family*."

Stavros' eyes softened and he leaned back and whistled. "You're a grown man and everything is up to you, son. I am proud that you are the kind of man that's standing before me today. I only hope you are making the right decisions in life for I would hate to see you be hurt."

"She won't hurt me, *Pappou*. It was I who hurt her so much."

"Well, make amends then. Get started on that family you've been dreaming about! I am an old man, Nikos. I can't wait forever for you to produce a great-grandson that I could bounce on my knee," the old man told him with an excited smile.

Nikos threw back his head and laughed. "I will, *Pappou*. I will."

Nikos returned to his wife who was dancing with Antonio as Elise danced with Alex. He also noticed that while Elise and Alex were dancing, Alex's eyes darted towards Isobel who was dancing with one of the youngest Senators of the United States. He looked at both of them as if he wanted to wring their necks.

When the song ended, he approached them and reclaimed his wife. They danced while she laughed and told him all of Antonio's stories about their antics when they were still on college. Nikos found himself laughing and shaking his head at all the embarrassing things he did in his youth.

Throughout the rest of the night, guests of the anniversary party watched with mixed amazement and curiosity how the previously estranged husband and wife laughed and danced close to each other. Surely, tomorrow this would be the headline in the society pages and not the ball itself.

Or maybe the headline will be about how a Mr. Alex Smith punched one of the Senators of the United States and dunked his head in a bowl of fruit punch...

Chapter 21
Surprise

January 18, 2013
Obstetrics and Gynecology Clinic
Athens, Greece

CASSIA stared at the pink walls as she waited for the result of the blood test that was done.

For the past week, she'd had nausea and she feared she was coming down with something. But she thought it was also something else. She prayed it was the latter.

Today, she finally had the courage to go to the local pharmacy after Nikos left for work. She bought five sets of pregnancy test kits. All five came back *positive*.

She felt like she'd won the lottery!

She wanted to jump up and down with joy but she feared it would jar her baby. So she just ran to her bed and screamed her glee against the pillows. Her joy lasted all through the morning.

But then she thought about the implications.

She was pregnant with Nikos' baby!

Would he be happy about it? Was she ready for them to be a family? Would this affect their relationship?

Having a baby felt very final to her. She was confused about everything else but she was sure about one thing: she was going to keep her baby and raise it well. She did not care about the rest of the world. If Nikos didn't want their child, then to hell with him. He was not needed in their lives.

Now, it was not a memory that she'd bring with her but a piece of him.

An hour later, she dragged herself out of bed and headed to the nearest clinic for her check-up. Her blood was drawn and so was a urine sample.

"Mrs. Demakis?" She was ushered inside the clinic and the doctor smiled. "The results came back. Congratulations! You are pregnant. We'll have to do an ultrasound to check how far along you are. Would that be all right?"

Cassia's grin was wide and she nodded. She was asked to lie down a narrow examination table and cold gel was placed against her abdomen. The probe was placed against her belly and she began to see blurred images.

"There's your baby. I would say you're about six to eight weeks along. Everything looks fine but I will be giving you prenatal vitamins you'll have to take every day. I'll also give you a list of what to avoid and food you can eat during your pregnancy so your baby will be absolutely healthy."

Cassia beamed. She felt as though she was floating on cloud nine. This was absolutely the happiest day in her life! Nothing could mar this perfect day!

The doctor gave her paper towels for her to clean off the gel and then went back to her desk and wrote down her prescriptions. She also printed out several copies of the ultrasound and handed it to her. Tears misted her eyes. It was her baby's first picture!

She sat down and the doctor continued explaining several things regarding her pregnancy. After her prescription was filled out, she returned home with a smile on her face.

She just couldn't wait to tell Nikos! She hoped that he would be happy about it. If not, then she definitely found her reason to leave him.

Her phone rang and she assumed it was Nikos.

"Hey! Guess what?" she blurted out.

"Cassia?"

It was not Nikos' voice but Hector's. In a snap, all her joy faded away.

"Hector? Where are you? Why haven't you called? I haven't heard anything in over a month!"

"I'm sorry, Cassia. We do not have time for this. I'll tell you everything once we're together. Meet me in Santorini. From there on, we'll go to Germany. I have a friend there who can hide us. We'll be safe. But we have to go now."

"What? Hector, I can't just leave like that! You don't call me for a whole month and then you expect me to drop my life and run away with you?"

"Cassia. We do not have time for this," he spoke slowly and emphasized every word.

"Make time, Hector. I am through being in the dark. I am done acting like your faithful lapdog and I am done with waiting for you."

"Cassia, what brought this on?" he sighed heavily.

"The fact that I've been blinded for a long time, Hector. I thought you were perfect because you stayed with me for the longest time, but that wasn't the case. Yes, you stayed physically but you were never there for me in any other aspect."

"I am sorry for my shortcomings. But I will make time for you now, Cassia. Run away with me and I'll give you everything you want."

She sighed as pain pierced her heart.

"Too late, Hector."

There was silence for a long time wherein she only heard his heavy breathing.

"This is about him, isn't it? You stupidly fell for Nikos Demakis again. He's using you, Cassia! He's using your kidnapping as an excuse to protect you, be with you then use you!"

"No. He cares about me, Hector. He's changed. After I was kidnapped, *he* bothered calling me, sending flowers and letters to make sure I was okay. I haven't heard anything from you! You do not care at all!"

Hector laughed.

"You're as naive as ever, Cassia. You did not learn from your mistakes ten years ago."

Something changed in Hector's tone and he sounded so menacing that a shiver of dread slid down her spine.

"Stop this, please, Hector. We've been friends for ten years...we can still be friends."

"No!" he growled. "What is it about Nikos Demakis that the world just seems to bow down to him? Why does he always get what he wants? I thought you were different, Cassia. It turns out you are like them after all..."

"Them? Who's 'them', Hector? What are you saying?" she cried frantically.

"All the others. It's not *fucking* fair!" he roared.

Hector Petrides flew into rage.

He remembered everything he ever experienced growing up as a bastard in the slums of Greece. He remembered how his mother died, begging for attention from his father. He remembered the tortures he had gone through trying to survive. He remembered how he vowed to make them all pay.

"You were the only one I've ever loved. I really thought you were different...At least tell me why, Cassia. Tell me why you choose him over me."

"He's there for me. He protects me. He makes me feel things I've never felt with you...he makes me happy! I'm really sorry, Hector."

"That's not enough reason for me. I know you're hiding something. Tell me!" he bellowed.

Cassia sighed and took a deep breath. She didn't want to lie to Hector especially when she hurt him so much already. But this was just it for them. She couldn't run away with him now because of her baby. If she did, she'd just endanger both of them.

So she opted to tell him the truth directly.

"I think I love him and I am pregnant with his child!"

Hector felt like the world came crashing down on him.

He closed his eyes as pain washed over his body. It was followed swiftly by anger. Once more, Nikos Demakis took what was his, and his rival won. He always *fucking* won.

"This is the ultimate betrayal, Cassia."

"I'm so sorry—"

"I've protected you from everything when I should've killed you from the start. It was because I thought you were different. Now, you and your bastard will die."

"Hector, what?!" Cassia shouted but Hector already ended the call.

Fear spiked within her and she walked as fast as she could back towards her bodyguards. She also took several deep breaths to calm herself. Hector just said those things because he was mad. It was nothing to worry about.

But his tone was not one of mere anger. It was one of fury. It was so extreme that it was not something that was just born today. It felt like he'd harbored it for a long time and she could not control the feeling of dread and sense of impending doom that slid down her spine.

January 18, 2013
Unknown Island
Greece

"Boss, we have something interesting to report."

Sebastian raised an eyebrow and lifted himself from the marble countertop of the bar to look at his men. He dragged the bottle of vodka closer and drank. He was drunk and he was causing a scene but he did not care.

"And what would that be?"

"The men trailing Demakis' wife reported that she bought pregnancy tests from the pharmacy this morning and then visited a doctor just this afternoon. We think she's pregnant with Demakis' child."

Sebastian threw back his head and laughed. He kept on laughing until people were looking at him as though he'd gone crazy.

"Excellent then. Get her and Demakis will pay us anything. Once we have the money, we kill her and let him watch the light fade from her eyes. Then we watch as he loses everything."

Sebastian grinned after he smashed the now-empty bottle.

A week from now, he'd get revenge.

And everything would be over...

January 25, 2013
Antoniou Winery
Santorini, Greece

She was finally going to tell him.

Hell, it'd been a week but she was really going to do it. She was not going to back out now. Nikos truly had the right to know. Besides, seeing him with little Anton confirmed that he was great with kids and she had a feeling he would be a great father as well.

Besides, the time she spent with him had been nothing but bliss. It'd been an adventure and she was glad that she took that leap of faith and gave him a chance.

She finally had everything she wished for in life!

She wanted to be a designer and have a great career. She had that. Cassiopeia was as successful as ever.

She wanted friends who would never ridicule her because she was different or judge her by her social standing. There were Anna, Jenna, Arlene and Isobel.

Lastly, she wanted a family. Nikos was hers and now they had a child on the way.

Surely, nothing could be better than this!

Now, she was back in Santorini where everything began. This was where their wedding was held and in this particular room was where they first shared each other's passion. For a week, Cassia planned everything down to the last detail. She wanted her announcement to be really special.

She went behind Nikos' back to make everything perfect. His friends were all in on it but they were sworn to secrecy. Cassia planned on telling him over a romantic private dinner then there'd be a baby shower with all of their friends after.

Nikos was due to arrive here any moment now and her nerves were eating at her. She was even more nervous now than on her wedding day!

Suddenly the door opened and it made her heart stop.

Nikos strode into the room wearing a huge grin. He quickly went for her and kissed her until she was breathless.

"Is this a second honeymoon, *agape mou*? I love it. It's brilliant!"

His eyes danced with mischief as he pulled her closer and began to kiss his way down her neck. Her knees almost buckled but she tried to be immune to his touch for once. She placed her hands on his chest and pushed him away gently.

"I was thinking we'd have dinner first."

She glanced behind him and pointed at the table laden with food and candles at the balcony.

Nikos raised an eyebrow.

"I really like this day," he whispered tenderly before he let her go.

Once they were seated, Cassia's courage ran away and left her behind again. As she stared into Nikos' green eyes, her mouth ran dry and her well-rehearsed speech vanished.

"Do you want to say something, *agapimeni*?" He looked at her with a puzzled but amused expression as he ate the salad appetizer.

Cassia, on the other hand, just pushed the food around her plate as she tried to find the words. She sighed.

"You can tell me anything, Cassia. Is this about your decision to stay?"

Shocked, she looked up, "Err...w-well...a bit about that."

Nikos groaned, "Please don't tell me you arranged all this just to tell me you'll be leaving me." His voice shook, giving away his fear. He reached for her hand and squeezed.

"No! It's not about that!" she hurriedly comforted him.

"Then what is it?"

She took a deep breath.

"I'm pregnant."

She handed him their baby's first ultrasound picture.

His jaw dropped. His knife and fork fell to his plate with a clatter.

He appeared as though he was in a trance as he stood up, crossed the table and went to her. His eyes were fierce with emotion yet his face stayed the same. He just looked at her for a long time.

"Nikos? Say something please...say you don't want this and I'll go —"

That snapped him out of his trance and he hauled her into his arms.

He hugged her tightly and she realized he was shaking. She pulled back and lifted her head to look at him. For the first time in her life, she saw Nikos Demakis with tears in his eyes.

He grinned, picked her up and twirled her around.

"Thank you, *glikia mou!* Nothing could have made me happier!" he shouted.

He set her down gently but he still did not let her go.

"Never think that I am not happy about this or that I would not accept our child. I want him or her. You're stuck with me from this day forward." Nikos smiled and embraced her tightly.

"I'll go wherever you go, wife."

Those words echoed in Cassia's mind until tears fell from her eyes. She hastily wiped them away with her fingers and looked down so he wouldn't see her cry. Nikos embraced her again and said nothing. He just let her cry on his expensively tailored suit while he rubbed her back.

"Is everything okay?"

She nodded.

"Can we continue our celebratory dinner now? I really love the food and the place you chose. But I do love your news a thousand times better."

Nikos led her back to her seat and they ate their dinner with huge smiles on their faces. He spoke animatedly about his plans for their future and she found herself agreeing with everything he wanted. He promised to cut down his work hours and delegate more especially after their baby came.

They only started to argue when it came to baby names.

When their plates were cleared, Nikos stood up and led her to the bed.

"Should I show you how I want to celebrate?" he purred.

Cassia giggled, "No. I still have one more surprise for you."

She took his hand and led him downstairs to the bigger balcony which overlooked the sea. It was where their wedding and the reception was held. It was also where Cassia asked all their friends to hide and wait for them.

The instant they opened the doors, the lights were opened, confetti was thrown and everyone shouted "Congratulations!"

Nikos laughed as he saw his friends wearing party hats in baby blue and baby pink. He hugged his wife once more and kissed her deeply.

"I said this day couldn't have gotten any better. I was wrong. What the hell was I doing with my life without you, *glikia mou*?" he whispered tenderly before they joined their friends.

Everyone was having fun when suddenly, there was a loud bang!

Everyone looked around and Cassia was the first to scream as the bodyguard beside her fell. There was a bullet hole on his forehead and his eyes stared up sightlessly. It was followed by more gunshots. It was almost drowned by the screams of the other guests as more bodies fell. Those bodies belonged to their bodyguards who were with them in the balcony.

Instantly, everything was in an uproar. Guest screamed and ran everywhere. Suddenly, the door was kicked open and their remaining guards who stood outside entered and ran to her and Nikos. Four of them remained and they circled them with their weapons drawn. Their eyes darted around the room as they herded her and her husband to the exit.

But their path was blocked by huge, burly men clad in black from head to toe. Their faces were covered with masks and they were holding guns. Several weapons were also strapped across their bodies.

Their bodyguards fired their weapons but the men who just arrived were much quicker. Plus they had the advantage of several snipers placed God-knows-where who first killed their guards in the balcony. Cassia whimpered in fear and Nikos held her closer. Slowly, they backed away from the exit.

"Everyone, on the ground now!" one of the masked men shouted.

Their guests immediately complied. Nikos shoved Cassia behind him and looked around. Dread settled in his gut when he saw that none of their guards remained. Antonio and Alex quickly moved behind him. Alex reached for his gun but one of the men kicked it away.

"What do you want from us?" Nikos shouted.

The man in the middle nodded and two of his men moved forward.

"No! Let me go!" Cassia shouted as they grabbed her.

Nikos, Antonio and Alex all tried to fight but the men kicked them back and pointed weapons at their heads.

Cassia's arms were pinned behind her and a pistol was pointed at her temple.

"We need one billion dollars wired to our account or she dies."

Nikos choked on his own breath.

"One billion dollars? Where the hell would I get that much money in such a short time?"

"We don't give a damn. But you should if you want your wife to live."

He sounded a bit familiar but Nikos couldn't recall where he heard that voice. Maybe it belonged to the leader of the group that kidnapped them?

"It's too much! I can't get that much money in a short span of time!" he snarled.

"Then we'll be holding on to her until you get the money ready. Don't do anything funny, Demakis. First your child dies." The pistol was aimed at Cassia's belly.

She gasped and so did all of their guests. Nikos had the urge to jump towards his wife but Alex and Antonio held him back.

"No! Let go of her! I swear I'll get the money!"

Tears fell from Cassia's eyes and every one of them felt like a dagger being plunged in his heart.

"You have fifteen minutes, Demakis. If we don't have the money by then, we plunge a dagger into her belly. Then you have an extra fifteen minutes. By the end of that and still no money? She dies."

Nikos stood there dumfounded.

"Clock's ticking. I suggest you do whatever you can."

The man took out his knife and ran it along Cassia's neck. She whimpered in fear.

Nikos reached for his phone without taking his eyes off her and dialed his assistant's number. He kept his movements slow so as not to agitate the men.

"James. I need to transfer money. One-billion dollars."

His assistant gasped with outrage.

"Sir! That's too much! It will take time!"

One of the masked men approached Nikos and handed him a slip of paper with the account number where the money should be transferred.

"I know. We have a situation. I need it now and I need it fast. Empty as many accounts as you can. Sell my stocks if need be or ask for a loan! Call whoever can help. I need it in fifteen minutes. Listen carefully, here's the account number..."

Nikos dictated the numbers on the paper and James repeated it to him for verification.

"But sir—"

"Lives depend on this, James. Hurry up," he pleaded.

"Tell your assistant that if he alerts the authorities, all of you will die."

His lips pinched in a tight line, he repeated the words to James.

Then, all Nikos could do was to wait. He prayed to all the gods listening that James could find away and beat the odds. He wouldn't let Cassia and his unborn child die. If they did, he'd die along with them.

Antonio approached him.

"Call my assistant as well. I can give you two hundred million."

A look of understanding passed between them. Nikos squeezed his friend's shoulder and breathed a sigh of relief. He called Antonio's personal assistant and asked for the money to be transferred.

"Eight hundred million to go," the leader remarked cheerfully.

Something in his voice was really familiar, even if it was a bit muffled by the mask he wore. He also made an effort to make his voice lower but still there was that niggling feeling that Nikos knew the man.

Ten minutes down on the clock and Nikos started sweating bullets. He kept his eyes on Cassia, and Cassia kept hers on his. He saw her love and her fear shining in them. His own eyes started to water for the second time that night.

"Time's nearly up, Demakis." There were just two minutes to go on the clock.

Suddenly, his phone rang.

"Sir! I managed to get eight hundred million right away. I emptied one of the Swiss accounts and called in a favor from the bank owner himself. Antonio's assistant called me and I already had the money wired to the account. Please confirm."

Nikos faced the men.

"My assistant says the money has already been transferred. Release her."

The leader tipped his chin towards one of his men. He had a laptop with him and quickly confirmed the money transfer.

"You have what you need. Please let my wife go," he begged.

"So sure that I already have what I need? Well, not yet. I've waited for this moment for a long time, Nikos."

"Who are you?!" he growled.

The leader pulled off his mask and revealed a mop of sandy-blonde hair, blue eyes and an evil smile. Cassia gasped while Nikos roared with rage.

"Hector? Why?" Cassia whispered.

"Why? That's a really good question. I'll tell you why. I was born the year 1975. My mother was from America and she chose to live in Greece. Why? Because she fell in *love*. She became mistress to Andrei Demakis—your father, Nikos"

Nikos inhaled sharply.

"Stavros Demakis hated my mother. She was an actress from America. It was not a noble profession for him and because of that, he refused to give us anything. Eventually, Andrei Demakis lost interest with my mother. He accused her of cheating and threw her out the street. He treated us like trash and we were forced to live in the slums."

Nikos paled for he knew where Hector's tale was heading.

"We begged Stavros Demakis for money. My mother just wanted to go back to her family in America. But he turned his back on us and didn't even spare a single euro. When I was four years old, Andrei Demakis married your mother and she had you. You became your grandfather's golden boy and he gave you everything."

"Hector—"

"Don't call me that! I am the first born son of Andrei Demakis. Everything should have been mine! All you have is mine! But what did I have? I had a life where I had to eat scraps, beg for coins. Eventually I joined the drug cartel and they took me in. They taught me everything. Most of all, they gave me the instrument for my revenge."

"Hector...don't do this, please," Cassia begged.

"Shut up! You're one of them now, Cassia! I thought you were the only thing he wanted that he'd never get. I was *wrong*. You fell at his feet just like the rest of them!" he roared. "I've waited for this a long time now, Nikos. I was the one who had you kidnapped two years ago, you know. I wanted revenge and at the same time I wanted all your stocks at the company to be turned over to me. I should be the one handling Demakis International! It is my right as the first son!" he shouted.

Then Hector shook his head. "But my people were so gods-damned incompetent and you were able to escape."

Hector sighed and when he looked up, there was a malicious glint in his eyes.

"I will kill your child and then kill your wife. Finally, I will kill you and take your head to your beloved grandfather."

Hector retrieved his gun and pointed it back to Cassia's temple while his knife was on her belly.

"Say goodbye," Hector commanded.

"Hector...don't," Nikos begged.

"Don't call me Hector. My name is *Sebastian*... and I do what I please."

He pushed Cassia forward. At the same time he pulled the trigger *twice*.

Chaos ensued.

Nikos roared and sprang towards him. Antonio rolled to the side so he could catch Cassia. Alex jumped from his crouch and aimed a kick at the man nearest him. The man staggered backwards and Alex wrested his weapon from his hands. He quickly turned around and started to fire.

The guests screamed and hid behind the tables. But in Nikos' rage, nothing else mattered. He dove toward Hector and the momentum bought them to the floor. He slammed Hector's wrist against the floor and he dropped his gun.

With his other hand, Hector swiped with his knife and Nikos dodged backwards. Hector was still on the floor and Nikos kicked his other arm causing him to let go of the knife. Nikos aimed another kick and this time it was to Hector's ribs.

Alex continued firing towards the men. Several of them dropped dead while more were returning fire. Alex ordered the other guests back and told them to stay down and call for help.

"Get down!" he shouted to them.

On the corner of his eye, he saw one of the men approach Isobel. He fired as he dove towards her.

"Get behind me!"

He crouched and crawled to the corner of the room where the buffet was laid out. He pushed her behind it and checked how much bullets were remaining. He only had two.

"Stay here," he told Isobel who remained silent and shaking from fear.

One of the men pointed his weapon at Nikos while he was on the floor in a struggle with Hector. Alex quickly fired and the man dropped down. Nikos tried to reach for the gun of that fallen man but Hector beat him to it. Alex used his last bullet and fired on Hector but the villain was able to duck.

Alex crawled to the other side of the room so he could get his gun that was kicked away earlier.

On the other side of the room, Antonio was behind one of the tables as he protected Elise and Cassia. Cassia had difficulty breathing and made choking sounds. She spat out blood and Antonio turned her to her side.

"One of her lungs is punctured," Elise murmured as she removed her sweater. She balled it up and used it to stem the bleeding from her wounds.

"My baby..." Cassia whispered weakly.

Elise removed her hand from her stomach and saw that it was where the second bullet went to. She had to be brought immediately to the hospital or she may never survive. But their exit was blocked by the armed men.

Antonio retrieved his phone and called for help immediately. He detailed their situation and he was promised quick response. He only hoped they came in time before any of those who were injured died.

"Are you really going to kill your own older brother, Nikos?"

"I have no brother!" he spat.

"You're right. We're so different, you and I. I'm scum and you're everyone's golden boy."

"Shut up, Hector. You're scum because you chose to be that way. Because you chose to involve yourself with the drug cartel. Because you chose to do this." Nikos waved a hand indicating the entire room.

"Not everyone is born with a silver spoon!" Hector kicked Nikos who staggered backwards. Nikos stood up but his side was pierced with agony. It felt as if one of his ribs was broken but he refused to back.

"You could have gone back. You could have introduced yourself and I could have given you what you wanted."

"I doubt that. I want everything, Nikos. I don't want scraps. I am the rightful heir of Andrei Demakis and I should have been CEO."

"That's your problem then. You're nothing but a greedy bastard who thinks he has the right to everything."

Hector roared and charged. He punched and kicked wildly because of his anger. On the other hand, Nikos did not allow his anger to rule him. He knew Cassia was hurt but unless they beat all the men here, they would not be able to escape.

"I'll kill you. But first, I'll let you watch Cassia die. I'll make you watch as I carve her chest open and tear out her heart. That's the time when I'll kill you," Hector snarled.

Nikos saw red.

He jumped towards Hector and punched him in the face. Hector spat out blood but still had the gall to grin.

"Every second you waste fighting me, she dies slowly."

"Shut up!" he roared.

Nikos charged and they exchanged blows once more.

On the other side of the room, Alex finally found his gun. He waited for the perfect opportunity. While waiting, he took out his phone and sent an emergency message to his team. They were the only ones he trusted and he knew they'd come as soon as they could.

Now, he just had to keep his friends alive.

He saw an opening and fired at Hector. He hit Hector's shoulder and the man crumpled to the ground in pain. Nikos kicked him in the back and the bastard sprawled on the floor.

"Kicking a man when he's already down? Going to kill me now, little brother?" he taunted.

"This is for my wife and my child!" Nikos punched Hector's face again.

Hector's left eye was so swollen that it was almost shut. He laughed still and tried to rise.

Nikos grabbed his half-brother's shirt and shook him hard.

"This is for what you did to Antonio and me!" He continued punching Hector even if pain shot up his arm with every swing. His knuckles might be broken but he ignored the pain. Once more, he punched Hector and that last one was enough to bring instant loss of consciousness.

When the men saw that their leader was unconscious, they started to retreat.

"Let's go! We already have the money!" the one who confirmed the transfer told the rest of the team.

"No one leaves," Alex snarled.

He carefully aimed his gun and fired. He kept on firing and when he was out of bullets, he rushed into the fray, pulling his knife out of his boot. He rolled to the floor and grabbed one of the scattered weapons.

One man came at him from the side and Alex quickly spun and jabbed him with his elbow. It stunned the man then Alex kicked him backwards before he fired. He threw his knife at the one who had the laptop. The knife hit the man in the back and he crumpled to the floor. The man tried to crawl away but Alex ran to him and slammed the butt of his gun at the man's head. Instantly, he was unconscious.

Alex quickly grabbed the laptop then retrieved his knife. He turned to help Nikos.

Nikos was about to rush to his wife when he heard Hector speak, "Kill me now, brother."

"No. That would be a mercy. You deserve to rot in jail."

"Then, I will kill you," he laughed.

Hector grabbed the gun nearest to him and aimed. But Alex fired first. He took his last breath and Nikos watched the light fade from his eyes.

He tried to feel remorse or sadness but there was none. He even felt as if a burden was lifted off his shoulders.

Finally they were all free.

The one who tortured him finally paid.

The threat to his and Cassia's life was eliminated.

Every inch of him ached but he forced himself to stand up and limp to the other side of the room. Alex's team burst in and they finished off the rest of Hector's men. They took the one whom Alex rendered unconscious. When he woke up, he would be their source of information.

One of them also took the laptop and reversed the transaction so that the money would go back to Nikos' and Antonio's accounts.

Minutes after Alex's team arrived, the police and the paramedics came.

Nikos' heart stopped when he saw his wife. She was pale and her eyes were closed. Her face was a mask of pain and her body was coated in her blood. Elise, who tried to help her, was also covered in blood. She cried as she held Cassia's hand.

Dazed, Nikos followed them to the ambulance.

"Sir, we need to see to your wounds as well," the paramedics told him and pointed at his bleeding hands.

"No. Her first."

He climbed inside the ambulance with her for the second time in his life. He winced at the thought but it was all over now. She would never be in danger again.

He took her hand and held tight even as the medics tried to do everything they could. They stemmed the bleeding, placed an intravenous line and hooked her to monitors. They also placed her on oxygen to help her breathe. Nikos saw her vital signs on the monitors. Her pulse was too weak and he knew she'd lost a lot of blood.

"Don't give up, *agapimeni*. Fight for me. Fight for our child," he whispered.

Then, Nikos Demakis bent his proud head over his wife's hand and wept.

Chapter 22
Hope

January 26, 2013
Athens General Hospital
Athens, Greece

"Mr. Demakis?" The doctor finally came out of the operating room and spoke to Nikos.

He stood up followed by Antonio and Alex. They all awaited the news with bated breath.

"She's resting now. Her vital signs are stable and we've retrieved the two bullets. Her right lung has collapsed but a few days of treatment, it will be as good as new. The other bullet went to her abdomen and punctured an intestine but it has also been repaired. So that means no solid food for a while. She'll be here for a long time but I foresee no reason as to why she cannot make a full recovery."

All three of them sighed with relief.

"And our baby?" Nikos whispered.

"Mrs. Demakis had a little bleeding. If the bullet went another inch down, it would have pierced your wife's womb instead. Good thing she was brought here quickly. Your baby's fine, Mr. Demakis. "

"Thank God!" Nikos cried out.

Alex and Antonio patted him on the back. His knees threatened to buckle so he sat. He moved quickly and his chest hurt agonizingly. He had several broken ribs but they'd already been seen to and bandaged tightly.

"When can I see her?"

"She's in the recovery room now. After this, she will be brought to the intensive care unit. If we do not have any complications, you may see her there. But I think she won't be awake for another two to three days."

"Thank you for everything, doctor," Nikos said as he shook the surgeon's hand.

"My pleasure, Mr. Demakis."

"The police and my team just need a statement from you, Nikos. Can you manage that before you go and see your wife? I just need that and then the part of my case about Hector Petrides is closed," Alex asked.

Nikos nodded.

"What's next, Alex?" Antonio asked.

Alex shrugged.

"Hector is just one of the many bosses of the cartel. There are still more. That's the only information I got from the only one from Hector's men that we got alive. After he said that piece, he killed himself." Alex shrugged and ran his fingers through his hair.

"I was just assigned to Hector Petrides so I'll say case is closed. If they want me to investigate further and nail the big boss of the cartel, then that's another matter. Another assignment for me."

A few hours later, Nikos entered the Intensive Care Unit wearing a sterile gown, gloves, mask and a cap. It didn't matter to him that he could only stay for a few minutes instead of sitting by her side through everything.

He'd take as much time as he could get.

He closed his eyes and fought a wave of pain the first time he saw her. She looked so fragile lying there. She was connected to so many tubes and machines that he feared to touch her. Her beautiful skin was now pale and covered in bruises.

He felt his eyes fill with tears once more and he fought them back. He would not be weak now. Cassia needed him and he needed to be strong for both of them. His tears would do nothing to help.

He took her hand and squeezed.

"*Koúkla*, I'm here..."

She looked so fragile yet still looked beautiful.

"Hang in there, okay? Be strong for me. I'll be here. I won't leave you. I'll stay here and guard you and our baby."

He kissed her cold fingers and brushed away the tendrils of hair from her face. Then, he stared at her while he prayed to whoever might be listening to give her a full recovery.

February 1, 2013
Athens General Hospital
Athens, Greece

It took five days before Cassia finally woke up.

Those five days were hell for her husband. Two days ago, she was already out of the intensive care unit and was brought to the largest suite in the hospital. Through it all, Nikos never left her side. He had Alex and Antonio bring his things and he asked James, his faithful assistant, to remain in the hospital as well.

When he needed to work, he worked beside her. He didn't want to go because he didn't want her to wake up without him in the room.

It paid off. When she opened her eyes, he was beside her holding her hand and reading a book. When her hazel eyes gazed into his, his heart missed a beat. When she finally smiled after looking around in confusion, he wanted to scream his joy to the heavens.

"How are you feeling, *koúkla*? Do I need to call the doctor?"

"I feel like I've been run over by a truck and that truck is still on my chest," she whispered hoarsely.

She turned to him and her eyes were wide with panic. Her hands immediately covered her abdomen.

"Nikos, our baby?"

"Relax, *agapimeni*. He or she is fine but the doctor ordered you on bed rest for about a month after this."

"Right now, bed rest sounds divine. And it's a good thing I don't need to be out of bed for my work," she whispered.

"I'll be right here. I'll watch over both of you," he said as he settled his hand over her abdomen.

"Hear that baby? Your papa will stay right here with us." Cassia grinned. "Wait. But what about your work, Nikos?"

He turned around and waved to the direction of the table behind him. His laptop was there along with several papers. "I brought my work here," he said with a shrug.

"How long has it been?"

"You've been asleep for a week."

"A week?!"

"Shh...don't stress yourself. You need rest."

"I'm fine, Nikos. I promise I won't overexert myself."

"I nearly died of a heart attack the moment I saw you there on the floor. I will never allow that to happen again, *agapimeni*."

His words made her smile. But then she remembered something else and it wiped all the happiness away.

"Is Hector—"

"He's gone. It's over."

She closed her eyes in a wave of pain. She'd been with Hector for a long time and he was one of her greatest friends. But she never knew his past or how troubled he was. If only he told her, she was sure she could've helped him.

She couldn't help feeling guilty. It was her fault that everything happened. She drove him well over his limit.

"Cassia, I know what you are thinking about. It's not your fault. It's his. He chose his path and what he wanted to believe in. He was rich, he was famous and he had you but he threw all that away for his revenge."

Nikos cradled Cassia close, careful of the tubes still connected to her.

"I just can't help wishing that I was able to help him, Nikos."

"I wish that too. I never knew I had a brother."

Then he just held her until she finished crying all her tears.

"What's going to happen now, Nikos?"

"We're going to start anew. We are going to forget everything that's happened and get on with our lives. Soon, there's going to be an addition to our family, Cassia. I want everything to be all set before the baby comes. We're going to start with us. I'm going to fix us."

She lifted her hand and traced his jaw.

"How are you going to fix something that isn't broken?"

He drew in a sharp breath.

"I told you I've forgiven you for everything, Nikos. The past is all a lie and a big fat misunderstanding. What matters is what we have now. I have you and I'm not letting you go."

Nikos grinned.

"I won't give myself over," he teased and his heart soared when she laughed.

"So what are we going to do after I'm out of here?"

"You are going to continue to rest. If the doctor says bed rest, I will chain you to our bed if I have to."

"Okay. Let's just say that I am cleared to go and that our baby's fine. What happens then?"

"Then I guess we'd travel. We'll go to Paris and you'll have one of your fashion shows there. Then we'll go to China and you can eat all the *dimsum* your heart desires. Hmm...then maybe to Hawaii because I know how much you love the beach. Or perhaps Bora Bora where you told me you wanted to spend a month?"

Cassia's eyes were filled with tears by the time he stopped speaking. "You remembered all that?"

"Of course. How could I not?"

She squeezed his hand. "I like that. Promise me we'll do all that?"

"As long as we still can, *agapimeni*. When you can't travel anymore because of our little one, we're going back to our island. I want my son born in Greece."

"Son, huh? What if it's a daughter?"

"It makes no difference to me if we have a son or a daughter. I just want him or her and you to both be healthy. If we have a son, I will teach him how to be an even greater businessman. If we have a daughter, you can teach her how to draw or paint and she could become a fashion designer like you."

She gave him her widest smile.

"I told you I can be charming when I want to be."

Cassia rolled her eyes. "Then you should have done that ten years ago. Maybe now, we'd have three or four children."

Nikos laughed and held her close.

"That is my one regret. I should not have believed the lies your grandfather told us. I should have gathered evidence. I should have believed what Antonio told me before. But because of my pride and my anger, I acted out. I'm so sorry, Cassia..."

"Don't be. I am a much better person now because of everything I've experienced."

"Then I am thankful for those ten years but sad that I was the catalyst. I should never have treated you that way."

"Yes. And you promised you'd make up for it every day of our lives."

"*Ne*. I promise."

He cupped her jaw and tilted her head up so her hazel eyes would clash with his green ones. He wanted her to remember this moment forever.

"*S'agapo i kardia mou einai diki sou.*"

I love you, my heart is yours.

Those were words he wanted to tell her for a long time now but hadn't had the courage to. Now that he blurted it out, he couldn't help feeling anxious as to how she'd respond.

Would she reject him again? Was everything going too fast?

"I love you too, Nikos."

Epilogue

NIKOS stood at the head of the table and began slicing the roast beef that his wife cooked for their Christmas Eve dinner.

His wife smiled and so did his two year old son, Theo. They were surrounded by friends and family. Costas was here and so was Stavros Demakis. Over the years, the two learned to be civil to each other. They both wanted the same thing: to see their grandson. Cassia and Nikos didn't allow them that privilege until they had settled all their disputes.

It took a long time but here they were.

Costas Andrade had been diagnosed with cancer a year ago. Now, he'd been told he only had about two years to live. So he began making amends. He apologized to Cassia and Nikos and explained everything he did wrong. He asked for forgiveness from Cassia and she told him he'd been forgiven a long time ago. But some things were never forgotten.

Then there was Alex and Isobel. They were married a year ago and they were now also expecting their first child. Beside them were Antonio and Elise with their son Anton who, by Cassia and Nikos' opinion, had grown up fast. Beside Anton was their second son, Gabriel.

"Oh, I forgot the mashed potatoes!"

Cassia slowly stood up and wobbled to the kitchen. Nikos stopped what he was doing and assisted her. She had a difficult time walking now since she was seven months pregnant with their twins.

Nikos still couldn't believe that miracle. He vowed he would protect Cassia and see her through all the aches and pains of carrying his twins, a boy and a girl. She complained all the time about how she had to pee and how it was so hard to walk and balance herself because her stomach was huge.

She always told him she felt like Atlas but was carrying the world in her womb instead of on her back.

Nikos listened to it all and he never complained. He even enjoyed giving her back and foot massages to alleviate her pain.

He shook his head as he realized how much his life changed. It was a full one hundred and eighty degree turn but he loved it. He wouldn't trade it for anything else.

Finally after a few hours of mayhem, they were alone in their room.

"I enjoyed that but I would have loved it more if my back didn't hurt so much. Theo is growing up and it's hard to catch him in my state."

"Don't run after him anymore, *agapimeni*. You might slip and hurt yourself. Just watch him and let his nannies chase him for now."

"I know. I can't wait for these babies to come out. I want to see my feet again. I want to bend over again," she laughed.

"They're the last."

She speared him with a glare.

Nikos threw up his hands and laughed.

"Let's close it on an even number. Maybe four? Six? Eight?" he teased.

Cassia slapped his arm and glared.

"Are you happy you married me, *glikia mou?*"

"At first, no. Which bride in their right mind would want a groom drunk enough to fall asleep at his own wedding?" she teased.

Nikos held his breath as he waited for her to continue

"But you know, you wormed your way into my heart," she added.

He exhaled.

"And you'll never leave me, right?"

"What makes you think I won't leave you? What if I get fed up by how you roar at me when you're angry?"

Nikos grinned. "Because you love me..."

She reached up and cupped his jaw. "Yes, I do, my *arrogant* billionaire. The first time I laid eyes on you on that ballroom when you rescued me, you stole my heart"

His heart melted at her words. He reached for her and kissed her tenderly.

"Back to my question...you'll never leave?"

"We're shackled together until we're old and gray," she whispered against his lips.

Nikos took out some papers from an old envelope. It was the contract that their grandparents agreed on but it was they who fulfilled the terms.

Nikos got up and threw it into the fire. They watched as it burned to nothing but ash.

"I don't need a piece of paper signed by two old men who thought they could play as gods and meddle with our fate to tell you that you are mine, Cassia. You're with me for the rest of our lives, Mrs. Demakis. We're not bound by a piece of paper worth billions but by our love for each other. I love you, *agape mou.*"

"*S'agapo, sýzygos...*" *I love you, husband.*

Cassia took a deep breath and continued.

"Our love is our new contract and it is beyond *any* price."

ABOUT THE *A*uthor

Alyssa Marie R. Urbano

is a Registered Nurse, blogger and a freelance writer from Quezon City, Philippines. She writes in an online publication site called Wattpad where her works were first recognized. Also, she is one of the Wattpad Filipino Ambassadors from the site. You can find her in this URL: http://wattpad.com/user/AerithSage or reach her as @AerithSage on Twitter.

THE

JAMIE HARRIS

Lives in Dundee, Scotland currently doing an MA in English and Creative Writing. He helps critique and or edit stories in an online publication site, Wattpad, while writing his own excellent stories as well. You can find him in this URL: http://wattpad.com/user/words_are_weapons.

GINYN NOBLE

Ginyn Noble is a full-bred Filipino bouncing between Makati City, Bulacan and her handsome beau's arms as her residences. She is currently working as a senior content writer for a white label SEO company with clients in the US, UK and Australia. Reach her as @ginynjanoble on twitter.

Acknowledgements

First of all, I want to thank my Editors: Jamie Harris and Ginyn Noble. This book is so much better after they shared their expertise with me.

Next, I want to thank my publishing consultants, Bronze Age Media. Thanks for recognizing my story and helping me through each step of self-publishing.

Also, thanks to my family who believed and supported me every step of the way.

Lastly, thank you to all my Wattpad readers! Without you, all this wouldn't have been possible. Thank you so much for reading my works and for all your votes and comments that truly encouraged me to be a better writer.

Made in the USA
San Bernardino, CA
16 February 2014